The Cruelty

A NOVEL

Candice Louisa Daquin

FLOWERSONG
PRESS

FlowerSong Press

ISBN: 978-1-963245-67-7

Published by FlowerSong Press
in the United States of America.
www.flowersongpress.com

Edited by Nitya Swaruba
Cover design by Christine E. Ray
Artwork by Frederick Middlehurst
Set in Adobe Garamond Pro

NOTICE: SCHOOLS AND BUSINESSES
FlowerSong Press offers copies of this book at quantity discount with bulk purchase for educational, business, or sales promotional use. For information, please email the Publisher at info@flowersongpress.com.

For the survivors.

There are many ways to die ...

During their lifetime, 1 in 7 women have been stalked by an intimate partner, to the point where the woman believed they, or someone close to them, would be harmed or killed. 19.3 million women in the United States have been stalked in their lifetime. 60.8% of female victims were stalked by a current or former intimate partner.

I wanted to write a story about generations of abuse and the danger such legacies of such violence can provoke in the lives of those who try to survive it. How abuse will continue, until it devours you, or you gnaw it off.

This story is based upon true events.

The Cruelty

Preface

"You are my blood-bride Camila. You complete the circle; your suffering sustains my rage."

In her minds-eye Camila saw a river of blood washing over white sand, the sand absorbing the blood, the sun baking the sand. That reddened, hardened sand turning into a figure. The Devil climbing out of the sand. The Devil pulling her after him, attached to his phallus by her mouth, his fist inside her, a grotesque mandala parodying goodness. They dance awkwardly, he shifts her, so he is taking her and she is bleeding. Always giving him her blood, her life. Enveloping the two of them so she is both mother and wife. *"He is born from me,"* she thought to herself. *"I keep him alive with my blood and I am the only one who can destroy him."* Camila woke up covered in sweat. The dream was so vivid. *It felt so real,* she thought, recalling the awful images. She couldn't get the nightmare out of her head. What did it mean?

She wouldn't have slept anyway. It was her last night of being alive.

Chapter 1

Can we be driven to take our own life? Camila thought so.

Standing unsteadily, the wind swaying her violently, she felt the push of fingers through the fabric of the world. She heard the sound of voices – deer, dislocated from encroaching suburban sprawl, leap out of foliage and streak brown and white across wet asphalt. 24 hours had passed so fast.

She stood alone. *I am not afraid to stop existing. I am more afraid of carrying on.* Now it was quiet, cars cold in garage did not make pools of water, kaleidoscopic and dreamy in red and yellow, in sleeping headlights. The air moved with little sound, an echo of deepest night swallowing humanity. Here was the hour of another life; able to see in darkness, crossing wastelands in search of human debris and cast-offs.

Her feet were hooked on the precipice of the bridge. Above her, the wrought iron effigy of mankind, breaking through nature without harmony. Camila felt herself letting go of all the pain she'd boxed up and sent to oblivion. Pain that had refused to be mailed, stood like a sodden reminder of her past. Now it opened and birds flew out, streaking across the chill water into high reeds and low branches. She felt release; a lightness that had been long denied. She was holding herself against falling and that was the last gate, the barrier that had been erected for so long, telling all never to throw themselves into the unknown.

Staring up into the sky, the endless wield of cloud and pending rain, muted color and fingers of light touching tree tops. Camila remembered being a child. Running out of breath downhill staring into the clouds, her heart thundering in her little chest. She remembered smelling moss and hummus and scat and the excitement of not knowing what her future entailed, with an infinite ribbon of hope flickering above her. Back then, life stretched out and was a vast and unknown entity, something beckoning her with the allure of a wide sky.

Why was the ending of a life in order to resolve pain such a taboo? She did not, in her eagerness to cross the gate, understand those moral reasons holding some back from the edge. Camila only understood the thirsting urge. The need to climb up over the railing, planting her feet against the ledge, and feel the tender fragility of life as her fingers slowly unclenched from holding on. One by one, loosening until she was free of any hold.

Her light-weight body fell like a thin stone hungry for the arms of deep water. Breaking through the shining darkness she sank steadily down without pause. Camila recognized falling through air, hearing the surprise in her bones as she became weightless, the rush of cold air barreling her toward glassy surface. Then a breathless smack, hard, breaking through, pain for a moment, then velvet darkness, descent, then nothing.

Chapter 2

Not being dead felt surprisingly gentle. Waking up slowly, Camila was first consumed by disorientation, the result of prolonged deprivation of oxygen and the dreaming void. If anything, she woke up the way you might wake up wistfully as a child; not realizing your house is burnt down around you. A child's capacity for fantasy. Thinking everything is as it was, when you were happy in your dream, without knowledge of what awaited beyond.

As the drugs lining Camila's mind with heavy wet rags wore off, she began to notice little things. Snatches of color and vague impressions, but she didn't recognize the full shape of her surroundings. There was a nag in the back of her neck like a memory, unable to complete its formation. The distant memory reminded her of when you leave the house thinking you have everything on your mental list and half way gone you remember the very thing you needed most you left behind. You don't have time to go back for it so you tell yourself, *maybe it's not so important, surely you should just keep going forward. You might be late otherwise.* Still the nag is there. Something forgotten, pulling on your clothes to remind you. Maybe as you left, you were also left behind, and that is what you had forgotten.

She didn't have time to go back for herself. She was already sprinting in the future.

Her death had occurred; she was ahead of it now, looking back. No way of knowing how she could marry the time of then with the time of now. Time had ceased anyway. She'd died, she'd come back, she did not exist. She stood outside the usual thresholds, peering in. Whatever was swimming in her drowned brain, took the edge off. The longing to jump off the bridge had receded like hunger after eating too much. She felt satiated, glutted on the idea of death. Her mind was almost empty of thought; like ice-skating alone, peaceful. It reminded her of when she used to dance, one song after the other. *So, this is how it feels to die?* She mused, the fear fading, growing water-logged.

Time didn't have a long hand, there was a clock, blurred somewhere on the wall. Camila thought it was humorous as that pretty much summed up her feelings about time in general. It could have been spinning around, or going backward, nothing really made sense when you tried to understand it through the mechanism of time. It was never linear, and it was never advancing.

She slept again, closed eyelids acknowledging the changing of light through a high window, from mauve to midnight blue and shades of in-between. There was no sound, the air was clean and smelt empty. She didn't exist, and she knew she didn't exist, so she endured. This was familiar and not as frightening, as if she had practiced for this in the stillness of depression. Losing herself, becoming nothing, emptying out.

Once you have died you have nothing to be afraid of any

longer. You've passed the biggest unknown. Like a heavy weight of water, a memory of sinking, Camila felt release and air, coursing through her, filling her with a new way of breathing. Like returning to the womb and climbing inside the salty haven of your own beginnings. A regression back to the point of origin and a new start, where scars had no time to form and possibility hung, a silver star in a night sky.

Somewhere, unhinged and distant, a constant and steady bleeping of a machine irritated the edges of her stupor. She found that she could bat it away, with the mental slap of a tired hand and the sound would recede with her consciousness, turning again toward dreamland. In her dreams she was not a girl who had flung herself from a bridge, and died, or survived. Camila's mind was a series of photographs flickering like a moving picture through the piano of her memories. Something addictive about being lost inside yourself, fingering fantasy and memory instead of coming up for air.

A steady supply of drugs that acted like an iron to the curls of Camila's brain must have been administered through the IV lines attached to her thin arm. This anemic-looking arm that had turned almost blue before it was reanimated and tucked beneath sensible blankets. Camila wondered how she could have survived when she had so certainly felt the unfamiliar press of death and began down the long corridor in search of release. Hands up, beseeching; *I have come here looking for closure, I am not afraid to stop existing. I am more afraid of carrying on.*

Days later, or maybe moments, the sun came up and bled orange and fierce on the tiles of her room, lighting the curtains with fantasy. She stared for a long while at the colors, seeing them play across her and turning back, wielding toward where they had come. Like herself; burned and then extinguished, she returned to her starting point and somehow, she missed *stop* and came around again to *go*. It was a marvel to be returned, as if she'd somehow hoodwinked the inevitable and surprised fate with her reappearance.

Back in the world that had receded, she recalled how sitting around sharing rolled joints, young people had often talked about how they knew what dying would be like. *I think it will be like going to sleep*, one said. *No, it's going to be like a seizure*, said another, *you'll see yourself and you'll know you're dying but it won't be frightening*. Camila always thought death would be a relief. That knowledge helped her when she stood at the precipice of the bridge and looked down to the cold swirl. It was important not to fail and end up broken-necked and drooling in a hospital bed. *How did she know she wasn't paralyzed now?* No. She did know, she could feel herself, whole. Physically unharmed. Somehow nothing hurt, and whilst she hadn't moved, it was more choice than inability. The catheter flowed down her leg and she felt her own urine, warm and reassuringly encapsulated in plastic, running against her thigh into a Foley bag.

Camila had adroitly spent her life so far, not understanding as much as everyone pretends to; seeing how others' confidences were just shallow masks; repeating thin assumptions. Unaware of the limitation of this closed-circuit way of thinking. A form of self-comfort because the things we know comfort us, and the things we do not know often seem daunting. Her father used to say, *As much as we say we want challenges and differences, we always return to what we know best*. It is no wonder that we can convince ourselves of almost anything if given clues with easy blanks that our assumptions can fill in. By filling in the blanks with our own dictionary of experiences, we can create entire worlds on assumption. It hadn't made sense then but it did now, in that creeping way that didn't feel good.

Camila's ratchetted mind grasped at familiar outcomes and

she wove together the most likely scenario by filling in the blanks. Had she been really examining things closely, she may have queried how odd everything was, but when hurt and tired, who queries deeply? That tell-tale feeling of hairs sticking up on our forearms when our intuition says something isn't right may be placated by our certainty that we are aware of ourselves. She was no more aware of her reality than perhaps she ever had been; reality shifting as she moved closer or further from confronting it. At one point she stood on a bridge and jumped so she assumed that meant she was seeing more clearly than before. But as the water took her under and she began to lose feeling, she could no longer see ahead of her. This underwater sleep was mimicked as she woke and began to collect herself. Was this a *way-station* in purgatory or a room in a hospital where they bring those who have failed to succeed in killing themselves?

As she had stood on the bridge, her bare feet cold against the metal, she could smell the unfolding of Winter. A remorseless chill in the air, fingering her calcium, dragging her into velvet boxes. Emptying trees silver against velvet sky; a series of broken compositions. Camila's own breath, the fast thrum of her heart, beating a countdown beneath her sweater. Her eyes glazed over, seeing the past: she's learning to ride her first bicycle without stabilizers, wobbling between the two small ponds of her grandmother's house, stinging nettles on either side. She starts to lose control. The bike veers right through bushes, past stinging nettles, into the larger pond, slugs kissing her face as she went down, into darkness.

Chapter 3

Now, in the hour of timelessness, a tall doctor stood over her. He had deep folds in the corner of his brown eyes and the skin of someone who preferred to be outdoors. He leaned over and palpitated Camila's neck, checked her eyes and mouth and listened to her chest. His own breathing is even and regular like an athlete, his breath like coffee and toothpaste. Camila wondered what her heart sounded like, brought back from watery grave to pound again, beneath her bones like fists. Before, when she wasn't dead, it had always been fast. Beating like a short-lived rabbit heart. Though she was relatively healthy she felt this was a legacy and spoke to the anxiety of her existence. Now she could not tell, her heart seemed to be far removed from her, as if every part of her earthly form had been taken apart and put back together, without feeling.

He removed her catheter slowly, it burned a little but slid quickly out, glad to be gone. The tall doctor showed her the bathroom, adjacent to her room. She didn't ask where she was, it seemed obvious; a hospital. Noiseless, maybe a sanatorium? He didn't say anything because it was obvious, she was a patient now. One of those death-seekers whom they had managed, through trickery or fortune, to save from their best intentions. She was on too many drugs to feel ashamed of her failure and too muzzy headed to want to talk about it. Camila figured there would be plenty of time for that, when the head-doctors decided to check in on her. For now, she just wanted to rest, and look at the world through half-opened eyes.

With time she saw that where she lay, this room, the doctor, even the light, was not a sanatorium or a hospital and it didn't seem to be purgatory either. It was a small cottage with stucco walls and one spare bedroom airy and wide, facing east. The doctor was not a regular doctor but a man who plucked things from the water. While he knew how to heal them, his real art lay in understanding they needed healing even as they did their best to outfox him. He may not even have been a man; he may not even have sought to heal. That may have been one of the assumptions a person makes when they think from the perspective of themselves and do not know the perspectives or desires of others, especially those who are quite different to them. People who can wear masks and walk through life unobserved. People who know the exact moment to push and the exact moment to pull. The puppet masters.

He wasn't a big talker, the tall doctor with the Asian folds to his eyes. His internal dialogue going over his personal observations were enough for him. He paid more attention to a bird breaking from tree cover, or the cry of a fox at night, than the confusing syllables from humanity. It seemed to him, the only noise humans made that was worth listening to, was music. Even then, it was the deep timber of the instrument and not the voice that brought from his deep-set eyes, a longing placed in the firelight.

The doctor's hands were rough and dry – he smelt of wood

smoke and cedar and his hair hadn't grayed or thinned, giving him ten more years of youth. During the night he read, voraciously and without moving, with an old brass lamp beside a La-Z-Boy and a ginger cat purring at his feet. In those moments the world seemed the best place he could imagine. With the sound of roosting birds and the strange cries of night, soothing the rough edges of day and cloaking it in away from enquiry. It was the only time a restless mind could quieten and enjoy the tranquility of inhabiting space, like smooth wood captures light and glows without bidding.

Her presence didn't harm his solitude. She didn't yet feel ready to acknowledge herself again. Her eyes would look away from him, not in anger but like a closed book, wishing for more time before revealing its plot. She was small and didn't take up much room, her selfhood so spare at times he didn't feel her presence at all. She was like a child tucking her legs up and turning into a circle again, imitating a fetus, unwilling to be born. She was his child, a child of the water, risen up and permitted a second chance, and he was ready to give it to her.

Camila was dead to the world and nobody noticed.

Chapter 4

When Camila's maternal grandparents had died on a cruise ship, Camila's mother, their daughter, hadn't reacted. The only betray of her emotions, the number of Whiskey Sours she consumed, standing outside in the frost, stomping her flat feet against the teasing cold. There in harmony with the ice, she'd watch hatching jackdaws take flight to warm their feathers, inking out the little light in the Winter sky. She would sit in front of her mirror and brush her long honey-colored hair until it was free of tangles, and Camila would watch her, always enthralled, seeing the mend from chaos to sense, freed in the determined strokes of a brush.

Her mother, tall and sleek like a thorough-bred, had class without being born with it. A natural poise and elegance that endured all the fists life pummeled in her direction. Her mother, always surrounded with friends, with a smile the length of a necklace, she belonged in a jeweled world, never a mundane one. Young Camila, a stranger in her lap, with her onyx eyes dreaming of a place she really belonged. Perhaps she had been plucked by the wrong harvest, placed in the wrong time. Maybe meant for greater things than the suffrage of their bland life, as mother and daughter, waiting for father to return from work. Camila could feel the desperation in her mother's throat, strangling her need to spin and dance beyond this. If she could have, she would have asked her to leave, *get out whilst you can, escape this net.* Swim, swim out until a new horizon breaks with dawn and shows you a destiny befitting your reach.

Privately, Camila's mother despised the weakness of dying; she didn't miss her daughter because she had no point of reference for her. As a child her daughter had been an unknown, bearing no resemblance in looks or action and that's what made it easy to leave. As an adult, she was at best, a slow disappointment. It was as if Camila's mother had given birth to a stranger and placed that stranger in another nest and left to fly off and find herself again. Nursing the pain of a sore birth only briefly before pushing it aside and becoming what she'd set out to be, before pregnancy had foiled her. She was proud of her ability to not be pulled down by guilt or obligation, she saw herself as a new woman, the kind who wasn't bound by duty or false expectation.

Many of Camila's mother's friends at the time had judged her, and that was expected in a shallow kind of way. It was easy to judge, especially when you pride yourself on motherhood, a quality she abhorred. She was a career politician, earning rather than marrying her way into the upper-classes. She wore expensive well-cut clothes and heels and was the opposite of frugality, choking in gold. It was the life she designed and she was owed it. Coming from a world of hurt where she could have ended up like her own mother; dying having never done anything about the bad things in her life. No. She wasn't going to make that mistake and motherhood didn't tenderize her heart as it might have others. She admired that in herself; she felt nothing and she felt maybe everything. Underneath her skin, unknown even to her.

Camila's father. A sorrowful, tall, preternaturally intense black-haired man with black crepe eyes, was a man lost in a high tower for as long as she could recall. He was never happier than when he was tinkering in the shed on some woodwork project or trekking up into the highlands surrounding his house. How he and her vivacious mother ever got together, almost impossible to understand, other than the adhesion of broken pieces – when recognizing the other and coming together to join imperfectly. Their relationship had been brief – an overstayed encounter rather than a marriage.

In Camila's infancy her father would farm her out for strangers to look after. When they were together, he was aloof and untraceable. She spent most of her time reading or climbing trees. Both her parents had many family friends, their daughter had no strings, or attachments, she hung off them like a bauble. Her mother told Camila once; *Look my girl, I made my way in politics with every obstacle. I didn't come from money, I was a woman, divorced and scorned for my choices. I did it anyway. That alone should show you, you can do anything you want by yourself. You don't need familial support. You shouldn't need anything.*

Perhaps that is why Camila moved far away from them. She disliked being reminded that she didn't matter. Going away made it easy to avoid confronting that empty feeling on a regular basis. With her discovered death, both parents resigned themselves. It didn't seem too different to how they had felt previously, as if Camila's existence had been no more than a peripheral aspect of their own, and not a center, from which their planets circled. Their independence as parents went as far as not really inhabiting the role that went with the word: *Parent.*

Neighbors didn't hear the news because the neighbors didn't even know they had had a child. Divorced and living separate lives, one married to her political career and place in society, the other detached from the world lost in the woods around his lake house, they were ensconced in their respective existences. That meant it was easy to carry on without a child that they'd never really made mention of. It was as if their whole lives they had diminished her existence *in preparation for her dissolution.* Two weeks after Camila's death, they received the paperwork. It was the paperwork of formality and legality and they inwardly marveled at the ease with which a modern person could die and leave nothing of themselves behind.

Camila did not own her house. She had never earned enough money on a steady basis to qualify for a mortgage. She didn't have any children, she didn't have any pets, her possessions were reduced down to a few boxes. What she owned was given away and donated to charity by neighbors who had hardly known her. On a long walk one Saturday, Camila's father found his face wet with tears, he had been watching the lake and without knowing, considered his daughter's body, discovered drowned and bloated. Whilst he did not really know how to feel guilt, he felt something, though he had no name for it. Maybe a disquiet in his soul, at something being ruined and wrong, without ever knowing why or what would have made it not so.

Chapter 5

By the third week, Camila was weaned off the strong medication that restored her mind. She felt lucid and clear headed, even a little exhilarated, to be in a space that had no expectation on her and no regrets. It was like taking a holiday from yourself if that was possible. Reveling in the peace of being somewhere strange and unknown where you could just exist without acting a part, or bowing to the pressure of conformity. Such was the relief of the sick bed. She'd known this feeling before as a kid, whilst her friends longed to get well and return to classes, she would linger and prolong her mild childhood illnesses. For another day, another week of peace, rolling in fever and entire books like a happy hedgehog.

The doctor with the sad eyes sat by Camila's bed and talked to her. At first, she heard the words like a cartoon – '*wa we wa*' – as if her head was underwater or swaddled in cotton wool. She found she couldn't capture comprehension, as if he were speaking a foreign language. When elucidation came, it was one word at a time: '*Brain,*' '*trauma,*' '*breathe,*' like staccato poetry. During the hours she was alone, she'd repeat the words like a haiku: *'Brain, trauma, breathe.'* It comforted her, as if the tall doctor were describing her cells one by one, creating her anew from dormant clay and breathing life into her muddy limbs. She was dragged from the river, covered in such mud, she carried it into her lungs, she could taste the residue of clay and sediment. A testimony to her drowning and her return to life.

The words he used were simple and slow. He talked to her of other things interspersed with herself. Putting Camila as a character in his stories, re-building her pathways with imagination leading back to reality. When her mind wasn't as wandering, she would hone in on his words as nourishment to her quiet days and listen without acknowledging, to the harmony of them. It was like music she thought, everything was like music depending upon how you chose to hear. She didn't hear the *meaning*; she heard the *feeling*. She was a cave, formerly without trespass, now laid bare from her self-imposed extinction.

He told her she was doing exceptionally well. It didn't comfort her because she had given away the part of her that cared how she was doing. Else how could she have ever made that last step, off the bridge's edge and into the void? He didn't know that perhaps. Though the seriousness of his tone and the downward pull of his eyes suggested he might know far more than she. With her addled senses coming back sluggishly like exhausted lovers returning after a night of tearing one another to pieces behind rose bushes, clamoring for the other's reassurance.

"You may not be able to talk the way you used to for a while. Do not be afraid, in time everything will come back to you. Your memories may be incomplete and that is good. In time we will work on emptying you of the memories that harm you and give you a new space." The tall doctor said.

She didn't know what he meant but she liked the sound of it. Like a robot bequeathed someone else's personality can march through life unimpeded by their own sense of futility or existence. If she could have cared less about those things, she would have opted for it, because the soreness she felt in her chest when she thought of her own being was like a punch to her heart, delivered unabashedly.

"Your arms may be stiff for a while but you will be able to use them again. Next week you start physical therapy." He waited for her to nod that she had heard him.

She hadn't lifted from her bed except to shuffle to the bathroom. When she did it would take all of thirty minutes there and back, even peeing was hard. Her bladder removed from its catheter was detached from her processing. It would hurt and stay full without expelling urine until she willed it, straining and gasping for breath, her legs shaky and unstable on either side of the toilet. It was humiliating but she told herself she'd brought it upon herself by her actions and briefly she wondered how she could have come back, when no part of her wished to.

Yet the birds outside would make noise and in the quiet they were the background color – she found herself listening for. Wanting to hear their call, feeling she was part of their migration to window sill and back. Wondering where they went as they flew off, shaken by sudden rain or change in temperature. She thought they were lot like her, easily startled by life, easily trained to act against herself by the poison inhabiting her being. The birds could take flight and shake it off, she could not. And yet, as she lay in her sweaty bed, her head feeling heavy against the double pillows, she knew she had already begun to change and nothing she had taken for granted any longer applied.

The physical therapy was excruciating. She wanted to claw her way out but had no idea where she'd go if she were able to summon the strength. She gritted her teeth and didn't think of the life she had before where movement came effortlessly. Camila tried to think of herself as the thick clay of the river bed, formed into a lumpen shape, hauled from the river, possessed of a chance at life, growing in meaning. Like the *Golem* created by the Jews, she would rise and take form. It would not be natural or easy, she would feel the pain others never felt and be powerless to articulate it. But she was urged from the river bed and given sentience, she had more purpose than the girl who flung her paperweight off the bridge, seeking oblivion.

Pain is such a strange sensation; it never becomes something you can ignore. With will you can endeavor to eat it and spit it out behind you, as you force your way through. It is a journey. For the dying, the journey ends with death and that is why they struggle against it. For the living, it can be endured because there is hope. Camila had not had any hope in as long as she could recall. It felt odd to realize, that through the pain she must feel something akin to hope to continue, as nobody told her she must and nobody told her if she didn't, it would be ruinous. Still, she strived, without pressure, to push through and come out, more a human form than the crushed shell of limbs she saw, reflected in the windows of the recovery room. Her small world now with its silver machines and distant radio playing songs from the 70s about endurance and survival and peace.

The old Camila might have lain in her bed and asked a hundred questions. The new her did not have the power of mind to formulate such questions. It briefly occurred to her that she'd been lobotomized and how that had been a former treatment of depression, in hope of easing the mental anguish of the stricken. She could see how not being able to think too deeply did help avoid depression. Maybe not eradicate it but draw a thin veil between yourself and it, masking off the unpleasantness of self-awareness and that clawing feeling in your throat that everything you did had no purpose. Camila only had the purpose of the moment and that was simple and that was good. She woke up, she ate, she voided. She practiced her limbs like a dancer trying to attain a perfect pose, and she slept deeply, not recalling her dreams upon waking.

The tall doctor visited frequently, Camila looked for him even without a clock at certain times in the day when the light would act as dial and he would knock on her door. After checking her progress on a handheld device, he would ask her questions; never about herself, but about politics, about climate change, about geography and history. It was as if he were massaging her mind to see what remained and what was lost; covered over with sediment at the bottom of a green and brown river, turning darker with encroaching Winter. He didn't ask anything personal, and she began to believe she had been someone before and left that person behind. Like a husk or skin sloughed off, no part of who she was now, reborn in brine and sunlight, striving toward emptying herself of melancholic hypnosis.

"*Today we are going to consider something different.*" He said, his eyes catching the sun and holding them in amber for a few moments before he turned into shade. "*We are going to consider doing something that will help you further, by taking the remaining memories away. If we do this you will no longer be the person you once were, you will be a new person. Obviously in the same body, at the same age, but without your personal legacy. We will only do this if you say it's okay to. It is your choice. I want you to think about it for a few days and let me know your decision, either way is okay. For my part — I think it is the best choice because if you stay as the person you are now, you will always find a bridge.*" This was the first time he had alluded to the incident, and Camila felt a shame creep over her face in hot flush, but said nothing.

Once he was gone, she got up shakily and went into the bathroom. There was no mirror either there or in her room, but she could see her reflection caught in the polished tiles. Her slightly green expression, pinched and revealing more than words. She picked up some tissue and wadded it in her mouth because for a moment she felt the familiar rise of panic and an overwhelming urge to scream, though no words came out. She couldn't think clearly. *Something didn't seem right.* Maybe it was just her. Maybe she shouldn't have survived, an ungrateful thrower of life. But she had. She didn't know which caused her more regret.

Chapter 6

A month later Camila left her small cottage room for good, and left behind in it, the woman she had been for 21 years. In her mind's eye, sore though it was, she would see an imitation of herself. There in her old life, still living the same repeated groove as before. Going nowhere spiritually or emotionally except closer and closer to that river's edge. It felt good to look at that imitation of herself and not attach the person she was, to that past figure. The recollections began to recede. The new medications in her brain were changing her and it wasn't frightening like the anti-depressants of old. They felt more like they were rewriting her to be someone other than that sorrowful person who inhabited empty spaces.

The tall doctor and Camila walked down the corridor, past the exercise room and into the front living room where she had briefly walked before. The outlay of the house was a miniature ranch style. You could see through the windows great plains of space, dotted with autumnal auburn trees and an expansive large sky. It was bigger there than where she had formerly lived but she had never asked questions. Strange because in the past she'd always been intensely curious but a part of her seemed to understand this wasn't about putting the pieces of the puzzle back together the way she had previously. In order to change, she had to even change how she approached things. She remained quiet and said only what she needed to, to keep herself engaged and growing toward the light the man shone before her.

They went outside; Camila didn't have any belongings and he didn't bring any either. The Psilocybin dosing in her brain ridding her of a need for usual expectations. They got into a Subaru station wagon, a dark blue that had seen many years of sun and was bleached and blurry looking. She sat in the front with him, there was a square of turquoise hanging from the mirror, and the seats were dusty and warm. Soon Camila slept as the man drove them from dusk into night and onward, through the almost invisible country roads, cutting smoothly like velvet ribbons with starlight as their only guide. The fields had been turned over in preparation for the coming Spring and their fallow darkness looked like curled ice-cream with a tinge of frost sitting atop and the odd black bird daring to settle.

Chapter 7

Loss was not something either of Camila's parents felt because they'd shored themselves against such feelings at an early age. During disappointing childhoods, where ego and confidence had been put in place to protect against any potential assault. It was an irony their daughter did the opposite and maybe a reason none of them fit well together. They were a family of origin that had splintered apart and stayed apart. As naturally as those who love each other seek the solace of that love, they were magnets placed to repel. There was so much loss, it was impossible to acknowledge.

Only her father's sister, Camila's aunt, expressed any horror at the events. She called and shouted down the phone in a hoarse voice, at her only brother. This only produced a silence on the other end and the sister felt the enormity of the chasm in their family, hating her brother for his inability to care and her own failure to be more of a relative to her only niece. She told her husband over dinner that evening she felt some families were cursed. Whilst not a woman of faith, she was a woman of superstition, and her own brush with breast cancer and the early death of one of her sons with Down Syndrome had lent her a wary eye at the fates.

Her husband had told her that some things could not be helped, which she found intolerable though she said nothing because their own marriage was savaged by a lifetime of petty squabbles. To cope, she had taken up fishing like her father, a hobby she'd hated as a child and now relished. The freedom of escape and the quiet of the act. *How sad* she thought, when we replicate our own parents' behaviors for much the same reason. How similar our outcomes, though we would believe we are all unique.

"*Camila never had a chance,*" her aunt said to her husband. "*She grew up alone. With the abuse from her neighbor, it was a wonder she ever got it together. Her mother, born in the wrong time, trapped into being a mother. My brother, her father? He had lost himself long before her birth. It's no wonder the child ended up dead, no wonder at all. Things are circular, we repeat history if we are unaware of it, she is only coming back through time, echoing her grandfather's suicide, because the same breakage within the family retains its damage and inflicts its fate on successive generations. This would never have happened had I been more involved.*" Her husband told her that regret was a response to helplessness, and it did no good. She did not bring it up again, because the empty pragmatism of man shut her down and held her tongue.

Camila's family were strangers to each other – she'd left because she felt lonelier with them than apart. The pain was handed carefully down through generations of people who didn't need or want that cohesion. She's spent years trying to find her own way, only to discover that the taste of water when you are at the very edge of drowning, can feel like a strange and wanted caress.

Chapter 8

In early dawn Camila woke, refreshed despite sitting in the passenger seat. No grit or exhaustion in her eyes, she felt she had slept an eternity and looked over to see he was out of the car and they were at a gas station, the pump making its undulating chant whilst she could see his silhouette paying in the store. It didn't occur to Camila to run; she knew he wasn't a proper doctor and she hadn't been at any kind of typical hospital, but she stayed put as if she were with an old friend. That's how in the guts of herself she felt. A relief at not having to put on any pretense or even make small talk. He was like a tree in that sense, strong and unyielding. A shade for the brightest rays of sun piercing her through the window screen.

They stopped a few more times, once for bathroom, another time for snacks at a roadside diner, where they ate in companionable silence and the waitress seemed to understand their need for minimal fussing. Camila ordered pancakes because her stomach didn't like savory food when she was in motion, and they seemed innocuous enough. He ate buttered toast and drank black coffee, betraying little fatigue, his eyes as clear as they had been the day before. As they left the diner, he told her they were nearing their destination and instead of feeling uneasy she felt glad that soon they would be able to stretch the aches from their limbs.

Another five hours and he turned off onto an obscure country road that looked much like all the rest aside the slight shifting in landscape as they came out of Texas and cut through the middle of the country upward. It had seemed an eternity, until in one long arc, reaching Oregon. Camila recognized the states more by their landscapes than names, because they kept off the roads. Despite this they made good time, reaching Oregon at the end of the day, with just enough moonlight to guide them through the thick forest road and up into the mountains. She had only been to Oregon once, many years before, for a business meeting. Had never had a chance to see the fabled countryside people told her about. It was breathtakingly beautiful and abundant in an Eden-like way. The moon looked almost like a supernova so close to the tips of the mountains, and shrouded in mist. The tops of great dark pines, spearing the light with jagged foliage.

Their destination was a house built from wood but not a log cabin, more Scandinavian in design with lots of large windows and a wide deck overlooking a lake. The first thought Camila had was *'the house is right by a lake'* and she surprised herself by feeling no anxiety despite the lake wrapping its depths around the shorelines, reminding her of her own watery assent. The second thought she had was realizing how tired she was and an overwhelming desire to fall into sleep once more and wake up to her new landscape. He showed her into a medium-sized room facing the lake on the east side of the house, and pointed out how to use the shower and what was where. She wasn't hungry so she said she'd just take a shower and then go to bed, which he probably wanted to do too. The shower was hot and strong, it rinsed away the grime of the road that she'd become accustomed to and she could smell eucalyptus and pine.

Afterward, she stood by the large picture window looking out at the lake. It was placid and the moon was reflected off it, causing an icy surface to shimmer against the darkness of the tree lines. Great natural hewn boulders, the color of slate, crept up the sides, and then dove down to small beaches of white shingle. Impossibly tall trees, ferns, lost willows, climbed around the other in a monkey puzzle of green. The water looked breathless, as if summoning silence to its core. It was a hidden marvel. The house alone must have been worth a fortune, she guessed.

As she lay down in the queen size bed made of pine and pulled the quilt over her, she felt a deep peace. Camila slept in a long t-shirt she found on the bed, having no clean clothes or much else, aside from a toothbrush and hairbrush that were left by the sink. In the silence of the house, she could hear a grandfather clock ticking and roving owls outside, among the canopy. She felt weightless in a way she had not felt in such a long time, as if she had already become someone else and hardly recalling the person she was, less than a month ago.

Morning came early – as it does when immersed in nature, and yet she felt good waking up with the light. It infused the room like reaching hands come to claim her awake, and she stretched lazily in the sun. In the kitchen he was making coffee and had toast on the table. She ate ravenously and they sat watching the birds glide across the lake surface. Finally, she asked him; *"What are we doing here?"* She didn't know why she'd felt the need to break the acceptance of her fate in his hands, or what urge caused her to say it out loud, but he replied as if he'd been expecting it. *"We're here to save you,"* smiling a slow, slightly crooked smile. *"Where are we?"* She replied. *"It doesn't matter where we are; it matters where we want to be."* He finished, and went back to his reading. With that she finished her toast and later they took a walk in the forest, looking up until their necks ached, at the great height of the trees, pointing toward the unblemished blue sky.

Though the clock chimed the hour, she didn't care what hour of what day it was. Time had ceased to matter to her, just as her sorrow had grown into a distant thing lost in the glimmer of water and light, touching space in-between. It was as if she was possessed of no wish other than to empty herself of all the toxins she'd been carrying within her for so many years. Every day she would take long walks into the mountains, sometimes alone, she'd grab a fallen stick and pretend she was striking out but always mindful of her return, she'd make sure to be back before light grew low in the sky. He cooked for them, or they ordered take-out which meant they were not so very far from civilization as she'd previously assumed. That was Oregon for you, a beautiful combination of unspoiled vistas and culture, living side by side with far more harmony than the fracking state she'd made her home for many years.

"Why did you choose to live in Texas?" He asked one day, as they were drinking coffee.

"I don't honestly know." she said, *"for me, answers are never linear and easy, they all relate to something else. Sometimes you try to run away, toward something better and you end up as stuck as you began. I'm beginning to think it's because you take all your stuff with you, so wherever you are, you're still dealing with it. Nowhere is far enough. It's as if anything I did wasn't really a single decision but a chain of decisions coming from one place."*

"What was that place?"

"I think the place was my self-hatred." She replied. Surprising both of them with her candor. This was the beginning of their conversations, and after that, as if something were understood

between them, they talked without reserve. He shared as she did and demonstrated a remarkable patience with her struggle to verbalize everything that brought her to that precipice in the rust of night.

"What was that place?" She thought, as the words circled her in the dark. The question was so much larger than a reply, it was a whole lifetime of feeling erased.

Chapter 9

One day, the kind of day few living things go outside, the world battening down its hatches and declaring us all hibernators of the worst of Winter's wrath, Camila told him; *"I mostly remember being in the asylum, I remember that us inmates smoked, because that's what crazies do, and it beats the tedium of being a non-smoker and crafting or collecting bees. We smoked anything we could lay our hands on. Wax, banana skins, dust mites, rags. If you could smoke blood, we'd have dried ours in antiseptic sun and sucked it back in. We were coming apart at the seams, faulty thinking, beat up youth, blowing raspberries at pain from an empty bottle. I had no feeling in my hands, the closer I got to people the further away I wished to be. But they made me feel less bruised by their own torn out minds, we were roughed up scarecrows, footprints in forest, stolen moments of hope breaking like crack pipes in snow."*

"Sometimes I thought I loved their sadness, the chimeric nonsense and sweet November souls, always among falling leaves. Their sadness helped me hide the voices of approbation thundering with tap shoes. Those voices said; Get your act together! Now I want to see you smile! Look how much better you would be if you just tried harder!" She

grimaced at the memory.

"Perhaps I was born missing the data entry for contentment, and I'd lost somewhere in school photos the ability to smile without crying. Like broken things mesh back together and you can nearly see the break? That was the rise of things, before melancholia made her rounds. I was told; Drink this. You will feel better. Swallow this, you won't get pregnant, looking down at boys emptying me, and refilling me, thinking; how fast you go, rowing back and forth between my legs like fevered hare. Told to smoke this. It will make you forget. Starve, purge, binge, cut, tear, break again. Now it's become familiar." So many years of prescription, she thought, without any hope of a 'cure.'

"All of us inmates, we all wore our pain inside out like family crests in disguise, hidden Jews, mannequins, pliable parts, stoic minds. Release valves with no identity but a shared knowledge of pain, skittering like fatigue over unlined fingers. When the others were released, growing roots and sprouting buds that hungrily faced the sun, they wished to be fixed, edited, repaired, patched, at any cost, and I was alone. Alone to be the last one whom intervention failed. Patient not responding. Treatments hopeless. Keep it quiet, maybe she'll fade into the wallpaper like a good little bottle of sorrow." She sighed. *"Does that sound paranoid? I suppose I was,"* Camila laughed with her mouth downturned in an ugly recollection. *"But can you blame me?"*

"I used to sing a little song about it; if I were a pill, I'd be a blue pill, if I were a car, I'd be a black car, if I were your child you'd regret me, if I were a balloon I wouldn't come back."

"But it wasn't easy, the swell of health about them, nobody wants to be reminded they too felt this bad. They lock their doors, keep the pets inside, something lurks in the woods outside and the worst aspect of sadness, ingrained wooden stakes become part of you now.

Just how you are, a shape that doesn't fit, and so long you've tried; it's stuck tight and sharp in your side. The worst is losing even those who walked your path, holding your hand, with eyes that felt the same. Understanding depression doesn't automatically come when you suffer, because nobody understands. That's why people choose to die and life glows on, a rolling stone seeking to gloss over any uneven edges."

He listened to her, without any comment. Camila talked on and on until she'd forgotten the first question or any of her responses and she felt instead a lightning within her belly as all the feelings she'd held on to – built into reasons for self-destruction, poured out of her, and lay flopping like fish hungry for the sustenance of water. She didn't know what to do with them, her flapping emotions. She wanted to put them all back in the river, but be no part of them, and let them die and cease flapping and melt into the floor turning into a mosaic of her life. She wanted to walk over them – feeling no delineation or proof of their having ever been.

"It isn't so easy to pretend things that have happened, simply didn't. Our minds tend to urge us to recollection, whether in our nightmares or conscience, we return. The only way to truly let go is to remove it permanently." He said later.

"What if I could? What if I could make it all go away?" He carried on. *"I mean everything, all the moments that crushed you. All the pain you carried that caused you self-doubt and insecurity, and finally, to feel that life was not worth living."*

"I'll come to terms with it. I don't need it taken away," she replied, *"I have a better life now, I'm content now, maybe all I needed was a change of scenery, someone to lift me out of my myopia and offer me a new doorway. You've given me that, I see things now, reasons to continue, hope even."*

"Do you really think it's going to be that easy?" He replied, looking at her evenly. *"Changing your life like a hair-style or a new coat? Do you really think you can shrug off the years you've inhabited yourself and the pain and let it go, without any residue or impact on the person you try to be now?"*

"I don't know" she offered, *"I would hope it could be. I didn't have hope before, now I guess I have some. I have read about people who overcame far worse, I have seen in texts on Buddhism that we become enlightened when we stop letting our pain and resentment dictate our emotions. I don't know how to do that yet, but wanting to could be a first step?"*

"It's very good to have hope" he said, *"but hope alone doesn't make things so. I learned that we may escape depression for a time, a vacation, a break from the norm; a spate of good luck. Sure, that might cause us to believe depression can be cured by improving our lives, but what if it's not true? What if it's like anything? When things are good – they are better and all our symptoms improve. But in time even the good will be dragged down by the persistence of the disease? This is more of a reprieve, a high from not having died. But one day you are likely to wake up and feel like dying again and when you do, you'll feel the most awful sense of betrayal. Both anger at yourself for your perceived weakness and anger at a world that permits a person to feel such agonies without sufficient answer for it."*

"You sound like the opposite of all the therapists I've talked to throughout my life, you don't have a lot of faith in change then?" she said, slightly irritated by his tone.

"Did the therapists help you? Did they stay your hand when you went to the bridge? You think they had the answer? Or is it possible the reason you're irritated is because you know I'm telling the truth and it rains on your short-term parade? Maybe it's not what you're accustomed to hearing, I'd say that was a good thing, given that what

you're accustomed to hearing hasn't helped you a great deal thus far, has it?" he replied.

She swallowed hard. *"Isn't that a bit insensitive?"*

"Only if it's not true. After all, truth is everything. We get caught up in the books we buy from the self-help section in bookstores, or are recommended by friends who swear they were in a terrible place and this 'saved' them. Haven't you heard that before? Take that pill? Swallow it down with the belief that if it helped them it 'must' help you? Did it?" His eyes looked like cracked marbles in the fading light.

"Well, I agree with that, truth is the only thing that saves me from anything but I would like to believe whatever the medicine you gave me when you found me helped me feel differently, maybe now I will get on the road to recovery, maybe there is a real way to feel differently." She thought about it. *"What did you give me?"* Her venture spilling out into questioning the last few months.

"That would be wonderful, wouldn't it?" He replied. Ignoring her question. *"But I'm telling you as honestly as you know that it is daytime and not nighttime with the certainty of one who has seen time and again, the falsehood of the proffered 'miracle cure' or life-changing text, that at best it will only ever be temporary."* His dark eyes catching the fading light of day and illuminating as he spoke.

"The real road to recovery is to get rid of the disease, cut it out, burn it out, eradicate it forever. It's like cancer, you don't live with cancer, you don't feed it, tuck it warmly into bed at night, kiss it sweet dreams. You try with every part of you, even as it almost claims you in the battle, to destroy it." He paused, watching her closely. *"People believe their experiences don't warrant extreme measures, that they're not worthy. But anyone who is struggling should do whatever it takes to feel better. At any cost almost."*

Chapter 10

She thought on all he'd told her on her singular walks. She'd come to appreciate nature once again as a soothing balm to the fever of city living, the way she had when at 17 she was sent off to be with her alcoholic grandmother. That had proven to be a strange but not entirely un-pleasurable experience, being away from everything she knew, at a time she was filled with questions and resentments. Her grandmother, a strict religious type and despite this tendency toward judgment, still youthful, energetic, with a great knowledge of literature. They'd take long walks with her border collie running ahead into the shrub and barking excitedly at the rabbits, which, startled, would bound out and leap for the nearby burrow.

Back then it seemed a wonderland, so far removed from the city. Her paternal grandmother had asked her to attend university there, but she'd declined, needing her own space, her own way forward. Many times since she had wondered if in her haste to be independent, she'd forgotten the value of belonging, at any cost. Her grandmother may have been a secret drinker, who locked her out in the cold some nights when the booze turned her cruel.

She may have been devoutly religious the rest of the time, forcing her to read books on why masturbation was a sin. But she had lightness to her, and a desire for family. Had Camila known what she knew now, she may well have gone into the deeps and followed her grandmother's penchant for gin at 4pm followed by Bible Study.

Family; *"Can I pretend I never came from one?"* She'd asked a therapist once. *"If that were possible, most people would do it."* The reply. *"But what of those perfect families you see?" "They don't exist." "I've seen them!" "You've seen what you wanted to see. People are good at putting on a show. But that's all it is. The heart of a family carries a darkness, no matter whether they leave all the lights on or not."*

Her family were beautiful and destroyed: Father's parents a rich legacy, half scalded in evil, half risen in brilliance. She often felt a greater attachment to their perspectives than her own parents who lived lives as if they hadn't had a child. As if the things her parents did not feel, her grandparents had somewhat compensated for, in their short, prematurely closed lives. For the millionth time she wished her grandparents were still alive. even her artist grandfather. Just one relative to deny the erasure of her family and identity. She had some really good memories of once having had a family but even those were lost when she thought of the neighbor abusing her. That unrepentant serial child molester who stole her soul and put it in a cupboard where little girls lost their innocence. That neighbor who always smiled but inhabited darkness like he'd named it. He would burn forever in her mind as The Devil and she owed him no fealty or devotion, only the loathing of the survivor. He who was never sorry and died still worming in her mind like a large grub, eating her finer feelings.

She thought of legacies and ancestors, the blue and the red pill of memory. Where we come from, determining so much of who we are, through the beliefs we carry before we know we carry them. She thought of her own family, the legacy of sadness that ran like a stubborn vein. When her paternal grandfather, sleeping forever in the blue room, switched off the light one last, certain time and winked out. How after he died, daylight bequeathed horror with toast and ghosts, already inhabiting the hinges like spectators to a wake before dying began. Her quiet, talented grandfather, skipping the obligatory explanation for his killing himself and going straight to his place among the hills. Maybe only there in quietude and undisturbed roll of thick grass could he spill onto page, the water colors of his imagination.

Her grandmother, sitting after his death at the wood table. Varnished hands still, the collar of her nightgown muddied with something indiscernible. For hours after discovering him dead, she hadn't moved. Her children and grandchildren absent, arranging as outsiders will, the process of grief in form. When she rose, she fed the ducks and noticed another broken egg by the side of the pond. It seemed a low mockery of her feelings, hemmed and constrained, wishing to slip into water and be lost. Camila, the drowned girl, always understood this feeling. She physically resembled her Spanish grandmother, though in her mind this was not a good thing, she didn't want any markers of her family, she wanted to be from somewhere else, from other people. Where the blood wasn't tainted and indifferent.

Camila's family were either dead or gone in a different way to death; the indifference of the living. Indifference is the true opposite of hate, and maybe it was that which scalded her the most. She wasn't a captive, she wasn't a guest, she wasn't ever at 'home.' She was nowhere and had always been nowhere and finally she made peace with that. For all the years she sought control in knowing as much as she could about everything, where had that gotten her? And he? What did it matter why this stranger had saved her? Why he hadn't taken her to the hospital but cared for her himself. *Fuck it.* Why did it matter what his motivations were when knowing never made a damn bit of difference? She thought often of the saying '*ignorance is bliss*' and how it had surely been her most hated expression before it became an accuracy. Maybe like a glove, she'd slip it on and see how it felt for a while.

Chapter 11

Though not proud of surrendering, Camila's conscience pricked her back into feeling she should be more responsible, once again take the lead, or at least the reins. When she expressed this a few times, he pointed out kindly that it had not done her so much good being in control. In fact, she may have suffered under the illusion she was, by micromanaging things and seeking understanding. Didn't she know? All along she was floundering in a sea of information that led her no closer to knowing anything of how to save herself from ending up on that bridge. He didn't say that to chasten her, or remind her of her past failings, as he didn't see them as failings but pathways that weren't achieving an outcome that didn't seek to destroy her.

She did wonder why her life was valuable to him. Sometimes she realized it probably wasn't about *her life* but the notion of saving *someone*. After all, hadn't Camila once saved near-dead things? She knew she had. She recalled the little animals and even a few friends, with that broken look in their eyes whom she would befriend. In her childhood, she didn't use computers much. Shuffled from strangers to relatives to her father and back again, she began to learn how to take up less space. She ate less. She spoke less. She was less. As the paintings that leaned against the wall had been forgotten and gathered dust, so did she. As the walls held memory in silent shape, so did she. She knew how to survive without food, water, or even air. She was an expert at it.

He eventually told her of the night he found her, as they lay in comfy seats facing the calm waters. He spoke in the dusk, of the day he went for a walk and saw her fall off the bridge. No one else had been around, he didn't own a cell phone, and he was afraid of cold water. But he dove in and pulling her by the tendrils of her hair, dragged her to the surface, feeling the cold threatening to take them both. He pulled her roughly out of the water and to land, in a series of grabs and pushes. Fearing he hurt her more with his frantic attempt to keep them both afloat but unable to be gentle. Surprisingly he reached the shore sooner than he'd imagined and they lay there, two mud-covered humans. Camila hardly breathing, he, breathing noisily like a child.

Still soaking wet, he had brought her to his house and nursed her back to health. He didn't contact anyone because he knew the reason she had jumped was because there had been no one to call and prevent it. Obviously if she'd had someone who had given a damn, she wouldn't have resorted to this. He figured she could do with stepping away from the toxicity in her life for long enough to regroup. He took the decision to cut her off from any potential source of further upset, by letting her die that night. Legally, metaphorically, there on the bank and be reborn in a new skin, beneath the sun the following morning.

At first he had fretted that Camila's parents would look for her, but another body had been found in the water a few days afterward. This body was assumed to be Camila, because her car and her keys and all her id were parked on the bridge. Picked out by disinterested neighbors who said *'yes pretty sure that's her'* because of the length of hair and the color of her skin, they looked no further. The police believed the body was Camila's and informed her relatives. The other person who ended their life stayed unknown, taking Camila's name in death. Such little things make us recognizable and not ourselves at all.

He'd gleaned this he told her, from the local newspapers. He thought maybe as she mended – she would come around to wanting to know how she could be outside of her old life with so little effort. She didn't say anything about the other body assumed to be her. It didn't seem to shock her. Maybe she didn't hear half of what he said. He could see every day he came to check on her, the good it did her soul to rest in anonymity and be far removed from those patterns that drew her toward taking her life. He didn't want to disturb that healing process. They had both focused on her getting well to the exclusion of usual considerations, falling into a companionable routine. When he decided to move her, it was upon the conclusion of her physical therapy, he said he wanted to take her further away from the distraction of the world and the nonsense of exposure, to reaffirm her existence in the healing waters of a lake that she would not wish to drown in.

Like a healing bone – Camila knitted together, growing stronger physically, her mind coming out of its hermetic fog. She began noticing once more, the world. Her eyes cleared, they took on the light reflecting from the lake, her cheeks grew fuller, she gained weight. Little things. She didn't wake up as late, and go to bed as early. There was a bloom of interest in her movement, she listened to birdsong, to his reciting some of the stories of his experiences living in the woods. She heard the honk of migrating ducks overhead, their fat bellies, sleek in flight, wonderful colored beaks a bright contrast against winter slough.

When she could walk, she would run her hands along the wood in the house, feeling the ancient thoughts of the house like a song. She would listen to the fall of light against glass, feel the momentary heat, and the hot chant of birdsong outside. The very air seemed to hold particles, filled with a quiet energy, coaxing her to observe. All the small things she'd forgotten in the years spent frantically trying to make herself whole, now lay themselves open like flowers. There was such an intoxication to simply observing. Walking through life like a quilt-maker, plucking color, sound, temperature, out of the air, and adding it to her pallet. It filled her with senses like she had begun to breathe different air. The tightness that had always held a stranglehold within her, loosed and grew soft.

And this is what they did. For months, felling time. Soon she would swim in the lake when the weather, crossing through Winter, began to warm and dissipate, giving way to the new season. He would join her on the lakes edge, reading a book and watching her grow stronger as she ventured further and further out. To conquer the fear of drowning when you have absorbed the very DNA of the river, was a feat indeed few could manage. Somehow, she did this unbidden – as deer coming close to water, drank long and it offered no resistance, only welcome salve for bad memories.

But the memories did come back … and he knew the only thing stopping a repeat would be to expunge them from her as you would rid moisture from a sea bed and dredge it for minerals. To find the untainted part of her, he would need to undo the parts that were cancerous, eating away at her edges, with every whispered entreaty they could muster. He knew as the surgeon inspects the blackened rot of cancer, starving away healthy tissue with its relentless scour, that she needed to be cleansed of her former wounds. Exorcizing the darkness and stitching her up, bright and clean like a new penny, glistening beneath water's surface.

"Did you know?" He asked once, *"in varied times during Psychiatric history, it was routine to electrocute even the underage patient to rid them of memories that caused them to fail to thrive. It was thought if a person began again, a fresh slate, we could amend our fate." "That's madness. I like that turn of phrase though; amend our fate." "Maybe … or not. For some, their aching minds, released of harmful patterns, went on to act upon hope rather than old habits. The damage to their neurons may be a worthwhile trade against the harsh winds of any recollection." "Still think it's madness,"* she replied, thinking of how years ago she'd read about this in some women's magazine. Now the abstract was her life. Camila grimaced in the inevitable next thought; if she plugged herself in and threw the switch, would she wake up light-footed again?

Chapter 12

When had the chains slipped around her neck and dragged her down? What moment in her life had started that slide toward eternal darkness? He asked her the same question and Camila took it high up into the hills, overlooking the lake and its certain weight, cupped in hands of rock and clay. She thought back to sinking beneath the water, the pain so far away she only knew it existed by color and sounds within her head, drowning out, getting fainter. What a relief it had been, what a terrible relief. To let go.

She always talked to herself, even as a kid. Acted like she had a friend inside her head, because no friends existed on the outside that really, really wanted to know what she was thinking. The make-believe friend wanted to know, they were interested: *"Maybe Camila,"* she muttered, tramping through the frozen mud, her limbs aching with the effort, "*The lethal pattern may have been configured during the years you were too young to recall. Don't we learn before we know we learn? Wasn't that what the Psych once told you? Do we act before we know the purpose or outcome of the act? Wasn't my childhood a fitful box of shards? How then can losing one's memory save one's mind, if memory is already fragmented?"*

"What the hell do I know?" She shouted out loud. The echo of her still crackly voice, echoing in the tall pines. *"I'm nobody, I don't know anything! Especially about myself – if I knew anything about myself, I wouldn't have done all of this. I wouldn't be the person I am. I wouldn't be this fuck up!"* Her too-thin legs submerged in mud, the mud going over the top of her borrowed rain boots (whose are these?) the feeling of mud between her toes, cold and then warm.

Because you do know he had said later that evening. *Deep down, you have always known, your mind is a filing cabinet; you extract memories based upon knowing what drawer to look in. If you have no map, you cannot purchase the memory but it remains, festering within you. Your subconscious knows, in the nightmares you have always had, in your unease. It affects you even when you do not know the combination.*

He told her; *"If something is unconscious how can it permeate your consciousness? Because so much of what we do is unconscious, for example our motivations are not always as clear as we think, our split-second reactions, our prejudices. We are an amalgamation of what we know and what we do not realize we know. So much of what we do is still harnessed by instinct and flight or fight response."*

"In your case," he continued, *"you are defined by what you have forgotten as much as what you recollect. If you are ever to be free of yourself, you have to empty yourself from the ground up, until you reach the very last memory you have, and extinguish the head of the fire."* He had a dichotomous habit of licking his lips after saying a lot, as if unaccustomed to thought, though his thoughts were fine and well described.

She could see what he was saying, *"But won't I stop being me if I lose all my memories?"*

"That depends upon what you define as yourself. I would say a person, irrespective of their memories, remains themselves but not so much that they do not have a chance to change. We believe we are the sum of our memories but they impinge upon what we're capable of being. Change doesn't mean not being you, it means not being you in that scenario drilled into your head." He replied.

"What if I repeat the exact things I did before, because that's the person I am?" She said. The thought of erasing one set of errors and just doing the same thing over again – seemed intolerable to her.

He didn't say what she'd expected to hear in reply; *"Maybe you will. But what you won't do is repeat the situations that caused you to become that person, as you are going to change those situations. If we say they are the cause of your reaction, then change them, change your outcome. You are as defined by what you experience as how you react to that experience. But if you recall your past, you are unable to truly experience anew. And be freed from the restriction of your responses."*

"What do I need to do?" She asked. There didn't seem to be a better question. She could feel the memories crawling over her at night, trying to find a way back in. She wanted to stay in the light, to watch the smooth water of the lake, to be able to hold her breath long enough to reach a shore that didn't have another suicide. *"What do I need to do?"*

"You need to die again." He replied. The wetness of his tongue on his lips, catching the fading light of day.

Chapter 13

Winter had taken hold prematurely in its second cycle during her time at the lake. Everything coated with a fine spit of frost, dormant colors rinsing through like crochet patterns. The wind was fierce and high, whipping the trees to cry out their wooden ache, and bend fitfully against the current like sleepy train passengers.

Camila had been dead for three days.

She read once of the Lazarus Effect, where people came back from the dead, sometimes thirty minutes later, sometimes two hours, the longest recorded being a full day. It flew in the face of science, though surely there was a scientific explanation, hibernation perhaps? It is said that one should periodically cease to eat, as Tibetan Monks did, to let the body recover from the exhaustive process of digestion. To be empty and go without, helped to maintain for longer, the vital organs.

She had been without food for one week, leading up in preparation. Light-headed and detached, hunger absent against the anxiety of the act. *This time dying hadn't been as easy.* When

Camila was in charge, when it was the culmination of suffering it felt like the easiest thing in the world to throw herself into the air and watch her body plummet like a stone into the resisting waters below. *I am not afraid to stop existing. I am more afraid of carrying on.* She couldn't even say she felt the murderous slap as she hit water as hard as glass and forged her way below. She knew she had submerged and risen, in fits and starts, as air within her, and weight of water without, fought to claim dominance. Eventually, like a dying flower sheds petals, she had simply sunk and at the bottom, rolled with the rip tide into a ball of gathered sea moss and mud.

That had felt like a dance she'd been preparing for her entire life. Somewhere in her psyche she had always known it would come to that, always known the road less traveled would beckon and she'd willingly submit. But this? This choice to die so brightly, with sense and reason on either side of her renewed vigor, it had not been easy. It had not been something she wanted to do if truth be told, though as much as she felt this, she knew he was right. The demons would return, they always did. They had begun to through the fabric of her dreams, lifting up the edges a little and peaking in like intrusive thoughts. She knew she would run on repeat until her battery ran out, so why not choose differently? Choose to live through extinguishing the monster claiming her.

The Psilocybin he'd been dosing her with was no longer sufficient, just as treatments of old, eventually failed. He'd believed initially the natural rigor of magic-mushrooms, laced with Ketamine, would erase Camila's worst memories from daily life. But she'd lived with them so long, they were good friends. More familiar to her than any future. Even at higher doses, the medicine he'd compiled wasn't sufficient. It was this or it was eventually, another ledge. Another deep-water submersion.

The pills he gave Camila were violet; she drank a full glass of water and watched the blue of the glass and the thin sunlight reflecting off, before closing her eyes and breathing slowly. Her breath was slow, then labored, then rapid, and finally, she simply ceased. Day turned to night. Winter claimed the remaining hold-outs of Autumn turning them into decorative ice-captured chimes, hanging from bare tree limbs, and overhead no birds flew. Choosing instead to stay in those places all living creatures find when outside is unwelcoming.

In her death she heard the sounds of the past. They rushed past her like hot-cheeked late dancers to rehearsal. She watched through a mirror within a mirror, her beginning and her end, until all of time was a circle. Then she could see it all at once, spinning like a ring within the theater of her electrical impulses, as they one by one, switched off and grew cold.

She saw herself as a toddler, plump, not resembling either parent. A wide smile and a frightened awareness of adult fickleness. Already she had known. She carried her patchwork doll to her room and clung to it, crying silently. The books around her were her companions as her parents' entertained friends in the other room. She learned how to be unwanted before she learned language. She learned how to know what it felt like to love someone who was aching to be released and how if love is real, you let it all go including yourself, until your world becomes transparent and you are not really there.

She saw herself as a small child, sitting cross-legged at the front of the classroom as the teacher read from a book. A little boy behind her, holding her hand, and a hard plastic doll, head lolling in her lap. She stung between her legs because that is when her neighbor had begun his play of her. Though she hadn't known it, the impulses of her always had, and had dyed her wool in the same mixture as that gray shadow of a man. The one who loomed over her bed at night, talking in tongues. She rose up to climb out of the window but he was fast, and he brought her back. Her hands scratching at the rose bushes that grew like captives,about the house and she heard her own cry, a single bird, taking a straight line, up into the night sky.

"*Why the hell did he choose me? What did I ever do?*" She'd asked so many times. "*I was just a kid and he decided to lay his disgusting hands smelling of exotic soap, all over me, invade places nobody should have touched. He ruined me before I knew what ruin meant. I was never the same afterwards, how could I be? I was disgusted with myself, more than disgusted at him, because he'd already placed the lie and stuck to it. I had to live with the truth, nobody wanted to hear it, nobody believed me. So, I quit saying anything after a while.*"

"*Maybe that's what began all of this.*" He replied.

"*No, no, no, that's not it at all.*" She tossed her head like she was drunk on anger. "*I can't give him that power by saying he caused this? That way he's won. Don't you see? I can't let him win!*"

"*If you die and you don't come back, then hasn't he won?*"

"*Not if he isn't the reason!*"

"*You can say that as much as you want Camila, but you're lying to yourself.*"

She threw something at him, the nearest thing she had, it sailed in the air past his head and she turned her own head, in shame for lashing out. "*It's okay.*" He said, patting her shoulder. She wanted to tell him to leave. She knew he was wrong. It had never been okay. Even dying hadn't made it so.

Chapter 14

In the Underworld, she saw herself sitting with her father on her narrow bed and her father crying, pushing the tears away like scolds. The only time he had ever cried in front of her, telling Camila that he didn't know how to take care of her, didn't know what to do. She heard her own voice, babyish but certain, assuring her father in the way little children sometimes can, that it was okay, she didn't need anything more, she was all right. Not believing it exactly, but deciding on that day, it was the only identity she could forge in her disintegrating family. She saw her neighbor smile at that, and pat the sofa next to him, whilst he peeled an orange with the thick yellowed nail of his little finger. Smelling of cigars, oranges, and something awful behind all the rest – he would ask her to watch TV with him but there was nothing of entertainment for her, behind the pillows and the cover of respectability. *I am not afraid to stop existing. I am more afraid of carrying on.*

The only-child's dilemma had lain flat like an ironed sheet on her back, weighing more than gold and costing more than saffron. It scalded like hot water poured in cold bath water, when the heater blows too weakly. The dilemma sank like a dark gray stone to a pond's end where nothing, not even light penetrated. She didn't know the answer, diving in, searching among slime and wriggling things of horror for its smoothness and reassuring weight. She needed to keep it in her pocket to prevent being swept away by guilt, a very red flag waving from a very distant shore. Unable to push it further away, she swam closer, listening to the yearning of time as, over water those who did not care for her called out*; don't be gone, you are the only one we have.* But this was just a sound coming from herself, nobody really called, nobody really missed her when she wasn't there.

They existed in many glasses of bitter gin, made in thick barrels out in redwoods where rain pattered on the sides and turned it to moonshine. She read her own fortune at the kitchen table, holding close warm dough before it baked against her chest to keep out drafts. Knowing then, longing does not return time for re-do-overs any more than we can un-birth ourselves from the set of our fate, tilting with sharp clothes hanger in narrow alleyways.

It was as if she had always been born of storm, some children are just weeds, let loose in seed, to find a pocketful of earth to sustain. Some children are born during violent storms, when the tin on shelves rattle and the woman turns away to the wall. Those women don't want to hear the cry, don't want to touch the outstretched tiny hand. *Take it away*, they cry, and so they do. Wrapped in afterbirth, the child knows before she can speak *this is what it's like, when you are born of a storm.*

"No! No! No!" She screamed, thrashing from side-to-side as he injected her again, and she sank again and she died again and he brought her back again. *"No! No!" Her chest convulsing, lifting impossibly, ceasing, restarting. "Come back"* he said, *"Come back here"* and she clawed through the treacle of her memories – through the fury of the neighbor's hands closing over her mouth.

"I can't stand it!" "You don't have to anymore," came his reply. The moon outside didn't waiver – the walls stayed straight – she devolved and swallowed her tail.

Camila had been sold by abuse into a purgatory of sorts. Sold women, purchased for a stone, bear children and rid themselves before bed sheets are burned. Women buried in exterior lives, vault internal demons and shut the windows to their souls. Prohibiting connection, they lie spread-legged waiting for the next customer, hoping they have enough pills to take the pain of their ripped insides away. Their children, like dogs, sense this and climb away, out into the unfocused world. This void is much like the echo of neglect within their own hearts. Such children become lost within a push and pull of longing for replacement and obliteration.

As a teenager, maybe 15, Camila had been this way, and used to dance at a club on weekends to whip away the pain. She was genderless, like nobody had taught her how to pick a side. Her short hair uncombed and thick like badger fur, her eyes emptied of empathy. She danced like she was naked but for wolf skin; raw and salted to the touch. She danced as if music were her own hero. And we? We were just insects climbing the walls. Her freedom was complete. Her capture? Inevitable.

"Fuck you!" "No." "Yes! Fuck you! Fuck you all! Every damned one of you!" "No." His voice was steady, like a pirate radio station in the dark waves, she tuned in, she tuned out, the fever was bright and blinded her. Days rolled, a storm within a storm. *"I hate myself! I want to die!" "You are dead. You are safe."*

She'd often thought about it in the past; When do children inhabit that space where adults are, and eclipse enviously, their thrones? When do children, rudely tossed to the side by glancing cars, strike out and shut down street lights with energy as fierce as stop signs? Who saves the child who kicks her pursuers with sharp metal boots, but is eventually swallowed by their need to drink from youth's fountain? There are demons in gentle hands, and salvation may lie at the release of a bottle. When you are feral you can't always tell.

In those days back then; Camila had the tired eyes of a 50-year-old street walker who had seen it all and her skin wasn't even finished blooming. She'd lived here before, in this incantation and in many, her movement a slide through time, mirrored back in different eras. She was the child they all kept behind them. A shadow of their hunger, itching to be fed, vampires feigning innocence. Until no longer, a marred and lost thing, she crept voiceless and became the red poppy, struggling to thrive by the road side. *I am not afraid to stop existing. I am more afraid of carrying on.*

If you took her to your room and undressed her scars and touched her when she's not listening. If you gave her water, made her lay down and open to you. You'd still be alone. Because you wouldn't ever capture her. Nor in your contemplation, understand the rhythm of her psyche, a wound beyond your grasp. You can enter her, mark her like the hound you are, thinking imprint means anything to children of descent. They've had your number their entire short lives.

That Camila. Her heart if she still has one, harder than flint. Her eyes if she sees, see through you. Her body, if she feels, has no recollection of your ardor. You are just something to wipe off, to hose down, to eject, as soon as you pay. Spitting you out, she opens the door and heads away, into fresh air, far from your stink. You believe yourself her Lord, you think you took something? With the drool of fetish, you keep hold of it, you think you own it, but your hands are empty. She has flown, she was never there, it was just a memory of something you will never have.

Chase her, pin her down, make demands, threaten, beat. Try to chase it out of her. She will look beyond you to another place, where she lives, free of it all in night glades. And when you tire of her wordlessness, when you find no voice echoes your own empty cries, when you try to hurt her and find she is laughing, you'll tighten the noose. You'll attempt to gain entry by squeezing and getting closer to her core. Up the ante. But even as her eyes glaze over and grow colder, she will outwit your chase. Be further than ever, because you cannot own her soul, it is free out there somewhere, blowing in the listless wind.

Eventually all the dreamlands Camila had walked through in her lifetime passed by and closed down like a candle is finally claimed by its hot wax and sinks beneath itself. The wick is only so long, and if we become liquid, we drown rather than burning ourselves out. She was done with knowing her secrets, carrying them on her back like a sun-bleached diviner of fortunes, with snakes in her pockets. She was bone and calcium, sea water and driftwood. Semi-precious metal and stone, she was undone and reworked in the shape of the ocean. Spreading out far and wide and losing herself in the crashing waves, breaking her into infinity.

That's when daybreak, mauve and pink, brought her back, in an emptied lifeline. She was no more herself, as she had been. Nothing remained but the shine of a shell much tossed by waves and sea. She glimmered in the rising light of morning, and earned her feathers, reaching out and taking flight; she joined the birds returning to the trees as they turned green again and once more, became whole. *I am not afraid to stop existing. I am more afraid of carrying on.*

Chapter 15

He was gone. She didn't know who he was, but she had not forgotten someone had been there. The voice in the pirate radio station, ransacking black waves. Now she was alone. Crimped into semi-straight lines, lying down even when standing up. Her head held a fog of no thought, reaching like a gardener scooping dry bags of leaves. He returned after a week and found her making shell necklaces and reading his book collection. In his absence she dosed herself from the brown bottle that contained the mushrooms and horse tranquilizer. They stayed like that for months, static in altered state. She read every book he gave her, tried every occupation, and he taught her the more complex skills as if she were a hungering child, sitting on his knee, begging for candies.

In a very short time, she knew as much as she had ever known, as her former self. Armed with this, unbroken by scars or history, she had a self-assurance she had never possessed before. She did not ask him why she had woken with an empty head and a hungry belly, as if a part of her through dying and being reborn had accepted this was her dreamcatcher and she was part of the spin toward the sun and back again into the moonlight.

I can't hate myself because I don't know myself. It is freedom. Terrible, terrible freedom.

Children learn eagerly and quickly, unencumbered by former knowledge, their instinctual drive to be filled. Taking on a brisk pace, they throw themselves into every pursuit without understanding restraint or how we learn to hold ourselves back even from pleasure, caused by those myriad fears that creep at night and render us silent. She was not the shy child who had abdicated herself, but a child of emptiness and thirst, drinking in the richness of the sky and earth. The cacophony of early birdsong, a quiet eve of bats taking warm current as they move in one long arm, out of their cave in search of mosquito. The rise and fall of life, patterning like silver around her eagerness to know all.

He let her become herself, without influence, she chose what she wanted to eat. She selected the plants she wanted to grow, she learned the ways of woods, breathing the aromatic chant of cedar and pine. Refreshing her senses, her long hair, blanketing her back like a river, her thin ankles muscled from walking uphill in search of things to know. She read alongside him, she drew what she saw with inky fingers and picked up on the change in season like a creature of the wilderness knows when it is time to bring in the delicate plants, or wrap them against coming frost, and when it is best to pick the reddening fruit and when to hold back for another day.

Her face filled out and burned slightly with the sun, it was peaceful and open. Sadness erased, she laughed, and ran, breaking into sprints for no reason but to feel her heart burn in her chest as she circled parts of the water where the exposed rocks permitted chase. She sang songs she learned in books for children, and hummed in return, the songbird's composition. Her hands were calloused from digging earth, her feet often bare on the wooden floor. She didn't feel the bite of cold as easily, nor shudder at impending change the way she had when she was held up by thin strings. A poor puppet to her own vaudeville and exposure causing her to fill with shame and loathing.

One night, she came into his room when it was dark and climbed into bed with him. He held his breath and pretended to be asleep and she stayed, huddled next to him throughout the night. He realized that much of what we believe is learned, is an innate desire within our manifest souls, for companionship and intimacy with other breathing creatures. She knew to treat the animals they found gently. She learned to ride a horse without needing instruction. Her mind was the natural mind he had cultivated in himself for all of his life time, only it was innocent and without deliberation. Following her needs as a child would claim hunger for a hug or second cookie.

They slept together every night afterward. His unspoken but abiding wish to find a woman untainted by others, renewed. She was a night flower, opening and revealing herself in unblemished trust. Soon her fingers wound on his own, touching the places that brought him unbearable pleasure. Neither considered this, they acted on urge alone. Her emotions were so clear now, so close to the surface instead of before, warped and lost. Now she did not know a source of misery, and did not require herself to consult it. It was a responsibility to create her memories, and whilst he felt confident to read to her and talk of what they read, or discuss what they saw on their walks in the wild, to touch her body and become part of her intimately, seemed a different universe.

They both decided it, moving every night closer, touching a little more. Eventually he could not help but grow hard and she could not stop from pushing her hips against his in urgent entreaty. She touched him between his legs and brought his hardness to her belly time and again, unsure of how or what she was doing, only that she longed for something to claim her. She felt his own longing and like putting pieces of puzzles together, she tried to fit them. Eventually he moved slightly and she found her own wetness, an opening, his passion against her, straining. She pushed without the timidity of the fearful, and he slipped deep inside her, enveloped against her warmth.

She had told him previously of how she hated intimacy, couldn't be intimate, never felt anything. Just that she was torn and bruised, sore and gaping after the many intrusions into her sanctum. She had told him that when others touched her, it felt like they were invaders and her body would seek to repel the sensation of penetration, like a weapon. He knew that she had no pleasure from the touch of others, even those who did not seek to harm her. Lying frozen beneath them, watching them take their fill, her own feeling muted by the errors of the past. Those memories erased, she moved now in time with him, gasping as he pushed deeper inside her. In many ways it felt to them both as if they were learning to hold their breath underwater for the first time.

He took her breasts in his mouth and wished she had milk to fill his throat. He opened her legs and pushed his tongue as deeply as he could, hearing her murmur the common language of lovers. He showed her how to pleasure him, with her mouth, her hands. Then on top of him, moving her hips, lifting up and pushing down until he could not stand the tension and released within her a flood of energy. He held her to him tighter than was comfortable until he could hear her heartbeat and her constricted breath and he would gorge himself on her need for him and her perfection as a woman without history.

Afterward, nothing was complicated, there were no talks in the night of the past and why people hurt and cannot be free with themselves. She did not cover herself, embarrassed of her body, or judge herself for the flaws that everyone possesses. Her mind was clear of doubt and condemnation. They continued as they had before, only now as lovers and friends. He knew after a year had gone by that this woman who had been Camila was different. He had succeeded in his attempt to create an unblemished mind; he could begin then to adorn her with his own needs. Then she would become the woman he sought to create out of the wet clay of the lake and the burning need in his mind, to forge her. He knew with his deepest sense, that nobody else would ever make him feel the way she did when she woke up in the morning and turning to reach for him, sighed with pleasure at first seeing his sleepy face.

He also knew he could not accept her to change, and grow from him as a child grows from its makers, and earns its first flight. She would not be permitted such freedom. He needed her too much for that, she was not one who would earn independence. Instead, she would earn her need for him and he would remain her maker. All that he had invested in her, the baptism of her death, her resurrection, her quickening. He was the only one now, her only lover, her only creator, he was a patient God who would not tolerate disobedience, or fickle ways, but rewarded dearly, the lover who worshiped him for the life he bestowed on her.

Chapter 16

Though not far from necessary stores and a few restaurants, it was a quiet area, even a neighborhood as their nearest point of call was a good five miles down the track on the other side. The land was rugged and much of it not easy to navigate, lending a sense of wild to the isolation and open space. At once they were part of the stretch of the lake and its reflective distance, and then they were small creatures, burrowing in their house, against the storm, holding light in front of them as ward against utter darkness. It felt right and simple, neither needed more or sought the companionship of others. She, because she only knew him. And he, because he only wanted to know her, or so it seemed then.

One day whilst he went into town to get provisions, she'd taken a different path and cut through some of the lightest shrubs toward an area she was unfamiliar with. Seeing a house in the distance she walked toward it, surprised that it seemed nearer than their neighbors whom she could see from afar and watch the plume of their log fire, set against the grey of sky. This house was small, more of a log cabin in design, dark wood and compact.

It had a thin steeple roof, lightly sprinkled with pollen from the highest trees and tall white framed windows with cream curtains bowing in front.

Outside there was a green truck and a chicken coop with heavy wire all around to keep predators from the hen house. She heard the sound of a radio coming from inside the house and saw the screen door was open. She walked up the steps and knocked on the frame of the door. *"Hello?"* A woman wiping her red hands on an apron stepped away from the stove, smoothing her high forehead stuck with sweat, leaving trails of flour in her hair. She smiled an embarrassed quick smile and said *"Well, hey."*

"Hi," Camila said, blushing a bit for her intrusion, *"I'm your neighbor. We live in the old farmhouse on Starcrest? A couple of miles south of here. I didn't know you were so close; I didn't know I had neighbors nearer than Ridge Oak up east."*

"Well neither did I!" The older woman smiled again, this time relaxed and brightly showing even white teeth. *"Come in! Good to meet you! How is it that we can live out here where it's so quiet and serene and not even know our neighbors? It's just not right, is it?"* She clucked her head and pushed out a linoleum chair for her to sit in, and automatically put the kettle on. The water must already have been warm, as it whistled lightly in its tin.

"I appreciate that," Camila looked around, she didn't feel particularly nervous, that's something you learn when you know enough to learn. *"What's your place called again?"* The new neighbor asked brightly, her quick intelligent eyes taking in Camila's bare chapped hands and untamed hair.

"Oh well we don't have a name here, it's just the farm house on Starcrest." Camila replied.

"Starcrest … Starcrest? That's the road off Route 73??"

"I'm not sure, I don't drive and I haven't been into town since we arrived but it's the main road out of town I believe, if that's Route 73?"

"Yep that's 73 alright, I must be losing my sense of direction because for the life of me I can't think of a road by the name of Starcrest. But no mind, my husband always tells me I'm a scatterbrain when I drive, so don't pay much attention to an old woman. Well, I don't feel old but that's what people see. Either way, you'll be wanting to try my baking though. Believe me that's one direction I got right." And Camila's new found neighbor let the stray thought go as you would some loose hairs brushed back out of your face. No longer wondering how a woman living in the woods was unaware of so much and why she would not know exactly where she resided.

They sat in the sunny, homely, yellow kitchen at the old wood table and talked about little things. The woman didn't offer her name, and Camila didn't ask either. They talked about the hens, about the weather, the surrounding countryside and how long they had both been living out here. They talked about the change in colors of the seasons, how each one brought an entirely new set of emotions and responses. How living close to nature made talking a little harder, a little less familiar and yet, the languages in the trees! The joy of the day, sweeping with an orchestra of music within the mind, freeing the need for little chatter. It felt easy despite their being relative strangers, like an unprepared conversation often is.

"Do you think you'll make it permanent? Living out here? You're pretty young for such an isolated life. Most of us around here are old coots I'd say." The older lady asked, grinning and showing oddly straight yellowed teeth.

Camila smiled at the question, feeling foolish for not really ever thinking about what things would be like in time. *"I, I haven't really thought that far ahead,"* she replied, smiling guilelessly. Aware because of the daily dosage of medication, her own mind did not seem to form questions that now showed themselves as natural and necessary. *"I take each day as it comes at the moment. That works for me. I can't seem to plan ahead as well as I can get through each day. That sounds ridiculous – doesn't it?"*

"I hear ya, I hear ya." The old woman nodded. *"I was just saying the same thing to my husband the other day. The world's gone to hell in a hand-basket. I don't barely recognize it. You're not alone. It's about right these days, too difficult to plan for anything, right? Who is to say any of us will be here a year from now, knowing the way Washington plays with our fates, oh don't get me started! So did you come from the city originally?"* The old woman responded.

Camila went quiet, her mind empty of answers, it occurred to her in a rush of embarrassment that she didn't know enough to answer some of the questions being put to her in the normal flow of a conversation and to cover her gaps of knowledge she shook her head either up or down, hoping it would suffice and feeling for the first time she could recall, awkward for her lack of knowing. The old woman did not follow up on any unanswered questions, she told her husband later on that day that a pretty young woman had been by, who lived further down the hill from them near the lake and that she seemed a little soft in the head, but a lovely girl, something about her though, as if she were not really quite awake and she'd never heard of the road she lived on, something beginning with Star, she was certain she'd not known of this road all the years they lived there.

"You're right, I'm not familiar with that road either and I didn't know anyone lived beyond us in that direction anymore," her husband responded, wrinkling his forehead and gazing down – as if parting the thick tree line. *"I never hear anything in that direction or see smoke, I wasn't aware of an active settlement now,*

or of anyone living there since Rafael and his wife but that was some years ago. I didn't know them, I only heard of the accident in town. Figured Rafael wouldn't stay out there after that, figured he'd be long gone so I expect that's it, the house sold, these are the new folk who bought it."

"Oh my, I'd forgotten all about that, "his wife said absentmindedly as she kneaded the pie crust and crimped the edges, *"But that's true. That poor man. I expect he sold the place on after the accident. The woman who came by? She is quite young; I can't imagine what she must do all day at her age. Those young folk think they can subsist on making jam all day, that wears thin pretty quick. Come to think of it, I didn't ask enough questions, it was unexpected to see her just appear on the door. We talked mostly about the woods and what it was like living out here. You know I didn't even ask her name."* She smiled up at her husband, noticing how handsome he still was to her, still able to make her heart flutter a little. *"I'm so dotty these days. I have no social skills!"*

"Well, I'll ask around when I next go into town," her husband said, *"Oh come here you scatterbrained old-girl, let me feel you in my arms"* and she laughed in a way that took three decades from her face, and they embraced by the fireplace, as the sun began to go down behind the mountain, filling the room with an amber liquid, much like a glass of scotch looks when it reflects against firelight.

Chapter 17

That evening when he returned and they set to work preparing supper, Camila told him about meeting the local old woman up the way on her walk and coming across their house. He went very quiet and walked out of the room. Ten minutes later, he returned and his face was composed, he didn't follow up and she didn't say anything more until they were sitting down to eat.

"The older lady, the one with flour on her face, asked me where we had come from and I didn't know. It made me feel silly for not knowing, or thinking to know." He looked up from his plate, his fork resting on the edge, and smiled reassuringly with his large white teeth. *"What did you tell her?"* His tone remained even and modulated. She felt uneasy, though she couldn't have said how, and replied; *"I just smiled and shook my head, because I felt, I felt I didn't know the answer, so I felt daft, not knowing what to say."*

How did you know when you first felt uneasy? If you could go back in time and recall the very first time you experienced that feeling, what would it feel like to your growing mind? Your mind, unaware of the emotion, trying to make sense of it. When do you first recall the moment an alarm sounded far inside you, warning that something in the serene landscape of your mind had been disturbed and there was a wrong infiltrating and changing things?

"What made you feel you were being 'daft'?" he asked calmly.

She floundered briefly before replying; *"well you know, when you see something move in the shadows you feel uneasy, like the characters in books, and that's how I felt, because the old-woman expected an answer and it only occurred to me right then and there, that I didn't have one."*

"You managed to avoid it pretty well," he observed.

"I guess I did but I didn't feel right doing that. It felt like I should have had an answer. On the way back I got to thinking why I'd never wondered before?"

"Wondered about what?"

"Wondered about anything before this, this time of you and I. I assumed this was the beginning. I didn't know that there was something that predated it. I cannot remember anything before this. How is it possible to be capable of thinking and not be uneasy with knowing so little of what's going on?"

"Why should you?" He replied, taking her hand in his and squeezing it.

"Because she said that she and her husband had lived in several places before retiring here, I've read in books about previous lives, and I know that many people do many things, but I assumed this was where we had begun and had always been and then it occurred to me how foolish that was. It is like I've been existing in some daydream for … I don't even know how long. Like my brain is capable of more,

but has settled for existing without questioning. It felt wrong when I actually consciously thought about it."

"Why is it wrong?" He asked, as his fingers touched her thin clavicle and traced lines into her cleavage, which if she were honest, seemed ill-timed when she was explaining her feelings to him, but she shook off the sense that he was not taking her seriously and continued.

"Because I'm not a baby, am I? I'm not a teenager, I'm an adult woman. I don't even know how old I am. We live here, without time and it seems to be such a good way to be. I feel so content like I'm in warm bath water. I didn't ever need to think about it before, but now, meeting this woman, and considering these things, I find myself realizing I took so much for granted and didn't ever question. What happened before this time? Before being here?" A tiny grain of fear ran up her neck as she tried to comprehend what she had just said aloud. The sense of disquiet and knowing she had an absence in her processing, alarming her enough to set the small hairs on her skin on edge.

He sighed and pushed back from the table, leaning back on his chair and resting his feet underneath it. *"I knew you'd ask this question eventually,"* he said, a great fist of sadness in his eyes. *"Selfishly I hoped it wouldn't be as soon as now, because I wanted it to go on as it has. We've both been so happy. Damn the need for humans to know more! But you've been here long enough that I can see how this would come up. It frustrates me to think of you seeing this old woman and her prematurely posing these questions in your mind before I was ready, before you were ready. But it's a valid question and I want to give you a full answer."* He took a long deep breath and planted his hands on his trouser legs as if a decision had been made.

"Answer me this, completely. What do you think you know?"

She looked down quickly and then to her right, out of the window, that was dark with night, and the merriment of night creatures come out to hunt. The tall trees were a canopy of sorts against the velvet sky, and light from the stars filtered in now and then, sending shocks of silver through the darkness like torchlights. *"It seems absurd now, us talking about it. To believe I've been going on without any need to know more than what we are now, it's like a spell being broken. I think I didn't want to know anything before, I reveled in the peace of knowing nothing. I didn't conceive of time even as I read about it, because it didn't seem to apply to us, here in our world, with one another."* She smiled up at him.

"I cannot think of anything prior to knowing you and waking up with you coming in with breakfast, I cannot say how long ago it was. Until recently it didn't matter because I wasn't thinking in the circumference of time, I was living, experiencing, I didn't need to know stamps like dates and days. But I recall every day since I woke then with you and nothing before. I knew how babies came into the world; I knew I was not a baby, so how did I never question my existence until now?"

"It may have been the medication" he said, pointing to the dark amber bottles on the countertop behind them.

"My supplements?" She said.

"They're not just supplements. They're medication to help you. You take a lot. You must have noticed I don't take the same number as you do. These are micro-doses of the meds you were given when we first met. Lower but still potent."

"Yes … I thought, no. Maybe I didn't think. They help with what?"

"Help you sleep for one, when we first met, you had a very hard

time sleeping without assistance, and help you maintain a life of joy for another."

"Do you take those types too?"

"No, I don't. I take my own kind and they help me in a similar way, but maybe yours also caused you not to ask the questions you may have otherwise. I must admit I hadn't thought of that." It seemed then that he was not so very surprised when he said that. It seemed then, that he was saying something that was not quite true and he had known a great deal about the *supplements* but neither of them remarked on this because one of them was not watching closely enough and had not the fullness of mind to comprehend the depths of deception humans were capable of.

Instead of any doubt or suspicion, she smiled, *"it's not your fault, you take care of me. But now I'm thinking on it, it's easier to keep thinking. Doesn't that make sense? I have found that I can't stop thinking about it and why it would be that I recall nothing prior to us, or how I ended up with you, when I have no memory of growing up and getting to this age. I don't know what age I am. They always talk about that in books but I never once considered it myself. I don't know what my full name is, because I never seemed to need to know. I didn't ask and you didn't say."*

"I call you my sweetheart" he said, touching her hand, his lips becoming slightly white.

"But that's not my actual name, is it?" She said, rubbing at her eyes in a mimic of her internal need to understand. *"I feel I've been in a fog, not a bad fog but one that has caused me to think of myself as a voyager. Like I'm watching everything, learning and absorbing but never asking of myself. I haven't considered myself outside of experiencing this life with you and it's been such a joyful experience, but I see how I am not entirely complete if I don't have the full picture of who I am and how I got here."* She did not notice

his pinched lips turning white with the strain of holding them from a snarl.

She looked downcast. It was the first time he had seen that expression on her since she had died and come back to him the second time. He felt a grave knot forming in his stomach, an urge to run outside away from the answers he knew he had to give. Fleeing away from her innocence, asking without notion of the answer. She was his perfection. Anything more and she would change and cease being so — untouched. *"Your name is Camila, Camila Ochoa. You are 22 years old now. We live in Oregon together in this house, our home with our dog and our dog is called Sam and I am called Rafael. Before you met me you were not well and I saved you from that and you were very sick and I nursed you back to health and brought you here, away from bad things. You are safe now, and always will be because you need me and we'll always be together."*

In his head he hoped wildly that she would not ask the next question. Still, he knew that she would. Because as much as we deny certain pathways, they come to us because the world owns them and presents them to us all. He thought of reading Milton's *Paradise Lost*, he could see in his mind's-eye, the fall of Eve. Angels without wings.

"Camila Ochoa …" she tried her surname out, saying it aloud, *Ochoa. "Before I met you where was I? I can't remember anything before we were together!"*

"Well," he said, trying to keep the dread he felt out of his voice, because he had to say it all. Almost all. *"It's been over two years that we have been together."* He was surprised at how level his voice remained. *"Before we met, you were lost, a drug addict. Your brain was destroyed and you were sick and you were going to die and nearly did. I took you off the streets and I brought you here and everything is very different now."*

She went quiet. Biting her lip. She ate the rest of her food and then excused herself and ran a bath. He knew that aside from when she menstruated, she didn't sit in the bath for long periods of time and rarely without asking him to come in and read to her or keep her company. He let her be alone because as much as he had planned for this, he was unprepared for any emotional backlash, he had his routines. He imagined a tear in a white sheet, there was blood coming through the hole. As the tear in the white sheet widened, the blood fanned out creating tendrils. In many ways, her questions represented the blood, the white sheet, her new purity, being torn slowly apart.

She was gone a long time and when she returned, she was wrapped up tightly in a long woolen nightgown that accentuated her thinness. "*It feels weird to call you Rafael because we never use names,*" she said. "*Why didn't I need to know details before? Is my brain really not working right? I can't tell that it's not working right. But I feel it's off. It's like I miss cues that others would pick up. I react in ways I think are different to others, but I didn't know it at the time. I've got no comparison.*" Camila's eyes grew wet and large. "*I feel like a freak but sometimes I don't even know I am one, it's like I have something missing in me, I don't even seek answers for things I should.*"

She looked like a child, her cheeks were flushed from the heat of her bath, her small toes flat on the wooden boards of their house. "*No. Camila. You nearly died, your brain was, almost literally, fried. You'd been banging those drugs for a long time. You already had cognitive decline from that. You were already unclear. I had to help you re-learn a lot of things. You may not remember that time because it was early on and you were pretty doped up on medication, I got to counteract the long-term effects of drug-addiction.*"

She looked down at her feet, her bottom lip hung loose as if it had become unhinged from the rest of her face. "*I really was a drug addict?"*

"Yes – you were." Oddly, Rafael felt strong saying that, he didn't know why but it pleasured him enormously to see the shock blanch like a slap on her soft brown face. A part of him didn't want to be so unkind and lie to her. The other part of him, the part he rarely let out; really liked the look of shame and shock that scolded her features. *If I can't have you the way I want you, I will have you the way I can control you,* he thought idly.

"And that means I was a bad person, doesn't it?" She looked at him with wide eyes, fixed on a point just below his chin as if she were ashamed to meet his gaze. *"People who do drugs all the time, they're fuck-ups aren't they? I mean, it's not like someone who is a drug addict is a success story?"*

He was tempted to *go there,* to wind her around him, like twine asking him to absolve her. But he couldn't do that *just yet.* He had to be careful of pushing too soon and losing control. *"Of course not sweetheart. Of course not. I don't know your entire history but from what you told me; you didn't know your parents."* In his mind he erased Camila's former life with the sweep of a hand over water. Replacing it with his own creation. *"You lived in the foster-system, which wasn't a positive experience, left as soon as you could, running away to another state. You spent time in several states, working menial jobs from around the age of 18. It wasn't easy for you."* He gave her eyes filled with pity. She looked away, hot-cheeked. *"Somewhere along the line you got hooked on drugs and took too many. I really think this is what caused you to live without much awareness of time passing or anything else. Then we met, and I saw that you needed to get away from everything, so I brought you here and now you are safe and well and healed and never going to be that person again."* The sense of control he had over her gave him an erection. He imagined being a God. He could see it. Creating people. Uncreating people. The way he could fit everything to his story.

Her eyes looked bright and feverish. *"It's not that simple,"* she said. *"I was that person. I have to own that; I have to know more about who I was."* She shook her head violently and slapped her small hands against it. *"I'm alive. But only part of me came back from that place. I don't know how to be 'normal' or what it means. Half the time I'm unable to even consider things like I am now, I walk in a fog, and I'm happy with that because it's like I don't know any better, but I should know better! Otherwise, haven't I just switched one addiction for another?"*

"Why? If it was a negative experience just leave it and move on, we have a beautiful life here, don't we?" He could see himself at the chalk line, on one side, their happiness, on the other, the anger he kept in a box underneath him, welded and shut. The anger that he had decided he would try not to take out since he'd found her. The anger that taunted him and said; *you will be using me soon Rafael. I am you and you like me best of all.* The anger he'd said didn't apply anymore now that he had his mind straight and she was his. Meeting Camila had changed him and Rafael wasn't going to take that box out anymore.

"Yes, yes we do," she said, smiling but this time her smile didn't seem as full as it had been. *"It's been wonderful. But this isn't who I am."*

He wanted to pound her answers to the ground. *How dare she?* He thought. His fists curled like cobras unbeknownst and the urge to strike was overwhelming, causing his whole body to shake. *How dare she?* Sounding like she's staying in a hotel, *'it's been lovely,'* talking as if he were simply a waiter in her life, needing more, always needing more. Why did people always need so much more? Such greed enveloping the intonations of her speech, his fist balling over and over, trying not to strike out.

"Of course it is darling!" He replied, false and insincere, his voice rising slightly. *"You actually would want to be that person? The woman I tried so hard to get you away from? You'd be her again?"*

"I don't even know who that person is!" She countered with equal angst.

He felt his neck get hot. He concentrated on keeping his speech modulated and smooth. He remembered to breathe. The urge to strike being pressed down. *"Why would you want to know that person when who you are now, is so much better?"* He kept his hands balled into fists, behind his back, they shook uncontrollably and his jaw was set beneath his lips as tight as a coil. *"Why would you want to go back to that person if I can help you be a far better person, here with me?"*

"Rafael." She beseeched. He found it loathsome to watch. Her desperation. Her stupidity. *"Don't you get it? Because if I was a terrible person, what did you see in me that was worth saving? Why me and not someone else?"* She was obviously unraveling. He could see the old-Camila behind her, standing in the doorway. He could see that Camila was infecting the new-Camila with her old, destructive thoughts and her old life. Fuck it. It wasn't enough, it hadn't been enough. *"Because* (he wanted to say, *you dumb ungrateful stupid WHORE*) *we're meant to be together, sweetheart, you know that."*

Her voice sounded uncertain, like she didn't mean the words she used. *"Yes, I do. But I don't understand. Help me understand? If I wasn't a good person, if I was a drug addict living on the street, what did you ever see in me?"*

Is there no end to a woman's vanity? He wondered disgustedly. He wanted to slap her hard across the face and watch the look of horror crawl across her. Instead, he stayed calm. He ate calm until it brought down his temperature and he was able to reply:

"I saw the person you would become." He said this patiently. Infinitely patiently. Though she didn't deserve his patience. She didn't deserve a good-Goddamn thing of his. She was just like the others. Still, slowing his breath, trying hard to uncurl his fingers from the fists he made, he continued: *"Being a drug addict is only a sign of unhappiness. You had no parents; you were very lost. You turned to drugs; nobody would blame you for that."* He forced a gentle tone into his voice, coming through his clenched teeth as much as his ire would allow. The bad impulses that sustained him, were buzzing in his head like Mayflies, the longing to hurt her, almost overwhelming, like a part of him had splintered off and revealed the part that had been waiting in the wings all this time.

She pulled her socks up higher on her slender legs and crossed them in the chair, looking like a little girl with her long hair falling around her. *"I just didn't know Rafael,"* she whispered. He wanted so badly then to hit her hard and shout *IT IS NOT YOUR RIGHT TO KNOW IT IS MY RIGHT TO TELL YOU DUMB BITCH*, but instead, he took her in his arms. Scooping her up and taking her into their bedroom where they talked of other things as if this had never happened, and they made love, whispering and moving like shadows set free from darkness.

Maybe human beings are not built for living without consideration of consequence or where they fit into things. Maybe those of us who do think out loud and within, are going to do so no matter what the circumstances are. We think to ourselves; *maybe I was that person because I am that person within me, and no amount of changing that alters my outcome?* All Camila knew, was that she felt uneasy at the thought of being someone she did not recollect, and not having any power over that made her just want to know more, as if she were in a Grimm's fairy tale, holding a forbidden key.

Rafael had feared this day would come. He knew he'd have to increase her micro-doses and probably add back the Ketamine during the day, to smooth out unwanted query. It frustrated him that he'd slipped in the dosage and believed she'd still stay 'under' where he could control how much she questioned things. He was angry they'd ever broken the calm perfection of living without a past and had ever had that conversation. Rafael didn't know how to erase it now that it existed. He'd tweaked her medication so damn carefully.

Camila hadn't ever manifested the notion she was being drugged into compliance. She thought it freed her. *What a little fool. His little fool.* Nothing else mattered, he'd invested too much in her rehabilitation to stop now. If she was going to be the perfect woman, *his perfect woman*, she needed to stay clueless, even if it meant she wasn't entirely aware. Better that than to slip further down the rabbit hole and become lost in *what ifs* scenarios bound to sink her.

He tried to bite his tongue and say little more on the subject. *Pander and they walk all over you*, he remembered reading once. Standing doing the washing up, he looked out at the lake, its glassy water, and remembered her sinking beneath the surface like a submerging sea lion, glistening and smooth in moonlight. *Is it possible a person's weft is destined to end, and if we save them from their fate, we simply return back to the same outcome because it is beyond us to alter it?* He wondered to himself. *Or do they come back so they can be ours, ours forever?*

Chapter 18

1988 was a hot year, the sun beat relentlessly down, bleaching colors and straining eyes, shifting from appreciation for its heat, to a weary hope it would cease. Everyone was tired, beaten up by the glare, moody and exasperated for the lack of adequate breeze. Nowhere was safe, even at night, the thick air was halted and weak, bleeding in like timid cats chasing their tails. Bedrooms with flung-open windows, still roasted hungrily and sleepers tossed off their usual blankets like angry children beating the mattress in their discontent dreams.

Camila was born that year, born unwillingly would be the best description. Her parents hadn't wanted children. Back then this was still socially frowned upon by the legions of families who felt married couples without children were missing something. Childless couples were subtly excluded from *family* themed events in neighborhoods. They took the roles of workaholics over the chiming company of like-minded locals who watched their children play together and grow up side-by-side.

Fortunately, her mother didn't care about those things. She'd never been a conformer, didn't do role-models or convention and shunned the idea that fitting in was a form of success. Socially forward and gloriously stubborn, she wanted to be part of society and to rise herself out of the pit she considered the lot of most of her peers. Peers with whining children hanging off their legs, holding them back from expressing their own worth and skills, whilst the husband got it all and excelled at work before coming home, the invariable hero.

Camila's father was indifferent, he may as well have not existed because his entire life he remained indifferent, without ever questioning if there was something missing in his appraisal of things. He simply breathed rather than experienced life. Going through the motions without knowing why, he sought no answers, he gave no answers. He acted like a person who did just what he wanted. Feral. Untamed. At times that included sleeping with other women when the opportunity arose. He had lost touch with any meaningful connection and lived in a castle somewhere in his own mind, where he didn't seem to need what everyone else did.

If he was discontent, it was the basic things that vexed him; not enough sex, not enough money, envy of others who seemed to do things quicker or better. He was very competitive, they both were, so they butted heads from the very beginning and it was a wonder they lasted as long as they did. Two strong-headed people, in a strained marriage and then she was pregnant and then they had a baby and then they both looked away. Both from opposite directions like a statue with two heads, straining to extricate themselves from their Siamese fate.

And the baby? Camila existed and, yet, did not exist. Any more than a painting left in an empty room is there, and is not there, if nobody looks at it, appreciates it. She grew, but only by default. She shrank and that was intentional and deliberate. When Camila's father was in the same room and happened to look over, she would pick that moment to speak to him, ask one of the hundred questions, whirling inside her: *"Daddy, will the river rise and drown us in our beds at night?"* Asking to understand the recurring nightmares that she experienced, as he sat, hungering to be with women, trying to placate her into going to her room.

Her father would reply impatiently; "*No Camila the river will not flood its banks and even if it should I would be here lifting you above the swell before you knew how to be afraid, such things cannot happen when I am here to watch over you.*" He reassured her with half an eye to another room. She learned then, the nature of words and the emptiness of words. She may have only been five or so, but the lonely sound of her father's absent step as he went across the road to the neighbor's bed thinking her sleeping, found a sad truth. He was even then aware, should the river break its bonds it would not be his life on the third floor with a single woman's limbs wrapped around him who drowned, but her, Camila, lying in her bed in an empty apartment. The inconvenient daughter, trying not to scream beneath the waves in a basement apartment.

Camila's childhood was part of a morally ambiguous time, a time of change and a time of greed. After the austerity of the Depression, people sought release, and drugs were *du-rigor* for the well-heeled. Ambition was once again a possibility for young-throated folk – who worked hard and strove to outdo their parent's shabby histories. Little was saved or held back, it was a rejoicing of excess and at times, a rejection of old ideals, in order to make way for the new. Parenting was looser, rules existed but were often broken. Kids could miss a lot of school and not have parents show up and still everything went on without breakage.

Camila the child knew, if they could, her parents would trade her for something other than a child. She knew if they could, they would go back in time and ensure the contraception didn't fail. She wasn't even as much of an accident, as an error. She didn't by default make them proud, because she hadn't inherited their self-confidence or urge for competition. She wanted to be free of the glare, left to her own devices – not torn down for failing to measure up to constantly shifting ideals that were nothing more than acerbic barbs at the mirror she held up, when they chose to look. It was no surprise then, that shortly after her birth they divorced and she went to live with her grandmother in the countryside.

Perhaps the best choice because the countryside represented freedom and expansiveness and the city was only a grave reminder of those who harnessed their souls to office cubicles and played the game so well, where they hoped one day to be ring-master. The countryside was without guile. It just existed and within its folds – Camila ran wild and untamed, at last thankful for the disinterest in her, so that she might flourish by herself. Is it so unlikely that a child can raise itself without the necessary involvement of adults?

Her best friends were a couple of sisters, disparate in looks but equally left to play outside and avoid bothering the adults within, who lived close by in a neighboring farm. They would meet at every chance at their hide-out fort in the hay barn, where beneath thick bales of hay they burrowed out a cave and hid themselves well when the farmer would inspect and finding no sign of them, move on, thinking the sounds of laughter were carried from other fields. They drew maps and pretending to be great adventurers reenacted their favorite books, taking on the boy roles more than the girl for this was the greater, more exciting part, and involved crossing great rivers and surviving on wits alone. In time that make-believe taught them much of how to actually exist outside of the framework adults made, especially when they were small enough to climb in through kitchen windows and pilfer food, faster than a dog seizes bone.

Those who exist in this way, know of no other way but self-destruction. Even paper, a wan thing, crumples in our presence, we crease sheets with our worn emotion, and wrap the rest of our fleshy hearts in newsprint, only nobody reads newspapers anymore, they glide through windows like mechanical birds. Because we know … in our marrow, that we are not of this place, we didn't come from here. That if we stick too long, our legs will be ripped off and we'll fall, catching the lime-colored glass of window panes, in our echo to oblivion and lie upside down in dirty sunlight turning to dust. Baryonic matter, capturing descent in abseil, watchful, watchful ever soft in hushed float.

The bee flying in behind us, they die too, never to make honey again nor feel on their fur that warmth come of freedom. We are all struck by illusions too thick for breath, wings like melting thimbles of glass, bodies as confectionary light as confession borne of a pure heart. For those who stand, unzipping secrets, they pour like treacle and affix us in place, witness to our execution of all that is safe. All that is secure. We are bound by the flight in our bones as the deer knows when it is born, it can never linger for long in one place.

Camila grew thin like a weed, slightly jaundiced by the wrong quality of light. This was how she began, the first steps toward her end. Though she strove to rework her weave, it remained a closed loop against interference, for the depths of her were mined and emptied by those who grew fat on eating her marrow. Many children start this way, it is hard to see them become adults, as they are fitful in development, lopsided and faulty, like mechanical dolls without a key. They may survive, they may choose paths of fire and absorb their legacy. But they will always remain, disfigured against beginning, imperfect for their witness of those who cared nothing of their existence.

"I love you, Rafael." Camila said into the darkness of their bedroom. She knew he was still awake. His breathing gave him away. He didn't reply when she spoke, he didn't say a word, he didn't hold her closer, he stayed completely still, and an unease, the color of Winter water, crept into Camila's thin chest.

Chapter 19

Camila's History

Even though Camila's memory was wiped, her dreams returned. In her sleep she dreamed of her grandmother who would tell stories of their family as she gathered the wool she'd knit with and smooth it into a ball. "*Did you know?*" she'd say, "*about your grandfather's past and mine? My mother used to tell me, 'We're not like the others in the village; our blood runs so thick the soil holds it sacred, we're descendants of the people who came from this clay. We forged this world, we belong to it, our family is special, you must act like you are worthy.' I suppose I grew a little fat with confidence on that. See, I'd always lived in my head anyway; people told me I was beautiful enough to be an artist's model, sure, I liked the idea of taking my clothes off to be admired, though at the time I didn't know anything about the true price it took to pursue such vanities.*"

"*Well,*" she continued, stroking the ivory brooch on her chest, "*Your grandfather you see, he was ten years older. He'd seen the war, lost his ear-drums in the boom from heavy cannon fire, trying to imagine how such heaviness could fly. In this, he lost his penchant for painting and his fingers grew softer despite being in the sludgy trenches. He had headaches that never left, and he took up smoking a pipe which seemed, all things considered, a fool hardy enterprise in the rivers of mud and gore, only a man who stood to lose little would choose it, and so he felt, a man hardly even there, except in explosive light behind his eyes as he tried to sleep, one hand always on the trigger."*

Her grandmother looked into the fading light and said; *"Upon his arrival home, there was nothing of the past he was drawn to; it was a repellant stranger, something mocking his blistered experiences. He had trained himself not to care; now he didn't know how to desensitize his heart, if indeed it still existed. His mother, who was an old lady from the day she was born, though she lived into her nineties, looked at him through weathered wrinkled eyelids and didn't say a word. She hoped that with silence he could mend those broken places within him. His own father, a flint the color of his landscape, ignored him. Maybe he felt undone by his son, because he was too old to see war, though nothing was ever mentioned. Only in the cold reserve at breakfast where – returning home seemed stranger than a faraway country and the constant shelling, arcing overhead like fireworks for boys without homes."*

"You see Camila," her grandmother said, *"In those days, I was the only beauty in the small town. Your grandfather admired my thin ankles and superior ways because he knew they were subterfuge and a sign of my desire for more. He thought if he won me, maybe between us we could find that 'more' and make it our own. I used to trip down roads in ill-hewn shoes of precarious balance, as if I were in some fashionable district, instead of buying half a leg of ham wrapped in yesterday's news. Despite this undoing, in those days I was imperious and confident, as anyone not knowing better can be in youth."*

"Your grandfather wasn't handsome but he was tall and straight, though years would change this, and his posture and confidence attracted me. I could feel the same loathing within him as my own heart, for something outside of our fate. My parents would say 'you were born for this' and I hated that, because I wanted to be free to be unburdened by any expectation put upon me. I hated how they tried to set me up with the young men who returned from war, startled expressions on their faces making them look more like my younger brothers. I hated how the minister would talk of reconciliation and peace, when I knew well those men were still in the trenches, leaving behind pieces of themselves, hardly returned at all, but in shadow form."

"Child, do you understand?" Her grandmother continued; *"My understanding of grief stemmed from losing my sister to the white plague. Consumption eating her fragile lungs into cobwebs until, breathing a horrible last breath, she died as white as a sheet. crumbling before the rot set in, like chalk cliffs, given over to sea water. The pictures I carried in my mind of the last day my sister was alive, the vivid scarlet of her blood on white bed linen. An impotence of everything, the hacking cough that sounded like life being suffocated. There had been nothing at all I could do, but check my own reddened cheeks for a sigh of the blight, and breathe guiltily, that fresh high air, that was denied my sister."*

"My sister who died, you remember don't you?" She said, and Camila nodded. *'I don't want to be born for your intentions,' I'd tell my parents, racing from the house, going deep into the hills and losing myself in blankets of wild flowers. There gazing at the sky and smelling the mist of birch and willow, I could pretend my sisters' fantasies were impatiently waiting for me, a heartbeat away, the freedom of a life created rather than born into. Much as a shackle, the loathed 'duty' I inherited, was a bequeathed rot I tore at with my fingers. I ached to leave it be, no loyalty inside me but that to myself*

and my need to carve out another way."

"Your grandfather's method was slow and certain. He ignored my interest and found his own steps to seduction in an aloofness that drove me wild. Increasingly I found ways to meet him and was spurned by seeming disinterest, my best attempts at beguiling, ignored and dismissed by a cruel quality I found alluring and different from the panting, heaving longing of men my own age. They always had clumsy fingers and horrible desperation in their eyes, turning my stomach into acid. I couldn't abide the desire they had for me, how superficial and wild it seemed, without any sense, without any control, like a mad thing."

Her grandmother would pause and drink from the glass she said did not contain alcohol but the child Camila knew, smelt like alcohol. *"Your grandfather seemed as cool as water, his bearing unruffled by anything, strength, an irresolute stance against the conventions that lauded over them like hammers driving in nails. He drove fast on his motorbike, he stayed out late, though nobody knew where he went. He didn't attend the usual events or functions, he was a stranger in his own domain, somehow above all those who joined in, he was a savage, I wanted so much to tame."* And she would smile then and Camila would see the young woman who smiled then.

"And this is the descent of many who believe; we can change or alter fate. Or in running, they do not meet themselves, smiling sadly from looking glass. I ran so fast from my tapestry, my fingers burned to change my face, my fingerprint, my place on earth. I felt I was too near to my grandparents and all the ghosts who lifted up and tried to pull me closer to the day I'd lie beside them. That fate, taking my place by their sides, as part of their kin and DNA. Salt-water on their fingers, from hard work as sailors. With coal in their eyes, from toil underground, they seemed to whisper to me; everywhere you go, there you are, everywhere you go, there you are."

Camila's grandmother had told the story of their blood. As heavy as the metal clasping her own heart, Camila saw only a ruin. Generation after generation. She had not come from a flourishing family but one that was ever ready to shut down like a series of dominoes pulled into synchronized fall. Was it any wonder that so many died early? Neglect and misery, her own destiny hardly altered from two generations previous. Was it any wonder sadness permeated every birth like a rotten legacy that couldn't be avoided? She didn't want to carry the horror of successive generations; suicide, depression, loss, loss, loss. When Camila looked in the mirror, she saw only the inhabitation of history. Generations come before her, without succor or success. This feeling of being caught in an endless cycle of failure and ruination built in her like an Autumn bonfire. She began to long to burn along with the leaves, bright and fallen. She saw herself no differently. She was a bright thing, fallen and dying. Why not just set fire to the whole bloody sum of her?

Chapter 20

The night Camila stood on the bridge was a night every other day had been waiting for. It was more familiar to her than her own memories, because the prospect had taunted her from her earliest recollection. *One day* said Death, *we will meet here, and you will be glad for it. I will take your hand and together we will step off and into air we will walk, falling, falling until we know no more than the peace of ending the charade.* Like a belief in God Camila couldn't help but find a compulsion in the allure of finishing her badly started existence. Blotting out the continuation of an error that had no fix. When it came to the actual day, it was only the next step in a long progression toward this end. The gleaming void scared her less than the solid ground beneath her shaking feet.

These people who tell others how to live – their cacophony of voices, grating against the cattle prod who urge in hypocritical chant; *Do what I say not what I do.* Camila was sick of it. The idea we redeem ourselves by generation? How? If each generation bears those they leave by the side of the road? How to redeem when so much has already been cast and dried? Can you ever go backward? If you smoked too long, drank too much, screwed too much, loved too little, and couldn't cook eggs in the morning? How? No, we are just left with broken chests and no bird resting on our rib.

Camila is grown, she can see the error of her thinking but you spend enough time longing, you'll take the first bus that arrives, even if it doesn't stop where you belong and in walking home you realize nobody waits for you to return. It's in that moment, that exact moment, the bridge is your solace. Camila was told when she was still very young that as you age, days will go by in such a rush. That in reduction, dilution, time gets away from us and those adults who warned her? She often wanted to ask them; "*What do you fear: dying before your time or not being in control? Do you need the structure of each year beginning and ending with goals to form an existence that feels whole?*" Like New Year, Resolutions, and Xmas presents, you need to mark calendars with bright X to signify your existence? Maybe the only reason the young believe time stands still, is because everything is encapsulated for them in an illusion of freedom, spun fine on an imagined loom. But they are simply waiting for their turn to toil beneath the clock and there it is; affixed to a papered wall, counting down the hour.

How did Camila come to the precipice? Where lay the precise moment the rain grew too thick to see beyond, she may never be able to say. But slowly I would suppose, like any awareness, or melting away of knowing, a knife thinly buttered, sunk in. The beginning, middle, and end, all one, no starting point – no seeming impetus. How small everything was after she saw. Her life was a dull eclipse – viewed in retrospect in a dance of plenty, just one voice amidst the fray, who else was listening? Even the stones we mark ourselves by will eventually be sold, slow poison working its way through, given with a kiss and an untruth.

Camila felt then as if she were standing in a river of ice water, previously a street, warm beneath her bare feet, the scent of copper in the air, and then she wondered how she had endured any of it at all. She felt breathless with her folly, almost giddy in knowledge that somehow this was it, she had really done it this time and nothing would be fixable beyond this point. Besmirched in the eyes of anyone who cared to look, it was then, she let go and fell into the reflection.

Like sugar water, from holding one of those paper flowers in your hand, gypsies sold. Watching the small petals unfold and grow soggy, colors bleeding into one another. Eventually losing distinction, until pulp, no more than pulp, to throw into the air and watch fall apart. She struck out time and time again. Until it became a lament how poor her intuition for harmful people really was. She made mistake after mistake. First a man, who never smiled, but who had enormous white teeth. He ate her stomach from the inside out, until there was nothing but mockery. Second, another boy, good at placing blame at others feet, good at entreaties and believable words. He clasped at others' strengths to girdle himself through life, like a many suckered leach – always feeding. So good at making promises and breaking them all over anyone else. That boy had no mercy in his eyes, he only had hate – and everyone saw it but her. She didn't listen, she just didn't listen. Her ears were pressed to seashells, divining the sea.

Other people's warnings were unheeded: How did they see what she had never seen? They had told her for years, *"do not go toward that boy he has evil within him, he is a broken person who only knows how to hurt, he will take you and spit you out, and roll you like ash in fire, and drown you like stones in water, and when you are unable to move, he will bury you alive, screaming under earth for abatement. It will never end, because his brand of pain is a rusty nail and a crucifix and all the hate he feels – will turn onto you. It will seem like hell then, it will be something you cannot escape, no matter how long you endure, how long you live. You will be dead, dead inside like the boy, with The Devil in his slack and withered breast."*

This boy with The Devil within. A loner – always alone in ways very few experience. Alone because nobody wanted him, they never have. They saw him for what he is, and Camila knew he was not loved and that has driven him mad. It has torn any good he may have possessed, replacing it with masks upon masks of untruths. He will wind you around and around, spilling your youth and your hope and your trust into broken glass and he will grind you up and feed from your hurt, like a wondrous flame, because to be burned is the only thing he knows. From the very start his own people mocked him, ashamed to call him part of them. They saw through him like she saw through a flimsy sheet, his ugly poison and lust for hurt.

It is no consolation to the broken that the boy's cruelty showed in his once plain appearance. Camila never understood the attraction. It was a sickness compelling her toward something she felt pricking at her, like a sharp knife. The boy-man grew old and fat, thin of face and wrinkled by his perpetual frown. His hair thinned and lost its former youth, he was dying in so many ways, plagued by a conscience he never possessed. Despite this, he resided as a torment, on the edge of her mind, worrying her sanity like a worm trying to eat its way through a rotten apple.

Do not long for his suffering they told her, as she tried to breathe from a hundred wounds, perforating her body. *Do not wish for his demise, this has already begun*; the slow descent has always paid attention and is now sucking him under, like a hundred claws flaying him for his sins. He may think he can see God; he may think he can be redeemed but we know his dark heart, and the evil he has been and all this will come to haunt his remaining days, with suffering and payment.

This Devil will not triumph, they said. For when he tries, it will drag him back, reminding him, nobody and nothing ever loved him. Then the whole world will bay for his destruction because he is a blight and blights must be eradicated. He knows this and it hurts him in a way to consider, even he cannot bring pain, because he who is a Devil is aware he matters not at all, to anyone in this huge, vast world. That knowledge, it is a needle, searing into his cranium, filling him with eternal emptiness. And as he is damned, so Camila, who survives only to not survive, is damned alongside him. For her acceptance that people can torture others, and those who are tortured do not survive, they stand by the edge, and prepare.

Chapter 21

This was Camila's history. The stories. The memories like tea stains at the corner of her eyes. The history of her people before her, during, and afterward. Times when she walked alone and found behind the masks of love, people who sought to tear her down.

Too often she was hoodwinked by promises and kindnesses, for what is kinder than someone who had an agenda involving you? Who is more giving than the thief who, once your back is turned, will rob you whilst smiling? These reasons drove Camila to the edges of herself and then to the bridge. And afterward? When Camila survived her suicide and the man who became Rafael brought her back … afterward. When he emptied her mind of her memories and re-wrote her life. Was she healed then? Or did her choices, hardwired into her brain, remain as echoes and suspicions, slipping slightly out of their bleach to tinge the day with some primeval consideration?

Camila was changed. Her brain tumor was the trauma of years and years of learned pain. And like those who are aware of their own deficit, Camila knew without comparison she was not completely formed. It didn't take long for her neurons to work out the micro-dosing she took, both in shakes at breakfast and pills with dinner, may have something to do with this. They weren't helping, they were holding her in cotton. Without Rafael's knowing, she began to hide the small sugar pills that Rafael dropped liquid onto, in a pair of never worn boots that stood dusty in the closet. Initially, nothing much changed. She was still operating through a slight fog, and when Rafael referred to her 'accident' she wondered if that was the cause of her aloofness from herself. Sometimes she wanted to capture a thought, to really examine something in her mind but she didn't seem capable of holding it for very long. Her light of inspection usually burned out before the thought was complete.

She wanted wholeness. She felt in her mind, an eclipsing unease, and whilst she could not frame the words to explain it, she knew it meant more than simply an impulse or mental quiver. It was as if she were grasping in deep water for some truth that eluded her. A murky shadow-self in front, swimming ahead, through the pitch and she, floundering unable to keep up. Every time she tried to call out to her retreating self, she got only the gurgle of water in her mouth. She longed to call out and be heard; *"Something isn't right, wait for me, I want to see what you see!"* Could this be herself, the shadow of her unconsciousness swimming ahead, unable to be tethered by her empty memories?

Panic crossed Camila like a silver arrow disturbing fog. She watched the arrow cut the air, slicing it to reveal questions that lay on the periphery of her consciousness. So many questions, a whole lifetime before this, placed in a jar and stoppered. Her ancestors, who drew her back and then away. The pain in their eyes, fading as memory became a much-repeated word without substance. Camila came from somewhere; she had been born of two people. But as with anyone who is lost, it is so easy to believe we have always endured alone, born alone, died alone.

Lost in her emptiness, Camila floundered. She did not turn out the way Rafael with his careful carving of her had hoped. Rafael the baker putting so much effort into his bread, watching it rise noting how buoyant and full it is, setting the temperature just right. Even ensuring he had used the very best flour, the very best oil. Then the bread comes out of the oven, picture-perfect but tasting strange. Even when programming is absent, it is hard-wired into us. The wolf bites, the computer spits out numbers. Camila felt an emptiness, and Rafael did not know how to retain her interest in being, the girl of his dreams. That one whom he could mold perfectly and make just the way he hoped a woman could be. She had a streak of rebellion in her, he didn't like it, Rafael didn't like it at all.

When next the urge for more came upon her, Camila climbed once more up the hill to see the old woman. She knew Rafael would not approve, though he never said as much, she could feel it as a dog can feel his master's ire and cowers under table to avoid wrath. She knew he would be displeased, though she didn't know why. It only compelled her to make the trip. Once more whilst Rafael was out running errands, Camila walked through the bracken and thick shrub, circumventing the thistles, and stinging nettles and knocked on the now closed door to the old lady's house, and waited for her to answer, with flour in her hair, and a welcoming smile. But nobody came to the door, and it was locked upon trying.

The truck that had been there last time – was still there. Everything was as it was, but the house was locked up against visitor and query. Camila walked around the four corners of the house, peering into the windows. In one, the bright kitchen with everything tidy and in order. Another window showed a living room, with two cushion-filled chairs. The third was a bedroom, the blind mostly down. She bent down to look underneath the blind and saw their bed, with two forms within, and no lights on. She thought of knocking on the window pane. It seemed real odd to be sleeping in the middle of the day. But something stayed her hand – thinking perhaps it was rude or intrusive to wake them, after all maybe older people needed to sleep more than she did.

What did she know anyway? Camila actually knew very little. Like a wiped hard-drive she strained at her erasure, feeling somehow that the worst of her, and the best of her, had been taken and stripped bare. Bare, leaving only the residue, a weak and sickly thing with little by way of opinion or courage. She didn't live, she just went through the motions. Cleaning his house, making his dinner, laying underneath him as he rose and fell, rose and fell, the cicadas outside, molting their skin and chiming in time to his careless thrusting.

As more time went on, this routine seemed to her, to be the very antithesis of growth and insight, and rather, a bland and ordinary life devoid of depth and knowing. Camila felt desperately lonely, even in Rafael's company. He was so quiet, so wrapped up in things he had to do in his office, with the door closed, or just fixing things around the house. Perennially busy, driving into town, always alone, leaving her behind, hand on the door frame of the house, watching him recede. There was a wooden doll on the mantle, and when you opened it a smaller doll and so on and so on, until the smallest doll was the size of her littlest nail. She knew there must be a name for this doll and that once she had known it. The label on the bottom was in Russian, the doll had a pursed red bonnet and with every reduction, her mouth appeared to turn just slightly downward. Camila could see in that wooden doll and all her inner dolls, her own desperate hollowness.

A week later she had another opportunity to visit the old lady's house and finding no one home, went around to the bedroom window and once more looked through. What she saw stilled her heart. The same two forms in the same position with the blind unchanged, and nothing altered. Stepping really close to the window – a strange smell emanating from the orifices of the house, as if the house had not brushed its teeth. Camila knew. She didn't know how, but she knew they were dead. *How could they both be dead?* Tucked up so peacefully in bed together, everything neat as if they cleaned up before deciding to die? How old were they? Old enough to die from natural causes? At the same time? What was a natural cause anyway? Her heart hurt in her chest, it beat too fast and she felt sick bile in her throat. Suddenly she wished with a burst of selfishness she'd never chosen to return, never found out they were dead, she was irrationally angry that they had died, and she fled back where she had come from, leaving wet shoe prints in the damp mud of the flower beds.

When Rafael returned from the stores, bringing soup for them both and fresh crusty bread, she was quiet and mauve smudged under her eyes. *"Have you been crying?"* He asked her. She looked at him slowly,

"Today I went up to see the old lady again, I hope you aren't mad?"

"Why would I be mad?" he said, his lips pinching into a thin line, *"how did it go?"*

"Well, the thing is I had gone before but I saw they were sleeping so I didn't want to disturb them. Same thing this time only this time, it's a whole week later. I saw they were still in their bed sleeping and I realized, they can't be sleeping, something has happened. They are

dead Rafael – it's got to be something like that."

"How could you possibly jump to that conclusion?" He said smiling evenly, his teeth biting the top of his dry lips; *"how old are they? People don't die together like that!"*

"I don't know how old she is," Camila shook her head, feeling the onset of a headache inching up her neck, *"she's not that old and she seemed mobile and healthy, I didn't meet her husband, but I thought that it was impossible they could both be in the exact same position a week later. Nothing had changed and there was an odd sour smell around the place, I felt it, I knew it, they were dead."*

"I'm sure they're fine," he waved her off, spooning hot soup into his mouth, *"older people sleep a lot, that's why folk choose to live out here, they like the serenity of choosing when to do what, and if they want to sleep during the day, well for all we know they are night birds who love to watch the moon!"* Seeing her face, a mask of anxiety, he continued; *"I'll go up there tonight and check for you, I'm sure they will be up and laugh at your concerns, but to put your mind at rest I will go check."*

"Can I go with you?" She asked, brightening.

"Sweetheart. I think it might be dangerous in the dark, I'm so used to this terrain I can make it in no time, I won't take long, I'll go after we have coffee." He replied. Camila felt a certain reassurance – though something damp still slivered along her neck, as if someone was watching her whilst she cleaned the plates away and tidied the table of food. Rafael put on boots and a warmer jacket and taking a large lamp kissed her on the nose and left. She watched the light trail up and up until it was lost in the skirts of the thick tree line.

He didn't come back for an hour, when he did his face was red and he looked bilious. *"I'm afraid you are right, love,"* he said, swallowing several times and going over to the faucet to pour a large glass of water, drinking it down in several long gulps and then coughing because he drank too fast. *"They are dead."*

She couldn't believe it, and she could believe it, a vindication of a gut instinct that she wished dearly she'd been wrong about. *"No!"* She shouted. *"No!" "Oh no, no, what happened?"*

Rafael shook his head slowly from side to side, *"I don't know. I got there, I tried the doors, I went to the back I saw them the way you described, I forced up a window, I climbed in. They were dead, you could, well you didn't need to check, you could smell them. I think they have been that way for a while, maybe longer than your first visit. I didn't go closer, it just seemed wrong. I called the police on the way down, using the emergency frequency on the CB radio and I told them. They will be there now. I decided to come back to you and I'm sure if they need to speak to either of us, they will come by."*

Camila was stunned. Although she had only known the old woman briefly it seemed a cruel fate for her life to be over. Even though she was older, she seemed full of life upon their meeting and happy with it, "*Do you think they died of natural causes? Surely, they couldn't both die on the same day?"* She tried to imagine. *"If not that then what? Food poisoning? Gas?"*

Rafael was rubbing his thumb against his chin, "*No I don't think it was natural"* he replied, wiping his mouth with the sleeve of his shirt several times, as if trying to rub something off. *"Could be bad food. Could be gas. I thought I could smell gas. I told the police that and left the window open. It's common in those old houses, happens a lot more than you'd think. That could explain how they died together in bed. It's not such a bad way to go, all things considering, but it's sad nonetheless. I don't know if they have family but either way, there's nothing more either of us can do for them. It's just a sad turn of events,"* he said, bringing her into his arms and holding her there. She felt his heart hammering in his chest, her own skipping irregularly and she felt lightheaded and wanted to break away and be alone but she thought that might seem rude and uncaring so she stayed still until her heart slowed and they turned out the lights and went to bed.

Chapter 22

A few days later, the police had not been by. They had no home phone, only the CB and he would use it irregularly to keep in touch with *buddies on my CB* mostly. Camila asked him if he thought it would be a good idea to go to the police station and find out what happened to the old couple, but he waved it off and said that if they had wanted to talk to him, they would. Camila found that odd, given that Rafael would be considered the only witness and a few days later, as if predicting this, he mentioned that he had gotten a call on the CB from the police station and they would like to see him down at the station the following morning. "*Do they want me to come as well?*" She said, realizing she was half excited at the thought and that maybe, for the first time since meeting the old lady, she craved another person to converse with. *"No, they only asked to see me,"* he said, and the way he said it, she felt it was unwise to ask more.

The next morning, he was out by eight, and Camila did a wash and hung the clothes in the washer-room because it was too cold on the outdoor line. She couldn't help but wonder what the police had found out, if they were at all suspicious as to why either of them would be at the old people's house. If it had turned out to be a gas leak after all. Around lunch time, as she was cleaning off her hands of potting soil with the outside hose, Rafael returned. He seemed relaxed, loose gaited and he brought some salami and French bread with him for lunch and a big container of Clam Chowder. "*Well, that was strange,*" he said, smiling, "*they said that the old couple didn't have any family and that aside from us, they don't appear to have known anyone around here locally. Looks like unless they find relatives, the state will have their house and possessions. It was a gas leak, they're certain of that. A very slow one that poisoned them over the course of the night, they said it would have been painless and neither would have known what happened.*"

Camila felt tightness in her chest, the opposite of what you might expect when finding out the truth of a story. It wouldn't go away even as she smiled and said that she was glad they hadn't suffered and asked if there would be a funeral of any kind as she would like to attend. "*They have already cremated them and put the urns in the part of the graveyard for cremations. It's done,*" Rafael said, his profile unreadable, and he brought out the paper and began reading the sports section slowly. Something, like a bur caught on your sleeve that keeps scratching, started to itch within her. As if music were being played slightly out of key, or everything had tilted by five degrees.

Camila began hosing down mud from the walkway and watched as the clots of mud turned from solid to liquid. She imagined the old people's house filled with gas, she imagined a match being lit, the entirety going up in one tall flame. Nearby trees caught fire, it raged and grew like a rumor, coming closer in the night to their home, eventually wicking at the heals of her bedroom window. She imagined waking up and seeing the whole world on fire. There was an odd relief in imagining this, which made no sense but hung around like a stubborn candle, spitting its way to oblivion.

"Would I be able to go into town and go to the library to get some books?" She asked the next day. She knew he wouldn't *approve*, it had become clear to her, after the flush of their first months together, that he intended her to be without company. He had, in a roundabout way, said this was necessary for a *period of time* until she felt she had really come to terms with everything and worked through the grief and pain of her experiences. When he first said that, taking the micro-doses every day, she hadn't given it much thought. But now she wondered what *a period of time* really meant? In the beginning she'd really just wanted to sleep long hours, stare out into the lake and go for long walks, sucking in lung fills of fresh air. It had felt like she was detoxing something within her and it felt right to have an empty mind and nothing to consider.

But as time wore on, the unease of having no origin, no memories before she had been here in the house in the woods, seemed disquieting, wrong somehow. Although she'd not talked to anyone else who could have affirmed that it was not a natural state, Camila felt nonetheless that something was not right. Perhaps it is the human gift and curse for consciousness that makes it so that we cannot live like the snow panther, alone and completely independent. That cooperation and perceived or real necessity, the tool of invention, harnesses some of our highest achievements. Even the protestor who ties himself to a tree to save the rainforest being cut down or the marches against animal vivisection knows that for all the negatives humans produce, in their greed and never-ending quest for betterment, none of it is done in isolation. We all, users of cars, gasoline, tarmac, paper, pen, contribute through our existence to the sustaining of dependency.

Like a prisoner, Camila's total absence from the world did not fit right, she had begun to feel constrained, trapped. She longed to just see another face, even if she didn't talk to them, or watch others doing something, instead of seeing her own hands knead the bread, or Rafael's return every day, eyes distant on the setting sun. It wasn't that she didn't care for Rafael. It was that she knew – in a way – he cared more for his control of her, his mold of her existence, than her needs.

Camila didn't need to ask him if she could go with him when he left the homestead. It was implied in the darkness of his eyes cutting away from her, that she could not. At first her head did not process the imbalance of this. But now, slowly, like waking from a stupor, she was able to piece things loosely together – she thought it was unreasonable, she did not know how to say that out loud.

Their house was set back far enough that walking, whilst Rafael was gone, to the main road and somehow making it to town seemed a shallow idea. It was equally disconcerting as Camila didn't know the roads well enough to make any certain guess of direction. The only other option was the cabin whose wood fire she could see burning far off. The neighbor she had known existed, some miles away, before she had stumbled upon the old woman's house. But how far was this neighbor? And what would they be like? She felt anxious because she didn't feel she had any experience with social situations. Everything was slightly overwhelming when she got to thinking about actually doing it, but weeks passed and she didn't let go of the idea. It rolled around in her mouth like a marble, becoming clearer and clearer.

Sometimes like an animal that has not yet been beaten, you know, by the tone of a voice or even the turn of head, and the way a pair of eyes settles on you. You know what those eyes say without words, the response you will get should you say, "*I would really like to meet some other people.*" Camila knew this. That he would disapprove and no good came of deliberately walking into such a conversation. Better to 'stumble' upon a friend, and then once ensconced, present that person as a normal aspect of life, rather than asking permission, which by its very default begs the asked to deny the asker.

Chapter 23

Rafael had gone to buy a new tire for the truck that had become bald and saggy, and said he'd pick up some things in town whilst he was there. Almost on a whim and without a definite or conscious plan, she set out in the approximate direction of the wood-burning cabin that she couldn't see except for the smoke, through the thickest of the brush. It was hard going, she was scratched and disorientated pretty quickly with the lack of direct access across, and the number of thick, spiny, coarse shrubs and bushes in the way. She tried to hack out a path and ensure that she would be able to find her way back based on the width of her path trodden down by her heavy shoes and a large stick that she used to bash branches into letting her through. Just to be on the safe side she also dropped pistachios as she went, their bright green skins showing up easily on the mostly brown forest floor. It reminded her of a fairy tale he had read to her not long after she had woken up.

Quite some time, if the light above her was anything to judge by, had passed. Camila was sweating and her hair was mangled around her with pieces of twig and leaf. It seemed a bad idea, but she didn't turn back. The more she went forward the more she wanted to ensure her success. Just as she had started to think she must have gone the wrong way for surely it was no further than this she saw not far ahead to the left of her a bright brick outdoor grill with black grates and a white fence that may have acted as a pen. Further in, the house became visible; a swat, low-sitting one-story house painted in natural colors, blending in with the landscape. She quickened her pace and almost ran up the white steps. If nothing else, this was all by chance, an accidental meeting, nothing planned or contrived and therefore, blameless she hoped.

The man who answered the door was much younger than she would have expected for someone who, it turned out, lived alone in the woods. He had black hair, slightly curling, dark brown eyes and deep brown skin, possibly Hispanic like Camila herself or Native American. He had high cheekbones and wore deep blue jeans and a matching shirt. *"Well, good day,"* he said as if he was not at all surprised to see a woman clambering up his stairs with leaves in her hair, "*how can I be of service?"* Camila felt herself blush, feeling stupid for her panic and urgency, and almost wanted to say nothing and run back, but he was calm and easy and stepped out onto the porch so that she didn't feel she was disturbing him.

"Hello" she said, trying to keep from stuttering, *"I'm your neighbor, we live down there, a few miles, you've probably seen our fire at night?"*

"Oh sure," he said, "*my only neighbor within five miles I do believe, the others, are way over the other side behind me, it's good to meet you ma'am"* and he stuck out his large hand and shook hers. "*You walk up here by yourself?"*

"I did," she said, "*I thought I would introduce myself, because I*

knew you lived here but we hadn't yet met." She felt dumb for the last part, as that was obvious to them both. Embarrassed to have to explain why she'd made the trek. Now she didn't know how to broach the subject, any subject. She wasn't used to talking with people she didn't know; she began to wish she'd stayed at home. At the same time, she liked how easy he was, nothing seemed to be brewing beneath him. She was aware that Rafael did not have that calmness, that something was always just beneath the surface when she spoke to him and she curbed her words accordingly.

"I expect after a long walk like that you'd be wanting a drink then," he said, opening the door and keeping it open for her to step through into his one room that served as all the room of the house, save the bathroom, a little closet off to the end, and a squared off bit she assumed must be where he slept. It was a cozy cottage, very small and warm, with bright light coming in through a sky light and five windows. *"Thank you"* she said, *"I'd love a coffee if you have one."* He went over to the open-plan kitchen and poured from a silver canister on the hob, it looked fresh and hot, and smelt like he'd flavored it with chicory.

They sat down in some upright wooden chairs covered with red and black Native American blankets made into cushions. *"So how long have you lived here?"* He said, blowing on his coffee.

"Ah, well I think it's been a couple of years," she said, realizing she'd never tried to actually assess how long she'd been here, as she had no frame of reference. In the countryside however, approximations of time were a way of speaking rather than a deficit and he took her answer without question. *"And you?"* She asked, *"how long have you lived here? Did you build this cabin?"*

"I did," he said, with a hint of pride in his voice, *"been here five years now, moved here from Chicago, when my parents died and left me a bit of money, decided I didn't want to keep in the city, bad*

memories and all. I picked up and came out here; I wasn't sure if I could make it but we're doing great." His brown thumbs ran over the countertops, reflecting the pride he obviously had for his new life.

"Oh, I'm sorry you don't live alone?" She said, looking around for a sign of a woman's things and finding on the bare walls no immediate sign of a woman's touch, everything was masculine, no flowers in vases, no tied back curtains or pillows on chairs.

"Well, there's me and Ben, he's my horse, and Jake, my dog, though he's not much of a guard dog, what with you coming up the way you did and he's still passed out on my bed over there."

She laughed, shy again, thinking of being here with this man, someone she didn't know, and aware that some pact prohibited her from making these decisions and she was doing something unsanctioned. *"I'm Lou by the way,"* he extended his strong-looking long arm and hand, she shook it.

"My name is Camila," she said her name out loud and it seemed odd to her, because she never used it and Rafael didn't use it much either. In fact, they made a deliberate point to avoid names and she saw names and time as belonging to the world of the past and those things she could not remember from it.

"Ah, Camila, and you are a secret Camila," he said, smiling, *"Did you know that?"* He winked at her; his lips crooked in a half-smile.

"How's that?" She asked.

"Because I have known Rafael, and we've been acquaintances of sorts since I moved here. I knew his wife, Carol and I knew their kid, think his name was Dylan? Well, I knew them before the accident that is. I thought more recently he'd been living up there by himself. I had no idea he had himself a new lady in his life, let alone one so

pretty. It's just like him to keep you to himself."

Camila's fingers went cold, the way you do, when you dip your hand into a really icy river, she felt like she had become heavier at a moment's notice. Deciding to keep a neutral smile on her face, she nodded and tried to make it not look like a dumb waiter nod. *"Uh huh,"* she replied, *"that would have been a while ago, right? His wife and kid?"*

"Well not that long." Lou replied. *"I mean time here; it goes slow as it is. A year can seem like a month, and all that, I'm sure you've noticed. I lose time here, always, quit wearing a watch as a matter of fact and no clocks on the walls, it's rare I need to consult one I can tell by the skies what time it is and not sure I really care about the day or month, that's half the beauty of it."*

"Oh, it sure is," she said, tight mouthed, the center of her clavicle ice-cold.

"But Rafael was with his family there when I came up this mountain and they were a tight bunch for sure, kept to themselves like most folk around here. We'd run into each other pretty regular in town, even had a few beers together. He's a nice guy. I had heard from Tom who runs the Pig and Slaughter bar, that they'd broken up and she and the kid had moved out, frankly I was shocked. Not that they'd moved out, it's hard for women by themselves on the mountain, but shocked they'd broken up. They seemed real close – I'd see her in town at first but then after a while not so much. Figured she was busy with the boy and all that, she being pretty quiet as well but he'd come by and we'd talk. I never knew how to ask him what happened, did what a lot of men do, made light of things, skirted the issue, talked about the game."

"I feel real bad now for doing that – because I found out some time later Carol hadn't left him, she and the boy had died in an accident, and I hadn't even asked him a lick about it." Lou paused

and scratched his cheek. *"The old grapevine here ain't up to much – sometimes gets it real wrong, a real damn shame, the boy so young an' all, they both were. But heck, he's back in the saddle, I'm glad he met someone else, did it quick too, did y'all meet online or something? Not much of a dating pool around here, that's for sure, but you must know that. Anyhow, yeah, I'd say I saw her around two years previous, that was the last time, doesn't seem so long ago though given I keep mostly to myself up here. Real glad to see he's found you though."*

Camila smiled and tried to think of a way to politely leave, drinking the last of her coffee quickly and wishing she had a watch that she could consult and make a pretense with, but those types of excuses, though she didn't know exactly how she even came to know those kinds of excuses, were not applicable on the mountain. Instead, she feigned ease and stood, stretching deliberately before saying, *"well I've kept you long enough"* which was patently not true, *"and I should be getting down before it gets dark, as my home-made path is rugged at best,"* she flashed a crooked conspirators smile, the best she could muster, brushed imaginary crumbs from her jeans, before wondering if that seemed somehow dismissive and rude, and had her hand on the door before Lou had a chance to answer.

Fortunately, Lou wasn't one of those who tried to control a situation. Laid-back and easy, he smiled graciously and said it was good to meet her, although strictly speaking that was all they had done and not even a proper get-to-know-you. He let her know any time she needed anything to give him a holler, and to say hello to Rafael and holler if she strayed from the path back and he'd come to rectify her. She thought it was a funny choice of a word as if his first language wasn't English and she found herself asking; *"are you Hispanic?"* It was an out-of-the-blue question, but Camila was Hispanic, she figured it was okay. A little pink flush on his cheeks hinted that she'd over-stepped and as sudden as it was, he shook it off like a dog, and smiled again evenly showing straight, white teeth. *"I'm as American as they come,"* he said, which neither confirmed or denied her question, and he closed his front door.

Chapter 24

On the way home Camila made better time as it was downhill and though she had to be careful of the branches that lay growing low or large roots growing up attacking her, she could tell she was making faster time and that eased her tension, she surely would be back before he arrived home. As she half-ran down the hill she had images of things in her mind, she wasn't sure what they were. One of them was a man, he was looming over her, she was on the floor, she felt wet and cold. Watching this was a little boy and the little boy was Rafael's dead son and she knew that even as he didn't say a word.

Rounding the corner into their garden she saw that Rafael's truck was still gone. She almost ran inside, pulling her clothes over her head. She showered like someone who had just had an affair hiding the scent of a lover. Only her lover was mud and small sticks, gathering in the circular drain of the shower, for her to wrap in tissue and hide in the wastepaper basket. Why the secrecy? Why did she feel she couldn't admit that she'd met the neighbor, when it was obvious Lou would tell him the next time they bumped into each other in town? Wouldn't that make it more awkward, as if she were keeping secrets, and couldn't be trusted? What if Lou told Rafael that he'd mentioned his wife Carol's accident? It would seem so disrespectful that she should find out via a second-party and she knew he'd be angry. Where did she get the idea about secrets and how did she know how to hide evidence so well? It was as if she were operating under the guidance of some invisible force, urging her to find out more about her blank mind.

When Rafael returned, it was fully dark and he found her in the kitchen, the lights hot and bright, as she kneaded bread and fixed the last part of dinner. *"It's good to see you darling,"* she said, lightly, thinking it necessary to point that out, and then wondering if it seemed false in some way. *"And it's wonderful to see you,"* he replied, his pupils dilated, and she knew he'd had a beer because she could smell it on his breath and she knew he had driven home wanting to make love to her and that it would be easier to just put everything on low and let him take off her dress. So, she turned the oven down to warming and already he was in the bedroom unbuckling his jeans and the moon caught his teeth and they were white and looked almost sharp.

Afterward they lay in the dark, eating dinner in bed, picking at it from their side-tables, in a decadent way, with a glass of wine on each side. She felt afraid for the first time. Of the power in his eyes, the way he could tell her to do something without speaking, and she would do it. The way her head always felt foggy at night and cloudy in the morning as if she were being fed an invisible potion. She longed to put her head out into the fresh night air and drink in the cold coming off the lake, and then she felt she couldn't move at all and it would be better to acquiesce and stay exactly where she was, with his hand possessively around her shoulders, and his feet, crossed over hers. She felt weighted down, like a full cargo ship, the captain proudly examining the load and declaring it good.

Over breakfast she made the first mistake. *"Did you live here a long time before I came to live with you?"* She asked, as innocuously as possible.

Rafael went tight and still, his body like a coiled spring. As if all the sound in the room suddenly sucked out and paused. *"Why?"* He replied, his voice without inflection, giving her no wiggle room.

Camila felt herself cringe. *"Just curious"* she replied, smiling too wide and probably transparent, realizing that curiosity was not a trait he expected in her. Wondering if that would mean the daily supplements would be changing. Fortunately for her, her stash was hidden and she found ways to keep it that way. Avoiding taking all the doses helped a little with the fog but she couldn't always avoid them, if he was watching her closely. The micro-doses he put in her morning shakes she couldn't avoid at all and that made her foggy at least half of the time, so it was a constant battle to find the her within herself.

"Why are you curious?" He repeated, his voice devoid of inflection, almost robotic, having turned to look at her, penetrating through her shallow question as if he were shining a torch at her soul and knew what she had been doing. She could feel her cheeks reddening and desperately willed herself to remain calm, not sure if she had succeeded or not, she said in her calmest voice, *"I had wondered how long you had lived here and where you'd lived before, because it's so beautiful here and I can't imagine you being anywhere else. I want to know all about you, before we met. Who you were all those years before us, I can only picture you here but I know you must have lived elsewhere?"*

That seemed to be enough for him and his posture relaxed. *"Well, you're right there. This was my parents' house"* he said, surprising her. Why hadn't he told her this before? Then again why hadn't she thought to ask (anything?) he didn't seem bothered that she'd asked, maybe it got boring for him to live with a doll who didn't know to ask questions. He seemed to be thinking, and finally he said; *"I was born here, in this house, my mother had me in the very room we sleep in, and we lived here all of my life."*

Rafael drank from his coffee cup noisily, and moved his neck as if it were stiff. *"She was a woman who never let pain stop her. The bed, our bed, was awash with blood my daddy said, but she labored without complaint, and when it came time, she tore almost in half and that didn't stop her getting up the next day and cleaning up. She was the kind of woman any man would be proud to call a wife. My mom, she had that pioneering spirit so many of these loose women have lost today."* His face took on a mask of dislike before he shrugged it off and smiled ingenuously. Camila had a mental picture of Rafael's mother giving birth in the bed they slept in. Her blood dried in layers beneath them as she slept or stayed awake staring out into the sky. It seemed like more than one generation were pressing her down, nights she lay there, compliant and trapped by her own empty mind and the heavy hand of Rafael as he slept soundlessly.

She hoped he would continue and tell her about marrying and bringing his wife here and having a child (and why he never mentioned them, and their deaths) but Rafael stopped there, saying nothing more. Memories hung on his face like a film for a moment and then wiped blank, he turned and began to roll a joint, with his feet out of his shoes and propped up against the window looking out over the lake. His lips were wet with the anticipation of smoking and his eyes were already removed from their conversation as if she had left the room. So, she did.

She went over to the kitchen to warm up some hot chocolate because the intensity of his proximity drained her, and she wanted to watch her own reflection in the mirror of the window. She wanted to ask; "*Why aren't there any mirrors in this house? Why don't you have a phone? Why don't we have a TV? Why don't you want to take me into town? Why don't you tell me more about myself before this time? How could you have had a child and not have a picture of him somewhere and say nothing about him?*" It made her wonder if the kid and he were estranged before the accident, hence the double-rumor about them breaking up and then being in an accident. It must be hard if you are broken up and then lose both your wife and child in an accident, *it's no wonder he doesn't want to bring it up. You're so insensitive Camila,* she chastised herself. She felt scared that he would find out that she knew and would clamp down harder on any inquisitiveness on her part. She stayed quiet and mixed the milk and chocolate around and around until they came together and you could not tell them apart.

Whilst she stood with her thin long back to him, mixing the cocoa, Rafael admired her legs through the diaphanous nightgown she wore, and felt himself growing hard again, which gave him some satisfaction to know his urges were not diminished by time or experience. He was a lusty man, needing sex regularly. It had taken all of his will power not to force himself on her when she first stayed with him, sleeping so soundly she may not have noticed. And yet, he noticed. Her body, her fine bones and the softness of her, drove him wild to imagine being with her, but he knew, slowly, like a hunter, slowly is the only way you tame the wild.

Chapter 25

Now she was his, she was completely his, and for the most part she was obedient and acquiescent to his lifestyle. He hoped her mind could not process anything other than this, as a blank slate, this would be eventually all she knew. He was careful what he allowed her to read, ensuring the only books in the house were ones he knew would not give her ideas outside of his own. He liked books by Eric Van Lusterbader, books about ancient Japan and submissive Geishas, with lots of hard-core sex. He gave her those books to read, to give her ideas and ensure she thought the amount he demanded was normal and not excessive. Because if she were to say no, he wasn't sure he could accept that. So far she hadn't, even when she was menstruating, he only had to look at her in that way he knew how, and she would acquiesce. He had needs, and she was his, and saying no just seemed a form of control that he didn't let her have over him. Fortunately for her, up until this point, she'd never said no. When he wanted her, his eyes signaled her and she would lift her dress and bend, as he'd taught her early on and he would splinter inside of her. The force of his urge, seeing stars and feeling the cool of water running down his neck as if submerged in the lake.

Rafael controlled what Camila knew and what she did not know. There was no internet. She knew what a phone was, but not a computer and not the internet. She didn't know that she knew how to drive. She didn't know that she knew how to look things up in the library because she'd never been. She had abstract concepts gleaned from generalized conversations and nothing more. When she asked questions, Rafael was the master of deflection. If nothing else, the violence in his eyes, quieted her enquiry and she remained still and let him take her again. This time he didn't wait and went up behind her as she mixed the cocoa. She flinched, as if she were startled that he should be there and then went slack as she processed what he wanted to do. Her unvarnished nails, her soft brown hands flat on the enamel of the countertops. The cocoa rising and threatening to spill over. He filled her with his anger and his rage and all the while, the light of the moon glistened over the placid water as if nothing could ever disturb it.

If Camila could remember what she'd read in her Psych 101 class, she might have seen parallels in her life with Rafael. She might have recalled what those books said; about how some of us like to be controlled, some of us like to control and most of us, lie in the middle somewhere. Usually happy to relinquish some responsibility and claim other parts, a balance of sorts. Sickness, missing parts in our psyche, broken pieces and psychopaths, share the common inheritance of being more at one end of the scale or the other. Either they are susceptible to being dominated or they dominate. In the case of psychopaths, the usual route is domination or avoidance, which isn't so much submission as omission.

Camila might have considered this if she had been talking to a friend over coffee in a city somewhere, and not locked up in a house in the remote countryside with a man who was a stranger just a short time ago. She might have remembered what her Psych teachers said about how it is possible to go many months — or even years, not recognizing in your life, that you are being abused. That you may think what is happening is not abuse, does not qualify because your limbs are not broken, your face not smashed in. Or you may believe you are deserving of their approbation or you may not even think the response is so very great. Depending so much on if you thought much of yourself, if you had any confidence, if you believed you were worthy. Camila didn't know who she was, she didn't know how relationships were meant to be. When Rafael screwed her until she felt tears on her cheeks, she thought she was the one who was overreacting, that he seemed so pleasured by her, surely the fault lay with herself?

When he first tied her hands up above her head, he made a joke about it. Her heart was beating fast through her nightgown, he tore it off, and joked again about it being time for another. When he lifted her thin legs above her, straining every muscle and pounded into her whilst her legs lay on either side of her cheeks, hitting the headboard above them, she did not cry out. When she felt bruises forming on her, and she felt him push too hard and too long, she did not cry out. She could see in his face, the emotion and the longing and she did not want to spoil that for him and a part of her did not want to acknowledge what was happening. She wondered afterward, as she tried to empty her bladder, if she was deformed *'there'* because of some part of her past. She could not ask Rafael; it would shame them both.

She shaved herself as he had asked her to do from the start. He said to keep her clean. As she pulled the razor across her pubic hair she wondered if Rafael were big, and she were too small. The next time he took her, she asked him if he felt she was too small inside, and he said he liked her that way because it felt so good for him. Really good. He did not ask her if it hurt, he did not ask her why she asked. This was never a question he felt necessary. She was after all, his, and he could have her any way he wanted her. He drove harder and harder, until against her will she cried out and then he climaxed, as if her cry of pain was the last thing he needed to complete his pleasure.

Camila might have recalled her text books that mentioned; Love takes many forms. Some of us like the sting of pain, the loss of control. But then there are those who are broken from their own journey with abuse. And it is those who are broken who are often preyed upon. As if the predator, adroit in their knowledge of prey, can smell the very hurt within their DNA. Rafael was such a man. He tasted the loss of self-respect Camila had absorbed into her psyche and lapped it up with his own raging desire. Camila was such a woman, that she thought only of pleasing others, and rarely of what felt right for her. In this way, prisoners are created, without the need for bars.

Camila first suspected she was pregnant when her menstruation, usually so regular and clock-work, skipped a beat and stopped. Not knowing more than that, she pondered if it could be true and kept quiet with a sense of mounting unease that she couldn't explain. The ugly feeling worming in her gut that this was all part of some grander plan. Rafael wasn't long to catch on. He liked to screw her when she was bleeding. In the second month when she hadn't bled, he knew he had implanted life in her, and he took her in his arms and breathing into her ears said *"Oh my only darling, we're going to have a baby aren't we?"*

"Yes, I think so," she said, blushing in the dark and feeling a muted joy, mixed with a far-off emotion she couldn't describe. It prickled like poison ivy on the fine hairs of her neck. *"Are you happy?"*

"Am I happy?" He answered, "*I'm so wickedly happy, I'm thrilled! Tickled pink! Here, I'll show you how happy I am. Open your legs,*" and he showed her all right. Not taking it easy, despite the news of the baby. Not saying anything like; *"I already had a son, he and his mother died in an accident, let me tell you about them."* Rafael was saying nothing at all except in his actions, rising above her in the darkness like a cloud, blotting out all light, as she held her breath longer than seemed possible.

Chapter 26

Camila's abdomen felt taut like the skin of a drum and she had bad morning sickness. She felt good otherwise, maybe better than usual, stronger and, somehow, more in touch with herself. She wondered if the micro-dosing had been reduced because of her pregnancy. With her only taking half and maybe Rafael reducing the dose, something in her had shifted. She was able to think far more clearly. She could process at a faster speed and keep up with the natural questions that came out of a thought. Instead of bringing those questions to him, she kept them inside of herself, tiptoeing around hoping somehow to find the answers without needing to ask. First, *where had his son and ex-wife been buried? What kind of accident were they in?* It sounded bad, but what happened? Second, *would he take her to a doctor to be sure the baby was alright?*

Her belly, which was always so flat, grew but not overly, and she remained fragile and thin throughout. Her small breasts stuck out through the linen of her nightdress as if they were already drunk from. Rafael found this intensely erotic and insisted on sucking on her nipples every night when they went to bed. Her answer about the impending birth came faster than she thought. Rafael brought home some strange tools and when she asked, he showed her and said; *these are for the home birth*. Camila felt shocked. He expected her to give birth, her first baby, at home? "*Without any medical personnel?*" she said. She didn't know much but she knew people gave birth usually in hospital and saw doctors beforehand to check on the baby's well-being. But he'd already told her the vitamins she took were sufficient for that, there was no need for checks. They were keeping it, nothing would go wrong, the baby would be perfect. Her stomach grew and grew, her back hurt. Camila was a small woman, and the bulge of the baby blew her out of her usual shape, causing her to ache and her ankles to swell up.

For the first time she really wanted to say no to his insistence they have sex every day, often more than once. Her insides ached; she was uncomfortable. She didn't want to be battered by his lust when she felt bloated and nauseous. Truth be told she'd never experienced the pleasure he seemed to. She figured it was because she was just fucked up. She wanted to turn him down. But something about the look in his eyes, stilled her from saying anything and she would bend at the waist compliantly and hope it wasn't doing any damage to her child within her belly. The child would be big, she knew that by her size, instinctively and was afraid of the pain and not being able to force it out of her when the time came.

Camila didn't know any history of childbirth in her family of origin, she only knew she had narrow hips and a small waist, and this baby seemed humongous. The idea of being in agony at home, miles from any help terrified her at night. She had dreams of bleeding out in the bed and turning the apricot sheets crimson. Rafael sensed her fear and reassured her that at the first sign of any distress he would drive her to the nearest hospital. She had no idea where that was or how long it would take and it didn't seem like a good plan at all.

"I've never had a baby before." She said one day. *"I'm really scared. I don't think I can do this at home."*

"How do you know?" he surprised her with his response.

"How do I know what? That I haven't had a baby before? Well of course I haven't and I'd just know." She replied. That wasn't the question she had been expecting.

"How would you know?" He repeated.

"I'd know because my body would show signs of it, stretch marks, something, and I don't feel that I have ever been pregnant before. How do I know I can do this? If I haven't had any practice?" She felt like crying but she looked away instead.

"Because you are stronger than you think," he said, kissing the top of her head, *"and anyway, you did have a child, when you were younger, and it died."* The words were like glimmering ash from a cigarette, burning her throat. Spoken as casually as if he'd been reading off a list of grocery items, with the blunt effect that came into his voice when he wasn't conscious of how he came across.

She couldn't believe he'd said it that casually and for a moment she said nothing, repeating what he'd said back to herself a few times to be sure she'd heard correctly. *"I had a child? Are you serious? How could you know that?"*

"I didn't want to tell you darling," he said, and his expression didn't seem like he was cut up about it though the tone of his voice imitated regret and yet, was a little patronizing as if he could not help himself. *"You told me when we met, you had a child in your teens and it was a stillbirth because of your drug addiction. I'm sorry. I'm very sorry."* Rafael looked anything but sorry, he

looked more self-satisfied, Camila thought.

"But the good news and the reason I feel confident about a home birth is that you've done this before. Let's not forget either, my mother had a home birth with me, and look at me, I'm as strong as an ox. This whole notion of needing to have children in hospital is just a conspiracy by the medical industry to keep them fed and well maintained with my hard-earned cash."

Camila's head ached and she felt nauseous. She couldn't believe he'd kept something like this from her, all these weeks of her pregnancy and even before that. It was as if her history was a Pandora's box and Rafael had the key and would feed her snippets of information as and when. How could anyone just tell the person they cared about that they'd had a baby they could not remember having and it was dead? *"But Rafael! What happened?"* she almost shouted out.

He turned, an irritated look on his face, with her tone; with her using his name. *"What do you mean?"*

She wanted to shout WHAT THE HELL DO YOU THINK I AM TALKING ABOUT? *"To the baby? TO MY BABY! Is it buried somewhere?"* She felt like she was going to pass out, the room was spinning, she felt simultaneously sick and furious at his lack of comprehension.

His face had become positively angry at her loud voice. He looked like he was going to strike her almost with the violence in his eyes. Just as quickly as it seemed to flare it went away and his eyes returned to neutral. "*No, they incinerated it in the hospital.*" He said, as if he were referring to the weather, clinical. Cold. No emotion, and he went back into the other room and listened to sports on his CB radio. He'd even said *'it'* not '*he*' or *'she.'* Camila stood, holding a wet tea-towel in one hand and her other shaking the air around her, as if trying to capture some understanding from nothing but filament.

She lay on their bed thinking of having had a baby during a time in her life she knew nothing about, because her memories were completely absent. Again, she wondered how she could recall nothing, nothing of her former past. Nothing of her experiences and yet know other things like the names of things, and the way to do certain things like cook, bake bread, write, pleasure him. Things you could only know if you had done them before, yet no memory existed of any before, nothing. Just the day she woke up in this room, with his eyes watching her in that intense way that he had, as if she were something he might like to consume.

For days afterward Camila tried to reach out to the memory of losing a child. Nothing beckoned back to her from the ether of her mind. Just emptiness. It didn't even feel like a familiar emotion. Loss yes. But the loss of a child? Camila felt she would know if she had lost a child. She would recognize that grief even if she'd been lobotomized or was senile. It was one of those things a woman never, ever forgot. Yet she had. Or so it seemed. Something false about that emptiness in her memory, as void as anything can be. Camila imagined her body becoming pregnant whilst still a teen, and touching her stretch-mark-free breasts and stomach, it seemed remote, like a story that someone had said and asked that she believe.

Chapter 27

Camila walked up the mountain again, waddling slightly with the weight of the child in her belly, this time it took her longer, and was exhausting, but the trail was still there. Lou was at home, cutting lumber in the yard, Ben the dog next to him, came up to her, without barking and sniffed her crotch. Lou turned and saw her and whistled through his teeth, *"well that's something fast now ain't it?"* He said, gesturing at her swollen belly *"and look at you, walking up the mountain in that condition. Is that really what you should be doing, young lady?"* She smiled and bade him hello, giving him some homemade jam and a loaf of freshly baked bread. *"Much obliged,"* he tipped his cap and winked, *"so you're going to be a Mama, are you? You excited?"*

"I am, I mean I think I am," she said, feeling flustered at being asked questions when she was never asked questions and always full of them.

"Well, that's good then – because it don't look like it's going to be much longer. You got yourself a doctor that's any good?"

"I'm having a home birth" she said, keeping her eyes on the dog.

She wanted to say *my husband is forcing me to have a home birth, I'm terrified and yet he says I've done it before. I don't even remember a before.* Instead, she smiled. Lou said nothing and wiped his hands on his jeans before opening the door and ushering her inside.

"*You been home birthing previous?*" He enquired,

"No, I haven't. This is my second pregnancy though. The first was still born at the hospital, so we thought a home birth made sense." As she said this, Camila's mind rushed through empty corridors trying to recall ever carrying a child in her womb before, and as before, her memory echoed emptiness back.

"You got a doctor or midwife least, to check on you?" Lou replied.

"Yes, I am taking all the vitamins and feeling good," she said as compensation, feeling the concern in his voice. It wouldn't sound right to mention she'd not seen a single nurse or had a single scan of the fetus.

"Well alright then Mama," he said, looking unsure, *"my Ma had four home births but she always had a midwife with her, mind."*

"I think Rafael knows how to deliver babies," Camila replied.

"Oh, that's right," Lou replied, *"he did tell me he delivered his son, I'd forgotten,"* Lou said. He looked at her quickly then, with a brief flicker of concern. But she paid no mind because her legs felt swollen and ached and her back was sore and she only wanted to sit on his porch and share the brief companionship of a moment. To rest from the fear and spend time looking out into the woods beyond and their tall wordless majesty.

Later on, as Camila left and walked back down the hill, she thought of what she had learned without asking. Rafael's wife had given birth in this house, to their son. His wife Carol whom he never mentioned. His son whom he never mentioned. Lou said that home-births were common but usually a midwife attended, but Rafael claimed he knew how to deliver. It didn't sound too good. She imagined the pain and tried to think back on a time she had been in pain like that, in her past, when she had delivered a dead baby and wondered why Rafael thought this time around it would be any different.

Coming down the hill she thought of Lou, how attractive he was. How he was more attractive than Rafael, and how in many ways, Rafael was not the sort of man she thought she would find attractive if she hadn't already been with him. But Rafael said it was she who had turned things romantic between them and she recalled that a bit. Yes, coming to his bed at night, it was her choice. She didn't know what it meant when you didn't really think about choice and did what you thought you should do, because your mind was empty and foggy. She didn't know if she wanted the touch of someone, to sooth the emptiness inside of her, or if Rafael was right and she had been lusting for him for weeks before. They had laughed about it at the time. Now she wondered if it just fit his story and made him feel good about himself. If Rafael knew that she found Lou attractive, what would he say then? She was not about to find out. She thought Lou liked her also, though he'd never lay a hand on her. She could see the way his eyes flickered over her belly, her face, the plains of her cheeks and brow. She liked how he would take her in, but then give her back, because when Rafael looked at her, he kept her entire being afterward.

Camila wondered: *If I had woken up alone would I have chosen Rafael?* Aware she already knew the answer. She did not like the way he felt when he pounded her, and bit her breasts. She did not like some of the words he whispered in her ear as he did it, or the way she knew if she ever said no to anything, he would do it anyway. She didn't like how he told her even when she was fat with child, to kneel whilst he stood over her and masturbated. Then climaxing in her face like she was a thing and not a woman. How afterward he would grow hard again almost immediately and ask her to take him in her mouth until her jaw ached and her back burned from her uncomfortable position.

She walked through the tall pines. It seemed the only time she felt peaceful now was when she was out walking. The reflection from the lake an omnipresent comfort. Home had rules. Outside in the wild, she had no restraint. It was funny to think of it as a restraint as it wasn't overt but still, Camila felt there existed an invisible restraint, a tether that held her back from … she didn't know. Being alone, without Rafael, she felt the tether lessen. Somewhere in her mind she recalled what it felt like to exist without depending on someone else. It had felt good somewhere in the past, a feeling of striking out alone, of feeling she could do things without someone else telling her how. The pines were so tall she couldn't always see where the tips ended and the sky began, it was like a fusion of color – green and blue. When she craned her head and squinted – she felt dizzy and had to look down. Her stomach protruded ungracefully through her clothing like a clock.

Chapter 28

It was not very long after visiting Lou, whilst on the toilet she felt a strange pressure, then an rush and water, not urine, came pouring out of her. She knew it had begun and she felt terrified. Rafael was out. Camila waddled to the bed and spreading out a big towel lay on the towel and began to breathe heavily. The baby, as large as her stretched, swollen stomach, how could it force its way out of her small hips? She wondered, trying to imagine the pain, and when she had asked Rafael one night, he laughed and abruptly shoved three fingers in her, painfully stretching her; *"see how big you can get? That's how!"* She thought his face looked ugly then and she felt wrong. She wanted to close her legs and tell him to leave her, but he was already mounting her, he was already pushing inside and trying to widen her with his thrusts. *"God no Rafael, not now,"* she said turning her head to the side, but the pain was so intense, she had no more words.

Camila didn't know when Rafael would return. The house was so quiet, only the creek and tick of the tall trees outside, swaying in the wind and the smell of water coming off the lake. Otherwise, nothing seemed to be alive, she was alone, increasingly she felt she was going to always feel alone. In the desperate moments of childbirth, this felt like the worst feeling she could experience. Irrationally she wished Lou were within striking range. She called out his name louder and louder, knowing it would be lost in the first winds to snatch it and send it careening over tree tops. The baby began to shift, her uterus felt like it was being split in half. Between her legs she could see blood and a terrible knifing pain started low in her groin. Camila screamed for all she was worth, a hopeless, fearful cry of terror.

The baby took a long time to come and she thought she was going to split apart. But it came, tearing her so much she could hear herself ripping and she screamed the house down. Screaming so loudly she was certain half the lake heard and the birds, disturbed by the noise, took to the skies in droves. She screamed and screamed and when Rafael finally arrived, he was preternaturally calm as if it was not a big deal she was giving birth alone in his house. He mostly stood back and watched. Hardly flinching, enjoying her unaided effort, with a strange look on his face. Once in a while he would get close and peer intently between her legs, and he would stroke her there, and say, *"Don't worry, soon. It's going to be real soon, you're doing great."*

Camila wanted to curse him, to slap him, to shout at him and say; "*how could you have let me have a baby in the middle of the forest?*" But she knew, without understanding why, that any loss of temper would be a catastrophe. Despite the pain, she buttoned her mouth against her torrent of accusations and questions. When the baby's head showed through the tears between her legs, so wide that she could feel the pieces of her come unstitched, Rafael told her to push really hard again. She pushed with every muscle she knew she had and every muscle she hoped she had. The stretching of her, so unbearable that she could not believe it possible for something that large to emerge from her and not leave her gaping and cavernous.

Briefly it crossed her mind that had she ever, ever done this before, wiped memory or not, she wouldn't have forgotten. Pain is something we rarely fully forget. Second-time mothers often joke that nature has a way of downplaying the pain in memory so that we are conned into a second pregnancy. But the truth is, ask any mother and they'll make the same face and say it hurt like hell. Such memories are more than things that we can wipe from our hinter brains. They become part of us, like a phantom limb hurts afterward. She felt if she had ever experienced childbirth before, even if it was a stillbirth – her body would remember it and everything told Camila that her body had never held a child inside it and this was her first pregnancy.

The baby was a big baby. Healthy, no jaundice. Round and already chubby, he had color and a loud piercing shriek from the moment he came, pulled by Rafael's clumsy slippery hands, out of her, turning their bed into a crimson lake. Camila was exhausted, from the pain that seemed to never end, and the effort of straining and straining until she thought she would burst in half. Rafael had put plastic underneath the sheets and towels, but there was so much blood. She knew she'd lost a lot and she could feel the disorientation of blood loss and exhaustion. Before long she was sleeping and the baby was on her swollen breast, already feeding. Rafael cleaned up and gave her an IV for lost fluids and one for lost blood. This he had known to do, which when she woke and saw them, she found less comforting than worrying. As if his control of her were so complete he scripted the birth story the exact way he had wanted it to be, with him in the starring role.

Chapter 29

It didn't seem possible Camila had woken up one day and been Rafael's, and now there were three of them. Two belonging to One. The baby slept in their bedroom; he was a good boy who rarely cried despite his squalling entrance into the world. She was bruised and torn down there, so badly that she found it hard to walk to the bathroom and agonizing to pee. *"I need to get stitches,"* she said, and he told her to lie down and looked, which she found humiliating, before announcing that she would heal just fine and needed sitz baths and chamomile. Camila took a very, very long time to heal and it never healed quite right, feeling irregular there, pain radiating every time urine hit her scar tissue. She begged him for the first time not to try to be intimate with her, and for a time he readily agreed, which surprised her greatly.

A month later, baby Joe and mother were up and around, walking the land. Finally showing Joe the wild geese on the lake, and laughing at the leaves that fascinated him as they blew around them like kites. He was a pretty little boy, with her brown large eyes and a healthy weight. He drank a lot of her milk, and was no trouble, didn't fuss and slept through the night as if he, like his mother, knew that any other option was not acceptable. He had an obvious preference for his mom. Rafael didn't tend to handle him, though he seemed happy enough, he was hands-off and always from a distance, approving, never close up and personal.

The time-off intimacy didn't last. She tried to explain she was not healed. Rafael said that it would be fine, and without a crumb of tenderness drove himself without foreplay or preamble between her legs, tearing some of her healed scars. Camila learned then that other pain aside from childbirth, existed with equal fierceness. Though Rafael didn't seem to mind her grimaces and quiet cries beneath him, she actually felt that it heightened his enjoyment.

Camila didn't feel like a mother, she didn't feel enough of anything. Sometimes she longed to press her hot forehead into the lake and submerge her fogginess, rinsing out its weak distinction. He spent time working on projects outside with large pieces of wood, building an extension on the house for the boy, a playroom. On the surface, like the lake, everything was calm, she kept her wilder impulses in check. Acted the part of docile partner, afraid of nothing that had happened but everything that could. Her child, little brown-eyed Joe was no trouble. He seemed born to bring delight and ease, growing fast and healthy like a tree needing no nourishment. Camila was both proud and afraid of what would come of this, how could they both live, as zipped up pockets in his large outdoor coat, appendages of Rafael's seething, unspoken will.

She visited Lou on occasion, showing off her strapping curious child, borrowing contraband books that he was not aware she had no knowledge of. Acting when she learned things outside of her circumference, like she'd known all along. Her mind gently spreading and growing with her son's mind. All the while, tiptoeing around her life like a seamstress, fretting over loose ends. *Where was Rafael's family? How had they died? Why didn't he mention them?* Lou continued to be respectful and courteous toward her, but she could see in his attentive eyes that if she ever reached out to him, he would take her into his arms without a second guess.

One night Rafael and she drank too much, the boy was in bed, the house was warm and the night, cool with a high breeze. It was the sort of night that tickled the dormant lust of any living creature, they felt excited for no reason, moving faster, happy to be freed of the closed windows of Winter. Invigorated by fresh air and comfortable fireplace, Rafael built the logs high and opened her for his pleasure. They drank three glasses, far more than usual for her, Camila felt heady and unpicked inside like cotton balls floating on water. Without knowing a moment before, Camila said it, she almost shouted out; *"Where is your first son buried? Where is your first wife buried??"* Once she'd spoken, she felt a rush of horror, but the words were out, she had tipped her hand irrevocably and the darkness playing in the trees seemed to have open mouths.

Rafael looked at her fast and furiously, his lips curling back, as shocked as she. *"What did you just say?"*

"It doesn't matter," she said, moving away, making herself busy, trying not to tremble, feeling the mistake hot on her face.

He followed. *"What did you say?"* he repeated, turning her toward his face, anger in a face like a red mask, no words needed, demanding. *"What did you say?"*

"Oh God Rafael, I was just messing around." She tried to laugh it off. But she'd used his name, she never used his name, and he saw her shaking. And worst, he'd heard, he knew she knew, there was no avoidance, no taking it back.

"You know then." He responded, his voice icy and without inflection. *"How long?"*

So few words necessary, Rafael's mind racing ahead of hers – she knew he'd beat her to it; *"I can only think Lou must have told you?"* Camila couldn't lie, it was all falling into place, she was half surprised but he was so fast.

"Yes." She said quietly.

"How did you meet?" his dead-pan voice asked. In an instant everything had turned around, from her original question, to revealing that she dared to have a friend.

"We bumped into each other."

"How does that happen living here? You're in the middle of freaking nowhere."

Tell me about it, Camila thought. *"I'd gone further up the hill, Lou had come down, we met in the middle, talked a while, no big deal."* She heard herself pathetically trying to play it down, no experience of lying, his gaze, a spotlight on her, scrutinizing the pulse, quickening at her neck.

"Good enough," he said, and turned away. She stayed preternaturally still, thrown by his words. All night she wondered how he had put the pieces together, as if suspecting all along. It terrified her that his response had been so calm, it felt worse than if he'd raised his voice.

A couple of days later, swift as passing head-lights on a car, reaching out into darkness, she woke up finding him touching her. She was so sore and asked him not to. He carried on, mounting her and hurting her with his urgency. When he finished, he asked her, in a cold voice, if she thought Lou was good-looking. Rafael put his mouth against her ear and in a slow, quiet, tight voice he asked her if Lou and she had been lovers and as he asked her, he pushed so hard into her, she felt her tail bone snapping backwards and she would have cried out. She couldn't cry out, his lips were crushed against her lips, his teeth cutting them. With each violent assault she went away into herself, away from the pain, away from his sharp teeth breaking the skin on her mouth. To a place where there was no sound, least of all the sound of a woman crying.

Then Rafael stopped, without finishing. He got up from the bed, still hard and stared down at her for a moment. Her head turned to the side – blood on the sheets and between her legs. He smiled a long, terrible smile, her blood on his lips, and turned and went into the bathroom and got into the shower. When Camila heard the water running, she put her fingers against her lips, they were swollen and hurt terribly, the ache between her legs she ignored, too afraid to know how bad it was.

The coldness of his love-making, the way he didn't listen when she said she was sore. The way he did what he wanted and let her know at the end he had been thinking all the while about her '*chance*' meeting with their neighbor. These things told her, with a certainty, that Rafael was not the forgiving type. He had a cold streak of possessiveness that stretched far longer than the span of their lake outside. She lay in bed, blood between her legs and aching and the unspoken message was clear. *Don't. Cross. Me.*

Chapter 30

The following week, slightly ameliorated by his apparent relaxation and lack of further rebuke, Camila threw caution to the wind and went up to Lou's house. The path by now, easy to follow, she cut a brisk pace through the bramble and shrub reaching the house rapidly and knocking on the unusually closed door. *Not again*, a voice unbeknownst to her, said inside her mind. *Not another closed door with death waiting*. She looked around as if someone had spoken to her, nobody was there. *You're being ridiculous Camila* – she said to herself. Trying the door, the door didn't open, the vehicles in the garage invisible. No way of telling anyway. The voice had been inside her head, where had it come from, what did it mean?

She looked through the windows, all the shades were drawn. *Do you think it's a coincidence?* The voice said again. This time a little louder. She clasped her hands on her ears, turning left and right, searching for anyone, but nobody was there, not even the fullness of herself, although the voice sounded like her more than anything else had in such a long while, how long she couldn't say. *How quiet does something have to be for you to realize it's wrong?*

The voice taunted her.

Tempted to break a window, Camila scouted the circumference of the cottage and then wondered, what if Lou's just gone into town? *Then check*, the voice said. She picked a medium sized rock and wrapped it in a black plastic trash can liner she found outside, and looking slightly away, she knocked out one of the panes of the French windows in the back of the house. It made a yielding hiccupping sound and her wrist went through the window pane. Automatically she withdrew it as if scolded, and her skin dragged quickly against the broken jagged glass. She began to bleed, it wasn't lethal but it was a deep cut, ugly. She drew her arm against herself, letting the blood soak into her sweater and she reached her other arm in, very carefully and undid the lock on the door.

The house was still, no tick of clock (what was it about time in this area?) no unusual smell. The dog, the man, gone. She began to think they were truly out, and would come home to find her needless act of vandalism. Just as she'd considered writing an explanation note, she noticed something odd. By the door, a handkerchief, the center stained by something that had saturated it. Camila bent down and brought it to her nose. It smelt really strange, a cross between aniseed and some clinical smell that she immediately recognized. *Ether* the voice said. *You should know.* The hair on the back of her neck stood up, a memory surfaced, unwillingly and vivid, she was breathing the smell, fighting against something, couldn't tell what, felt panic. Felt like she was going to be sick and pass out..

She let go of the handkerchief suddenly and gasped, it fluttered to the floor, like a discarded thought. *Don't leave it there*, the voice said, she scooped it back up and stuffed it into her pocket and raced out of the house. No sign of anyone, nothing wrong, no disturbance. *They're just out, they could be visiting family, he wouldn't have felt the need to say anything. Then again, then again...*

The smell stayed in her nostrils, stinging the edges. She felt like she was light headed and a sudden terror gripped her chest like someone was sitting on her, she breathed slower, deeper, nothing helped. She was hyperventilating, running through the forest, away from … toward … the voice, it spoke louder than her heart beat, *don't let him see the handkerchief.*

As Camila ran away, a reel in her head played. Unbidden images, pictures of Lou smiling on his porch, pictures of his hands going up to protect himself – from …? Something heavy hitting his face. Images of Lou looking at her in that way he did. His fingers lifting her skirt, his hands beneath her underwear, unbuckling his jeans, his hard chest and soft lips. The way he turned her around and entered her from behind, and then Lou was Rafael, and Rafael was tearing through her like a savage train and the blackbirds were all crying out. A terrible din and Camila running barefoot in the forest and trying not to fall. Then she saw the grave – she saw Lou's hand rising from the soil and as she ran away, she screamed and screamed. Because they were only figments of her imagination and they were terrible and they weren't real and yet. The forest had turned red and she couldn't see well and she kept falling and falling and falling.

Camila felt like her hands were covered in red paint when she got home, that Rafael could see exactly what she'd done and that he knew it. Neither one of them said anything but in her mind's eye she went about preparing the food with her bright-red-painted hands and he went about pretending he didn't know when it was clear to them both. He knew she'd checked Lou's house, and she knew he knew. How, she wasn't sure; maybe he pretended to go out and stayed around the corner? She could tell how paranoid she was becoming, could envision anyone else laughing when she said that someone had hurt her neighbor and she feared it might be her lover. She even laughed at herself and chided herself for her overactive imagination, but despite that, the lingering doubt grew in her stomach like an unwanted child.

Then unexpectedly, after they'd finished dinner Rafael announced he would be buying them a boat. *"Are you excited darling?"* He asked, showing her a catalog with a second-hand boat for sale that looked brand new and had all the trimmings. *"It's a really good deal, only fifty miles away, I can drive and hitch it to the truck, drive it back in no time. We can build a boat ramp, the three of us, sailing on the lake. Isn't it worth it when we live so close and we never take advantage of the water the way we could?"* He seemed to be asking her but she knew he was telling her; she didn't make decisions. She smiled at his, and told him that she was very excited and it would be terrific because he could teach them how to sail as neither knew. *"My boy will have his sea legs sooner than any other kid around here,"* he said with a note of pride, and he went off to his study where he spent time, and preferred she not disturb him.

For all you know he does have a phone and it's in there, the new voice in her head informed her, as she removed her make-up and undid her bra. *For all you know he's got it all in that room and you're too feeble to even dare to go in there.* Was she going mad? Camila wanted to reply and tell the voice that she respected privacy, but just as she thought it, the voice heard and replied, *I'm you. You don't need to say it consciously, I hear everything you think, and you're wrong, because you have no privacy, so ask yourself, why do you think he needs some?* She felt angry at herself for never considering this. *The micro-doses make you into an idiot*, the voice said, it seemed to mock her, in her own cadence, as if frustrated with her lack of effort toward understanding. *You used to be a smart woman, now you are an obedient puppet, how did that happen? Ever wonder what exactly he puts in your morning shakes? When did you get so dumb?*

The next morning Camila feigned nausea and said she would rather not drink the shake he always prepared for her and left beside her coffee. If he's dosing her in everything she consumes, how to reduce the dosing? *"Now, you can't do that,"* Rafael said roughly, *"you didn't even do that during your pregnancy and now isn't the time to start. This is your best nutrition. You need this for life, to heal the damage you once did to yourself and avoid ever getting sick as a result, don't argue, drink it."* His tone was not an option. She had begun to actually feel nauseous despite it being a pretense, the idea of swallowing drugs lacing her mind with fog, it felt repellant and wrong. She gagged a few times before swallowing it down. *"Good girl"* he said, in that patronizing tone he thought was endearing, and rinsed the glass at the sink. *"Don't think you can avoid it, you need to always be vigilant because your body took a premature beating in life, this is how you stay healthy."* She felt what he was really saying was not referring to a shake but her entire conduct with him.

Camila wondered what would have happened if she had actually said, *"no Rafael I'm not going to drink the shake, don't make it for me anymore."* Though she'd never actually crossed him, the nearest being when she begged from a reprieve from sex until she healed, which he took surprisingly well for a short time and then utterly disregarded. She didn't know what he would say but something within her told her it would be very ugly and Lou's ominous empty house, neglected in the trees, sent a shiver of fear down her spine.

She closed her eyes and opened them in her imagination; in front of her Camila and Rafael stood, Act One: Camila was telling Rafael she didn't want to drink her shakes, Rafael was lifting Camila up by the neck, Rafael was throwing the glass across the room. Act Two: Rafael was striking Camila across her face; Rafael was beating Camila with his closed hand. No Act Three. The

End. She closed her eyes again, against the horrible imaginary scenario and opened them to an empty room and a racing heart that knew, imagination takes its source from somewhere.

Chapter 31

Although Rafael never outright said anything, if she displeased him, he found ways to punish her. He knew she did not like to be touched on the first day of her period because of the pain, and when her periods returned after Joe's birth six months later, he made it a point to *make love* to her on the first day of her period. She would tell him that she was bleeding and he would say in a voice that knew what she was really asking, *"Oh darling you are so beautiful every day"* and pretending to be ignorant of her pain, though it was clear from the pain killers she'd asked for hours earlier, he would be especially rough and take her for a long stretch of time. Many times, he'd hold on to his climax until she was dry inside and it felt like he was sandpapering her aching womb with a hammer.

The next time Rafael went out, Camila didn't go walking up to the cabin. A part of her, *not the voice* but something like instinct, told her it would be futile. Nothing would have changed; nobody would be home. The forest, once comforting and familiar, seemed to have gained eyes. She wasn't sure what Rafael observed and what he did not, she was treading on eggshells. Even as nothing actually rose, it was there, under the quiet of their life, as angry as anything she had ever felt in another person. A crimson rage that seethed just below the surface and with the scent of a wild animal. She could smell it the way she smelt her own menstruation a day before she got her period. Rafael had that smell especially when she was not metaphorically painting herself white and binding her feet.

Instead of going to Lou's house, she went to the door of Rafael's mystery office and tried the handle. She could not believe she'd never even tried the door before, so acquiescent to his wishes, it was drilled into her to steer clear. The door didn't yield. *He locks it*, the voice said, *why would he need to lock the door?* She had no idea what to do next and then it came to her, a book she'd read, given to her by Lou, talked about a woman who had locked herself out. As the woman knew the key was on the other side of the door, she poked it through so it fell on the floor and slid a piece of paper there, so when it fell, she could pull the key underneath the door on the piece of paper. *Surely it wouldn't work* she thought, books aren't life, they make everything up. But there was no key on the other side of the door surely, else how did he lock it? *Maybe there are two keys and he keeps one in the door to prevent you picking it*, the voice said. *Don't be silly* she replied, comfortable having internal conversations by now, with the other new part of her that was emerging. Why would he need to do that? Then you couldn't open the door from the outside. *Try anyway*, the voice said.

She looked through the keyhole, sure enough there was a key in there. How had she known? Camila tried the method with a piece of paper she found, and heard the key land on the floor with a thud that sounded like it had muffled on paper rather than the wooden boards. She pulled the paper through and a key was on it. How did he get out? She wondered, taking the key and opening the door. What she found in the office answered her question immediately; there was another door, it led outside of their house, and could not be seen on the outside because it appeared to be completely invisible except on the inside. Why does he need another door? She began to sweat under her arms and the sweat dripped down her waist and pooled at her hips. She felt unclean the way you do when discovered doing something wrong. *But it's not wrong, it is research*, the voice responded. She felt nervous and shaky and her senses were on high alert hoping not to hear the sound of his return. *He's gone for several hours yet*, the voice said, *why don't you use the time productively?*

The office was a small room, the outside door went out into the back garden, it opened with the same key, so she figured he had two copies and he'd accidentally left the key she had in the other door, and last used the outdoor exit, when leaving the office. How had she never seen him leaving by an unknown side door to the house? Why hadn't she even heard the door opening and closing? She tried the door; the hinges were well oiled and unlike the front door to the house it opened without any sound. He went outside at night when she didn't know and did what? An image of the old woman and her house flashed before her mind, then another picture, the two shapes in the bed, the blinds drawn. Then another flash, Lou's house with the shades down, nothing out of place. Flash. The handkerchief on the floor was the only sign, she smelt the smell of ether and felt woozy and nauseous all over again.

It was a mistake then, she reassured herself. Usually – he'd take the key out of the door, or it would be impossible to get into the study from the interior of the house, but he last went out by the other door and he mistakenly left the key in the lock. The office itself was very confined, just room enough for a desk, two shelves and a computer and separate screen. How did she know it was a computer when she'd never seen one in her life? The word came immediately, she recognized it and knew how to use it. As if being controlled by strings in her arms she touched the keyboard and mock-typed a few words. *I've used a computer before*, Camila thought. We've never talked about computers; we've never mentioned them. I have used one in the past, the past I cannot recall. She checked the machine, it was hooked up to Wi-Fi (yes, she knew that too) and the modem was active, there was a separate bigger screen, and several books beside the computer on coding. *Maybe he used to work with computers and didn't want me to get bad habits,* the acquiescent side of her said, *maybe he's keeping things from you*, the new voice said.

She touched the screen, it was cold and had no static, he'd not used it this morning. She tried to think how many times he came into his office. Maybe once a day? Usually after he'd had sex with her and left her in the bedroom. He'd say he couldn't sleep yet and he'd tell her he was going to his office for a while. By then she was always so tired, (*what does he put in your shakes? How much microdosing does he give you? Even if you hide half of what he gives you, how much is he still drugging you?*) Camila never questioned Rafael getting up afterward, it was a relief, it meant he wouldn't try to screw her again, and she was fast asleep by the time he returned. *What if he does it every night? Even the ones where he pretends to sleep next to you? How do you know? If he doesn't sleep much, how many hours is that? What does he do with that many hours?* The rational side of her tried to make rational explanations for herself; he's probably working, he has to make some money surely, it could be a hobby? *He's allowed a hobby like this and you aren't?* The new voice replied. *Don't you want to know what kind of hobby?*

On the shelves there were many books. Some leather-bound personal albums, with his name on the front in ownership, most of them dog-eared and obviously not new. The first shelf had books on hacking, computer programming, computer coding, website design, the dark net, and navigating the web. The second shelf was entirely devoted to pornography. Flagrantly shelved neatly as if books on knitting and pottery. Except these books were hard core. Dark stuff, things she'd never considered in her entire life, even the one she didn't remember. She'd remember this. Books upon books on S&M, sadomasochism, art books of Japanese girls who looked under age, tied up, tortured. Art books on exploitation, Robert Crumb's beautiful and sickening cartoons of women with enormous breasts and thighs. Manga art with scenes of torture and rape, school girls being anally penetrated whilst another man *cums* on their smiling or screaming faces. Books on underage girls, barely pubescent, hard-core porn, thumb drives, presumably more porn. An entire world of it. A treasured collection.

Camila had never seen porn up close and personal that she could recall, which didn't mean she hadn't. But something about the way the basic stuff was familiar and as it grew worse and worse, less familiar, was shocking beyond what she might have anticipated. No, she hadn't anticipated this. Perhaps a little naïve as she may have no memory but she knew Rafael's urges, and she knew after her pregnancy he hadn't touched her for a short while. *So maybe this is just his way of coping when I couldn't sleep with him*, the acquiescent voice that she had begun to hate said timidly. *"Yeah right,"* she said out loud, tempted to get a match from the kitchen and pull them all off the shelves and burn them. *"Because raping teenagers is a perfectly normal desire, isn't it?"*

Rafael had a magazine open on the desk, each page showed underage girls, thin and emaciated, bound and gagged, with older men, fat and pot-bellied, thrusting into them. It didn't look staged. The girls had genuine faces of fear, their pain was real.

They were barely grown, not even properly formed, their small genitals were hairless and in some of the photos you could see they were becoming red and irritated. The men wore masks. One of the men had a birthmark on his thigh in the same place that Rafael had the exact same birthmark. Camila knew it had to be a coincidence, that was obvious, but what surprised her, was why it didn't shock her that Rafael liked to look at images like this.

Why didn't it surprise her? When her empty head knew so damn little and her experience was confined to the walls of this cabin and her secluded life, what comparison did she have? Was it enough that she could feel his hungry violence every time he took her, or notice in her own small body, the similarity between herself and these children? Or how when she had been healing after giving birth it only made him more insistent that he fill her with his anger and leave her piecing herself back together as if she had just given birth to his rage? Camila knew this wasn't love. That she was in fact one of these girls. If not literally, then figuratively, and also, she was the doll on the mantle, the one whose lips turned permanently downcast and had forgotten how to smile.

One book in particular, *Dreams of Young Girls* by David Hamilton was initially a beautiful book. Hard bound, very artistic, circa 1970s. Gorgeous young girls, on the verge of puberty, in long flowing outfits, sometimes half dressed, sometimes more. Nothing too overt, no actual genitals opened for the viewer, but even more disturbing because of its beauty and erotica. Camila thought she actually recalled that book. It was like a piece of lint caught in her mind. She had seen it before, had a conversation about it, looked at the pictures, studied them. Trying to conclude if they were simply beautiful artist renderings or something that was at its core wrong and loaded with innuendo. How did she know this book? Where in the deluge of her mind was the memory that would bring it back? She stared at the photos. Then she remembered her first serious boyfriend, the one who had begun to come back to her. His cruel and sharp face, still a blur, more of a feeling, it was him. He had owned a copy of this book.

Just as she was about to turn on the computer to see what was on the thumb-drives, she heard the sound of Rafael's truck. Panicking, she scurried to lock the door and get out, realizing too late that she now held the key on the outside of the room without any way to replace it back in its original position. *Shit! Shit! Shit!* She said, furious at herself for not considering this, and gathering the piece of paper from between the door, she put the key on it, pushed it back and then jerked it suddenly so the key fell on its own on the floor and she could remove the paper. That way, hopefully, he would think the key had either fallen on its own or he'd dropped it, and not recall leaving it in the door. As she ran into their bedroom and tried to smooth her hair and rinse her face, which was hot and sweaty, she tried desperately to recall if she had put everything she had touched exactly back the way she found it. Anxious, she found it hard to remember but she knew herself, she always put things back where they belonged, that was her nature. *What else is your nature*? The voice in her head said. *Is it your nature to survive?*

Chapter 32

In the long run she'd made it easier for him. Rafael hadn't had to go around to the side door and open it to let himself into his office. It didn't presumably occur to him when he found the key on the floor that it meant anything, because both doors were locked. It made it possible to enter via the interior door whilst Camila was awake, which he did that night. Spending time behind the door, whilst she pretended not to listen for every sound. *I wonder why I never hear anything?* She thought, as in her mind she ran through the details of the room over and over, recalling how clean it was, as if he spent a lot of time in there, moving around. How she had put her hands on the seat, wondering if that is where he sat whilst he viewed his pornography. *Well, he wouldn't be the first man,* she thought. *Maybe I'm being unrealistic. There are worse things in life than pornography* but the new voice didn't agree, the new voice thought it vastly depended upon the message. The new voice told Camila she was a fantasist if she could justify what she'd seen.

Camila thought of leaving then. But where? Her whole life, according to the snippets she'd teased out of Rafael over time, was a series of disasters. She should be dead. In many ways she felt she was. Trapped in Purgatory, where a Demon who said he loved her and treated her like a poppet, kept her imprisoned in a beautiful home. Part of her said *be grateful, he saved you. He says he loves you. Who else would ever love you? You're not worth shit.* The voice knew better and told her so. At times it was easier to fall back on bad habits. Rafael had said the micro-doses would stop her self-loathing, that he told her she used to have really bad. But she developed a new kind of self-loathing. The anger of a woman who knows she is worth more than being a *thing* of man. Battling with the two sides within her, Camila had no idea if the stronger side of her won, how she would leave and where she would go. *He's all you have*, the beaten down side of her said. *Better The Devil you know.*

Rafael was rough with her more and more. It could not be described as *love making* any longer. His hands around her throat, trapping her air flow enough that it was uncomfortable but not causing her to pass out or have marks on her neck. He pushed into her like he was somewhere else, his eyes fixed on the bedframe and not her. Moving robotically, as if he were performing a distained duty, though she knew, the only one choosing such a duty, was him. She wanted to say, *"if you don't like it, why do you do it?"* But she already knew the answer. He did it because he knew she didn't want him to. Because it was part of the game, and it was his way. He owned her now. Being inside her, all of the time, confirmed this and her unwillingness, coupled with his domination, gave him a thrill no amount of pornography probably would. She didn't doubt he did that too, now that she knew. She'd desperately try to stay awake and feigning sleep would hear him leave the bed every night. She didn't know how long for, but it was frequent enough that she longed to return to his office to find out what else was in there.

There was no way of returning. The next few times she tried, the key was not in the lock and she had no other method of gaining entry. She tried the outside door when she figured out where it was hidden, subtly carved out of the wainscoting so it looked like it was part of an old design rather than the seams of a hidden door. She tried picking the lock and laughing to herself, said out loud, "*well one thing we know about you Camila is that you were never a thief in that life of yours you cannot recall.*" Her boy during all of this, slept well for a young child, often taking long naps during the day, and never waking at night. She could be sure of his complicity in her endeavors to find answers, because he did not demand too much of her time, leaving her enough to poke around every corner of the house in hopes of finding something else.

Soon enough eventually she did. Underneath the kitchen sink there was the usual mat to keep water from warping the cupboard floor, and yet, it moved slightly. Lifting up the mat, she noticed that the floor of the cupboard was faux and could be pulled up by inserting a pencil into a small hole on the lower right end. Once lifted up it could be pressed back flush against the wall, revealing a hidden interior about one the depth of her arm up to her elbow. She pushed her arms into the darkness, feeling around, touching cobwebs, dust, particles that had been trapped and hoping she would not feel in her blind fingered search, the carcass of a roach or spider. *There.* A box, she pulled it out. A filing box, with a spring to keep the papers flat.

Camila took her find to the kitchen table, clearing away her plate with half-eaten toast and nervously checking out of the window for any sign of his return. The box was A4 in size, marbled on the front, and inside were lots of papers within plastic envelopes. The first envelope said *'Carol,'* she opened it. A piece of paper was actually a photograph, face side down, a blown up close up of a woman's face. A beautiful woman, with a high brow, black hair, sad large eyes and full lips. She looked to be in her late twenties. Could this be Rafael's wife? Along with the photo there was a marriage certificate. He'd married her six years ago. In the same state, or maybe not. There was something odd about the certificate; it didn't seem right, as if someone had copied it and written in their details.

A bundle of letters with Rafael's name on, in woman's handwriting, on lavender paper. They were love letters, talking of her love for him, excited to have the chance to build a life by the lake, how they would have a boat and spend days sailing in the sun. She signed the letters *'your Caro'*. There was a will, it had her name on it, the last will and testament of Carol Rosa Garcia, leaving a house, to her husband and child. A letter, written by her attorney to Carol, expressing concern that she hadn't been in touch, could she please contact him as soon as possible. Lastly, a death certificate, Carol Rosa Garcia, died two years ago, around the time Camila woke up. Cause of death: Suicide.

The second envelope said '*Jacob*' and was again, a large photo, this time of the same woman holding a little boy, around 2 years old, in her arms. He looked the spitting image of Camila's own son Joe. No birth certificate, no vaccination records, no death certificate. Just the picture of mother and son both, staring out, looking a little pensive, a little detached, as if neither of them felt quite comfortable enough to look directly into the eyes of their photographer. Once again Camila had a memory of her first serious boyfriend. A memory that kept coming back through thick waves of forgetting. How her ex-boyfriend had always told her he loved photographing her when she looked sad, and from behind the camera he would almost plead: *Don't smile, don't smile, stop smiling.*

There was more, but Camila ran out of time, and was certain

Rafael would be due back soon. The light was changing in the kitchen and her hands were shaking as she put the papers back into the box, returning it to its secreted hole and closing it up. She was trembling so badly she tore off her clothes and stood underneath the shower letting it get too hot and almost scald her. Rafael came into the bathroom as she was finishing up, wrapping his arms around her naked waist he said, *your timing is perfect.* She wanted to push him off and felt sickened by the smell of beer on his clothes, and was that cigarette smoke? How did she know that smell when she'd never smelt it before? That she could remember. What an absurd thought. She could remember so little. Her mind was a mosaic with yawning gaps. *That you can remember*, the voice said, and Camila walked ahead into the bedroom, knowing Rafael was already taking his clothes off.

The photo of Rafael's previous family haunted her. *How had Carol died? Why had she died? Where was their son Jacob? How had he died? Didn't Rafael say the house was his? That his parents had lived here? How then, was it Carol's house?* She stared down at her own child, sleeping peacefully in his cot, and wondered at the chance of the two boys looking so alike. It was as if he were able to facsimile himself into everything he sired, and control even, how they looked. *I often thought he told you to be a good boy from the moment you were born and you obeyed,* she said, softly, touching her son's fat cheeks and smiling involuntarily. *If the other boy is gone, and the other wife is gone, how long will it be before that's your fate?* The voice said. This time, it didn't even seem like a new voice or a voice that wasn't hers. It was her own voice, a little bolder, with a shake in it, and a really, really good question.

Chapter 33

Camila knew she had to try to get away. On the one hand it seemed absurd, there was no evidence of anything, it was ungrateful for all he had done for her. She wasn't a prisoner (*yes, she was*). She wasn't forced to stay (*do you really still believe that?*). She could leave whenever she wanted, she just had to ask (*and what do you think will happen when you ask? Glug glug*). It made her think of a cartoon of Popeye eating his spinach and the sound he made *'glug glug'* as he opened the can and quaffed it down. *"Oh my God! I remember!"* Camila saw herself watching a TV, she'd not seen one since, but here was a memory of her, she could see herself laughing at the TV watching the cartoons. *"I remember!"*

It made her feel heady to recall something, even if it was as silly as a cartoon. Until now, any recollection was like a ghost on the periphery of her mind. She knew now that if there was one distinct clear memory within her, there were more. She strained her mind to try to think of anything else. *"It's an association, isn't it?"* She said out loud, "*I have to remember by seeing something that triggers the memory, like when I smelt that ether or said 'glug*

glug' but of course, it's not that simple, you cannot just deliberately trigger a memory if you have no idea of what the trigger is." She was running out of time, even without a clock she knew that, and yet, how could she hasten the broken parts of her brain to come together faster? *"Maybe if I read things he hasn't prescribed I will remember more, because they will remind me?"* She asked Rafael again if he could bring her library books. He said he would and brought the ones he had decided were okay, they didn't tell her anything, they didn't trigger anything, they may as well have been coloring books.

The voice in Camila's head had felt at first like it was not her own, then it merged to become her one voice. When she considered who had lived in the house before her, what might have transpired, the terrible pain locked in the walls. She imagined Carol, his first wife and maybe even Jacob, his first son, were part of that voice. Urging her to break free before she joined them, at the bottom of the lake or wherever they were. She imagined Carol, her familiar features, being held underneath the water, her face growing slack. The last images captured on her watery irises, of a clear sky containing no moon. She hoped that Carol and Jacob were somewhere far from pain. She thought it would be nice to meet them, but not by sharing their fate. Camila's urge to live was powerful now. It ran through her veins like warm coffee, she didn't want to endure, she wanted to live, to survive him. To survive his desire to dampen her and fashion her into a wax figurine, malleable to his whims.

Not long afterward, when Rafael was again out, she went under the sink again. This time she knew he'd be gone long enough that she could go through everything. She felt nervous with a mix of excitement and dread. Seeing the pictures once more, it shocked her, appalled her, to think he could have been married previously. A completely different life, in which he had a son, a family, and somehow, upon his wife's death, hid the entire existence from Camila and the world. How did Carol die exactly? It said suicide. Rafael didn't think to mention the coincidence of his first wife and now Camila, both suicidal? His son Jacob no longer in the picture. What happened to him? Was he dead too? Rafael had found Camila, and started all over again as if neither his wife or child had ever existed (*that's what he would do to you, if you died. Yes, you could die. So easily, yes you could*).

As she said that in her mind, the word *death* jolted her, and she almost fell backward. She remembered standing on the bridge, she remembered wanting to die! She felt beneath her bare feet the cold, cold stone of the bridge. She felt the longing to end the pain within her. She felt the muddied thinking of her mind and how it urged her to the precipice. Camila saw in her mind's eye, herself standing by the edge of the bridge and willing herself to fall like a stone. *Death. A longing for death. How much you wanted to just let go and stop.*

"No, I wasn't a drug addict!" She said, moving quickly on the spot, with nervous energy, "*I was never a drug addict! I tried to take my own life! I jumped into the river! I drowned! He got me out, he brought me somewhere, he made me better, I was moved here, I've been here since then.*" But something wasn't right, something like a large plaster over a cut, was distorting the story. What was it? She remembered! Her discussion with him. Rafael had said, in that slow way that made her think he cared, that she would never be free until she forgot who she had been and started over. Her acceptance. *Yes – I understand.* She didn't understand anything! Too high on medication. Grossly sick from nearly dying. Messed up from all the reasons that led her to try to take her own life. Still foggy and clinging to comprehension. Saying *yes, I understand.* Then nothing. A blank. That must have been when he did it. Like his computers. Wiped her clean, started over. Rebooted.

A computer! She had been cleaned out of her viruses as you would a computer that runs slowly. Rafael had saved her. Instead of taking her to hospital he'd taken her for himself. Making her well, causing her to owe him, to feel gratitude and trust. Then convincing her the only way forward was to forget everything of who she had been and start over, with him. She didn't remember it all, there were big spaces and gaps. It helped that she tried to avoid as much of the micro-dosing Rafael gave her. It helped her head. Everything was indistinct. But she saw herself waking up in this house, recalled how empty headed she felt, as if she'd just been born, wondering how she could have just been born if she was in an adult's body. Finding it hard to do things, having to re-learn certain things. Helpless.

Camila remembered after the accident, a catheter, feeling like her head had been set on fire. Pain everywhere, especially her throat where the river water had poured down and filled her lungs. She remembered Rafael wiping her down, sponge-bathing her. Touching her between her legs, and her, letting him, because she was nothing, nobody. Because she could not recall anything other than his face, looking down at her. Smiling. His teeth so white in the poor light, they glowed.

"So that's what happened. And now I'm here and Rafael would like it if I never met or spoke to anyone else. But why? Why save me only to keep me like a doll in this house in the woods?" Camila felt the stone of certainty in her throat. It was impossible to believe this was an act of kindness anymore, it smacked of obsession, derangement. No normal person would take advantage of a suicidal woman and imprison her in the wilds. *"What is Rafael hiding me from? Myself? My memories and past? That can't be. He said I was a drug addict, implied I was a prostitute. Said I had a child before who died in a still birth. Made me give birth to our child at home unaided. That's not protection, that's control!"* the voice

that had integrated itself as one voice, told her, calmly and with a certain relief that Camila no longer had two competing voices.

The worst part of her recovering memories? Camila thought of his face, and his dark black eyes and his curly black hair and something struggled to the surface. An overlay between Rafael and her first boyfriend, whose name had not been Rafael but who bore the uncanniest resemblance to Rafael. So much so, that when she overlaid the two faces – aside the haircut, the facial hair, weight gain, tan, age on his face and a slightly different slant, which could as much as anything be changed habits – Rafael looked almost identical. *But it couldn't be.* She thought. *It just could not be him.*

Camila tried hard to pierce the fog of her returning memories. She saw herself with her first boyfriend. He's smiling at her, the same teeth. He had his similar hands around her neck, squeezing. She saw herself free of him, but alone without any support. Alone, falling deeper into despair, she remembered going to a therapy group and talking but nobody had anything to offer. They were all broken like she was. She recalled typing out words of despair online in a suicide chat room and some man on the other end, someone she didn't know, responding and telling her he admired her for her courage to end her unhappy life. That he thought more should have the guts she had. This unknown man had used such familiar words, his language so similar to …

Camila saw it all, in a basket of thought within her, spilling out, disordered and making sense at the same time. The voice in her head, her voice now, showing her the relevant images as they tumbled out. Marking them in her new mind: Exhibit A. Girl pushed to the edge through manipulation and careful selection. Exhibit B. Girl drowning. Exhibit C. Hero saving girl. Exhibit D. House of lies and control.

Chapter 34

Camila's heart felt like a stone plunged into icy water, no sense of safety remained. All sounds were dangerous, even the pounding in her chest, and the dampness beneath her shoulder-blades. She thought of Rafael's hands rough inside her, taking what he wanted. Of kindness laying on the surface of fire. She saw the cruelty beneath because she had seen it in others. Long before him, she had grown to understand that some people were broken from the start and their appetites included eating you alive. She knew the scourge evil could do to the soul. She understood finally why she had given up and knew, with the entirety of someone who has walked through fire and survived, that she would never, ever stand on the precipice of her life again and throw it away. She meant to overcome it all.

Afterward she looked through the rest of his papers; they were mostly old things, newspaper clippings of when Rafael was at school and in the football team, their wins, their victories. Blurred pictures, nothing finite, no way of seeing if he simply *resembled* her first serious boyfriend who had been such a tormentor, or if he was indeed, the very same man. People can look similar. Time can distort memory. Camila needed to be certain. A picture of Rafael around eighteen, handsome, tanned, smiling arrogantly for the camera, team captain, but wearing eye-protectors and a mouth guard, everything out of place, unrecognizable. There were a bunch of those and a bunch of old photos of someone, presumably him, as a baby, not recent, in black and white, faded and dog-eared. His beautiful dark-eyed mother. His father. Both parents were always slightly to the side, it was about Rafael. He was the focus; he was the pride and joy. Then their death certificates, side by side, same cause of death. Vehicular homicide. The report read: Elderly couple were driving at night, neighbors reported hearing a crash. The following morning, they were found already long dead, flung out of their car that had turned off the road and crashed into a ravine. One survivor, their son Rafael Morelle. Not in the car at the time but at University in New England.

So, Rafael had lost his parents whilst still at college, and he lost his wife and possibly his first child. Why wasn't Camila feeling bad for him? Instead, she was only feeling afraid. As if this was a runaway train, some kind of out-of-control chain reaction and she will be next if she is caught doing anything outside of Rafael's set rules. After all, it's clear now, he's the ringmaster. Not just of his own life, but others too. Camila gathered everything up, stuffed it back in and closed up the secret paneling. *So many secrets in this house, I wonder what else it can tell?* She mused, and went to check on Joe, whom she realized could not stay here, any more than she could. At this point she wasn't even sure who Joe's father was. The cruel boy who mistreated her as a teenager, who had driven her in many ways, to bad pursuits and eventually into giving up. Or someone who bore an uncanny resemblance to him, and in so many ways, possessed the same habits and penchant for control.

People will often say things like; "*If she knew she was in danger, why didn't she just leave right then and there?*" We might scream at TV characters in exasperation for staying, yelling out; "take the damn child and run!" But should our own lives be televised, we'd soon understand, staying and leaving are not simple doors a person walks through. They are life-altering decisions, ones not lightly made when the person in question has little memory, no money, nobody to turn to and no understanding of what they are truly capable of. We need to be able to first and foremost, trust ourselves, or trust someone else, in order to make that leap. It is rare we do this unassisted in some way, falling backward without any safety net. But in those cases? Those desperate times where we run with the clothes on our backs and our children in our arms, there is without exception, a sane reason we choose to leave and such instinct should never be second-guessed.

Camila thought of her own mother, her beautiful dark-skinned mother with long hair the color of honey that ran down her back in a thick plait. She recalled how long it took her to leave Camila and her father and that a part of her had understood her mother's need to leave. It was her own survival and those who say that is selfish do not understand. We owe it to ourselves to survive, and if we can, return later to collect the remains we leave behind. If we all sacrifice for the sake of what is *expected*, what is considered moral (*to endure, to endure, to endure*) we lose ourselves. Trapped behind glass, the butterfly mounted and displayed, without a mouth to describe its pain. Camila had always admired her mother for her independence. She carried that same resolve, in herself, curling upward, like a vine seeking light.

She planned little, because there were few options. She decided the only one that worked was to just vanish. If she left on foot, with the boy, Rafael would track her down. She had no money, her memory was not complete, she didn't know where she was or where to go. The only option was for him to think she wasn't going anywhere, because she no longer existed.

Chapter 35

The boat. She had to arrange an accident of her own. She was a strong swimmer, so was the boy, but how? He'd brought the boat and they'd taken it out several times. It really was a beauty and it felt wonderful to sail on the glassy surface of the lake, seeing it from different vantage points and watching the birds overhead – fly through the clouds. *A little piece of heaven, isn't it?* Rafael had remarked and soon he was dozing on the deck as they drifted, hardly any wind to move them in any direction. The only way was to leave then, for him to think she had drowned, just like the night they met, and he'd pulled her to life out of the darkness. Only this time he was the darkness and she had to pull herself free.

Being a strong swimmer is only part of the reason a person can leave a boat in the middle of a lake and hope to swim to shore undetected. The most important part is having an urge stronger than anything you have felt in your entire life. With enough distraction to ensure you are not caught red-handed. And carrying a small child not even two years of age complicated matters almost impossibly. Until she realized she had the very answer in her possession. Her brown bottles of micro-doses. Her medicine! She would grind them up, put them in his 'maritime whiskey' that he liked to nip on as he took the boat out, and it would hopefully act the way it had many times on her, and put him into a deep sleep. Not enough to cause any harm, but enough asleep that he'd not hear them leave, and she could pull her son in something buoyant to the shore.

A real escape: he'd think they'd drowned when he woke, and the best part? He wouldn't tell *anyone*; she was very sure of that. Whom could he tell? He'd killed the old couple, she knew that now with a horrible certainty, and he'd probably killed Lou too. That meant he didn't want any witnesses and certainly no police. She was sure he'd never spoken with the police. It was all a ruse, no doubt he'd reported their deaths but anonymously. They'd never known about their cottage nor thought to come looking to check for potential witnesses, realizing that it was a gas leak overdose. He'd have known that it was a death by gas all too well, given he rigged it in the first place.

Camila realized it was an absurd plan, but none other existed. Totally unrealistic. But what other option was there? Time, though it did not exist on the lake, had run out, for them both. She also knew she would betray herself, some slip, some look, and he would know she knew about him. Whether Rafael was her first boyfriend grown up, which she began to think seriously he could be, as crazy as that sounded … or just some man who bore an acute resemblance. Either scenario worried her because she had none of the memory defenses to be sure of anything and that was deliberate on his part; either way she needed to get away. She was not anyone's possession and much as all of us may like the idea of someone needing us so very much, this was less need than control and sought subservience. The time was now.

Her son had floaties, which she'd taught him how to swim in, he still used them on occasion but could swim without them. She ground the pain-killers Rafael used to give her that she had been saving, into a fine powder and added some of her micro-dose medication into some whiskey so that it would disguise the chalky taste of pills. Camila knew there were a thousand things that could go wrong. He could taste the doctored whiskey. He could say he wasn't thirsty. He could decide to dry-dock the boat and not go out any more. She felt like there was a clock in her head, ticking urgently, the chance of escape away.

Miraculously the perfect time presented itself. On a day that was a little darker than usual and not brightly lit as most days he wanted to take the boat out. Camila slipped the mix of whiskey back into his bottle and shook really hard. By then, micro-dose, pills and whiskey were one and there was no cloudy residue to give her away. To be sure, she sipped it and it tasted the same as it had before she'd spiked it. To be additionally careful she asked him if today was a good day for sailing given the clouds, but he assured her they would burn off by midday. His mind was set and Camila knew, what Rafael wanted, Rafael usually got.

They all put on their life preservers and went out into the water. It was as serene as ever, the boat seamlessly gliding through the water like a butter knife. Joe delighted at the reflections and air whipping through his dark hair. Rafael, smiling absentmindedly whilst nipping from his bottle, seemed lost in his own thoughts. Camila held her hands tightly to her sides, conscious of trying to seem calm. As carefree as she knew she had to appear, it was also an impossible feat. It must have been around midday when Rafael's speech became looser and his eyes a little cloudy. He dozed off, woke up, dozed off, and finally, snoring softly, fell into a deep sleep. Camila's hands were shaking badly as she left their life-jackets on the side, they'd all discarded them as they were prone to do once the temperature rose anyway and she couldn't take them with her, because then he'd wonder where they were.

The perception that we have drowned has to be done right. We can't afford to get anything wrong. It must be believable or we're ruined, she told herself. Her son followed her every move with his large dark eyes. Too young to understand, nevertheless he didn't say anything, as if he knew what his mom was doing and understood it was the right thing to do. Camila put his inflatable wings on his arms, having smuggled them aboard and she took off their sandals and hats and her sunglasses. She blew up each wing on his little skinny arms, and lowered him first over the side of the boat, and into the tepid water. He didn't make any noise, she came quickly afterward, gingerly trying not to rock the boat or cause any noise. They were both in the water, silent as night birds, she pushed off and started to swim as hard as she was capable of, with her son alongside her, pulling him like a duckling, with one hand, whilst kicking her feet under water and using her other arm to propel them both. The boat receded slowly, too slowly, as Camila tried pushing through the water as fast as she could without creating a sound.

It took a very long time, she kept looking back, terrified to see his head lift up and enquire for them. It would destroy everything if he woke. Every interminable moment in the cool water, pushing forward in vain, the boat seemed to stay near for far too long. A taunt. Rafael could stand up any moment and the gig would be up. Yet there was no movement from the boat, her nerves caused her swimming to be spastic and broken up. She knew she needed to be as fast as possible, because even if Rafael bought the idea that somehow – they had both gone overboard, he'd only look so long in the waters before considering the shoreline. What would it really take for him to believe they were dead and stop looking?

Reaching shore eventually she threw a last look back at the boat. It was pretty far away now. She could just see the top of

Rafael's head. It didn't seem to have moved. Her heart was in her throat. She was exhausted. She pulled her son out of the water and took off as fast as her legs, shaky from the swim, would take her. As she ran, the urgency of flight lending her stamina, she tried to look back regularly enough to ensure no footprints or sign of their leaving the water could be discovered. They had landed on the far shore; she could see their house to the south of them. Camila knew Lou's house was due west, and she figured if she headed straight up (north) eventually she'd hit a road.

By doing this she was going away from the direction Rafael took when he drove into town and this was deliberate. She knew that would be his first calling point and anyone seeing them would be bound to report to him if he enquired, that yes, they'd seen a damp looking mother and child out on the highway. Her only chance was hoping there was a mountain pass, to the north, that had a road, and traffic and she and the boy could hitch a lift with someone as soon as possible. She knew the risk was horrible. Anyone who saw them would be suspicious, the longer they were out, and nearby, the more risk someone would tell Rafael they'd seen them if he enquired. If he knew they'd deliberately run, he'd never stop hunting them.

The walk was exhausting. Her son, uncomplaining, sat on her back as she pulled her aching limbs up the hill side. The land was as irregular as her own and she had to beat back the foliage to cut a path through. She tried hard not to leave any trace of her climb, which made the going that much harder. Each time it felt like she couldn't keep going at such a rapid pace, Camila would think of Rafael, hurting her where he knew it would hurt most. The extreme pornography and under-age girls. She would push beyond her limits and climb faster. The thought of him finding her, was as terrifying as anything she'd ever feared before.

After a while she was too tired to carry on with her son

straddling her shoulders and she pulled out from her shorts a shawl that she wrapped him in and bundled him on her back. She'd never done this before but it seemed to make sense and she'd thought of it before they left, he didn't seem to mind and soon she could hear by his breathing, he had gone to sleep. The way was rocky beneath and scattered with low-lying tree branches, so she slowed down and became methodical, knowing one false move and they could both fall. What good would come of a twisted ankle, causing her to be unable to flee? *Slow down*, she urged herself, though every muscle wanted to speed up and get as far away as possible.

Much as Camila wanted to, she didn't look behind her anymore. As she climbed steeply, she knew the lake would be visible and a part of her was dying to know if she could see the boat and get some idea of whether Rafael had woken up. It occurred to her that he would be instantly suspicious, that he would think it unnatural to sleep so heavily during the day. She berated her short-sightedness – but what other plan had existed? She hoped that the hangover of the pills would mimic an alcohol hangover and he would attribute his hard sleep to drinking too much in the sun, which he often did. Of course, he would be instantly suspicious that they were not on the boat. Camila knew him well enough to know that his first thought would not be that they had drowned, but that they had escaped. That was his nature, suspicion. But as he saw no sign of them – he would begin to wonder if indeed, her nature had reasserted itself and she had drowned them both. It was the only time in her life she was glad for having been suicidal once.

Given that her memories were coming back and Camila had given him no idea of this, Rafael would not assume she had a good reason for leaving. Nor that she had seen what he had in the office, or put two and two together and figured out he'd caused the deaths of their neighbors. He would not think she was anything but maybe a little frustrated living out in the middle of nowhere and that is why he'd bought the boat. His natural arrogance wouldn't let him think she didn't feel pleasure when he had sex with her. Even as he knew he hurt her, he would assume she loved him, such was his narcissism.

Additionally, she hoped, Rafael would probably think his son too young to make it to shore, he didn't know how proficient he'd become with his floaties, or how desperate Camila was to get him away. Whilst he would look for them, she hoped he would eventually begin to give up hope and this was what she desperately counted on. That and the decreasing light making searching for them harder, but also harder for her to keep going. Fortunately, the way evened out a bit, still crowded with trees but older growth trees whose lowest branches were above her head, and thus, she could make faster progress, despite draining every ounce of her energy, than when they were threatening to slap her in the face.

Camila knew Rafael existed for the control he exerted upon them both, especially her. Without them to control and restrain, he would grow irrational, out of control. With nothing to glut and sate his urges upon, who knows what he would be capable of? But what could he do if he couldn't find them? What could he do if they were able to escape undetected and all he had was the certainty that they couldn't have made it that far on their own? As she walked, she told herself: They were going to make it that far and get out. Escape from his snare that he had crafted around Camila before she knew how to think. *Poor Joe*, she thought. Born into a cage. We both need to get far away; I don't want to be pulverized every night underneath him. I don't want Joe to grow up seeing his mother used like a vessel, drowning on dry land. I want him to grow up and admire his mom the way I admired mine, a woman of singular design and strength. I am half of her; I can do this. *I can do this.*

Chapter 36

The vastness of the mountain-side and all the space and air around her, caused Camila to feel almost dizzy with the magnitude of what they were attempting. Adrenalin dumping into her veins, propelling her leaden, damp feet forward. She recalled a long walk she'd taken with her grandparents before her grandfather took his life. She thought of how he showed her some of the forest vegetation; which were poisonous, which were good in soup. How she'd felt she came from them then, a family, a procession of people throughout time. The irrevocable loss of such kinship when everyone fractured and tore apart, going their separate ways, dividing and dividing again like individual cells with little relation to one another. How she felt she was left, on the curbside, wanting for some sense of belonging. A home, people she called her own, ancestors, a hand reaching down claiming her.

But we claim ourselves when no one else is left. When we bear our children, we hold them tightly and carry them through life, no matter the cost or the dissolution of others. We are the strong ones, who hide the real pain of life from them long enough that they may grow tender shoots of hope for themselves. Swaddled in some belief that life can be good, they leave our side and try for themselves, knowing we stand there watching them, arms open should they return. That is the strength of a parent, knowing their role, standing firm in all weather. A lighthouse for their progeny, swimming out in the unknown ocean. Camila was aware she had this within her, and it lent her strength to know she would stand strong for Joe, always, until he didn't need her any longer.

She talked to herself as she went ever upwards. Shoving a power bar in her mouth at some point when she felt her blood sugar drop precipitously from her uncommon exertion. But the power of a mother is something no man can understand and her urge to get them to safety ran on guts and instinct alone. Before it grew completely dark, Camila reached the top and there she saw a tarmac stretch, a road, dark and empty. The best sight she'd seen since she'd first looked into her sons face after he was born. Freedom. Even if the chance is the slightest slice of moon, she would take it over the prison they inhabited back at the lake house. There where Rafael's dark eyes, bore through her and threatened to extinguish every light she lit within herself.

Her thin legs strained under the weight she carried, and her stomach lurched with anticipation and dread, a sickening mixture of fear and excitement. She could feel every scar inside of her; the ones from her baby, sleeping soundly against her now, and the ones from Rafael, as he clawed out the light within her and filled it with darkness. Every step was a step away from him, every strain and ache, a promise she could live a different life. No matter how hard, it could not be the prison she experienced lying beneath him as he stared into the distance and hit her from the inside out.

The quiet long stretch of tarmac wasn't foreboding. It was beautiful in a way. Not like the forest and its thick canopy of green. But as a means to an end, a possibility. Camila didn't remember everything, but the veil grew lighter every day, and she had begun to recall things from before. She remembered walking down empty roads as a teen. Watching the rainbow patterns of spilt oil on the road. Seeing when it rained, the pattern of diminishing vehicle lights in the distance, play across water. There was something romantic and sad in those images. She recalled sleeping in the back of cars, perhaps driven by her father years ago. The stretch of time and memory seemed to play up the long, long road. It was her only hope now.

The 18-Wheeler came through once weekly and it happened on that day, at that time. Like the fortune of serendipity, watching us hurl ourselves at fate and beg for clemency, Camila saw the reflection of its chrome markers first. They were shiny against the bright of the moon light, and then she heard it, powering toward them. Still out of sight on one of the bends, she wasn't sure if it would see them, she wasn't sure if she should risk standing out into the road. Should it not be able to stop, what would she do? She tried to recall anything she ever knew about the stopping distance necessary for large load carrying vehicles, but her adrenaline was already leading them out into the road. Her son still strapped to her back, warm against her skin that held a little of the dampness of their swim, she had nothing to lose. Rafael could be behind them, he could have worked it out, he could be coming for them.

Camila waved her hands frantically, thinking at the last minute she'd do anything to get attention. Although it was loud, like a big rig, she second-guessed herself. What if it was Rafael? What if he had known and this was his truck, loud against silence? She imagined seeing his face in the window. Running, knowing she couldn't get far enough away. But the sound of the 18-Wheeler was unmistakable, her new-found memories were certain. She began to move her arms up and down, wishing so much she had some kind of light source, other than the moon. But the moon sufficed, the driver saw them as he came around the bend and acknowledged with pressure to the breaks. She could hear the break being applied and the truck slowing ahead of them and thought she would scream with relief. The truck stopped a little further than she had been standing, she moved to the side as he came close, and then ran up to catch him, afraid he would play chicken and speed off again.

"Oh God! Thank you, thank you, thank you," she said, not asking as she climbed up into the rig and sat down in the cab. *"You are a real life-saver Sir, a real life-saver. Oh, thank you dearly for stopping, I was hiking with my son and we got badly turned around in the woods and ended up coming out here. On the road in the dark."*

The driver was a sixty-something bearded man with kind eyes, he had a clean smelling cab, with no lewd pictures of topless women plastered inside, and he wore a company hat. *"You're real lucky I was passing, nobody comes up this way this time of night,"* he said, already reengaging the truck, *"I can't turn around. I'm on company time. But I can take you as far as Lampasas as that's my first town, if that's helping you any? My name is Javier,"* he shook her free hand.

"I am so very grateful to you!" She beamed at him. Pulling her son around onto her lap, he was still sleeping, and holding him to her chest. *"You're a life saver, you have no idea."*

"That's what I'm here for," the older man said, smiling, showing a perfect set of dentures, and increasing his speed as they left the trees and danger behind. The road looked so black it appeared wet, and glistening like a molting snake. The unease lying behind her, reflecting off the lakes surface, began to lift slightly from her tight shoulders as they made headway, and miles from her

confinement. For the first time, Camila did not feel she could be slapped at any moment, although she could not recall him slapping her, it was always what she expected him to do. Why was that? The memory of him mixed indelibly with the distant recollection of her first boyfriend, the one who liked to inflict pain and did it so very, very well.

"How far are you going?" Camila asked after a brief silence.

Javier studied her face, maybe an unasked question on his lips and replied, *"I'm driving through to Vancouver ma'am and then the next, turning right around and heading all the ways back to Monterrey, Mexico."*

She smiled thinking that it must be a very tiring job to drive those big rigs across three countries on a consistent basis. *"I'm sorry. When I say this might be rude of me to even ask, and I don't have any money at all I'll be upfront with you about that. But my son and I are leaving his father, he's a very abusive man, there's no other way of putting it. We need to get as far away as possible; the next town isn't going to be far enough. Is there any way, any way at all we can ride with you to your final destination? We need to get really far away from this man, Sir."* Camila's cheeks burned with the shame of telling a stranger her experience. What else could she do? What if throwing herself on the mercy of this stranger failed? He could be as cruel as Rafael for all she knew. Looking down at little sleeping Joe's face, she knew she had no choice but to try.

Javier turned back to the road, squinting at the headlights spotting birds flying out of trees as they passed. *"Well. I don't like getting involved in anything domestic see,"* he countered. He looked uneasy. She put her hand on his forearm and said *"Oh God please, I'm really desperate. I have no family. I have nobody else to ask, nobody who can help me. Just me and my son. I can't go back to his father. I can't. I'd literally rather die than carry on living like that."* Javier turned briefly to look at her son sleeping in her arms and took in their disheveled state. *"¿Eres Hispana? ¿Eres Mexicana? ¿Hablas español?"*

"Un poco. Si, soy Hispana." Camila took a deep breath. *"He estaño viviendo como prisionera. ¡Por favor, ayúdame!"*

"*Dios mío. ¡El mundo hoy!*" Javier exclaimed quietly.

"You say you have nothing with you? Nothing at all?" He asked softly.

"Nothing. I don't have anything but the clothes on our backs," Camila replied. *"I took my son and we left. I had no chance to do anything else, this was the best shot we had and the only one."* She realized that everything depended upon this man, she hated that idea because she didn't want to depend upon anyone, but she knew without his agreement they'd be dropped off locally and it wouldn't be far enough away, it wouldn't be nearly far enough. It was possible he was a predator also, that he would take her vulnerability and rape her in the woods and leave her there. What would stop him? He owed her nothing. She was a stranger, he had no obligation and if he hurt her, nothing would come back upon him.

"This is what I will do. I'll take you to the border, but without papers I don't think I can get you across." Javier said finally. Chewing on his thick lips. "*I don't want to be breaking any law; I can lose my license doing stuff like that.*" He looked at the sleeping child in her arms again, and then sighed deeply. *"Can you make it work at the border?"*

Camila tried to think clearly, but she was damp, tired, physically worn out. The adrenalin that had kept her company during her flight was fast wearing off, she felt unnaturally tired and muddy headed. "*We will have to find a way,*" she said, looking at her son, who despite his turbulent hours, slept the way children always sleep, an envy to every adult. "*We will find a way. We just need a chance.*"

They drove and drove, the countryside beautiful even in the darkness, a different kind of wild to the house, and the lake. This was energy, moving under the stars, seeing the entire expanse of sky shift and linger between dips and valleys. Camila began to nod off but a part of her, the part that was coming back to life said, *no, not yet, not yet.* She stayed awake through sheer willpower. After a few hours they pulled into a weigh station and she got out and met him at the roadside diner. She didn't have any money but she figured if he bought her a cup of coffee it would warm her a little. Even though his cab was cozy, she felt cold inside, maybe the nervous energy draining out of her.

"You look like you could do with something to eat," Javier pronounced and ordered two breakfasts and a little kid breakfast, *the kindness of strangers.* They all three ate ravenously and Camila thanked him profusely which seemed to make him uncomfortable and happy at the same time. *"I have an idea,"* he said, wiping egg from his beard and drinking a long swig of hot black coffee. The waitress was generous and had already topped them both up three times.

"Oh yeah?" She asked. He grinned like a little kid with a plan. *"I could unload a little, that way the weight would come in at the right weight and this time of night, on this road, going into Canada they're not checking. If you went in back of the truck as we came, say 25 miles to the border, and kept the little one real still and quiet, that's got to happen or this won't work, you think he can? He seems a good boy."*

Oh God could it work? Could they make it to Canada? A whole new country. Rafael would never, ever not in his wildest dreams think they'd got to Canada. If he even thought they were still alive, he'd never look for them there. They would be safe. Camila shook her head up and down like a child. *"Yes, he is. Joe's such a good boy. He's very quiet."*

"He doesn't cry much?"

"No, he's a very good boy my Joe, he doesn't cry." Camila thought of the horrible reason behind this. What Joe had instinctively known about his father from almost birth. How sometimes children know before they can articulate how they know, what they must do to survive.

"That's a blessing for a boy his age for sure," Javier said, smacking his lips with a memory presumably of his own experiences with toddlers. *"Okay then."*

"Okay?" Camila said with incredulity. Could this really happen?

"Yeah, I'll do it. I never did approve of men who need to lay a hand on a woman or child to prove their power. No that's no good, my father didn't raise me to let that be okay. If you feel all right about being in the back some, as we near the border, I'll get you over. We'll have to drive a ways – before I can let you out and 'cause it means you'll be in a different country with no papers, that's not easy, not easy at all, but if your minds set on it, well I'll help you get there."

Chapter 37

Camila felt so relieved. How had the impossible, happened? Javier, a savior in an 18-Wheeler, coming through the darkness like avenging angel. How could it be a stranger would be kinder than family or people you have known for years? Yet how often this was the case. Such a horrible irony. But maybe why we had to continue to believe in others? Yes, it was madness. Canada. She didn't think she'd ever been to Canada but she needed to be that far away, if not further. For long enough to know she wasn't going to be brought back to that house, to those secrets, and the lies she knew Rafael had in the pitch of his eyes. Now that she was away from him, she let herself admit how afraid she had been. Every day holding herself like a porcelain statue, hoping to get through. It seemed odd, given that he'd never outright hit her, but some violence is implicit. It's just part of a person and like an animal, we smell it on them, we taste it, we know it and we bow our heads like wolves and let the pack master take control.

It wasn't a life she had ever wanted, to be the geisha to his warped fantasies. She remembered she had nearly died, that she had actually wanted to die and he had saved her. But he had saved her for the wrong reasons and that nixed anything she may owe him now. Besides, she couldn't get it out of her head that he was somehow her ex. How that could be possible she didn't know. Maybe it was the drugs. But the similarity was impossible to ignore. Either returned in deed or actuality, they were one and the same. Rafael was also a murderer, what had really happened to his wife and son? And the neighbors and possibly others, part of his body count. If she put a foot out of line, she'd be next on the chopping block, she'd known that and been living with that for a very long time. With an empty mind she responded differently to the way others would, she relied more on instinct and the instinct had a voice and that voice said, **run**.

Closing on the border, Javier threw out some extraneous things from the back, stuff he said he was keeping because of habit not necessity, by the road side. It was mostly packing and boxes and once gone, making enough room for them both – she climbed in, with Joe, and they went right to the back of the truck. There, there was a packing blanket and they curled up in the blanket and within minutes, surrounded by the comfort and security of walls of boxes, they both fell asleep. They stopped briefly at the border, but she didn't notice and didn't wake, nobody checked the back, the papers were in order, the weight rang true, Javier drove through and they were on the other side and in Canada sooner than seemed possible. The countryside was much the same, maybe a little more ordered, less scrub. They drove a while and then he pulled over and Camila woke up as he pulled up the gate of the truck and they got out and drove again in the front, a little proud, like conspirators who had pulled off a heist.

As day broke, they reached the outskirts of Vancouver. *"This is as far as I'm going mi amiga,"* he said. *"The drop off is about two miles up here, before you get into the city proper. You want that I take you into Vancouver? With no money you're going to have to find a shelter for you and the boy. I know there's battered women's shelters, they'll do you a service I'm certain of it."*

"I would be so grateful Javier. I can never thank you enough," she said, feeling so grateful for this stranger's kindness and wondering how she thought she would ever have succeeded if she'd not been picked up on that tarmac road under a full moon, soaking wet with a sleeping child in her arms. *"You are divine intervention Javier and I hope you know that,"* she told him, and he blushed just slightly underneath his facial hair. Camila thought, maybe it made him as happy as it made me, to save someone.

Happiness, that illusive beast that comes more from the kindness of strangers, or helping others, than ever from the luxuries this barren world offers us. A full moon lighting its way home, better than any fancy car. A helping hand and home-cooked meal far more valuable than a rich hotel. Such is life, simplicity being our greatest joy, as Citizen Kane considered when he said *Rosebud*, his sleigh, at the end of his life. Camila understood why she had been unable to be happy in the past. Too welded to notions of what she *should do* rather than doing what she *needed to do*. Too empty from her own pain, to see the value of others reaching out to help. Too scared to have love, until her son was born and he gave it to her without asking. Happiness is always simplicity, and never the complex notions humans make up when they convince themselves that if they just have a bit more, then they'll be happy.

Javier looked up the shelters in Vancouver on his cell phone. There was a woman's shelter and a battered woman's shelter. He felt the latter would be more helpful because they'd have means to put women back on their feet and not just a roof over their head for the night. He got directions and they got there quickly because it was on the same side of town and slightly on the outskirts, probably because of price. A tall building, turn of the century, painted in light colors, to liven up the tired brick. He pulled outside, which made them both smile, seeing the absurdity of dropping her off in an 18-Wheeler. *"I'll come in with you both, make sure you are situated"* he said, unbuckling.

"No, I'll go in by myself, it might look better that way, nothing against you but you know how first impressions count, and anyway, they can't really turn us away. Not now we're here." She replied.

"Okay, are you sure?"

"I'm sure," Camila said, *"and thank you again, so much, I can never thank you enough Javier. Would you consider giving me your number for when I get settled? I can at least repay you a little or let you know how I'm doing?"*

Javier wrote the number down and gave it to her, *"now I don't want to hear anything about repayment. This was my pleasure. Sometimes God gives us ways to serve that we wouldn't expect. I'm grateful for that. It gives me a good feeling to know I got you away from a bad situation. Real good feeling. But you let me know when you're settled or if you need anything I can help you with. That would be a kindness for sure."*

"Deal." She said, and kissing him on the cheek she climbed down with Joe strapped on her back, awake and playing with her hair, and watched as Javier drove off into the coming dawn. The big rig, strangely quiet on the silent roads, a long rush of silver, slick on wet tarmac. Camila felt a lurch in her stomach, the kind you get when you stand completely alone on strange ground. A foreign country! The last person you knew has left and you need to find within yourself that strength to start over, with nothing in your hands except yourself rising to the challenge, conquering the fear that starts to take over and spin its yarn. Camila swallowed once, ensured Joe was fastened tight to her, and opened the door to the shelter.

The Battered Women's Shelter was far nicer than she could have envisioned. She was fairly certain she'd never been in one before, but not knowing for certain was bothersome. Like wondering always about yourself, if you knew everything you'd done and been. A kind-faced woman in her fifties with big thighs and a hard hug, manned the front desk and when she saw them enter, didn't seem in the least surprised at a walk-in with a baby strapped to her back. *"Well, you look like you could do with a refreshment young lady,"* she said. *"Welcome, let's get you a hot drink, and we can talk in here."* They went into an adjacent room and the friendly lady came back with water and coffee and sugar and creamer. Shuffling some papers – she pulled a pen from behind her ear and said. *"Take a load off and tell me what I need to know."*

How to begin? Sitting opposite a person, you think might care, if they knew you, and because of what they do, but not sure, not sure of anything. How to start and what to say and what to not reveal? Camila's imperfect memory made this part hardest, so she decided to stick to everything she knew and hope for the best. At least she was nowhere near Rafael. At least she had a chance now. Even so, if you've ever told a painful story, and you struggle to even remember details, you fear each time you tell it. You fear the looks people may give you, or worse, no expression at all. Exposing yourself and your pain to another person, is something many avoid at all costs, it is only when we are with our noses to the ground that we usually feel we have no choice but to tell all and throw ourselves on the mercy of others.

Camila began with; *"I'm American. I don't know where I am from originally, I have some memory issues. I know I lived in Texas at one point. My memories, they're coming back but a lot is still gone, so bear with me. What I do know is I came here because I think the man I was living with, his name is Rafael, he will kill me if I don't get away and stay away. He is my son Joe's natural father. It's not even a legal matter, as I had my son at home, he's not registered anywhere, and so there is no legal bind between myself and this man and my son. Most of all, the reason I ran, it's a feeling I have here,"* and she touched her stomach, *"because since I lost so much of my memories, I only have my gut to go on and my intuition and I've given this a lot of thought and I had to run, because I knew, I knew, if I didn't, I'd never survive."*

They talked for about an hour and a half. Camila told the kind woman about what she did recall. Her suicide attempt, though she did not know all that drove her to that point. How Rafael resembled the first boy she had a bad relationship with years before. How she thought they may impossibly be the same man. She told her about the not being taken to hospital, being kept in a house, eventually moving. The choice Rafael gave her to stay suicidal or wipe her memory and start over, how she agreed because she didn't know what to do. How she woke up after 'dying' a second time, with no memory, and gradually learned to live a life with him in an isolated house in the middle of a forest in Oregon.

She told her that they'd become intimate, that at first it seemed okay. That she wasn't thinking straight enough to really process thought so much as just living and existing, and gradually discovered that she was being drugged. She explained this was different from what she had been told about 'healing micro-doses that could help her stop being suicidal.' This was real drugging to keep her compliant, willing. She told her about her pregnancy, and her son's birth at home, despite her protests. About the neighbors and how they died and her suspicions and her awakening mind, and the other neighbor Lou and how when he went missing. How she knew it was just a matter of time until she was next. She told her about the photo of Rafael's wife Carol and her *apparent* death by suicide. His missing first son. All the connections with suicide and premature death around Rafael including his parents whilst he was at college.

Camila said that she believed in coincidence, but not in ignoring your gut and that even her son, at two years of age, seemed weary of his father, as if he knew, just knew, something was off. Finally, she told her about the locked office. The violent porn and torture and the many questions she had, but the danger of staying any longer to find out more. *"It was just a matter of time before I did something that really set him off and that would be all it took,"* she said. *"So, I pretended to go overboard and drown. I don't know if he bought it, I suspect he didn't, but what else could I do? I drugged his drink with my pain-killers and some of the micro-dose and escaped, doing my best to hide my tracks. An 18-Wheeler picked me up and got me into Canada after I told him what happened. And that's it. Here I am, I have no money, no papers, no legal residency, and only my child literally on my back. I have nowhere to go. No family that I know of and still an impaired memory. Please. Please help me."*

"Well!" Said the kind lady, crossing her generous thighs and taking a long sip of water. *"I think that about beats any story I've heard in a while. We get some pretty incredible stories here of survival. I don't mean to be glib, but it's a wild one for sure. God Bless you for being alive."*

"I know it," Camila said, not sure if she should laugh or cry, not really feeling like either, but rather, a numbness at recounting her experience that sounded so impossible and unrealistic, she feared that nobody sane would really believe her. Would you?

"I want you to know," the woman said, as if she were reading her mind, *"first and foremost I want you to know one thing and hold on to this, all right? I believe you. I believe you because I wouldn't do what I do if I wasn't prepared to believe each and every one who*

comes through these doors and believe me, there's a lot of stories that are out there. But I also believe you because I've gotten good at reading people and I can tell the liars from the truth tellers, pretty easily. I see it in your eyes, you're literally terrified and you didn't come in here and spin a tall story to get a bed for the night, this I know."

"What does that mean?" the lady continued, *"Well it means I'm going to do what I can to help you. It's not easy, because you're not Canadian, but you don't really know where you come from, so we can work on the premise that you 'could' be Canadian. It really doesn't matter in cases of abuse, they work under an entirely different visa system anyways, a bit like asylum cases for those mistreated in another country. It helps because we can cut through some of the red tape almost immediately and get you temporary rights to stay here. I assume you want to stay here for the time being at least?"*

"Yes, I do," Camila said. *"I do very much. I need to be as far away from him as possible, he's only in Oregon, even here doesn't feel far enough, I feel he would and will do anything to get us back. He doesn't let people survive him."*

"Well, he's not even going to know you're here because the first thing we're going to do is give you an alias. You'd be surprised, lots of women are trafficked or run away from abuse, and many times they cross borders, in desperation, or because they run out of choices. There is a special provision in the asylum laws for women in peril that allows us to use an alias. At no point will your given name be on documentation that he could potentially access."

"Let's not get into all of that right today, today I'm going to do the paperwork after we stop talking, and I won't even need any details of yours upfront because the basic paperwork is self-explanatory and mostly for us to explain your circumstances second-hand. Your job for today is to rest, have a shower, get cleaned up, eat, and sleep. How does that sound?" She was so kind, merciful in a way that she was

not used to, Camila felt her eyes welling up and looked away, embarrassed at her emotion.

"Thank you." she said, *"thank you so much."* She wished there was more she could say, to the kind lady, to the truck driver, the unknown angels who helped her when she had nothing to give in return. It humbled her, through the loss of herself, she found the wealth of humility and thankfulness and it filled her deeply. She didn't know if she believed in God, or just used the words as a way of describing good and evil, but she knew for a long time she had thought only evil existed in the world. Now she understood, there were people who did good for no other reason than because they felt it was right. She was miles from Rafael in another country. But Camila still felt unsafe.

Chapter 38

Her room was not a dormitory bed as she had suspected, but a private room, given to all the women especially those with kids, unless space was an issue. "*We have 40 rooms,*" the kind lady, who was called Ruby, explained. *"Sometimes it gets real busy – other times we're half-booked. I think unlike a hotel that's the best time because it means less women who are being beaten and forced out of their houses. Before you say anything, I know 'battered women's' shelter implies physical abuse and you may worry since you didn't say he laid hands on you but believe me, the worst abuse can be psychological and we see that many times, it can scar just as bad as any beating ever will."*

Camila was left to shower and bathe Joe. Their room was small and made of pine, with a big picture window and sill with some ivy growing on the outside. It overlooked a parking lot, and wasn't very scenic, she didn't care at all. Keep the lake, keep the gorgeous view, she wanted safety and her own locked door. They now had that, the two of them, washing and laughing for the first time in what seemed like forever. Getting all clean and rinsing the road off them, before falling into bed, exhausted and sleeping the sleep only the weariest emotions are capable of inducing. When she woke up it was dark and she was starving. The shelter had a canteen-style food setup with serve yourself, and there was no charge. She had a big bowl of soup, Joe had crackers, a small bowl of mash potato and carrots and a little chocolate pudding. She ate bread with her soup and even a small chocolate cake afterward. It felt like the first time she'd ever eaten without looking over her shoulder.

The eating area was pretty quiet, maybe it was later than usual for eating, she didn't know since she wasn't accustomed to time, something she'd have to learn to get the hang of quickly if she was going to return to the world. Outside, the world looked still and open, in a different way to how the lake had. Camila realized she'd been holding her breath for years without acknowledging. A part of her, the feral part, untamed by learning, had known something was wrong long before the conscious elements of her knew. "*This is something I should hold on to,*" she thought. So many people live for intellect and what they have learned, we forget what we already know, in our bones. We forget to listen to that voice that is telling us insistently, when something doesn't feel right. We walk into it because we don't listen, we only obey reason, but there is nothing in reason that can explain someone who seeks to destroy you.

It was then she realized Rafael had meant to destroy her, she didn't know how or why but it was his urge. Maybe that's all it was, a lazy urge to destroy, and she could have been any girl jumping from a bridge. Maybe he justified it by saying had he not saved her, brought her back, she would be dead now, in a watery grave. Or maybe it was something more sinister. Camila represented for him another shot at marriage, another chance for a family. Though he would destroy them as he did his first, as was his habit, as was his design. The worst part about memory loss is how much you distrust yourself. You cannot reliably state without doubt almost anything, and in time you rely more and more on instinct, which is harder to justify if cross-examined. In a sense a loss of memory turns you wild, feral, instinctual, and watchful. Like a deer never really stops looking around as they cut through trees and bend to eat the tender shoots of grass.

If Rafael had indeed been her first boyfriend, what did that mean about Camila's ability to gauge things? How could she not have known? Her first boyfriend was someone she had been close to. Years ago, yes, but how can you forget someone? Not recognize it? Was Rafael years later, slightly different looking, her first boyfriend come to find her? How was that even possible? Who does that? Had Rafael somehow been tracking Camila's movements to the bridge and became her 'hero.' If so, was this all part of his plan? Driving her to the edge, watching her unravel for years afterward. Letting her try to end her life just so he could walk back into it again and control her. Did the layers of sickness go much further than she had even anticipated? How was that possible?

There was every reason to believe Rafael was indeed her first boyfriend, years later. How could she not have recognized him? Yet on so many drugs, was it not completely understandable? Was that why he wanted her to lose her memories so completely? Rafael had so much of the same personality. The need to control. The need for perfection. The sexual appetite and rawness of his urges. How stupid she had been not to see sooner, the echoes of the past. But of course, that was one reason he wanted her to wipe her memory, to avoid that ever happening and her ever putting the pieces together and accusing him. Equally it served his interest if she was beholden to him. Emptied of her own resistance and knowledge, reliant upon his control of her, absolute and unquestioned.

As she thought back to their first weeks together, through the fog of the medication she recalled Rafael standing up. Moving in a way to catch her attention, admiring himself and wishing to be admired. He was confident, overconfident, nay in love with his body and his prick and his entirety as if he were a God seeking believers. When he *made love* to her, which now she thought of as abuse, he would stroke himself hard and push her chin down, opening her lips, watching her take him in her mouth. He would get off on observing the act, of worship on his phallus like an Egyptian God beckoning slave. She understood he was a Narcissist, the kind who worshipped only himself and could not accept anything less from a lover. And she was his to mold into the acquiescent partner he craved to sustain him, at any cost. With every day away from Rafael's control Camila unraveled more of the game and saw things starkly for what they were.

As time moved on, she began to understand time in its orderly, human form, she got a watch, she checked clocks. It was a novel thing, and it held her like a straitjacket to the world, in a way that timelessness never had. But Camila was glad to be held, by something, by anything, other than the isolation of Rafael's dampened rage and expectation. Sometimes she'd wake at night and see instead of her safe little room, the lake, and his eyes, saying nothing, speaking volumes. Other days she longed to find out more, to ask him directly: *"Why did you do this? Why did you let this happen? Who are you? Why did you kill the neighbors? How could you? Did you kill your own parents? Did you kill your wife Carol and your child Jacob? Were you going to end me and your son Joe?"* And she imagined him responding, without emotion. *"What did you think? You knew me even if you denied it, you recognized me that first day. That you get to keep coming back? How many times are you going to die? I want to ensure you will stay dead."* She would dream of his hands around her neck, underwater, fighting both of them changing space in the freezing lake, first her, then him, taking turns to drown.

Life has an enduring way of reconstructing itself; even as you lose everything, you continue forward. She had lost the memories that had brought her to want to take her own life, in some ways, she understood his logic in believing this was the only way she would ever recover from whatever legacy had pushed her to self-annihilation. Camila didn't seek to know the horrors that exposed that impulse to die, but she did wish to know the parts of herself she thought might not have always sought death. After all we can want to die in a moment, and in the next, as it passes, wish again to live. She thought of all the people who had tried to commit suicide and failed, and how when asked they inevitably said they were glad for their second chance at life. It just shows that what we think we know, we do not know, she thought, as she tried and tried and tried to maintain a sense of normalcy without really knowing what *normal* felt like.

When for so much of your life you have lived in fear of the instability of your mind, an endowment from the fragility of your upbringing where you could not rely upon anything or anyone, you are like a plant that is afraid to stretch toward the sun. You shrink back from the greatest things because you neither believe yourself worthy nor that you could succeed. When you are never told that you have done a good job, when you are not rewarded for your hard work but instead asked, *what you could have done better*, it forms in you a negativity that runs so deeply you do not seek to find out how far you can go. You don't know what you can do, until you are pushed to the edge and you fall and then of course, you have nothing to lose.

The shelter bent over backwards for them both. Enrolling Joe in subsidized kindergarten gave Camila more time to fit the pieces together. The paperwork had come through and she was granted asylum based upon imminent threat of death, and a judge signed and stamped this, allowing her to apply for Canadian Residency which afforded all the rights of a citizen *bar* voting. In the meantime, Canada had socialized healthcare and support systems for indigent and struggling single parents, and within a week Camila's name, her new name, the one she gave as a pseudonym, Joslyn, was on a list for housing. Now Joslyn, she'd begun to get checks, small sums, to give her the semblance of an income and afford her a few of the many things they did not have.

The shelter had outreach programs and connections with other organizations. *Dress For Success* brought over bags of clothes for them both, other charities chipped in and she had before long as much as if she had been buying for a whole year. It was odd to own things, to possess anything that she could say was hers, because she couldn't recall ever having anything she deemed her own. The feeling wasn't entirely welcome, she had liked the idea of being without anything, it gave her a sense of freedom from responsibility but she knew that was childish and an effort to avoid reality. As Joslyn, she tried hard to embrace the roles she knew she would long have had to adopt, had she been part of the real world.

It was odd to imagine in idle hour, how long she'd been out of the world, a stranger to most things, including making a living and paying bills. Maybe some women would have liked to be utterly controlled, she thought. It takes the worry out of everything, and at times, when she considered how far she had to go, it did feel overwhelming. But not once did she want to go back to the chains of Rafael's rule book, because in so doing, she would lose herself again, and rely on him for everything including her own life. No. That was never going to be an option. Her counselor, who had been assigned her the first week, asked many times if Camila considered going back. She knew the high rate of return among battered and abused women to their abuser, not because they wished for the abuse, but because they'd been broken and had no self-worth and felt *better The Devil you know*.

At first Camila didn't understand how any woman could do this, but when she thought of the comfort of the familiar, even the bad familiar, she could see how struggling in a strange world could be overwhelming, and how returning to a bad but known world was often perceived. If you do not believe in yourself, her counselor said, you often feel you deserve nothing better than the mistreatment of others. You feel you ask for it, with your existence, and that justifies it and permits you to take it for years. She understood in a sick way how she felt when he slowly shifted her perspective to put him first, to ignore her own needs. When without asking he shifted her perspective where he had become the center of her everything. Through persuasion and inflation, he was the shrine and she the worshipper. Unable to leave, for without him, Camila literally did not know who she was.

She was learning so much. She learned to be more independent. She got a job at a coffee house not far from the shelter. During the days she worked, and filled in forms during her breaks and in the evenings. Joe made friends in kindergarten, they both learned how to be around more than one person. For Joe it was easy, he was still young; for Camila it was hard because she had no social clues and would often remain quiet and just absorb the social dynamics of others. But it felt good, not to be alone all the time, wondering what would happen next and having no power to affect the outcome. She found she really liked working, it filled the day with routine and gave her pride in earning the little money she brought home each week. Something within her was flowering and it felt like it had been wanting to do so for a very long time.

She wrote to her savior the truck driver Javier and updated him on everything, using email for the first time since (when? She wasn't ever sure) the past where she had presumably known how to do a great many things. She made friends with one of her neighbors at the shelter, a woman about her age, who had been in an abusive relationship with her boyfriend and finally been kicked out half dead onto the streets. They bonded over both having small children and finding it hard to ask for things when you had always been controlled and told what to do rather than given options and choices.

Judy, her neighbor, had grown up in Trinidad before moving to Canada with her family of origin. She'd met her boyfriend when she was 15 and he'd indoctrinated her with a warped idea of life from the get-go, she found it hard because he'd trained her so well to be obedient to his abuse. But in the end, she'd found her way to the shelter and begun to reevaluate how she saw herself in the scheme of things. Perhaps their mutual shyness and unfamiliarity with the rhythm of things, caused them to understand one another and form a friendship that was the first balanced and trusting friendship either had experienced in some years. The strange feeling someone else understands those parts of you, you don't want to share with anyone. It erased the invariable shame of feeling you'd been gullible, naïve. The kinds of dark feelings narcissists know how to plant deeply and watch grow.

Chapter 39

As life gradually built around her and Camila, within it, thrived, she would still feel anxious, she had to look over her shoulder at the slightest sound. Irrational as it may seem, often thinking that somehow Rafael was on her trail. Logically she knew this was impossible, she'd changed her name, she didn't leave any clues. She had no clues to leave with no family to contact, no trail to follow. Despite that, there was one remaining thorn. She kept thinking of Lou. He loomed over her like a carved edifice, branded in her mind. Wondering if indeed he had been killed like the old lady and her husband, considering the body count of her lover. They were all innocents. Camila was scared that she'd simply run away and left Rafael to continue his quiet rampage in the Oregon hills, perhaps obtaining another girl like herself. Someone who wouldn't be missed, someone easy to shut away and control.

"What if he's doing it again?" She said to Judy one night as they ate with the kids in front of the TV sitting on her bed. It was Asian noodles, Vancouver having a high population of immigrants from Asia they had excellent Asian supermarkets with

inexpensive tasty options. Joe was a big fan of noodles, he called them 'oodles' and jumped up and down when she announced what they were having for dinner.

"Don't you think he'll lay off because he knows you've escaped and he might worry that you're watching and will call the police at the first sign of anything?" Judy said. Like Camila, nothing surprised Judy, she'd seen more than most her age, she'd survived. She knew what certain people were capable of.

"He'll known I've run. Eventually he'll figure it out. Especially with no bodies. He's perennially suspicious of everything. He's too smart. If he even believes I'm still alive, he'll know I've gone as far as I could. He knows I can't report him from so far away without risking his finding out where I am. Either that or maybe eventually he thinks I'm dead. Either option isn't good because they both permit him to start over."

"What makes you think he'd start over? He's had two sets of families now, neither worked and you left him. Whether he believes you died or escaped, you chose to go, and he might have learned what that signifies about his relationship style. Wouldn't that teach him to avoid doing something like what he did to you ever again?" Judy replied.

"Exactly. You said it. I left him. That's unacceptable. That's something he'll never let go. Psychopaths don't just suddenly switch a switch and change and decide they are going to be respectful and not do what comes naturally. The whole point is they lack empathy. I may not know what brought me to the point in my life of wishing to take my life and falling into his hands but I know from living here, there are many vulnerable women out there, and he only needs to find one."

Judy responded, *"True. A man of his nature isn't going to quit satiating his nature. If he preyed upon you then he'll do it again.*

Especially if he's capable of those kinds of double-manipulations where even smart people like you get caught up."

"Needing sex alone would lure him to find a woman. Rafael literally couldn't get enough and I told you even I wasn't sufficient. He was a serious sex addict I'm certain of it, and who knows what else? Maybe his trips into town were to be with other women, maybe he had a backup all along? Who is to say that he fished me out of the water by sheer coincidence? I always thought it was unbelievable that he happened to be by the side of the bridge at the exact moment I jumped and happened to dive in and 'save me' – don't you think something is really missing from that story?"

"Yeah, it's definitely weird as fuck. But like what?"

"Like how he knew I'd be there, and how he witnessed my attempt and how he was able to save me? I thought at first it was just coincidental and fortuitous that someone had seen me jump, but as I recall more, I remember noticing that the whole area was empty and abandoned. I had chosen that deliberately because I didn't want anyone to save me. So, he came out of nowhere? That suggests to me Rafael was hiding and he had been watching me. If there is any truth to my suspicion, then it means he was stalking me well before I decided to kill myself. What if he even had something to do with that? I'm not saying I know how, but it makes sense in a mad way. A bigger picture that I can't properly recall yet. What if he orchestrated the entire thing to work in his favor?"

"Isn't that a bit paranoid?" Judy said, with an apologetic but kind expression on her sundial face. "*You're telling me that somehow Rafael had the power to cause you to become suicidal, and happened to be able to stalk you so well that he knew exactly when you'd try to kill yourself and was able to rescue you? That would take some doing."*

"I know how it sounds. I wouldn't believe me. Why do you think

I question it so much? You're right, it would take some doing. But I think if anyone is capable of that level of orchestration it's Rafael. You don't know him, he's manipulative in ways I can't even articulate or understand. He knows how to control you without needing to actually verbalize it. It's like he's playing chess with your life."

Judy smiled a sad smile; "*Oh girl I do know that feeling, remember I was in a similar boat?*"

"I know love, I know, and I'm sorry. I don't mean to be insensitive and all about me. It's just that my gut tells me there is far more to this and Rafael. This isn't a one-time thing; he's got absolutely no reason to stop now and every reason to carry on. A God needs worshippers. Sometimes truth is stranger than fiction."

Camila stayed with that thought for a long while, it began to burrow deeper into her until she had gone through every possible scenario her mind could develop. *A God needs worshippers. A God needs worshippers.* At the same time, she and her counselor worked on her memory, her counselor urging her to put the pieces back together. Camila began to remember her family of origin. She remembered being estranged from her parents at an early age, one set of grandparents' deaths, her grandfather's suicide. She remembered her experience of sexual abuse at the hands of the neighbor, how everyone looked the other way, the legacy of alcoholism and depression that ran in her DNA. But despite this it didn't explain why she'd follow the pattern and take her own life. Nor did she ever recall having a child, still born or otherwise, and she became convinced that part of his story was fabricated as an excuse for Rafael ensuring she had her son at home.

"Why do you think you'd decided death was the only answer for you?" Her psychotherapist asked her one evening as they sat in the peaceful twilight in two facing, comfy chairs.

"It's so hard to say without having a full recollection," Camila

replied.

"I'm sure it is, but what I'd like you to do is give me the answer you believe most likely. Don't try to remember, try to feel the answer." Camila let go of her roving through her incomplete memory and tried to release her emotions. The answers that she *felt* rather than knew.

"I feel I did it because I felt alone. I'd felt close to my father growing up but he wasn't an interested parent. He had other people in his life and he didn't have much time for a kid, I was an appendage at best. My mother didn't have a maternal streak. I think I used to resent that but as I've gotten older, I see that some women don't and it's not a flaw or deficit it's just how they are. She taught me a lot; she taught me to believe in myself and to try for anything I wanted. I'm not sure when I forgot those lessons." Camila said.

"I don't hate either of my parents, I just always felt so alone despite them existing. I knew they never thought about me the way I thought about them. After a while I couldn't stand that so *I left and I moved a long way away and that just isolated me further. Before I knew it, I was making a series of bad decisions and stumbling further and further down a hole of my own making. It's like I had run away only to find the very thing I was running from. I discovered that too late. I didn't realize it had nothing to do with them and everything to do with me and how I handled the world."*

"Are you sure it was a bad choice and not just a different choice?" The therapist asked.

"It was a bad choice, and when you make a hard choice and it turns out to be either wrong or just not right, you have two alternatives. You can return with your tail between your leg and confirm that you have shamed yourself even further in their eyes, or you can endure the choice you made and make the best of it. I tried to go back, but by then they'd moved on. I did it in the first place

because I felt they didn't need me and I was right. I decided that I'd made the choice, a hard choice and I was going to do my best to make it work. Who knows if that was the right decision? After what I just experienced, I'd be tempted to say no, definitely not. But then who can ever say an alternate decision wouldn't have ended badly? We just don't know, we do what we think is best, with the limited information about future possibilities and the rest is a gamble. I have never liked to gamble and I suck at it."

"Did you ever think it was normal to expect your parents to want you and that whilst they might not have thought so, your need to be wanted and loved was normal?"

"Yes. I knew it when I had Joe and even before him. The feeling of being a parent or wanting to be a parent. I knew it wasn't abnormal to need my family. But it was something that hurt because they didn't feel the same way. What was I going to do? Keep hanging around hoping it would change? It never did. It hurt me and I began to hate myself for wanting that so badly. I felt weak. I wanted to strike out on my own, prove to them and myself I could. Maybe at the back of my mind I thought I would make them proud of me and they'd change their mind. I pretty quickly figured out that wasn't going to happen. Then I saw it for what it was. I just wasn't their type. And it all escalated into this feeling of worthlessness, despair, invisibility."

"You never blame them and that's a good thing." Camila's therapist said. *"Blame only transfers guilt, it doesn't obviate it. The point of healing is to see that there is no need for guilt. With guilt comes feelings of worthlessness, self-denigration. The only way we heal is when we can stop hating ourselves for the way our lives turned out. In our society we're held to account for everything and it drives us crazy. It's one thing being responsible for ourselves. It's another to believe we're responsible for everything. You're not responsible Camila for your parents not loving you. Nobody is. Not even them. It's in your family like a legacy. Before you were born. That's not something*

you could ever have controlled. It was already enacted before you existed. Probably before your parents existed. We continue histories without even knowing how much of them are not our own choice."

"Did you know," Camila told her therapist, *"Rafael told me once that when I died neither parent came to claim my body, I was cremated. It wasn't me who was cremated it was the girl who had been in the river whom they thought was me. But she represented me, that poor girl whom nobody will ever give a name to. She lies in my grave, and she is me, for all intents and purposes. Knowing they didn't come to my funeral well, I didn't have a funeral, but didn't come to be with me, I suppose. It reminded me of all the times I felt that way as a kid. I don't think there's anything there anymore. It broke for good. If my parents are still alive, I hope they are well but I don't see the value in re-connecting. Sometimes you just know things are broken. So maybe that had something to do with it. The last fragment broke inside me to imagine they would not have turned out for my death. At the same time had you asked me, I'd have said I knew they wouldn't have attended. It was their way."*

"You're saying loneliness kills?" Her therapist countered. *"Starting life feeling you aren't valued by those closest to you, who usually would. Then going through life carrying that feeling you don't matter, builds loneliness, until even when you're in a room with people you feel alone?"*

"Yeah. I think that's true; we spend our lives alone even if we don't know it, but most of the time we can convince ourselves we're not alone. When you know you are alone and you have nobody to talk to. It builds up and after a while you start looking at death as a haven. I don't think like that now. It's strange how much I have changed. Sometimes you have to lose everything before you realize what you have. It's not that I was ungrateful then, I was suffering and I won't ever condemn myself for my decision then, because until you've been at that precipice of despair, you cannot understand how hard it is

for people who feel that way to consider living another day. But I'm glad I feel differently, it's almost a miracle to overcome a lifetime of sadness." Camila said. *"But it's almost like I chide myself for ever having felt it on some level. Like I threw my life away, which I know logically I didn't, but I can't get over the feeling I deserved what happened because of how I saw my life."*

"Do you thank your abductor for that?" the therapist asked. *"You say you feel differently now; do you think he's responsible for that positive change?"*

Camila felt unsettled. *"What an odd question. I suppose I did at first. I know that even now some people would say he didn't abuse me so much as save me. He lied and said I was a drug addict,* a *prostitute. He told me I had a child and I was responsible for killing it because of my drug addiction. He re-wrote my memories with ones where I did what he wanted me to do and learned to be compliant and submissive. I didn't realize so much of what he was doing was unhealthy because I couldn't remember another life by then. Now that I know better, I see that sexually he abused me, mentally he kept me unknowing, and emotionally he controlled me. Do I thank him?"*

She breathed out, *"Am I grateful he technically saved me from dying? Yes, I am. But not grateful to him, grateful that it happened. That's part of the twisted manipulation otherwise. As for the rest? It was a nightmare. I was heavily medicated, my thoughts were not my own, he sought to have a bride of his making, a girl who would open her legs at his bidding and sleep through his other darker desires. I had no idea that half of what he did was unacceptable and worst yet, I'm certain he killed people. I don't know how many. I may never know, but our neighbors almost certainly and I strongly suspect, his parents, his first wife and child, maybe others. I can't tell you how I know he's capable of it, but I do. It's more than supposition. I saw him strangle* cats *that came to the house, I saw him gut fish without flinching. He was more than a mountain man; he was a killer."*

Her counselor didn't disabuse her, but urged her to consider herself in light of her survival and reincarnation as a woman who had a new lease on life. "*Do you think he helped you find that?*" she asked. "*What if you are placing blame on someone who helped lift you out of the darkness you had found when you felt alone?*"

Camila felt something crawling across her forehead, a memory, an unease, something tugging. "*Why are your questions centering around my being grateful toward him?*" She looked up. "*I mean I get how we have to see things from every vantage point, but it feels a whole lot like blame right now.*"

"*No blame. Just questions. To help you understand your experience from every angle like you said. Because a part of you may struggle with the idea that he actually helped you just as much as he abused you. Whilst this is not absolving his crimes toward you or saying they didn't happen and are not valid reasons for you leaving, you may have a part of you that also recognizes out of a bad situation you survived and became a more resilient person.*" Camila's therapist replied.

"*Ok I get where you are going with that. Yeah. Yes, I suppose I did. I remember as we climbed the hill from the lake, I had a strength I never thought I'd possess, and it was a wild and wonderful feeling. I was shaking with fear and cold, but I kept going, knowing if I could just crest the hill and find a way, I'd be free of him. When I first met him, I had neither liked nor disliked him. I didn't have any radar, I was too disorientated then, too drugged. It feels strange considering now all I see when I think about him – is the first boyfriend I had who mistreated me. I can't ever be sure if they are one and the same.*"

"*Back at the start, I thought him kind and gentle. He was at first. As time went on, his kindness slowed down and his gentleness evaporated and without my even noticing he began to be less gentle, less kind, and more controlling. If it is slow enough, gradual enough, you don't realize what's happening until it's actually happened. I can't tell you when it shifted enough that I was aware, when the trust I had initially, turned to* fear. *My mind was clouded, my memories, almost absent, I was like a reworked wooden doll."*

"What started you believing you were in danger? How did you know what danger was?" The counselor asked.

"I think when the old lady and her husband died. Something wasn't right at all; it was badly wrong. I told you before, when you don't know much, you tap into instinct, it's something those who know a lot often lose or ignore. Yet it's our most valuable asset and nearly always right. I felt something was deeply wrong. I felt Rafael had something to do with it. I couldn't begin to say why, other than it seemed maybe too coincidental. Why I thought him capable of something like that? Instinct. I felt that also, in his touch and dominion of me. When we made love, which really isn't the correct term for what he did, he totally controlled me, I was his vessel. I had no point of reference, no compass, but I felt that the way he touched me was not with love. Did I say anything? Absolutely not. Because to do so would be to let on I knew something wasn't right, and again, in my psyche I knew that would be the end of me."

"So that's when you started to prepare to leave?" The therapist queried.

"I started to consider the pieces, to form a picture, to work out why I felt what I felt. When I had given birth to my son at home, I was in so much pain. I knew Rafael had done that so I would be off the books, our son unregistered, my existence, unrecorded. I worked out that he kept me from the world not just so I would be completely his, but to ensure nobody asked questions and found out I didn't have a whole lot of choice."

"What would have happened if you'd asked to leave?"

"I think he would have caused an accident to happen and I would not have survived." Camila licked her lips; they were dry but her stomach was in knots, she didn't want to drink any water.

"Would that have applied to both you and your son?"

"I think so, because we were a package deal. Rafael didn't even really care for his son, he never picked him up, didn't play with him, he liked the idea of owning us. I was the mother, I breastfed Joe, I cleaned him I fed him. Rafael watched us, he would watch me breastfeeding and then he would drink from my breasts – initially, I wondered if maybe he did that out of homage to my being a mother. But it seemed more like he wanted to ensure nobody, not even our son, did something with me that he couldn't do. Control, it was all about control. When he took me sexually, it was rough and it hurt, and I didn't say anything because he squeezed hard around my neck and felt if I actually spoke, he'd choke the words out of me and carry-on squeezing."

Camila breathed in deeply trying to calm herself as she recalled. *"In a way I was like a wild animal, sensing and feeling his moves, like chess pieces, and the lake was a reflecting glass echoing my instincts back at me. When I ran, I didn't think I'd succeed but I'd decided anything would be better than waiting for everything to collapse. After I saw a small fraction of the pornography Rafael kept, I knew he was shaping me to be like those women in the pictures. If I wasn't able to do something about it, my son and I would be prisoners of his warped world for our entire lives. That's if we even survived it."*

"What if you didn't get away?" She turned to the counselor, surprised to be asked that question and thought for a moment, of what it would have been like to have been caught.

"It would have been awful."

"How would it have been?"

Again, Camila thought it was an oddly specific question and one that didn't seem necessary, *"I don't know,"* she said impatiently, *"I just know it would have been awful."*

"Would it have hurt?"

Now Camila looked at her counselor fully, questioning her with her eyes, and asked, *"Why are you asking that?"*

The counselor, instead of being embarrassed or awkward or explaining, didn't say anything.

"Why are you asking that?" She repeated, a slow icy hand on her neck as she spoke. *"Why?"*

"Why do you think?" Rafael's voice answered, and Camila screamed.

Chapter 40

After Camila tried to escape and jump over board with the boy, Rafael had dragged her back with a fishing hook and tied her to a bed in the spare bedroom. The bed had metal rails. Joe stayed in his bed, turned to the wall, unnaturally quiet, with the bars of his cot raised and captive. Rafael infused Camila's veins with heavy medication, pumping her over and over with drugs to erase every word she might have had in her defense. She couldn't move, couldn't think, couldn't process her existence. She wet herself, her bowels loosened, and he left her in her own filth for days, with the room locked from the outside and the windows nailed shut.

Camila's wrists were bound with leather straps, so tightly that she could only lie in one position, her legs apart, humiliating her. She was naked, her body marked with the struggle. The story was in her drugged mind. A story of escape, nothing more than drug-fueled fantasy. The 'counselor' was Rafael all along. Dredging up her fears about him, forcing out her secrets. Controlling her as he was so good at, by knowing all there was to know and without anything held back, leaving her helpless. Something more than physical torture stays longer with us, the exposure of our inner selves.

When someone you hate knows you so well they can mimic your thoughts before you think them. Then echoing back any power you have, as if you have lost control of yourself, and are a drooling patient in their care. Evacuating your secrets like bowel movements to be flushed away, exposing the recesses of your fears and in knowing your fears, the monster knows how to control all the better. Worse than what Camila could have ever imagined had occurred, she hadn't escaped and been caught, she'd been a prisoner all along and now Rafael knew everything.

After days, many days, he dragged her up by her matted hair. Forced her into the shower on her knees, poured bleach over her body and scrubbed her with a hard bristle brush until her skin was raw. He pushed his fingers between her legs, ostensibly cleaning her but with hideous violation and harshness. Camila felt every orifice was pulled open and hurt. He opened her mouth and poured bleach into her mouth. He rubbed her hair with something that smelt bad, and shoved her back into the room to curl up, cuffed with leather restraints to a chair whilst he stripped the bed. *"You're so damn filthy,"* he said, and he took the sheets off the plastic under sheet, burning them in the garden in a metal grill, filling the air with the smell of shit and urine.

Covering the bed with new sheets, Rafael tied her back, spread-eagled and then he raped her. No doubts in her mind about consent. Three times in a row without stopping, as forceful as he'd ever been, with such violence she screamed out, against the thick skin of his hand. His heavy hand cutting off most of her air, as her nose was blocked from crying and her eyes swollen from his fists. When she screamed, he boxed her ears, her head ringing and the world spinning. She could hardly see; she could hardly breathe. Again, and again – he pounded her until she cried out, again and again and he hit her each time, with closed hands. His marks of violence leaving huge welts on her cheek bones and swollen lips twice their size. He bit her, he filled her with his hatred of her. The picture of Canada and all the good people who helped her in her dream, splintered and cracked open and ran away, like spilt egg yolk.

"Now that we have both taken our masks off Camila, we can get back to the way things should be. That involves you, doing what I say, and if you do that, we'll get along superbly. If you break that rule, you know what happens now. Don't doubt me Camila, don't doubt the sincerity and longevity of my investment in you. I knew you as a teenager, I was the first boy to have you – bitch. I broke that thin piece of skin over your private-parts and I own you and them. And I will be the last. You left me back then, telling me I hurt you, but you didn't know hurt. You caused me pain, and I found you again, years later, ruined by life, seeking death. You nearly died you dumb bitch and I saved you. But not for you to find yourself again, for you to become mine and make amends."

Rafael surveyed her like a lump of meat, turning her over, probing her, he lifted her breasts and pronounced them unfirm, pinching them tightly. He pulled her open and stretched her with his fingers, *"slack,"* he slapped her ass, *"you're turning slack Whore, you should be so grateful to me, that I let you live, that I let you near me, when you are so dirty, so slack and stupid. You will obey me; you will do my bidding. I will have everything of you, every morsel of your soul belongs to me."* He put his mouth over hers, his breath foul, and he bit her around her lips, in a horrible parody of kissing, and shoved his tongue down her throat far enough that she gagged and tried to jerk backwards. But he pushed further and further until she thought her neck would crack and all the while he put so many fingers inside of her that she thought she would split apart and have another child and could hear the edges of her begin to tear against his fist.

Rafael held Camila's throat, tightening his grip until the corners of her vision began to blur. She could not make a sound his tongue shoved down her throat, his fist within her, brutalizing her insides. He shoved harder, as if punching her within. She began to retch from the pain, jerking against him, but he did not let up. He punched and he punched, she felt it like the bruising of her womb being cracked by thunder bolt and her mind floated upwards and over the tree tops and into a cloud where people spoke to her through the cloud and she strained to hear, but all she could hear was the scream within her. Trapped and sagging against life like a captured lizard stills in his imprisonment until he hardly seems to breathe.

Camila lay there, her bruised and bleached skin hurting so bad, and tried to process the nightmare. She'd nearly drowned again. Her son had nearly drowned. The freezing waters had been too much to swim through. He'd known her trick all along, what a fool she had been, and he'd pretended to drink far more than he actually had. He was sober all the time and not drugged. He'd easily foiled her pathetic attempt at escape, she'd tipped her card and he knew she knew. How much didn't matter now the gloves were off. Rafael didn't have to pretend to be solicitous anymore, he could be the destroyer he'd always been and it suited him far better. At heart he was a sadist not a lover. He loved his role. Neglecting his son who grew thin and pale, torturing Camila in ways she could not have imagined. All the while thriving on the cruelty of his person, he drove himself deeper and deeper into his depravity and rage for her disloyalty.

"I gave you everything. I gave you your life. And you wanted to leave me? You thought you could? That was an option for you? The only way you leave is if you die again, and if you die again, it will be more painful than you can begin to imagine, and you won't be

coming back." His voice was The Devil and Camila believed every word. She knew he would do it and she was completely certain; he'd enjoy doing it. She wondered why he hadn't already done it, was sure he would almost any day now. But maybe her being alive, was the best result, he could reveal himself, subjugate her. She would exist but only if he willed it. Complete control. As she did not exist legally any longer, she did not exist without his permission. Like the slave in the dungeon, she would rely upon him with that sick love a captive has. He told her, "*I owned you once, I own you again, you are not leaving me, I gave your life, you are mine Camila,"* and he closed the door and bolted it, from the outside, the lock sounding like a drum within a drum within a drum.

Chapter 41

Camila felt her mother nearby, her tall mother, dark-skinned with the eyes of a wolf - grey and calm, looking down at her. Her mother told her she needed to fight, for the sake of Joe, for the sake of what is right. "*You need to fight Camila,*" her warm skinned mother said, and she reached out for her but she could not move her arms enough and her mother, stepped one step back, then two, then three, and was gone. She opened her eyes again, nobody was there, she could not hear a voice within her and only the howl of his rage, bursting her ears, roaring down her throat like liquid fire. Every part of her was violated, every part damaged and crushed. She stopped feeling, she rose out of herself, and looked down and told herself, this did not matter, this was a vessel, the real her was more than that, the real her endured.

The light off the lake spoke of days passing, otherwise she might not have known. All the work she'd done to recover herself, diminished by the power of drugs coursing through her at rapid pace. Rafael was a chemist of her mind, obviously knowledgeable about how far to go before going too far. Sometimes she wished he would slip up and dose her beyond survival so she could slip into the lake once and for all and become frozen below the surface. When she became too disorientated, he would let her come up a little from her stupor, enough that she always knew what he did to her. Was conscious of the shame he bestowed with his calculations of pleasure at her expense. Her body ached distantly, covered over by the drugs, it felt separate to her, as if her mind, soul, and body existed separately and not at all.

Camila had read once, in some memory almost crushed and lost, that those who are captives, form attachments to their captors. Some odd long word for that. Patty Hearst had had it, she thought. Camila couldn't formulate cogent patterns, but she knew something happened. A transformation, the survival instinct kicking in, beseeching the captive to be grateful for their life. Turning gratitude into bond with the only person holding their existence in their hands. A gnarled sick twist in the right way of things. Long days of isolation, too much time to consider things, the mind explodes, cannot cope with reality, decides love and attachment are needed. The captor is imprinted upon, becoming the source of any good feeling as well as bad. A savior in reverse, like ducklings following the first thing they see, be it mother duck or man, encouraged to connect, to form a bond.

She didn't feel that way, so maybe the theory was obsolete or just plain wrong. Camila felt hate, as deep as she'd ever felt, more powerful than any she thought she must have felt when her neighbor abused her. He may have been a repulsive human being but he still resembled a human in some ways. He didn't take her down to this level, where covered in her own excrement she would be led by her matted hair to shower in bleach and scalding water or icy cold, shivering and shrieking like a wild animal, pulled out of the woods. She didn't feel anything but a loathing as strong as his own toward her. With her closed mouth and buttoned soul, she obeyed because the alternative was worse, and she lay still when he violated her, because to move would only bring more pain. In her deepest mind, where little but emotion and reaction lay, the wildness built a fortress and she grew her claws and her teeth as sharp as the thorns of suffering he threw her broken body on.

Rafael would pay. Camila would destroy him. The idea to run away had been wrongheaded. She was bound to be captured, the fantasy was just that, a fantasy. Nobody would help her, nobody would care, or pick her and her son up by the side of the road and save them and take them to another country. *Who was she kidding?* This world was built on the indifference of others. Good people who look away when they should move to halt the evil. Surely, she'd always known that, from her parent's disinterest and her own pathetic need. Surely a sign that the natural order of things was upended, and wrongheaded. They were not civilized kind souls, they were wild animals and the more you struggled against that legacy, the more likely you were to be taken down by the pack.

She had to create her own pack. If she couldn't do that literally she had to do it by being more than a victim, more than a survivor. She had to be an *avenger*. And with this ire burning in her chest and between her legs where fire longed to blaze him out of her and shut him out forever, she writhed and built her bonfire, high and dangerous. The only torch in the darkness of her confines that kept her believing there was purpose to opening her eyes and taking breath. For why is someone who is denied everything, still able to endure and live? In the days Rafael left her chained to the bed, where presumably he drove far away and did what he liked to do without apology. He left her starved and defecating on herself, much to his amusement and her fragmented disgust.

Her drugged head would clear enough that she knew the

memories long denied her, were being forced back into the sore space of her consciousness, perhaps despite the drugs, urged by trauma and survival instinct. Camila was certain something, someone, other than herself, kept her alive. Maybe that instinct was almost independent, the opposite of self-control? A self-hood borne of some hungered need to endure, irrespective of how bad things were, longing to survive and outlive the myriad reasons to die. She'd flipped 180 degrees, gone from the girl who'd willingly plunged into the river, to a snapping, violent shadow thirsting to undo her manacles and wring the neck of her captor, before supping on his lifeblood.

In her withered recollections, she remembered a Jew called Viktor Frankl, a book she'd read, impressing her with the courage of those who survived concentration camps. That man had endured the very worst a human being is capable of experiencing. No one had known how in such horror a person could survive and his explanation had been that we have a will for meaning. An enduring need to continue, even when our own families are annihilated around us and we see no end to torment. Still, we survive in spite of this, and sometimes, if we are very fortunate, we get to come out the other side and are granted a respite to our torture. Instead of giving up because we have nothing, we build again, on the foundations that are broken and destroyed. Because that's the human way, to live even when we have every reason not to.

Our instinctual selves, like a badger or fox trapped in metal hunter's manacle, will chew its own leg off and escape leaving a trail of blood and no regret. Camila had read about explorers who ate their dead when they had no choice. The impossible things men and women do to survive. When she'd first heard that she'd said to herself that she didn't think she had that survival gene. The lasting endurance of those who wanted to live at any cost. She'd thought she was the very opposite, a person who was born without much longing to live, always on the cusp of death. Always seeking it in that romantic way the youthful do, as a way out of her own consciousness.

Camila surprised herself by not being that person any longer. What had changed? What shifted to build within her, the jaws of need, hanging on to anything no matter the cost, she couldn't say. But she'd certainly gone from being a person who didn't hold on tightly to one who wouldn't let go. Maybe anger was the reason, a need to exact revenge. She didn't care if that was it, it didn't matter the cause, or the rationale. There is no real intellect in survival, you just do, analysis is obsolete. It is funny to consider how many people have tried to intellectualize the reasons for why bad things happen and people survive. There's no true answer that will be logic-driven or fit into an equation.

You cannot quantify the madness of being. And that is what Camila was. A mad thing, driven to the edge. The edge not of a river, but her own mind. Coming back in pieces, chopped up and unwell, striving only to fight back with every molecule of her consciousness. *"The day would come, and he will pay. If I die in this, I will die trying. If I survive it, I will dance on his grave in red shoes and a red dress and he will be dammed."*

Her ancestors, who let her down by dying early or never being alive enough to warrant relying upon, now was their time to lend her the courage to survive. Her grandmother who had endured her grandfather's disinterest and when he died, blamed for his death and held accountable for his selfish suicide when things hadn't gone as planned. The rejection of her grandmother by her sons, her isolation, and turning to God. She may have seemed desperate, but she survived by knowing what it would take to survive.

At any cost she bequeathed over time. At any cost you hang on until you can climb another rung. You keep climbing, until you reach the top of the pit and you leap out and close it over and you never go back, ever. Maybe she'd fallen a long time ago into that pit, causing her to try to die, and now she saw the light glimmering at the top of her imaginary trap, and she knew, if she could reach that light, she would always possess it, and never grow dim enough to wish to turn it off permanently. Never again.

Maybe Camila didn't come from a lineage she could be proud of, or who would be proud of her. Maybe in losing them, she'd lost part of her reason for being alive, and felt rootless and cast off like a tumbleweed rolling down an empty highway, catching in the desert bushes and growing wane with lack of nourishment. But there were choices and she knew she could carry on even as she had nobody to catch her if she fell. She'd found someone far more enduring than even her parents or her relatives who watched from yellow graves.

She'd found herself. That self who had been denying her all of her life, turning away, changing her identity and keeping her at arm's length. When we're told to love ourselves, she'd always thought that was a trite and shallow proclamation without much substance and she had been so wrong. Her lack of love and faith in herself had translated to a loss of faith and trust in the very fabric of her existence and her place in the world. She wasn't able to survive because her soul did not have a spine to hold it upright, so she sagged like a loosely filled doll, void of the substance it took to battle through and be left, still standing.

Even as a prisoner she'd changed. She'd come to know herself in ways all the previous years she'd cast off, and avoided. Maybe her self-hate, the reminders in the weft of her chin and hang of her cheekbones that reminded her of past souls whose DNA coursed within her blood. Instead of pride, she'd inherited shame and emptiness, like a house whose windows never closed grew cold and unwelcoming. She'd abdicated love for herself and acted like she was her own worst enemy.

If you fight yourself, you don't need enemies, you're already doing such a good job of unpicking your making, you can kill yourself without any assistance at all. Of course, it wasn't that simple. Other things; betrayals, people who said one thing and did the other. They all added to the kindling that set her on fire. But she chose to jump and she knew now, she would never, ever choose to jump again. Never. Unless he exposed his throat in unguarded moment, and she had opportunity to leap up from her shackles, stretch far enough to sink her sharpened fangs into his pulse and extinguish him completely.

Chapter 42

Her son Joe was in the other room. Camila never saw him, or even heard him cry but she knew he was alive because she heard him being addressed and talked to. She hoped dearly Joe's youth would salvage the horror of his days and prevent his tender soul from being crushed flat and useless. His existence made her sure she would not quit the fight until he was freed. Even if it meant she died in the process, he had a right to a life, though with both parents' dead it wouldn't be a good start. It was as important that somehow, she made it out too. For his sake. But how? How to free herself from the leather that chaffed her wrists raw and left permanent rings of welt and burned skin as reminder of her captivity? How? To escape the shackle and break him out, to trace the land not in fantasy but actual flight. To gain them both the wings necessary to break cover and seek over mountain, the freedom they had never known.

What a person is capable of, is usually not revealed to them unless they are forced into a situation that is intolerable. At such juncture, like a cloak lifted off a ball of crystal, they see how far they are willing to go, to reduce their suffering and break their chains. Women have lifted cars off the bodies of their children, reducing science to guess-work by their urge to save. Men have cut their own limbs away to escape snare. Girls have put razors in their vaginas against the spoils of war, when soldiers pinned them down and reduced them to ash. Young boys, hardly old enough for words, have worn bombs strapped to their chests, and walked into clearings proclaiming the prophet. *We do what we must* or what we deem necessary in the madness of war. Be it actual or within us, a scour of sense and safety, we survive like a rabid dog will run from captor, knowing it is dying, seeking only to live one more day.

One day Rafael untied her and told her she'd start to do more around the house. *"He wasn't going to do every goddamn thing."* He hit her open handed across her face, stinging her already tender skin and leaving the heat of his strike as reminder: *You cross me once, disobey once, and you will surprise even your worst imagination.* Camila carried the leather restraints, unchained, on her wrists and after cleaning up, was given a list of chores she needed to start doing daily around the house. *"I'm too busy to be doing everything,"* he said, and went into the office. Instead of locking the door as he used to, he'd taken the door off the frame and she could see what he did, it was impossible to avoid.

Rafael told her not to check on her son, other than to give him food, denying her any time with him aside the most cursory of moments. In those brief moments she saw that Joe was clean, had a bed, some toys and even a TV that had been brought in presumably for some weak entertainment, in lee of any parenting. Her son's eyes were flat and distant, she couldn't bear to look at them. Imagining how he must feel, that he must assume he'd been abandoned by her. Yet Joe's eyes still held the thoughtful intelligence they always had, maybe deep down, still rooted to his instincts he knew she was trying, trying so hard to get him back.

Whilst Camila was let out of her captivity for a while she scrubbed the floors, cooked, mended, cleaned, fetched for Rafael, and did everything around the house. During this time, Rafael would sit in his office with his hard-on in his hands and masturbate over and over to disgusting pornography on his computer. She did not see it but she heard it, the slick slide of his hand over his unending lust. The screams of girls being tortured on the screen. He did this in front of her. He didn't turn it down; he didn't apologize or hide it. Now he was out in the open, The Devil in a scarlet dress, showing the depths of his unending proud sickness.

It helped Camila to know she was not alone in the world, that others like her were punished for their gender, their existence, their trust. She knew it wasn't so much punishment, as exile from goodness. Like stepping into quicksand and being enveloped before you can pull yourself out. She knew she existed in a twilight zone of terror, spun by his evil and longing to flay her. Seeing the others that got him erect and violent, explained how his mind worked and linked him to all the other violence in the world. Violence perpetrated by glutted monsters who felt they had the right to go out and take what they wanted without regard.

She saw he had snuff movies, too realistic to be mimics. They were illegal, real depictions of killings, where women were strangled to death. Their corpses gang-raped. She saw that he had torture movies where women were stabbed in their genitals, and children molested with their school uniforms still on. She saw children as young as her son, put to death after extreme torture. She saw the same looks in the eyes of the men who raped, sodomized, and murdered their captives as in Rafael's eyes. She saw a film with a woman with dark eyes. It was Carol, his first wife. She saw Rafael in the room, undressing, and she saw Carol naked on the floor, the same chain around her neck. She saw

Rafael strangling her, letting other men violate her, ripping her apart until she lost consciousness, waking her up and starting over. She saw Carol mouth her sons name, before a man pushed himself down her throat.

"You see what will happen if you cross us?" He said, referring to the other men in the film. *"You see the power I hold in my fist, the power of this fist cut through you and deciding whether you live or die? You see why there is no choice, only obedience? You are lucky not to be where Carol is now. You are lucky I keep you living. You will live and be mine, totally and if you refuse, I will find a way to destroy Joe in front of you so that your heart explodes in pain and you die as you are dragged to another hell. I am your hell but I am the only way you survive Camila."* She knew he spoke the truth. She knew Joe's fate lay in her ability to survive Rafael and become his every need. To sustain his interest so that he did not strangle her to death as he had Carol.

She wondered how anyone could become such a monster? How does evil truly bloom? It seemed less important as the days dragged on, because what good would knowing why he chose his brand of violence, ever do for her and her son? Camila cleaned and cleaned, often her own blood, his pleasure, streaks of it mixed together. Like arterial spray all over the walls when she'd finished for the day. When everything was tidy and the dishes washed, he would take her into her room, beat her with his belt leaving large red welts like bolts of lightning across her back, rape her, and leave her chained to the bed shaking uncontrollably.

Often, she would bleed violently afterward. Both from her mouth where her teeth had cut the sides of her cheeks as he forced himself too deeply and caused her to gag. He would push her head as far as she could, and she'd desperately try to concentrate on not suffocating, knowing if she did not please him sufficiently he would take her from behind, until the sheets were crimson.

After he'd closed the door, she could hear the films still playing, it seemed he never tired of watching. Like he didn't have enough time to survey cruelty, and was addicted to the never-ending cycle of hate spewed on screen.

During those hours and well into the night, she pulled out one of the metal spatulas she used to cook with that he didn't notice had gone missing. She worked it against the metal of the bed frame where she'd formed a sharpness, and it could be gradually, painstakingly, fashioned sharp. She imagined stabbing him over and over again. She imagined herself like her mother, straight-backed and tall, riding a horse, slaying the men in the films. She thought of gathering Carol and all the others, who died beneath those men, and saving them. They were ridiculous fantasies, half-maddened, they were the only things that played in her mind, as she desperately tried to cut away the horror-show he inflicted every day.

Eventually as her hands developed calluses and her eyes strained in darkness, her home-made weapon grew sharper and sharper. The edge able to penetrate her own skin when she tested it. Afterward she hid it beneath the bed to the very edge of the floor boards where flush against the side nobody could see it, in the darkness of the shadows. Then she worked on another piece of metal, taken from inside the toilet bowl. A part that permitted her to thin it into the size of a pin. When completed she held it tightly between her sore fingers and picked at the locks on her wrists, until she learned how to open them and close them back up. It took an excruciatingly long time to develop but she had time, and her desperation impelled her to work far harder than had this been a matter of choice. In time she was able to unlock herself. Whilst this alone did nothing to aid Camila's chance of escape, and only encouraged her to be killed breaking his rules, it was one part of a longer plan.

He slept in their old bedroom, right next door to her, so being quiet was the only attribute she needed to perfect. He didn't sleep deeply like she did when he poured the drugs into her water, to punish her for too much consciousness, or because he just felt like doing it. Other times he forgot to drug her and she'd be able to stay awake all night. He on the other hand slept lightly but soundly, except when he'd been drinking. Usually, he woke early to go jogging for about an hour, before returning to release her and demand breakfast and for her to bend over for the first time that day.

Camila had one hour when Rafael was guaranteed to be out every day, sometimes longer if he chose to stay drinking. Other days when she didn't know how long he would be gone, a whole day, even overnight, or a few hours. She could not risk releasing herself and getting away, without any certainty, but there was no way to know how long he'd be gone. The idea struck her that she had to find out when next he planned to be gone at least a day. She released herself from her chains one night after he'd been sleeping for at least an hour and trod as quietly as she'd ever been, hardly allowing herself to breathe, into the now open office.

He didn't know how much memory she'd *recovered*. He knew enough by her confession to her 'therapist' and her original attempted escape and desire to leave, but nothing more. He wasn't curious, such was his confidence that he had her on her knees, destroyed physically and mentally. She surprised herself by being able to go into the office, shaking so badly she grit her teeth against her fear. Mindful that any creak or wrong step could cause an end to any escape plan and cause her and her son's punishment and death. She couldn't boot up the computer in the house, it might make a sound. She opened the door that led to the outside, knowing it was silent, and took the computer outside and far enough away that it might still be able to read Wi-

Fi but not be heard from his bedroom. Booting up the computer she was rewarded with silence, the sound was muted, nothing played loudly in the silence of the night from his previous feast of gore and sex. She found the internet and tapped it, and it came up requiring a password. She nearly screamed and went into the main frame and found another internet browser, the default, and clicked on that, no password required.

Online she realized she didn't know what to do. Was there even a 911 online? What was her exact address? If her neighbor hadn't known the name of the road, was it possible the road's name and everything else she knew, was made up? How can you ask for help without a tracker to show where you are, or any ID? Especially if the world thinks you're dead? When you have no email address and no real name to use? Who would believe her? They'd think it was a really sick prank. She recalled his license plate number and googled '*slavery rings in America*' being sure to remember she needed to delete the browser history after use. A website for tips on slavery rings in America was the seventh option, she clicked on it, and it gave an option to *get in touch* with a screen for typing in information appearing.

She wrote: *"Help me, I'm being held captive, in Oregon. I don't know my address; my name is Camila Ochoa. The license plate of my captor is SAK 293 and my captor's called Rafael Simone. Only my son Joe and I are here and in desperate danger. We will be killed. I am being tortured. This is not a joke, this is serious. I can't tell you more because I am afraid you will dismiss this as a prank. Please believe me that this is true and find a way to track down his license and get his address and please, please come to the house. Do not come alone, but with law enforcement and weapons. I am in the spare bedroom chained up or I will be hidden if he knows you are coming, and my boy is in another room. Please, please help us."*

Sent. She deleted the browser history, and signed off. Terrified that she'd taken too long, she stole back into the house, with the turned off computer, careful to put everything back where it was. She crept back into her room, redid her bonds, and tried desperately to quell the rapid beating of her heart, thundering in her chest. *Would anyone come?* Days went by. Nothing. She figured if someone took it seriously, they'd contact the police. The driver's license would be run, address obtained, and they'd be here in a day or two.

Nobody came. It dawned on her, what if his address wasn't this address? They'd been at another location right at the beginning. She'd recalled that after a while, remembering her previous existence, being brought out of the lake, recovering, being asked if she would be prepared to die again, to be reborn without her legacy of reasons for suicide. Then the whitewash. The place she'd been in originally, she had no idea of where it was, than it was in Texas. How stupid to have assumed his license would be altered! He probably kept a house there, family money or his parents will. They wouldn't even know about any place in Oregon. Worse, if he heard the police were snooping around his Texas property – he might piece things together, figure out somehow, she'd tipped them off. Exact revenge.

There was only one other option because nobody was coming to save her.

Chapter 43

The next day Rafael took her into her room and was going to chain her down for the night, but she stopped him. Gathering every risk she'd ever dared take, Camila reached out with her manacles, and touched him through his trousers. He looked genuinely surprised and not unhappy. *"I want to be a good wife,"* she said, forcing her voice not to shake, *"I want to touch you and pleasure you"* she said, as beguilingly as she knew how. Knowing he would be suspicious that it was a trick, Camila knew she had to do this for a while before he stopped thinking she was trying to butter him up. Maybe she could convince him she'd snapped and her mind had fractured and she'd finally snapped inside and come to love her captor. Maybe his sheer narcissism would be gullible enough to believe he was irresistible, even with everything he'd done to her. She relied on his wanting to be wanted. She knew it was his weakness, just as it was hers.

Camila stroked him free of his pants, he was so easy to get excited it sickened her. She bent down and sucked him as deeply as she could, feeling his fingers push her head into him, and trying so hard not to make gagging sounds. Without him asking she turned around on all fours and offered herself to him. Showing him what he wanted, trying in her rags and her welts to be a little more attractive than the dead-eyed doll he usually abused. She had put spit on herself. She glistened and felt his intake of breath.

He took the bait. Though his thick hands remained around her throat, warning her that he would crush her wind pipe if any of this was a trick. She let herself pretend to enjoy him. Instead of crying out in pain, she cried out faking an orgasm, shuddering with feigned pleasure as he drove himself into her aching insides. He climaxed immediately afterward, obviously turned on by her compliance. As much as he wanted to hurt and humiliate her, the narcissist within him wanted to be desired. Her overture surprised him at how much he needed her to want him. After this, he did her again, and again. She falsified her sensations and pressed her muscles into faked climax, tightening around his erection with every fiber of her being, ignoring the sick feeling in her mouth and belly, stinking of him.

For a week she acted this way. Impatient to reveal the truth. Knowing she had to go slow, an agonizing dance between acting and reality. Pretending you like being abused by a psychopath may sound easy on paper, but in reality, Camila struggled to feign interest and longing for him, that she knew was required to bring him out of his suspicion and guardedness. But what a woman is capable of, to secure her freedom, is boundless. Soon her acting skills were as convincing as the real thing. Camila writhed, she bit his fingers, she even opened her mouth against his lips and kissed him with the passion of her hatred and loathing, approximating desire. He was after all a man besotted by himself and his violence. What better bait than a woman who responded sexually to his repulsion and lusted for his pain?

He drove harder, wanting to split her in half. Turned on by her false screams of pleasure, she willed herself to shout out harder so he lost himself in the game. And afterward to cover him with kisses as if he had been the most gentle and kindest lover, instead of a murderer of her soul. There is never a right time, there is never a moment you can say *this is the moment I take the next step and I become what you are*. Evil is evil, good is good, but the two must cross in order not to cancel one another out. The evil chooses good to get what they want, and the good chooses evil to survive evil. An eye for an eye, isn't so Old Testament at all when faced with few options, all of which are desperate.

Camila chose the moment she least expected, because if she wasn't expecting it, she figured, he sure wouldn't be either. Pushing her hand down the side of the bed, as Rafael pinned her beneath him from behind, sweating over her like a wraith. He was diving into her with his sword, she faked pleasure and took him to the point of his own orgasm where she knew he would close his eyes, release and let go of any consciousness for a brief moment. In that moment, timed against the terror of her failure, she lifted the fashioned weapon from the side of the wall. Lifted slowly, as slowly as a dancer, avoiding falling. In one movement that seemed in slow motion, Camila pulled it over her head, and in the direction of his back and struck him with all the force she could muster.

His scream was high pitched and shocked. Like every time he speared her with his anger and loathing. As swiftly as Camila could, knowing he'd begun to trust her not to be chained whilst he fucked her, she turned as he fell on her. Meeting him facing forward, she brought the weapon that had come smoothly out of his back into his neck and opened him over her. Blood poured like a well of oil released into the air. Falling down and spraying her with warm, surprisingly thick and foul-smelling life. His existence was as rotten as his actions. She started to retch alongside his convulsing dying body. He had infected her, with every spurt of blood she was covered and turned into a red demon, created by him out of the wax of his ears.

Rafael's scream grew week as his life ebbed out of him into the sheets, which were crusted with his semen and her pain. She pushed him off her, noticing the pathetic shrivel of his angered member, dying alongside him like a weed on his inner thigh. She saw the hole in his neck, pulsing blood and the red of his eyes, leaking loathing as he sputtered and convulsed. *"I hate you! I hate you!"* Camila heard a voice yelling, not his, but her own, loud and unrepentant, she screamed the years of her abuse, the nightmares of her days, until his ears were dumb to any entreaty or insult, because he no longer heard anything, or felt anything, or was anything, but an empty vessel, devoid of life.

Afterward she left everything as it was. She knew legally she was dead. They wouldn't come for her. She knew her fingerprints had never even been on file so they wouldn't know that death can rise again. Her son Joe was in no database. They were two people who didn't exist, and this had been bad and now this was good. Camila picked up everything she thought she needed, including the money in Rafael's wallet, a credit card with the pin stupidly written on the back, and necessary things. She grabbed a binder in Rafael's office that held photos of the girls she thought he'd harmed. She took nothing else. She washed herself before she could stand in front of her son without gore and death marking her for her actions. She let the water scald her, she felt no shame, it was gone, as the blood rinsed away down the plug hole. She didn't think there would be much sign of her left after the fire. Maybe they would think the killer of the mountains had really existed and Rafael was another victim. He somehow had been both killer and victim, it made so much sense.

Camila would take his truck, knowing this was the only way to get away. She would drive until she couldn't drive anymore and then she'd keep driving, even though the last time she'd been behind the wheel of a car and in charge seemed like, a lifetime ago. But it didn't matter, it didn't matter because she knew if she could do what she had done, she could do anything. And she would, until she got them away and never coming back, in dream or deed, the house would burn. She would leave, it would cease to exist, along with him, along with them all.

She poured kerosene on the door and window frames, and as they left, she lit the match. She knew it would burn some of the countryside and she felt bad so she ringed their garden with foam from the fire retardant, in hope the trees would not catch and the fire could be contained. They would know it was murder. But they would not know Rafael was the murderer and they would not know Camila was the victim. Everything was so upside down and drowned, it could be used to her advantage and that was exactly what she was going to do. The house went up in flames like dry thin paper and the shape it made in silhouette against the lake was like a Rorschach picture of a moth, opening its wings and jaws against the savagery of existence.

Camila and her son Joe drove themselves out of their nightmare. They drove without light until they'd thought of new thoughts and begun to smile again. The smell of blood gone from her nostrils, her son playing in the seat next to her, the sun beating on the old leather seats. Rafael had money in the cab, a lot of money. Ten thousand, in a metal tin beneath the driver's seat that she'd found when she pulled it forward to fit her shorter legs. His blood money from his killings and who knew what? It would become the stuffing necessary for them to stand upright in a world they hardly knew. They were two illegitimate children of fire, come out burnt but still alive, seeking refuge in a world that hadn't known they existed.

Chapter 44

Five Years Later

Camila loved the days her son would hold her tightly before she waved him off on the school bus and checking the flowers growing near the post box, would walk slowly back into the house, feeling his arms around her. He was the best child she could ever have wished for. *I'm sure all mother's think that,* she found herself saying before smiling wryly at the untruth of that, aware her own mother had never once thought that and it was okay, it was really okay. Her chance, her turn, that was all that mattered. They lived in the sun, he and she. The two of them against the rest of the world, a world that could be filled with horror, but also joy and peace. Like when the end of the day came and everything was soft and quiet and they lay together, two peas in a pod, under a patchwork blanket watching their favorite shows on TV. As if nothing of their former life had existed, though the shadows, always on the side of every day, knew otherwise.

Her son Joe was growing into a beautiful little boy of seven, with dark skin, lighter hair, and huge brown eyes. He did not resemble the monster. He looked a lot like Camila's mother with his honey hair and he had the gentle heart of Camila with no residue of his father's savagery. At first that had worried her, but she knew we did not have to be facsimiles of our pasts, or our parentage. The more we thought that, the more likely we'd become that through giving in to the temptation to repeat history. But she wouldn't let him know his history. He was too young to recall, he would never know what happened, he would grow up thinking his father was someone she didn't know. As bad as that might be, it was nothing compared to the truth and she was okay with the deception.

They lived in a small house, rented, but homely, on the outskirts of Albuquerque. She'd chosen Albuquerque because she'd never been there, had no history there, and it beckoned her with its wide-open space and ceaseless sun. She didn't want to be anywhere near water again, much as she had loved to sail and swim – they were now tainted things. Much as she could try to redevelop a love for them, she decided there were other things in this world worth nurturing, than repeating bad memories. They planted chiles in the back and watched them bloom and turn to fruit, red, orange, shades of the sun that nurtured them. They put a paddling pool in the back-yard and Joe would circle it in the water, whilst she watched his little boy's body, grow even more tan under the sunlight.

Albuquerque was also affordable and laid back and strangers were welcomed. It wasn't a scrutiny to move there, and people didn't assail her with questions about who she was and what she sought. Many people there were without the right papers. For a price, with money she had from the tin, she purchased identities for them both, giving them the start they needed to grow roots. She didn't have much money left so she had sold Rafael's truck to someone who took stolen vehicles over the border. She didn't get much for it but she didn't own it, so that was the price you paid. With that money she bought a second-hand car, that worked and was reliable despite its chipped paint job and basic appearance. She'd long stopped caring about those things, she only wanted the sunlight on her face and the sound of her son's laughter as he played in their small backyard.

Joe learned because he was young, to live a different life. Not one incarcerated in a room without light, but the normalcy of childhood. He didn't remember the nightmare. It was a blessing to be young, she thought, where we can recreate ourselves without assistance because we are still growing upward. For herself, Camila knew the scars ran deep. She saw them every time she showered and she faced them, rather than turning away, for nothing else would save them both, but the truth. She saw in her own eyes, her mother's. For the first time, her strength and determination. She knew even if her family did not exist for her, they existed within her and she could mine that and tap the good parts for her own life. At times it seemed unfathomable that she'd survived Rafael. That life had existed afterward, after the melting down of everything. How had life left her standing, Camila couldn't fathom. But she chose life. She chose life with every pore of her being.

Her hair had started to grey, she didn't color it. She let the strands of grey infect the darkness and contrast like snow on black mountains. It was the outcome she said, of her survival and like a scar; she wasn't going to cover it up. We prematurely age with horror, but ageing is a sign we still endure and we survived. She wore it proudly like a badge, after all, she wasn't going to get involved with anyone so there was no need to be anything more than she was. A woman who had come out of the wild with her cub. The Native Americans who lived in the area in larger numbers seemed to understand and respect her. They looked at her with their knowing eyes especially the women, as if they could read straight through into her chest and hear the stories of her heart.

There was a lot of abuse in the Native American world. Both from whites who still believed they had the upper hand and would use their resources to rob the Native Americans of their land, and among themselves, as outcome of desperation, limited resources, poverty, and alcoholism. These things Camila understood. Her own life being no dissimilar. And whilst she may not have been native, she felt she had the soul of one who had grown into the land and been reborn. Able to stand like a corn maiden and see the fertility of life again and respect that life, as given by the wind, the spirits, the legacy of ancestors, and the fates.

Camila kept to herself. Getting a job in a local mini-mart, nothing noticeable. She took online classes using a grant for single mothers, to earn a certificate in bookkeeping and then she began to do the books for people she met, at the mart. She started with her boss, and going through a connected chain of people who had flunked out of math at middle school – it was a discipline that kept her from dwelling. She saw the value of numbers, and liked how she could make them bend to her will, and rely upon them to make sense. Human beings didn't make sense. Evil didn't make sense. Death and maybe even life at times, didn't make sense. Her haven became numbers and she eventually earned enough to just work at that and quit her mini-mart job, giving her more time to be at home when her boy came back from school and asked her if she'd made any cinnamon toast. She had.

Their life went along like the desert, stretching, changing color, burning in heat, cooling in night. She was not growing like her son but maybe within her, her soul was still reaching out, with color at the tip of her fingers, painting the landscape as the sun set every day. They got a dog. The last dog she'd seen was his dog and Rafael had strangled it in front of her, just to see her eyes when he choked the life out of it. But her son wanted a dog and this was a good guard dog so she took him. A little huskie mix, who growled at strangers and slept on her or Joe's bed at night with one ear pricked up for sounds. Sometimes she thought animals were so in tune with the world and humans, they knew when someone needed protecting even when they did not know themselves.

Some days Camila let herself think about her past, which had almost all returned to her. She saw that person who had existed then, as both part of her, and no part of her. She did not recognize the impulse to die, but she neither rejected nor mocked it. As the native Americans said, death and life, they are part of the same system. She saw it that way, as being a time in her life she needed death as much as now she needed life. Having her child helped her live, she knew without him she might not have had reason to, though she hoped she'd have still tried. She didn't want to make much of herself other than to maintain the peace she'd gained in the last years, and stay far from any reminders of harm. But as with anyone who has walked through fire, fire has a habit of becoming your legacy and perhaps before that, your fate.

It was a little after Christmas. The desert was cold at night and still quite warm during the day. Some animals were hibernating but unlike other parts of the world, it was easier to go through the year unchanged in the desert than anywhere else and she didn't always notice the shifting of seasons the way she had in Oregon or even Texas. Camila had strung their small adobe house with chili lights, and some Mexican bunting, in pinks and reds. On the stove, a pot of beans, for a hungry little man who liked chili beans for dinner, and in the oven some fresh bread. Every time she baked bread she thought of Oregon and the beginning where she learned to make bread from scratch and he ate it, with white glistening teeth and red, red gums, smiling with pleasure.

Funny what you know when it's over. She knew she was a wolf. Just like she knew she was supposed to be consumed and managed to overcome her fate. It was like living on borrowed time but she chose to see her life as being for her son rather than running through a sand dial. If he was okay, she was okay. If he survived, she would survive. Maybe it was unhealthy to invest so deeply in him but not unsurprising and the exact opposite of her own parents, therefore, to her, it felt right and it felt good. She loved accomplishing things and having a career, but ultimately her heart sought the refuge and unabating love of a child. Holding Joe in her arms, she had felt a depth of love she'd never known previously.

Her son was due back at 3:40. Joe walked home from his school because it was less than a block away and all the kids walked on their own. It was daylight and safe, and mothers took turns to watch out. The kids could be heard from streets away, playing tag and being light-hearted and laughing the way children always do. Camila listened out for his voice amidst the others. But he didn't come home at 3:40 and he wasn't home by 4:00 either. She went outside and saw some of the kids he was in class with, she called and asked if he had been with them or kept behind by the teacher, they said the words no parent ever wants to hear. Joe hadn't been at school that day.

Chapter 45

Gone. Camila's reason for living, her reason for waking and sleeping, only to start over again. Gone. She ran like a mad woman to the school, screaming inwardly at herself for not collecting him each and every day, although no parent did. She ran through the emptied rooms, frantically shouting at teachers his name, where was he? They all said the same thing. *"Joe had not been at school all day, he did not come to school that day, he was absent, nobody had seen him arrive that day."* He was lost. She knew how she must have looked, streaking through the rooms, her face purple with fear, her eyes rolling in her head, but she didn't care, where was he? Where was he?

Camila spent the rest of the day down at the police station. It was the first time she'd ever been to the police. Their papers were bought, they were not legal; even in the country of their birth they were outcasts. She'd never wanted to risk discovery, but now what did she have to lose when Joe was gone, who knows where? She had to tell the police the whole unbelievable story, something she had never ever done out loud or even in her head. That her death by suicide was faked by a man who abducted her and held her captive, another suicide taking her place and being misidentified due to the decomp. How Rafael had taken her. How in all likelihood he was the same man who she had first gone out with as a teenager, grown up with a different identity. How he tricked her, forcing her to have a child at home, keeping her captive.

How she had killed Rafael and set fire to the house and run. How Rafael had killed his first wife Carol and there were films of it, most likely lost in the fire. A stupid thing for she knew now she owed it to his victims to find the other men. But she had acted so fast. So terrorized she wanted to just get out of that house and burn it to the ground. The policewoman who took her statement stopped writing several times, in stunned silence she was not aware her mouth was open, the virulence of her story so compelling that it had to be believed. They brought in a detective from Santa Fe the next day. Camila came in early, having not slept but sticking his picture to every street corner and calling everyone she half-knew from school and searching everywhere she could think of.

Others, neighbors, acquaintances, store owners, searched the backs of their stores and cellars. There was no brush to search in, no forests, no lakes, but they looked in every empty and obvious place they could find, all without finding a single thing. The detective was another woman, about fifty. Native American with the kinds of cheek bones that look like they were upside scoops of ice-cream placed on top of bone. She had a beautiful calm presence and straight hair that fell like water. *I just want him back I just want him back*, Camila repeated over and over, uselessly because she'd begun to believe Joe had never existed that it was another madness. Another torment. A dream that had turned, a wolf that had snapped, the death impulse in her rising again and swallowing her whole.

"You have to tell me everything you know from the start," the detective said, the turquoise in her earrings reflecting against her mahogany skin.

"He's just seven. His name is Joe, he's dark like me, he's got honey-colored curly hair and light-brown eyes. You have four pictures of him, he goes to Amarillo Middle School. I've asked every friend of his, every parent, every teacher, every local, nothing. Nobody has seen him. If they didn't know who he was I would think he had just vanished and never existed."

"It sounds like vanishing was what you and your son did five years ago from what I have read," the detective who was called Miranda said.

"Yes. Yes, we did not leave that's true. We got out, we vanished. We had to. Listen, lock me up for murder if you will, but you have to find my son!"

"I don't think anyone is going to lock you up for murder for two reasons," the detective replied. *"The first reason is because if what you say is true, you were being held captive and you fought to escape, making a death, an act of self-defense. Secondly, and you need to brace yourself for this. We tracked down the house. It was in a news article five years ago in an Oregon newspaper online. But here's the crazy part. Yes, there was a fire. Yes, the house burned somewhat. Yes, it was Rafael Simone's home. Yes, he was registered in Texas but had a second residence in Oregon listed in his diseased wife's names. But no body, no body was found in the wreckage."* Miranda said.

Camila felt her entire being turn to stone.

Chapter 46

How could he be alive? Rafael died. Camila saw his eyes fade and his life wink out of them like The Devil lifting his coat and turning into flame. He could not have survived the mortal wound to his neck. The back wound alone would have incapacitated him. The house fire must have burned everything, including him. She hadn't put gasoline on his body, she didn't have that black heart necessary for the depth of violence that entailed. But the room he'd been in? There was no way out. They hadn't stayed to see the fire eat itself out, but she saw the flames. She saw the way it exploded into a thirsting flame, nothing and nobody could have survived both those things, *"It wasn't possible,"* she told the detective over and over, *"he was dead, he had to be dead."*

"I agree with you" Miranda replied, *"by your account Rafael could not have survived. But what if, drugged up, sick with abuse and torture. Brain damaged; memory impaired. What if your recollection of the events is incomplete, or perhaps less than accurate?"* She looked at Camila with querying eyes and gently said, *"Please know this, I'm not accusing you of lying or embellishing in any way,*

I'm trying to come up with a reasonable explanation for how no body was found and yet, you stabbed him, and set fire to the house. I'm trying to come up with a plausible reason for how your son Joe, who has no living relatives who are aware of him, and has never run away from home, could be missing?"

Miranda smiled sadly; *"In my years on the force there are only two compelling answers, and unfortunately, it's always the same. A family member has your son, or a stranger has your son. You want it to be a family member because if it's the latter the chances of ever getting him back alive are minimal and you know that, knowing as you do, the survival rates for child abductions. I'm working on the premise that without a body, your ex survived this fire and his wounds, perhaps they bled a lot, perhaps he did nearly die but somehow – he survived and it is he, Rafael, who took your son."*

Camila thought of the fire, the way it caught and went up into an almost perfect triangle. She thought of Rafael, lying there in his own rusting blood, seemingly without a breath left in his body. But she hadn't checked! She hadn't gotten close enough once she had thrown his bleeding, choking, convulsing body off her own and run to arrange her escape. She didn't dare, he was The Devil, she wanted to burn him, burn him back to hell. And run.

There was one thing she kept seeing in her mind's eye, one thing that stood out among the fire and his closed eyes and slowing respiration until it seemed he did not breathe at all. The one thing she saw through the fire and blood, a door leading from the office to the outside. A door so secret that even people who knew its secret would forget its existence. A door that had no gasoline poured on the outside or inside of it, only around the window frame. A good five meters to the side, a door, that led away from the house. Heading behind the house, where she, in the truck, turning around, seeing the fire take hold, could not see.

"Oh my god," she said, and covered her red face with her dry hands. *"Oh my god. He's still alive."*

Chapter 47

The Devil takes many forms. Some of those forms are even beautiful, some are grotesque, some alluring. Some speak to what they are, whilst a few appear the very opposite. The well-dressed young man who came up to a little boy on the street leading to his school, did not seem like The Devil. The boy Joe did not recognize him, or the scar on his neck that had faded into a silver cusp. The boy did not think a man who was smiling with nice white teeth and warm brown eyes and a clean white shirt and friendly crinkles on the corner of his eyes was The Devil. Joe believed him when he said that he was a friend of his mommy's, although if he'd really thought about it, he knew his mom didn't have any actual friends. Nevertheless, he knew she worked with people who liked her and looked out for her.

The nice man said he worked with his mommy and he needed to get him to come with him to the bakery to pick out a cake with him because they were going to give her a big surprise cake for doing their books so well and he wanted her son to pick out her favorite flavors because only he would know. The boy was proud to be asked, it made him feel adult, and special to be relied upon and the only one who would know something like that. He wanted to do something like this so his mom would see he could be relied upon to make grown-up decisions, and he also liked the idea of making his mom smile because she had a really beautiful smile and it always filled him with a good feeling when she smiled.

The nice man showed him where his truck was parked, a clean, new-looking dark blue single-cab truck and he said casually, *"hop on in partner, the bakery is just a few blocks away but rather we take my truck to get there fast as possible so you won't be late back to school."* The boy felt secure in this plan, he'd be back for school he wouldn't get in trouble and he'd make his mom proud. It sounded like it was going to be a good day and he hopped up into the passenger seat as the nice man sat next to him and put a foul-smelling rag over his face that smelt of chemicals and made him blink out like a used bulb.

The nice man who was The Devil had found Camila easily. After all, she was his. He knew her memories, he was inextricably part of them, from being her first ever sweetheart to the father of her child. He'd known Camila in Texas when she suffered from crippling depression and he'd talked her into taking her life. Typing on a suicide website about how life was meaningless and death the ultimate release. He watched her through the camera in her computer, he watched her from his vehicle, he followed her every move. She was his mark, his target, his possession before she knew she was possessed. He tipped her fragile mind over the edge like a china statue, falling and breaking into hundreds of pieces.

It was the easiest thing in the world – to break a person – and it felt so damn good to do it again. Easier than lifting weights, easier than walking 20 miles, especially if you knew their sore spots and exactly where to poke. He was The Devil; he knew everyone's sore spots. Especially all his dolls, all his whores. He was adept at manipulation and enticement, he could take any face, any form. When Camila wrote on the suicide website, that she was becoming sure death was the answer, he told her that she was brave and he admired her. He stood as she fell from the bridge, and watched as she drowned, and dived in and brought her back. His poppet to stick pins into, as much as his heart desired.

His plan was always greater than anything they could conceive of. His evil deeper than their worst imaginings. He created the world and he would destroy it, one woman at a time. One reflection of his sister at a time. Winking out like stars over a perfectly black sky. Just like he'd done twice before, he reeled Camila back into his pit. Her son Joe, their son, whom he didn't care about at all aside his worth as a tool, that son whom he briefly fantasized about stabbing and leaving lifeless outside their sickeningly domesticated home, with stupid bunting and chili lights. Their son who carried his DNA but not his hate, their honeyed-haired sissy son who had Camila's beautiful eyes. He also had her weakness, her life force, and, thus, the power he had again over her. He knew with this prize he would wield any outcome and he already knew what the outcome would be.

So, no he wouldn't kill her, because that would be too kind, that would be like his first mistake. The first wife, the first child. His burning all-consuming itch to destroy them, taking him over, choking them out like extinguishing candle wicks. Then, emptiness, nothing to hurt, nothing to make suffer. No, he would not deprive himself again of a longer pleasure. The Devil was a lonely man, he needed blood, he needed to make it last. He needed it to last a lifetime, because in that he destroyed more than any easy death. He was, after all, the hunter of *souls* not of lives. He wanted it to be indelible and everlasting. He was able to do anything; reach into the viscera and pull out the beating heart, tattoo it with his blackness and return it, destroyed and malfunctioning to blow up in the sleeper.

He took her son, he took her weak-eyed son to a hotel room outside of the city, drugged and unconscious. He bound him and injected him so he would not wake up. He felt confident in his disguise, the facial hair, the dye job, the contact lenses. He wouldn't be picked up by anyone who had a picture of him (and anyway, nobody was looking). The only one who would recognize him would be her, and yes, she would. She had the feral heart of a mother and she would recognize the abductor as she would her own child. Aside that, he was invisible. Now he knew how delicious it felt to be absolutely invisible, cloaked by certainty that nobody and nothing was going to stand in his way.

Time was always the great fragmentor of minds. Parents of missing kids will attest that it's the not knowing and the hopelessness of time that kills them the most. He wanted to bequeath this pain to her, like a bouquet of flowers. He knew for every day she didn't have her son she would imagine the worst and he would delight in her pain. It was a drug to him; every time he'd hurt anyone it was the most magnificent high. Being born with so much money in his family, ensuring he kept it all when his parents began to worry about his predilections for killing animals. Even when his cousin came to his parents accusing him of rape, he thought he had control, but their eyes began to waiver and so they had to go. They had to stop suspecting, so that he could take control of everything and become the man he knew he'd always been destined to be. Nothing could stand in his way. It was incredible how nothing ever did. That's how he knew he was a God. Better than a God, a fallen angel who needed no Master. He was his own Master, and Master of anyone he chose.

He had loved raping women, girls, and even boys. It was

how he remembered always being. Just his nature. Nobody in his family seemed to be the same way, it wasn't caused by abuse or terror, he had a good childhood. It began early, as soon as he was large enough down there, he tired of touching himself and began touching others. He didn't care if they let him or not. He knew how to take. It was usually younger kids who wouldn't say anything if he told them he would gut their parents with a knife if they did. Such an easy way to instill terror, and what a delight to watch it rob souls.

It was ludicrously easy because he was a kid, and nobody suspected kids would hurt other kids. How feeble minded that was, he laughed to himself as he enjoyed their terror and their tight little assholes with his greedy fingers. He was no fag but a little boy was so like a girl, clean, soft, hairless, they looked almost identical before hormones kicked in. Of course, afterward they disgusted him and he had to hurt them some more for his own sake, but the little girls, no he didn't hurt them afterward. He told them he would be back and he always was.

A reign of terror inside a family can go undetected for decades. He knew that better than most. He'd met Camila at a support group for sexual abuse survivors, she'd gone trying to exorcize her own demons. With his ability to disguise himself, she had no idea he was her first boyfriend from all those years ago. She didn't know he was the same person who had been writing to her on the suicide chat site that she had turned to in desperation. She never mentioned in group that she visited this site, because she knew what they would say. He knew more than anyone else but he didn't over play his hand. He waited her out, like a panther, patient because he could see the desire – she had to end herself and he was dying to lap up her remains.

That time, Camila didn't disappoint him, on the one hand unable to trust, on the other, so stupid in her assumptions that

The Devil was not sharing her life. There he was, sleeping in her bed, all but infecting her with his whispering until she began to do his bidding, weak, useless woman. During the support group sessions, she'd talked about what it felt like to be sexually abused by a family member. He had always had to touch himself afterward because it excited him so much to consider violating her again after so long. He liked that she was a victim who had been hurt, he wanted to carry on their special tradition, to see the widening fear in her eyes, and he inwardly applauded her rapist for their good taste. The other survivors in the room told their stories too and gave him fertile hunting ground for his long taste in mutilating the lives of others.

Often times the best torment was to go out on a date with someone from the group under the guise of caring, and then date rape his victim. The special power of knowing that they were a victim, knowing their secrets, violating them mentally as well as physically. He was certain, this time they wouldn't go to the police, they'd know better. This time they'd know what would happen if they did. He told them what he'd do to them as they clutched their torn clothes, going further inside of themselves than they ever had as the horror played on repeat; *"they won't believe a dirty little bitch like you who has already sucked your families' cocks for years."* And they'd realize the truth of what he was saying and their bodies would go slack. Lifeless. It was a way of murdering without having to clean a knife.

"They won't believe a lying little whore who spread her legs for one of her fellow sexual abuse survivors, I'm so good at this. I'm really good. I'll tell them that you came on to me, that you were drinking and we slept together and now I'm really messed up about it. You'll probably get in trouble, they'll shame you, they'll never believe you, look at those scars on your wrists, you think they will take your word over mine? Bitch, I'm squeaky clean. But you? You have a mental

history, you're a crazy whore, nobody will believe you, did your own mother believe you when you said your brother had sex with you? What makes you think anyone will now? Maybe the policeman will get turned on and he'll fuck your dirty little hole too. There's nobody you can tell, there's nobody to tell."

And just like that, The Devil scripted the play. Time and time again. He almost lost count. The delicious aftermath, they'd kill themselves, or quit the group and start using drugs again. He loved to see their destruction like a magician admires his own tricks, or a conductor watches his own hands raise and lower the swell of music in the choir pit like a ring master. He controlled them all, he was Punch and they were endless Judy. He made the rounds, abusing them over and over until they could never say it was rape because they didn't know how to say no anymore. Forcing their ugly little mouths to suck on his hardness – until he filled them with poison and went home to watch his violent porn. He good-God-damn loved his life, he loved to hurt others, he was so damn good at it sometimes that alone got him hard.

Chapter 48

Camila hadn't known it was him, hadn't known what he was like. When he dragged her out of the river, she didn't recognize him from their teenage years, her first boyfriend who broke her heart, relishing the peal of pain on her young face when he did it. Didn't recognize him as that quiet man later in group, because he'd removed his disguise, and altered his voice back to its original. He'd never spoken much, the group was big, he was just a mass of facial hair, she hadn't been looking. People in pain tend not to look that closely at anyone. To Camila he was just a guy who plucked her out of the river. *No harm in that, right?* The rest? With the suggestion of drugs, was easy to facilitate and soon she'd died again and then become truly his. Being in control of another person committing suicide had been his biggest rush yet, but now he was trying something cooler. He wanted to bring her back to life and make her die again, waking like a doll without a memory for him to harness and use as his own.

She was surprisingly pliant to the idea of another death. He filled her veins with poison and her heart stopped, he brought her back with another injection, this time right into her heart, yes that felt good, stabbing her hard. And when she recovered, he administered the drugs to wipe her mind and whilst unconscious he electrocuted her brain over and over like psychiatrists do in asylums for PTSD. He was a damn genius. And she knew nothing of what had happened. He wiped her clean, for his dirty use like one of his laptops.

Then she was as malleable as a doll, a Stepford wife, obedient and beautiful, he could teach her everything. Teach her that screwing her hard was normal and loving, that pain wasn't what she was feeling; it was pleasure. That having a child in the middle of the forest and nearly dying was normal and loving, that pain wasn't what she was feeling, it was pleasure. He got off on her disorientation and stupidity, she was such a stupid, stupid little bitch and she was his stupid little bitch, his play thing, his whore, his hole, his defilement. When he watched his porn and the snuff movies, he would then use her like his surrogate, careful not to snuff her out, though many times he longed to drive a knife into her mouth instead of his phallus.

Forcing her to have his child was just another method by which he controlled her. Of course he was going to knock her up, he was a prince, he could bring life to anything, however ruined. His first wife hadn't been able to have children with her previous boyfriend that was why they had broken up but with him she got pregnant in a month. *One month! He was a God.* Carol had been really shocked but he wasn't at all. He knew he was so virile he'd beat any statistic; he'd plant his seed so high inside her womb she had no choice but to turn it into life. And mind you, he truly hated his first wife, for her weak love of him and her innocence and her stupidity and her trust. Well, guess he'd shown her! Her mistake that's for sure, and as she died, he'd spat in her face and come all over her, laughing all the while, telling her the truth about their children that she had never known. She couldn't do anything, nothing at all, he heard her struggling to speak, and then wink out, eternal night, goodbye.

Some wars are fought overtly, over land and objects, clashing and blood spilt. The most lasting wars are wars of hate, they infect everything that comes into contact with them, they last generations, staining the soil and ancestors with the crime. Camila felt this. Unable to sleep, unable to eat, dead in her wake for her son's return. Voices punished her perpetually with scold, they reminded her of every mistake she had ever made. How when we think we are well, we are proven wrong by a slip that reveals our inner hatred. Or maybe it is like anything else, when we have no explanation for evil, we attribute it to our doing *we must have done something to bring this upon ourselves* to explain, to justify, to excuse, the horror we cannot explain or excuse.

Camila forgot how to speak or think, her mind a blank like a wide mouth screaming. Neighbors would drop by and see her blanched face, her unmoving hands, her empty chest; and they would mutter words of consolation like *he's bound to show up, he's a strong boy*, as if they helped any, and then they would leave, sensing it did her no good to have them around. And it didn't, she only needed one person in her entire life. Before him she had not been needed and learned how to return the emotion, needing no one. When people came and offered condolences, she wanted to shut them out, pretend she was one of the condolers and not the victim, the mother without a child. Anything but that! Anything but victim again! Hadn't she promised herself? Hadn't she SWORN she wouldn't ever be a victim again? But that was before her son was gone. Yet, wasn't it obvious? So damn obvious this was going to happen? How could she not take him to school every day, how could she lower her guard even for one moment, one second? Didn't they live in a world of violence, why hadn't she learned that?

What did it take to learn that?

She wanted to rip open her arms and let her blood grow him back and die, watching him live. She begged the Gods she didn't believe in, to bring him back; *"return him to me, I'll do anything, I'll be anything, I'll even go back to Rafael!"* And that's when she knew, with the cold certainty of a knife against your throat. That was it. Rafael had taken him. This was the price he demanded. Joe was the pawn, which meant he was alive, and Camila could save him, if she destroyed herself. *Oh God it was so obvious once she thought it.* It could not come quickly enough. She wanted to write out a big sign that read *I know it was you come, and take me I will do anything*, but of course that would not work. He was staying away, taunting her, making her pay, hurting her the way he knew. If he'd had strings attached to her heart, he couldn't have pulled them any more tightly.

So, a game again. Both of them, somehow back to facing one another. He the tormenter who had come into her life and never left, a scar on her, a permanent brand. And Camila absolutely completely thought she had killed him. She had stabbed into his neck and thought he bled out and died, leaving them free to live without his taint. How then did he survive? Why did he survive? What God permitted someone like him to live? The fury she felt for him when she plucked up the nerve to stab him and defend herself, soared through her again like rising blood pressure. She only felt that emotion and nothing else. He had her son. She would do anything, anything to get him back and see him safe. But that price would be a price nobody would have considered possible when this all began.

We think those kinds of scenarios belong only to fiction, but they are the bread on which we rub our butter. Well-worn stories of manipulation, one-upmanship and control, as old as humanity. Why do we find them so fascinating? Because the sickness we as humans are capable of astounds our sensibilities. We tell gruesome horror tales as part warning to our children, part wisdom; do not be as stupid as this person, learn from others' mistakes. For if we do not learn, we fall into the pit of those who prey on the vulnerable, the blind, the easily deceived. And innocence? Innocence means you are the most vulnerable, hence why it is said, the good are first to be hurt in this life of pain. If that is true, it is because, when you are good, it is far harder to fight someone who cannot be turned from their course by any rationale or any plea.

Instead, you submit. When the life of your own flesh and blood is at stake, it's not even a question. You just find yourself falling to your knees, leaning your neck out, waiting for the blade. How many mothers have thrown themselves on the bodies of their children to protect them from slaughter, how many have offered themselves in their place? And father's too, though this father, this father with eyes as dark as tar, he did not offer himself to anyone but The Devil's hearth. There he felt most at home, and ruled the world with the crush of his fist that knew no compromise and only, the pursuit and joy of destroying.

Camila had fallen asleep finally, a gun next to her bedside, loaded. The Devil came into the house, breaking in through the bathroom window, climbing through the bottom half that appeared too small but was slightly bigger than it looked for men with narrow hips. Rafael was quiet and she, exhausted and ragged with sleep deprivation did not wake up. She did wake up when the blade was at her neck, when reaching with her other hand instinctively the gun was not on the side of the bed. She knew before her eyes focused in the dark, she smelt him, a wounded, vile odor she never thought she would have to smell again. What do you say to someone you hate so much and had tried to kill? What is there to say? *"Give me my son, I will do anything."* That's all she could say as she looked up at a man who should have been a ghost and wondered, perhaps all along if he was.

Chapter 49

"Y*ou have to do two things Whore,"* Rafael said, his features obscured with the darkness, but his shape, his movement, as familiar as her own. *"If you want Joe to live, you have to devote yourself to me, for the rest of your life, I own you. That's the first thing. The second thing, you may find harder. I want you to kill. I have a target, a woman I have been with since you left, a filler, more beautiful than you and a better body than your worn-out flesh. But she's not you Whore, her pain isn't as exquisite as yours. If you come back to me you need to take her place. I can't deal with two of you. I'm going to ask you to kill her. If you do it, successfully this time, because you really didn't do well killing me you dumb bitch, then I will let Joe live. He can grow up in foster care for all I care, he may share my DNA but he's got your weakness in him. I'd only end him eventually if he stays with us, so the way to get you to return, is to let him go."*

Rafael smiled, his white teeth shining in the darkness of the room; *"I'll do it and I won't ever lay a hand on Joe unless you leave me. If you do, all bets are off, I'll gut you slowly and I'll gut him after he watches you die. He's a soft boy, a pathetic creature, he's not really part of me. I disown that, anything part of me has strength, vitality. I see none of that in him, only your weakness, your thin skin and pathetic victimhood. Do you agree? Will you do it? You have one chance. It's more than you deserve. Tonight, you come with me, or you never see him again and I leave you to die emotionally for the rest of your damn life."* Camila didn't even need to answer. She lifted up off her bed, left her home, and everything she had gathered all the years she'd been free thinking Rafael dead. She followed him like a possessed ghost, in his truck, out of town, and far, far beyond anyone who could or would help her.

Rafael took her to Colorado, she'd been before, skiing with friends from work at 18. That had been a happy time, this was an awful parody. Everything when you feel sad, turns ugly, even when you really try not to let it, it infects your soul with a hopelessness and nothing solves that except if you can find a solution to your misery. But this was round two, or was it three? She'd lost count, she'd given up, there was no re-match, he'd beaten her, in every way possible for a person to beat someone. That said, when someone has nothing to lose but their life, and they've already done that, maybe the tables can be reversed.

Re-visiting a place that holds good memories, when you are going under the auspice of grief and suffering, is the bitterest feeling in the world. Camila recalled the easy joy she had experienced last time and now, the weight in her heart. A scythe cutting through her innards with every step, knowing she was as sure dead as perhaps her son would be, but still, with the determined march of the condemned, hoping for a reprieve for him at least. Any hope, even one percent, being better than facing a reality of Joe's death. No, she couldn't do that, if he died, she knew she would blow away with the wind and that would be that.

They stayed at a hotel that had been rebuilt after the storms, between Denver and Boulder. It stood a way up in the mountains, isolated and rugged, there was a stream running down, snow still on the mountain tops and a small winding country road. Rafael had a cabin at the back of the property, she thought Joe would be there, but nobody was. He told her that he'd have her son found by police when she'd proven to him that she would do as she said. "*What will that involve?*" she said, barely able to stand to look at his smug face and the scar on his neck that reminded her of her failure. *"Oh baby, you know what it will involve,"* he said taking off his jeans, *"come here Whore. This is going to really hurt."*

It was fair to say in all five years since she'd been free, Camila had a fair number of flashbacks, of their struggle, the blood, Rafael raping her, shoving in her mouth making her gag as he thrust down her throat. But in all that time she had never thought she would experience it again. It took a lot of work, coupled with counseling that had helped her to keep a lid on the panic that would rise up unannounced often at night, cavorting without control across her nerves. Here they were in the day light, the yellow walls of the hotel, the cheap stinking carpet, she on her red knees, opening her mouth to him again like the animal he saw her as. No, she didn't think this was how it would ever be again. She knew she'd forgo anything to avoid a return to being anyone's slave, but she hadn't counted on Rafael being alive. She hadn't counted on this being all about saving Joe.

After Rafael brutalized her again, a hideous familiar feeling that left her numb, she lay with her torn clothes facing away, not even caring what he saw of her. *"Your body isn't as good as before,"* he said carelessly, *"but it doesn't seem like anyone's touched you since me, which I don't find surprising, you're not going to be desirable for much longer, you're lucky anyone wants you,"* he mocked, slapping her thighs. *"Fortunately for you I want you although I haven't worked all that out yet, I might still just slit your throat, but to keep you compliant I will promise you this. From the word of a murderer, I will not kill our son. I will keep my word and Joe will be free, that's on my honor.* He laughed sadistically. He was having So. Much. Fun. *"But you keep your end of this bargain Whore. You have to kill first. And I want to watch and I want us to fuck in her blood as it cools on the sheets after you've done her."*

Does it seem strange that Camila should be so calm, knowing what she faced ahead? Yet a strange calm was all she felt, nothing else. She was powerless to make any other choice, it wasn't a choice. She only looked forward, to ensuring somehow, at any cost, Joe survived. She knew Rafael would kill him just to destroy her. Whatever it took she had to stop this outcome. The only way was playing the game. *"Why do you want the other woman to die?"* Camila asked, knowing the answer but hoping she could talk him out of it.

Rafael rolled his eyes. *"I can't deal with two of you full time. Sexually sure. Easy. Two whores or one, doesn't matter. But the rest? I'd be always looking over my shoulder. It isn't worth it. Better to have one in the house, and get what else I need outside where I don't have the hassle. I can always buy pain. It's cheap and plentiful."* Rafael grinned. *"How many truck stops have I found the kind of delicious pain I like to consume? How many snuffed out just because I can and I will? There are so many vulnerable, desperate souls out there – Whore, you're nothing special, you're less than special. With you it's personal. I want you to hurt more than kill you."* Rafael said.

"But I don't want to bring the hassle of taking care of you. You nearly killed me last time. I need to keep my eye on you better than I did. I can't relax if I'm always watching you Whore. Since you are the one who got away, you get to survive, aren't you the lucky one?" He laughed. *"And her pain isn't as exquisite as yours, I don't find myself hard imagining her face and the torment in her eyes, it doesn't run as deep. In your eyes it runs so deep, I've never looked into more*

tormented eyes in my life, it feels so damn good to place torment there, time and time again, to see that it comes from me, that it is all for me. You make me feel like I'm your King and your God every time you look at me. You can't help it you're so weak, you love me despite yourself, and I like to be worshiped by debased creatures like you it helps me when I need to kill others, to know I have that worship to return to and bask in. You are my blood-bride Camila, you complete the circle, your suffering sustains my rage."

In her minds-eye the nightmare Camila had all those years ago before jumping from the bridge had returned. So visceral it felt like it was replacing reality. Camila saw a river of blood washing over white sand, the sand absorbing the blood, the sun baking the sand, the reddened hardened sand turning into a figure, The Devil climbing out of the sand. The Devil pulling her after him, attached to his phallus by her mouth, his fist inside her, a grotesque mandala parodying goodness. They dance awkwardly, he shifts her so he is taking her and she is bleeding, always giving him her blood, her life, enveloping the two of them so she is both mother and wife. *"He is born from me,"* she thought to herself. *"I keep him alive with my blood and I am the only one who can destroy him."* He saw in her mind, him turning back to sand, the blood rinsing clear, the desert clean and unspoiled again. She understood the nightmare she'd had way back then at last. She saw the power of her.

Before something happens, the anticipation is always more detailed than the event. Two states of mind: pre-anxiety, then a change. We put on our battle masks and prepare in ways we cannot believe ourselves capable of preparing. Clenched teeth. Uplifted jaw. As animals, our adrenalin, an inner cocktail of chemicals releasing. The Berserker, the warrior, the survivor, we don a mask. Surviving atrocities, watching ourselves from afar. Those who are raped will attest, they know it is happening but they are also somewhere else. We climb inside ourselves when violated, wait it out, returning only when pulled out and re-born into the world. Or we fight. Both responses to unacceptable trauma. Because of Joe, Camila could not afford to withdraw. She could not permit any hesitation; this was a bloody war and she needed every fighter standing. What we can force out of ourselves, the unlimited well of our being, tested only when comfort falls and hell knocks at our door.

Chapter 50

The next day they drove further, soon there was little traffic and lots of logging roads and unfinished dirt roads leading off to private land. Rafael had another track of land with a gate in front and a long drive down to a small cabin built behind a ring of trees. It was beautiful, he seemed despite his depravity to have an unending source of money and good taste. Rafael had limitless income, despite not working, surviving on the inheritance of the dead she presumed, a tract of land this large, in Colorado, must have set him back. How long had he owned, it, was it even his? *Or did the skeletons of the real owners, lie beneath them*? As they pulled up to the small house and she knew, this beautiful place, was likely to be her final resting place, unless somehow, she were able to take control again. How unlikely given he held the one card she would never jeopardize, her flesh and blood, and his, though nothing of him poisoned the goodness of her son.

He dragged her out of the car by her hair, told her she would be expected to grow it so he could pull it more easily and threw her into a cage on the outside of the house, that looked a lot like a dog pen but with more locks and security on it. There was even a camera pointed at the center. *"You'll sleep out here until you've done it, I'll give you two weeks to get your courage up, meanwhile you eat, crap and piss here, unless I ask you inside for my needs. In which case you say nothing, do nothing other than what you're told. Understand?"* Camila nodded and curled into a tight circle. Instead of thinking, she tried to focus on the sounds around her. Learning everything she could about the way everything worked, she needed the intensity of the wolf to find her way out, to survive this. The rest did not matter. She knew pain. It was familiar to her. When you are your most dangerous, you are honed in on one thing and one thing alone, the rest is invisible. You are a sniper; you have your finger on the trigger and your eye sees its target.

The night was bitterly cold, she thought she would die, naked but for a blanket she grew so cold she began to hallucinate. She saw her son, Joe was crying, asking her why she let him die? She saw a girl's face, covered with blood and saw herself pulling out the knife. She woke knowing if that was what it took, she'd do it. No part of her wanted to, she wanted to sink the knife into his neck all the way through like she should have the first time and she cried silently, berating herself for not having finished him when she could have. *I will never get another chance*, Camila despaired, her feet and hands bound, he would never trust her enough to untie her and with the ties she couldn't hope to escape. Inside the cabin she heard screaming, a voice not unlike her own. Camila closed her eyes and screamed back, silently, inside her mind where nothing else was tethered down and everything floated, lost and terrified.

It occurred to her that she should have done more, more to prevent this and then she chided herself for the blame that inevitably came when she felt helpless. Turning on yourself, only keeps you down, you become your own worst critic. When the world seems to hold everything against you, blaming yourself only heightens the feeling that it's personal. But when bad things happen, they are rarely personal, and whilst Rafael had hunted her and her son down, she had not failed them both by a lack of vigilance. If someone really wants to destroy you, chances are they'll be able to take a shot, but no outcome is set in stone. She breathed, her son breathed, if there was a way, she intended to find it. The fear she'd held toward Rafael all this time apart, burning in her sub-conscious, had become a ghost by which he'd found her. If Camila had underestimated him, she only did so to avoid him suffocating her waking thoughts. When brutalized, we try to push our violators away, somehow, they always find a way back until we face them and we destroy them, once and for all.

With so much time to think, it was impossible not to. Camila retraced the years that led to her being tied up in a filthy cage outside in Colorado weather. *How did it come to this Camila?* She asked herself time and time again. *You were a normal kid, a normal person, and look at this! This is anyone's worst fear. This isn't even possible.* But it was. And Rafael was real and he'd hunted Camila down again and stolen her life, and her son's life. Was she that weak she could only be Rafael's victim? No. She knew after everything, the one thing she wasn't, was weak. But still, it was her in chains, not Rafael. Rafael survived everything; Rafael snuffed out so many lives she'd lost count. How could evil thrive so abundantly? What had she ever done to deserve this kind of life? Feelings of hate, fear, and rage coursed through her mind as she lay in her own excrement. Three days went by, she began to cough and feel slightly feverish, but at least he left her alone and she was glad for that. It gave her time to build, within her mind-palace, her resolution to take it as far as it would go. *Whatever it took*, she whispered, over and over and over, her lips blistered and dry from lack of water.

Eventually he came out of the cabin, naked except for a pair of dirty boxers, which were well worn and stained. Camila knew that when he turned back to slovenliness he did so because he'd unhinged the corners of his mask and let his bloodiest monster out. This was when he was most dangerous, when he would not hold back, when his appetite for pain flourished. Despite herself she began to shiver uncontrollably. She wasn't sure if it was worse not knowing what he would do, or knowing only too well what he was capable of. He unshackled her and brought her inside by a chain around her neck, forced her knees to the floor and told her to lick the floor clean. She began to lick the floor, her mouth was dry and calloused from punches to her lips, it was disgusting but she did it, because she knew the alternative was worse. At some point as she made progress along the floor, she felt hot urine cascade over her shoulders and head, he was pissing on her laughing, she tried hard not to swallow any, and say nothing, but the urine splashed down onto the floor and she had to lick that up too. You might think you can't do these things, but you really don't know what you can do until you're in that position. Camila knew she was capable of doing things she couldn't even speak out loud.

He did this intermittently. Every three or four days as she could reckon. Time lost itself. Camila recalled an article she read about disassociation and how to protect itself, the mind detaches from reality when traumatized. That made sense. Sometimes it's just too much, and it was too much, and had been many times before. Try as she might, her mind kept a spark within it that knew what was going on. *Maybe it's the part of me who won't give up and will find a way out of this*, she thought, dully. But there seemed no way of overcoming Rafael a second time. She'd blown her one and only shot, and failed to kill him. How would she ever get a chance like that again? All she could do was find a way for Joe to escape his father. If she could just do that.

Soon enough, on one of the days Camila was brought by a chain around her neck into the house, Rafael brought out a girl from a closed room. She was almost anorexic looking, and a doppelganger for Camila. The same dark skin and eyes, the same long dark hair, except she looked even younger. Her tiny breasts were emaciated and there was blood smeared on her thighs. She was filthy and wore the drug-addled look of a long-time captive. *"You may wonder why I haven't drugged you,"* Rafael said, smiling, kicking the girl in the groin so she doubled over making a strange sighing sound. *"It's because it bores me to have such dumb bitches. I liked that you were a fighter. This is going to sound strange but I think it turned me on when you stabbed me, the guts you had. What a gutsy bitch you were."* Rafael grimaced, touching his neck. The scar tissue was puckered and ugly looking. *"I only wished I had been more prepared; we could have stabbed each other until one of us won. I would love to run a knife up your insides and know as I did it, you were dying to kill me but I got there* first." He laughed loud and ugly.

"*You can't kill me. You know that now, right? You Just. Can't. Kill. Me!!!*" Rafael's eyes bulged as he roared those words and both women cowered at his awful pitch. *"I really have to control myself or all the fun will be dead, ha ha ha! Get it? I can't kill my play things; you bitches are getting harder to find. Too many people look out for their little girls, fortunately nobody wanted you two disgusting Whores. All the more for Daddy. Right? Someone has to take you."* Rafael kicked the nameless woman again – she crawled away from him and he yanked at the chain around her neck until she choked. *"Say it!"* he screamed. *"Say it! Or I'll bust you up so bad you won't pee for days!"* She was hiccupping with terror, trying to catch her breath. *"All the more for Daddy,"* the girl rasped, hardly able to articulate.

"Didn't it ever occur to you, stupid Whore? You never asked questions? The girl who took your place in the lake? The girl who drowned and they thought was you because her damn head was bashed in and the only identifying marks were your ring and the stuff in your truck? She was one of mine, the one before you. She pissed me off royally. The mother of my first child. Carol then dared to have a damn miscarriage. She killed my baby! It's true. I've ended some of my kids, even deliberately rather than through neglect. But for her to miscarry, that was pure disrespect." Rafael looked so savage with the memory, Camila thought he would explode, his face beet red, his neck bulging with veins. *"Another freakin Whore, like the rest of you. I showed her though. Carol was scared of water; it was the perfect death. And with her death, she let me have you. See its fortunate I have such a type, reminds me of my mam. Mam was dark eyed, dark haired, dark skinned. Beautiful. I guess I can't get away from a certain look. It was easy to replace my mam and Carol with you."* His smile was feral and hideous. *"I can do it again, so remember that. You're not indispensable. Not even close."*

Rafael was always a bragger. He loved to hear the sound of his own voice. He loved and craved his own success. It didn't matter how debasing it was, he wanted to share it. He liked it if it made you uncomfortable. Camila had always known that about him. She should have seen how it was a red-flag; she thought – as she lay watching him boast of his depravities. *"If you find girls who nobody wants then you can get away with anything."* He continued. *"It's no fun if they want you to. Some of them are that sick they like being hurt, I prefer it when I can hurt them and see the terror in their eyes. With you though … you, I confess, I did like it when you pretended you were hot for me. It was different, exciting, but maybe I knew all along it was an act and was just waiting for your calling card."* He laughed again. Feckless and without a shred of remorse. *"Fuck me I didn't know you had it in you and making a weapon? Seriously I was proud of you. For that I'm giving you a second chance, and this Whore? Well, you know your mission. As for now, carry on cleaning the floor, be sure to get up all her blood, it tastes really, really good."*

Rafael left them alone on the floor of the kitchen, the similar looking girl seemed to be unconscious. Camila carried on licking but when she was sure he wasn't watching in the doorway she would feign licking and spit instead, rubbing it with her finger, so it cleaned but not with her tongue. *"Are you conscious?"* She asked the girl, who said nothing in return and lay as if unconscious in the fetal position. *"Hello?"* No reply. She pushed her but the girl didn't move, she must have passed out, he must have dosed her with a motherload. No surprise. She'd been there herself. But how glad she was Rafael had chosen to keep her conscious. As much as the pain was worse, the knowing was better. What you know can hurt you. What you don't know can hurt you worse.

She thought about what he'd revealed. As he unraveled mentally, he seemed to reveal slightly more. The woman found in the river, whom authorities had assumed was Camila had been one of his. His first wife Carol. That's how she died then? Not in a car-crash. Not buried in an unmarked grave. Rafael been intricately involved in the entire process. Orchestrating it like one would a symphony. What incredible energy, Camila thought. To devote such time and energy into revenge against his first girlfriend. It seemed an impossible feat. Only the patience of a true psychopath would go to such lengths, invest so much time. This was a master plan, years in the making. Camila wasn't just 'any' girl she was 'the' girl Rafael was determined to destroy. It was personal.

A series of deliberate twists and turns. First dating Camila as a teen, angry to lose her. Rafael then spent years seeking revenge against her. Re-connecting unrecognized as an adult. Hearing her sorrow, pushing her toward suicide and when she jumped, when she had nobody to stay her hand and say, *no don't*, he was there to witness it. A sick mimicry of kindness. Abducting her, ensuring she was off the grid, dead as far as anyone was concerned. Finally, to become the perfect playmate. Camila could have stopped this ever carrying on if she had checked Rafael was really dead in the house by the lake, but so much blood, she'd been sure he couldn't survive. What did she know about how much blood a human can lose and still survive? Perhaps she underestimated him because he was neither human nor alive, but some kind of reanimated monster with one agenda. Her destruction.

Chapter 51

Now Camila was again under his yoke. She had become his investment, reclaimed and subjugated, licking his floor with her tongue. She knew far worse was in store for both the girl and herself. Here was a girl Rafael had taken to keep his bed warm in her absence, her abduction could have been avoided, if Camila had just had the courage to put her fingers on his neck and feel for a pulse. But terror spurs the runner, and we are brought up to believe fire will wipe anything from this earth. But not those who are born of fire, who live in fire, not those who make it their pilgrimage and their destination. Surely, he was a demon, not a living breathing man, but one who had returned to claim her again. Camila, the girl who was supposed to be dead and shifting under river weeds.

Rafael returned after she'd finished the floor and woke the other girl up by throwing water on her head. He pulled her roughly up and told her to fix dinner, which slowly and in a dreamlike state she did, as best as anyone could with their hands in chains. Meanwhile he took Camila back to the new girl's bedroom. There was blood all over the bed, dried and fresh and

Rafael told her it was time for his first course. He opened her legs and rammed her twice before punching her in the face over and over until she lost consciousness. When she woke up, they'd eaten and the girl was back in the room with her, lying in the corner in a ball, tied to a stake. Camila was still on the bed, her legs shamefully spread, blood pouring down from her nose to her navel. She had no clothes left to cover herself with and her arms were chained above her head to a post on the wall. Rafael had installed a lot around the house to make it easy to chain them as was his need.

After humiliation there is usually numbness, and a relenting of the soul. But in Camila's case, she had decided humiliation did not apply where Devils were concerned. She'd survived one Devil when she was abused as a child, she knew she had it in her to survive another. She was not going to be torn apart mentally and stuffed into a nameless grave. If she died – she would die knowing she was a good person, someone who could not be consumed by his fire, and burnt out. The pain was excruciating but it focused her on the task ahead, to survive him, to endure past and find a way. If not, then she had no guarantee of her son's freedom. It was bigger than that now. Because Camila knew, if she died, before long, two new girls would be in this room, humiliated and shredded and she could not have that on her conscience.

She slept, fitfully. No longer confined to the cage outside, maybe Rafael had changed his mind, maybe he forgot. She thought he did drugs, the way his eyes looked. Unfocused. He seemed a little slower, she hoped it meant she had inflicted some damage when she cut him. Those injuries, presumably Rafael had never been seen by a doctor. She only hoped this would give her an opportunity, anything, because after she killed the new girl, it would be too late for both of them to ever come back. Maybe that was fate, how many times can you cheat your destiny and return from your own death bed? It reminded her of her grandfather, his quick suicide, robbing everyone of a chance to ask him, *"Why did you choose to leave us? What did we do to make you want to go?"* How at the time her father had starred off and she saw in his eyes, the pain of a little boy who would never be able to tell his father what he had felt, all those years, growing up in his shadow.

When you thought about her life, was it any wonder, that she had ended up here, in a cage? When her entire time on earth she had been either trying to get out of one, or building one to hide in? Perhaps she was a coward, for all her stories of strength she always returned to the abyss one way or another. Somehow someone else would have escaped. Somehow others would have fought him off, killed him right, prevented this. She was bound on a wheel, reversing into water to dunk her, time and again; *the witch is dead* – with his vision of penance, though she knew not what she should be sorry for? Surviving him? Was it possible that one person had the belief their life mattered most? She felt all were equal and only actions disturbed equality, but what of her actions? By trying to kill herself, had she tipped the balance and broken her allotment of forgiveness? Was she paying the price for her own sin of once wishing for death?

Chapter 52

Rafael told her a few days later that he'd called the police and told them where their son was, not mentioning any names. Joe would probably be identified, but either way, it didn't matter, he was foster care fodder now, she'd never see him again, and he thought that was brilliant. A day later he showed her a newspaper from New Mexico online, on his mobile phone, that talked about her son being found, to prove to Camila he wasn't bullshitting her. *"How do I know you're not to going to change your mind and hurt Joe in the future?"* Camila asked him. *"You don't of course. But you should feel lucky I did this for you. I could have gutted him like so many others." "Why didn't you then?"* She asked, wiping her sore eyes. *"Because he's my son and I want to see what potential he has growing up. You never know?"* Rafael grinned. *"Maybe he'll end up taking a cue from his ole pa."*

"*Now you have to finish your end of the bargain,"* he threatened her as he unzipped his trousers. *"I want to watch, I want to see you turn from the good little woman into a slice of me, because I know it's going to hurt you more than it's going to hurt her. The pious always hurt the most, it's the bothersome conscience, it just can't stay quiet.*

Fortunately, empathy and conscience aren't my concern but I do enjoy watching others lose theirs, and stare into evil, realizing we're all just a heartbeat away from it." Rafael began to stroke himself.

"You can be my acolyte," Rafael said, his eyes were on fire, he looked completely unhinged. *"Yeah, it's an enormous role and I want to see your gratitude. It means I know you have it in you, I saw it in your eyes when you stabbed me with the knife. It felt good to feel your rage, to see your power, little as it is, better than these wet rags I keep finding."* He starred at her like he wanted her to nod her agreement. Camila didn't meet his eye. *"Whore, you had a little piece of my rage, it turned me on, as I lay bleeding out, I wanted so badly to fuck you. Maybe I couldn't then. I had to wait until you left so I could get out, and bide my time and find you again."*

He grinned his terrible grin of rage and spite. "Whore, I've waited so long to let you know, how much you moved me, how much it meant to me that you had it in you to do that, and I decided, you'd be the one I'd teach. Yeah, because it would hurt you so much to be taught and yet, you'd do well, I'd be proud of you, I would reward you, you'd grow to like it. When you got ugly and I couldn't fuck you anymore we'd fuck them together, we'd do them together, like a true man and wife." Rafael was so excited by his plan for them both, he didn't even need to hurt Camila in that moment to feel pleasure. She could see him getting more swollen with pleasure and she felt sick to her stomach.

Rafael raped the new girl in front of Camila. The new girl lay there as if unconscious, being assaulted limply and without any fight, as if her spirit had already lifted away and found some refuge in the tall pines outside. Camila knew that feeling. So many times, unbearable emotions would suffocate her, she would try to take herself off into the healing void of imagination, where if she tried really, really hard, fate dealt a different hand. In that fantasy world, the world was kind and forgiving, her parents had loved her, her family was whole, she was safe. It felt like a beautiful agony to pretend and then come back to earth, when the rope cut a little too deep or the sound of screaming became your own. Losing yourself in the trespass of your mind, sometimes saves you from throwing in the towel and holding your breath until you suffocate on the unacceptable. But sooner or later, reality returns, the well-worn record, tracking over and over, capturing you in its sticky net and binding you tight.

Watching Rafael brutalize an alternate version of herself was worse in a way than him brutalizing her. Camila strained at her leashes, she wanted to ask him to take her instead but she knew that's what he wanted to hear, and he'd only hurt the other girl more for it. She could see the topsy-turvy inside-out warp of his mind, the way he turned things wrong into good and things good into wrong. How he got off on pain, on the subversion of goodness. Like a wolf devouring a new born, licking gladly the life blood of its fresh skin, and savagely tearing out its jugular as the mother runs, too late to stop anything. She saw how the young woman jerked with him buried in her like the hilt of a sword, and was flung like a dead thing on the end of him, this way and that, until a thick stream of blood ran from her.

Some days he stayed away from them as if they were infected, dirty things, and did whatever it was he did without them. During that time, they had hours, stretching out, timelessly in the flick of changing light. Bound in contortion with hardly any room to move, forced to evacuate where they crouched, it was a dehumanizing imprisonment, reducing them both to the sheer husk of humanity, and nothing more. A dog would be given more. Camila saw in the cruelty, a design to rape them of their souls as well as their freedom and with every ounce of strength she silently resisted, building a world inside of her head. A world that was good and strong, a fortress to keep out the mad man who had scaled her defenses and robbed her of her liberty.

"You know what?" Rafael said, after he'd finished debasing her, "*I don't change my mind often but I have about the two of you. I really like having you both here. It's variety, it keeps me guessing and when I get tired of your slack hole, I can renew myself in her tighter hole. I might just take it back about ending her, there's something about different pussy that keeps a man young I reckon. I could always turn the lights out and do you both and see if I can tell the difference. Ha died, ha! It's like being in a harem, I'm a powerful man I don't think one whore is enough for me, I don't owe you a damn thing Whore.*" His eyes looked glassy and feverish, she could see him bulging in his groin, "*I only wish I could sate my lust to kill so we'll have to think of a way of doing that too*" he smiled as if he'd been talking pleasantly about the weather.

"Maybe if I hobble you both then it will be the equivalent of having one to worry about and I can keep both of you. I'm going to look up what it takes to hobble a bitch and then we'll see, okay?" He was gone some time and when he returned, he had a hammer and a knife. *"Well, I've read two ways work. You can either break the ankle or you can break the knees. I'm thinking the sound of your pretty little open knees being broken would be a real turn on but how could you stand to do your chores? I figured the answer was do one leg not both, that way you're not going anywhere but you still serve as slave and can clean up and cook."* He smiled. *"As long as you still have holes and tongues to scream with, you'll do me fine."*

Without giving Camila a moment to think or react, Rafael raised a hammer with a large metal head and a firm wooden grip, down fast and smashed the brown knee cap of the girl whose name was Julia. Camila heard it like a sharp crack and the highest scream emanated from the almost catatonic girl before she swooned from the pain. Camila's terror in watching this, knowing she would be next was unbearable and she felt herself let loose a stream of hot urine on the carpet despite herself. *"You dirty bitch!"* Rafael said, laughing and laughing as he made her lick it up. Then, as she shook so much, he had to steady her with the large hammer, ramming it into the back of her ankle and left her screaming and throwing up on herself.

Neither of them healed well. Julia's entire knee was ruined and deformed, it swelled up and turned purple and made cracking sounds when she tried to move. Camila's own ankle was in bad shape, it bled like crazy. She wedged the mattress cover on it and in time it clotted over but not being in a cast left the entire ankle useless to stand on. It was as bad as being one legged. She couldn't put any pressure on her second leg at all so she couldn't stand at the counter to cook and had to kneel on the floor with the food and then ask Julia to put the pans of food on the counter to cook. Julia could stand because they had bound her knee and she could side-ways prop herself at an angle but she couldn't walk except by dragging her leg. She couldn't even do that really and had to walk on her hands and feet. It was pitiful and Rafael loved it. They had no underwear, he would humiliate them as they crawled, and sometimes mount them like pigs.

At first Rafael had left them alone to heal, but predictably that didn't last long before he came in to get what he always wanted. Both were in excruciating pain so he dosed them with high pain killers for a couple of weeks which helped but left them out of it, unable to tell the passing of time. When alone at night he chained them to separate parts of the room so they could not touch or hear each other without being too loud. Neither talked, there just wasn't any point, they were hobbled, covered in excrement and blood and probably going to get infected and die. Camila began to realize she would rather die than kill this young woman. Now that her son was free, the only thing she could lose was her own life and suddenly, that didn't seem such a big loss after all.

Rafael would leave them shackled to the wall most of the time, they'd have to pee on themselves and then clean it up once he returned. The room stank, the carpet was stained irrevocably with blood but he didn't seem to mind the state either of them were in. Camila noted that what turned him on most of all were naked women with dark hair and dark skin, naked and bound. All his pornography had been that, and all his films. He had a type and he kept raping and raping that type like he was unable to punish it enough or hate it sufficiently. He'd alluded to his mother, to his first wife, and it seemed there existed a desire within him to kill and kill the same woman over and over.

One day, his eyes clouded with drugs, Rafael told her about his sister. She died at ten, *an accident* he said, with an exaggerated wink. *"She looked a lot like you, so did our mother, but I never touched mama, that would have been really wrong."* He feigned disapproval by putting his hand on his mouth in mock outrage and then breaking into a smile. *"My sister on the other hand, yeah she was young it's true, but you still got a hole when you're underage,"* Rafael laughed and slapped his thigh with his own joke. *"I think I always missed her so much it's good to have her back. Now I have two sisters."* He giggled. *"A happy family all over again!"* Camila had never really seen the madness in Rafael when he talked. Just the physical propensity for violence. But now she saw an unhinging of his mind, in the way his past and present came together more and more. With the mask off, he was deranged; barely capable of pretending normal.

After the pain became bearable, he weaned them both off the pain killers. Probably it was hard to get a large stock of them given that they were so strong. Camila realized that she should have paid attention to things like that. Where he got his forgeries, where he got his land, where he got his drugs? Had she been able to do that she might have discovered that others helped him. She'd read about pedophile rings, who was to say there weren't torture rings? People in touch with others, who did similar things; abducting women, torturing them, keeping them slaves for years, unknown to anyone. She thought of the film she'd seen back at the house, angry at herself for not taking it with her, recalling the snuff film of his wife's death and others, he was part of something bigger. After her escape she'd read about it happening in every country not just the ones you might expect. Modern slavery was alive and well and she was part of it.

It pricked her conscience that once free of Rafael, her and Joe had returned to normal life like nothing happened, like they hadn't been slaves to a monster. *What was normal about ignoring something like that?* Not going to the authorities? Not helping others avoid becoming slaves. *Why didn't she do anything to help others?* Camila wondered again and again at her uncharacteristic years of selfishness. *I know I'm not a selfish person* she said. But something about living through that. She'd just wanted to get so far away. She'd wanted to pretend it had never happened and didn't want to touch anything that would ever remind me of it ever again. *Maybe that's why I'm here now*, she thought. *Because I didn't do anything to stop it.* The recrimination and guilt were easy to place around her neck, just as the chain Rafael put around her was.

Chapter 53

With clearer heads they were able to lean toward each other and whisper just loud enough not to wake Rafael up at night. Alone without anyone else, they formed a bond of kinship, tentative and a little untrusting, but the only thing that wasn't painful. Julia told her she'd been living in Vegas alone, had no family. At first, she had worked at burger joints, even did a stint in one of those drive-thru marriage joints. But Vegas wasn't kind. Nowhere ever had been. The idea you can make a living wage working low-end jobs is a myth. Eventually her boss cut her hours, she lost her apartment and was staying with friends. She ran out of money and got into dancing at clubs as a last resort. *"Maybe it wasn't a last resort after all"* Julia said. *"Girls like me, who are abused before they can recall. I remember a therapist I had once, telling me we ran the highest risk of going into sex work. Makes sense. What else are we good for?" "I'm sure that's not what your therapist meant when she told you those odds,"* Camila said. *"Well no. But that's what I feel."* Julia replied. *"I kidded myself dancing in a strip joint wouldn't lead to blow-jobs, but that was naïve as fuck. The money was too good and I was alone, nothing else made sense."*

Camila looked at Julia. So small and young and having lived so much already. *"If you are expecting me to judge you for doing what you had to do to survive, well I'm not going to,"* Camila said and she meant it. As a woman she knew how vulnerable you were. It took one bad illness and you could be out on the street no matter where you came from and what background you had. But obviously the harder the background, the more at risk you were. How could that ever be faulted? Who asked for that kind of life? Julia looked at her differently then. Like she knew she had an ally not a judge. She wasn't as defensive and closed, she didn't avoid her eyes. Later on, she told Camila how she'd been picked up and taken to a cheap hotel by a john from the club one night. She'd blacked out, no memory. Woken up here, sometime later and ever since, slave to Rafael's wishes. Julia said at first she tried to escape every chance she got, but he said he'd gotten wise to the escapee tricks and he gave her no outs, and terrible beatings if she stepped out of line. Eventually the pain and isolation wore her down and she began to actually ask for more drugs to dull her consciousness, giving up and growing slack jawed.

The insertion of another female in the house briefly gave Julia hope until she figured out Camila was supposed to replace her. Fortunately, he'd changed his mind for the meantime and though this was little solace, she wasn't looking at immediate extinction. At times though, Julia confided, it didn't matter if he ended her, she was so tired. *"You're too young to be tired of life,"* Camila heard herself saying. *"Like you're much older than me? Anyway, that's hypocritical coming from a suicide attempter,"* Julia retorted, she'd obviously been privy to some of Rafael's words, and knew a little of Camila's former life. It stung. Hearing this from someone she didn't know well. Her privacy violated by Rafael in every way possible. But how long can you hold onto insult, when there's a streak of truth in it?

"I know." Camila said. *"You know how an ex-smoker can be the most adamant about people quitting smoking? That's not hypocrisy, it's learning from your mistakes. I made a mistake, I wanted to die, but I don't now. I want to live and I want us both to live. Trust me, I'm further along the road, if I've got a reason to live, so do you."* Camila badly wanted Julia to not give up, it was enough that she suffered but if she gave up, they had nothing. Right now, the only thing keeping her going was her own fury and she didn't want the light in Julia's eyes to be extinguished. After all, Julia wouldn't even be here if Camila hadn't gotten away from Rafael all those years ago. Unbeknownst, she'd left a monster unleashed.

Despite her extreme youth, Julia had a backbone that she kept hidden when Rafael was around. If he'd seen any strength in her, it would have urged him to cut it down and break it into pieces. Show yourself, reveal your remaining strength and be crushed. Julia knew how to appear pathetic, cowed, destroyed, and that appeased him, causing fewer flying fists to land in her face. When he was gone, the color of her eyes changed, she took on the darkness of the room and she could see fury burn there, urging them to fight back. Alone, they may both have given up. Even with Camila's son's future dangling lost in the world like a torn thread, she might have taken herself out by holding her breath until she was cold and beyond his threats. But together they had more, they had each other. Yes, strangers once. But with every night spent chained in the same room, a familiar. Someone who even without speaking, knew what you were feeling and reached out across the battlefield. The intimacy of the captives, locked in their destruction, considering how he would make a meal of them.

Having someone witness to your extinction binds you tightly together, as captives sharing the same experience will attach to one another with a lasting fierceness, recognizing the shared intolerable agonies of their circumstance. People trapped in an elevator may bond, but those forced into slavery of one kind or another, they become a family of sorts. Forced by disgusting scenarios, to sooth one another, as a way of trading morsels of comfort in order to live through one more day. Camila recalled seeing a documentary about child-sex-rings in Asia and interviews of 12-year-old girls, bound to beds, raped by 30 men daily, all their 'income' kept by their traffickers. At the time it had horrified her, but seemed so remote. Now she knew better, slavery and abuse were in every corner of the world, underneath the surface maybe, but not so very far.

She considered their situation in the same light. They were hostage to a psychopath but he bore many of the same proclivities as sex-traffickers. She wondered if he used some of those underworlds to ensure his survival and get his drugs. Since she'd known Rafael, he had never worked, but he'd always been up to something. She told Julia it would not surprise her if he was involved in trafficking women across state lines, how else did he have access to those films of people being tortured and killed? Rafael was involved somehow – maybe taking the ones he wanted for himself, and giving the rest to others like himself. Julia confirmed this by relating that she had seen evidence of this when she was with him alone. Other girls coming in for two days at a time, a few men coming to pick them up. Hearing people talking and screams, in the adjacent room. *"He kept me because he said I reminded him of you. He kept you because he said you reminded him of his sister, whom he killed. His mother, whom he killed. His first wife, whom he killed. He has a type, we are it. The others are a means to an end or to satiate a passing need to exterminate."*

"He killed some of them too?" Camila asked.

"I think so," Julia replied, *"I saw one girl come in once. Really*

young, still a teen, she was a fighter. That's how I learned not to be, watching what happened to her. She really kicked, bit, and screamed. It pushed him closer to the place he always wants to be, but holds back from, that awful place that crushes life. I heard her fighting him, the noise of their struggle and then it went quiet. Later on that day, he dug a hole out back, I couldn't see from where I was chained but it *was a deep hole and then he covered it. What else could it be? I never saw him take her out, I'm thinking he did her and that's what made me react to him the way I do, because any kind of protest is what awakens the beast within him that urges him to take a life. I had that happen before, with other men. I could smell their violence and I would let them do what they were going to do. Fighting isn't always the way out, believe me."* Despite her youth, Julia looked haggard beneath the dirt on her face. She looked like she'd stared into hell and it had stared back.

Camila thought about that, about how women are taught to fight their aggressors, to learn ways to disable or escape. For many who are attacked, the first instinct is to try to fend off the attacker. But some violent people seek that response to justify their own extreme violence, it is the reaction they long for to justify their end result. Maybe with experience, a woman can tell if it is not worth fighting or if she has a chance. But what are you supposed to do if you don't know what kind of savage has his hands around your neck? If you could escape by fighting, by reasoning, by being passive? Where is the rule book for abuse?

And still the authorities will say; *she did not fight her attacker*; they will judge the survivor as if she didn't do her part sufficiently. As if her choices were real choices and not a series of dead ends with question marks. Camila thought about how little the system understands about the moment of danger, when a decision may mean the difference between life and death, and instincts take over and we act. In that moment, we act without consideration of what we have learned, but with the impulse only to survive and see another day. It comes in many forms, and each one is as valid as the next, the legal system be damned.

Julia was gutsy in a way Camila didn't think she had ever been. Though quiet, she had a strength come from her experiences of living on the street and having to take care of herself, a harder shell and less room for self-pity than most. She told her she'd also tried to commit suicide when she was younger but she'd woken up in a hospital bed, being criticized by an angry nurse, who told her that too many '*useless druggies like yourself*' decide to '*crowd the people's resources with your pathetic cries for help*' and if she decided to do it again, to be sure she succeeded because she didn't want to see her in the ER again. Wasting the doctors time with her pathetic life. Julia said after that, she realized, people's charity and mercy tends to be reserved for the private, high-paying sanatoriums and places the moneyed send their depressed kids. For the street kid, there are only differing hues of the same horror.

Despite her experiences, Julia didn't judge Camila for her own story. *Abuse doesn't come in just one flavor,* she said. Camila told her about her reasons behind the suicide attempt and Rafael's manipulation and Julia nodded, understanding immediately the level to which he'd gone to re-claim his teenage lover. *"What is it about you?"* Julia said, once, *"why does he need you to exist so badly? Anyone else done what you did to him and he'd have ended them, no question, but he almost admires you for it."*

Camila thought about that – not offended by the candor of the question, because it was one she'd asked herself. *"I don't know." "I think I know,"* Julia said, *"I've thought about it and I think he didn't mean to kill his sister. I think his sister was his first love, the one who got away by dying and he's been seeking her ever since."* She paused. *"Because you look like her and you met when you were teenagers, he's been hunting for you and her back ever since. Just like with his sister, one day he won't be able to help himself and he's going to kill you. That's for definite. He's going to kill us both, and then he'll start over again, with someone else, when he finds them. He's never going to stop."*

They were like two scarecrows, at strange angles against their shackles, dirty and ragged, necks bent at awkward degree, uncomfortable always, fitful and filthy in their excrement and piss. Somehow when they talked, it freed them from their circumstance enough to stomp through the despair coming every time they woke and realized anew where they were. Talking to each other became the sustaining bread they ate, the only light in darkness, something tangible and depended upon. Camila feared Rafael would realize this and take Julia away, or worse. She asked herself why he'd allowed her inside. But with the first snows, if he'd wanted to take her outside again, she wouldn't have survived it. She figured he was too high to remember to chain up two girls in two separate places. Easier to have them together. What could they do to him anyway? Chained to separate walls?

Camila remembered taking a class in high school where they talked about *hybristophilia*. She only recalled the name because she used to have a prodigious memory and it sounded like a variation on pedophilia. Her teacher told her hybristophiles were people who were attracted to those who raped, murdered, and were violent. At the time Camila asked her teacher how anyone could ever be attracted to someone like that? *"Think of those women who write letters to prisoners like Ted Bundy and want to marry him,"* her teacher had said. *"I never understood that either,"* Camila replied. *"Why would you be attracted to evil?" "Maybe it's not that you're attracted to evil so much as someone who exhibits evil because you equate it with power? People are turned on by power, power attracts."* Her teacher had responded. But it had always stuck with Camila, the wrongness of such an attraction, that was a profound sickness of spirit to find a rapist or murderer appealing. Now she knew Rafael was aroused by rape and murder, it was as reasoning with a madman.

They tried hard to keep their conversations unknown to him, always at night, never during the day. If Rafael thought one thing in their lives was a solace, he would murder it. It would bring him intense pleasure to strip them of the last bit of humanity. But Rafael figured watching each other, they saw a horrible reflection of their future. It was a worse horror than being alone. He let them stay in the same room – time moved on; seasons changed. A foul routine of subjugation, humiliation, and horror became normal. The only sliver of sustenance was knowing they were together.

With the moon coming in through the bars of their prison they sought each other out and spoke like sisters lying in bed, staring up at the stars, wishing for a future that may never come. Of course, it was an absurdity. Their life was worse than anything any horror film could have portrayed. Julia told Camila about watching horror films as a kid. *"I've seen the best ones. Believe me, nothing is close to this."* She didn't say it with humor. There was no humor, no break in the horror. It was just varying degrees. As much as they say you get used to the intolerable, there are some things nobody gets used to, and torture is one.

"I'm guessin you had a real different life to me growing up Camila," Julia said. *"I get a sense that as sad as growing up made you, you didn't need to fight for your life every day the way I did. Maybe that's why I accept the chains easier."* Julia raised her eyebrow and bit her lip. *"You saying I had less reason to justify being sad?"* Camila asked. *"I'm not saying that,"* Julia replied. *"I'm not saying that at all. I don't own suffering. It's just been my experience; others haven't had the bad I've had, and they aren't as used to it like I am."* Julia's

eyes were resigned, cold, haunted. *"Don't assume others haven't had bad times just because their experiences were different,"* Camila replied. *"We suffer differently that's all. But irrespective, you think because your childhood was horrible that somehow justifies what he's doing to us?"* She felt angry. *"No, not justifies,"* Julia replied. *"I'm just accustomed to bad treatment. That's what I meant."*

"Don't assume my life was perfect before this," Camila said defensively. *"It's not a contest and you wouldn't necessarily win if it were." "I know,"* Julia replied. *"I know … Ah hell, maybe I don't know. Maybe I have a chip on my shoulder about suffering like I gotta own it or somethin. That's all I had for so long, almost like a pride for having survived. But what kind of fucked up pride is that?"* Julia sighed. "*Any survivor should be proud of surviving. It's the one thing we can do and we can do it well. If we survive, and thrive, we beat the odds. Many abused people don't make it, we owe it to them to try to."* Camila said passionately. *"Yeah. I think my allotment for giving a shit ran out a long time ago,"* Julia responded. *"I don't believe that Julia. You can't stop caring because your life sucked and people weren't there for you."* Camila responded. *"You don't know what I went through."* Julia replied. And they didn't say more for a long time after that.

Being near Julia reminded Camila of how as a child she'd wanted a sibling. It was unusual for Hispanic families to have an only-child, but Camila was already too many kids for her parents. She grew up envying the clans around her, the kinds of parents who doted on their kids, siblings who were best friends. It was probably an idealized view of families, looking in from the outside. But spending too much time alone as a kid, Camila knew anything had to be better. Julia and she looked enough alike they could be sisters. It was a pathetic comfort to have her near, even as Camila knew it was a sickened thing too.

It became their habit to talk of ways they might break out

because talking about life before this hurt too much. It felt almost like talking about how you'd spend the winnings of the lottery. A fantasy. Camila held little hope of success given how she'd revealed all her tricks first time around, didn't seem likely that she would ever find a way. *"There is a way,"* Julia said one day, after he'd been especially brutal, forcing himself on her and busting her nose for crying in pain. *"There is one way, and it's really dangerous and has a really small chance but it's the only thing that could work."*

"What?" Camila asked.

"We pretend we're attracted to each other."

"Why would that change anything?" Camila said. *"Because it would give him a new toy."* Julia replied. *"Rafael likes new toys. You know that, you've lived that. Why do you think he let me live? I knew he wanted to end me. But he kept me on for variety. Nothing, nobody is ever enough. And in time, even horror isn't going to be enough. He's always trying for a better fix. Let's give him one. Men love lesbianism. I'm willing to bet he's no different."*

"No that's not going to work." Camila replied wearily. *"I already tried that first time, to try to get him interested, it wasn't successful because he was on to me and I didn't manage to kill him, and now he's clued to it. He won't fall for false attraction. He won't think we're capable of liking each other in these circumstances. We're disgusting, we're raped every day, it's the last thing on our minds. He might be mad but he's not stupid."*

"You're right" Julie said, *"Maybe the last thing on our minds but not on his mind. Remember, sex to him is the life force. You're not alive unless you desire. Why do you think men think so differently to women? Sex even in stress. I had a friend once who would jack off every time he was stressed, he said it was the big stress buster. Sex has a heightened place in Rafael's mind because he's not only a*

sadist he's a sex addict. So, yeah, we pretend we're attracted to each other, out of desperation and fear. Started off clinging to each other then it got sexual, because we're warped and sick, lost and desperate. We make out with each other. We keep doing it until he thinks it is sincere. I know him well enough to know he doesn't like to share his girls; he likes to be in charge. If anyone gets more than one option it will be him not anyone else. He won't like that we have anything pleasurable. We pretend to do it behind his back, that enrages him more; he'll likely beat and rape us but he might also do something else – and if … if he does, we have our one chance."

"You don't think he'll kill one of us for that? I've thought he would kill one of us if he even suspected we got any type of comfort from being near each other, so imagine if we're intimate? It might be the tipping point; he might decide to end one of us then and there. It's too big a risk. It's a bad idea. What might he do beside beat us and rape us?"

"What I'm hoping is that he might want a threesome."

"So freakin what?" Camila said, infuriated and not understanding, *"are you seriously here to get your rocks off, because I don't think either of us are, and that's a really shitty idea."*

"No. No you don't understand!" Julia replied, trying with her manacles to put her hands up in a placating posture. *"That's not it at all. If he decides he wants a threesome, he will have both of us at the same time. That might gross you out but I worked the streets I know it's something johns always seem to like. I reckon he's not so far removed from the typical john, only more disgusting and more depraved, if anything that means he's more likely to do it."*

"He fucks us both at the same time, so what, what does that achieve?"

"BECAUSE when there's two of us, even with chains, and one

of him, we have finally got a chance to overpower him." Julia said.

"Are you serious?" Camila couldn't believe it. What an idiot. *"Julia. You don't know him. You haven't lived with him like I have. You seriously think with us chained to the walls, with little leverage, not even enough to wrap a chain around his damn neck, that we could get the better of him? When he has a knife next to him at all times? No way possible. Rafael will cut both of us to ribbons and mind you, he won't cut our necks. He's said enough times where he would like to put his knife and it's not on my neck. I think in his anger he'd do it even if we did die and bleed out."* Camila replied. *"he's told us he can replace us. Do you really think risking something like that will do anything but increase the likelihood we're not surviving another day?"*

"Maybe, and that's why I said it's a small chance, but it's the only real chance we got." Julia said. *"But Camila, think. You know he's going to lose control and kill one of us soon anyway. We have to do something. You got a better freakin idea?"*

"It's a lousy chance," Camila said, *"it stinks, we got nothing to protect ourselves with, no weapon no plan, what will we use for a weapon? Our bust-up mouths?"*

"No not our mouths Camila, we're going to use our legs." Julia said.

"What do you mean?"

"Well, when he rapes us, he usually keeps our legs chained and just takes us from behind, right?"

"Right."

"What if we're doing it to each other? We need to be between each other's legs, can't do that with the length of chain right? He'll play it out a bit, give us some leverage, maybe.

"Okay …"

"Okay I know that's disgusting but forget the idea of that, it's a means to an end, we're not doing this for pleasure, you ain't ever done worse? I'm talking about the end result. He takes the leg chains off, he still feels safe as we're tied at the hands, we can't do anything."

"Okay, Julia, but we get our legs free. What we going to do? Your knee is bust pretty bad, my ankle has healed enough to stand on but that's it, nothing better than that, I'm always going to have a limp? How do we do this? Yank the goddamn chains out of the wall? Somehow, I don't think so!"

"No, stupid, not that. We use the strength in our thighs not our lower legs, like I said, two of us is stronger than one. At the same time, we pull our thighs over him and around his neck, or near enough and we pull ourselves back as far as possible so if he reaches the knife the thing that gets cut is our legs not our face or neck. We squeeze and we squeeze. He passes out. We get the knife, we stab him, and this time, he dies." Julia smiled and her face looked, in the half light of their small room, almost relieved.

"Great fantasy kill idea." Camila said half meaning it, half thinking of the James Bond film where Pussy Galore kills in a similar fashion *"but even if my thighs are strong enough to strangle someone which I seriously doubt since he cut my Achilles and bashed in your knee, and even if we both can turn into gymnasts and strangle him. He'll have cut an artery before we started. Remember one of them is in your groin area, he probably knows that given the amount of medical shit he knows."*

Camila frowned, and went quiet. *"But … if we can kick the knife away, and then lock him in a head lock, then he's got no weapon but his teeth. He can't reach our thighs if we hold ourselves a certain way, maybe we even break his neck, the two of us trying together?"* She thought about it and the more she did the more it seemed like the one and only possible way they could free themselves. Sometimes there is nothing worse than having no choice except one single, really bad choice. However, having a way, even if the chance of success was miniscule, stirred something in her she thought had died.

She looked at her thighs, they were thinned and hollowed out but the muscle was still there. It had compensated for her bust ankle and grown if anything slightly stronger. She tried to flex her muscle, and pressing them over and over, she forced the muscles in her thigh to contract and hold. She did this again and again, feeling how it firmed the skin with every contraction. Such a small thing but the only thing they had. They worked, each night, each moment they had. Building the fragile sinews of their wasted thighs, into the one weapon they may shape and fasten around him, the one chance they'd have to fight back.

Chapter 54

The only and bad idea took hold and they made plans because there was nothing else. It would have to start slow. Times he'd come in and they'd be nearly touching, trying to touch, one of them crying, the other with soft eyes, giving him that feeling that they are growing close. Afterward, he comes in and they're touching, straining to be close. Then times they're let out of their chains, working the house, he finds them embracing, cuddling, in each other's arms. They knew he would fly into a rage. They knew he would beat them until they could not walk, but this risk might be worth it because what if, as a result of his rage, Rafael also got turned on? They could work with that. Camila had to believe Julia, with her experience of certain types of men, that she knew what she was talking about. It wasn't that she was squeamish about being with a girl. In their current state, that seemed the least of it. She only worried that this would be yet another failed plan and it would be a fatal one. On the other hand, they had nothing else, and time was not on their side.

Days were slow like molasses – the imprisonment of chores and hours spent chained to the wall. Rafael seemed to find a deep satisfaction in having total control over them both. Perhaps he hadn't known what he liked until he got it, Camila thought, as she watched his evil smile as he chained them after they'd finished the morning chores. She stayed inside her head when Julia and her were at risk of being overheard. She remembered her childhood, the snatches of freedom she felt as a young child climbing a hill and looking down on all the world, as it felt back then.

Back then, there was this ever-present idea of freedom in what she would do in the future, that portend of possibility, which seemed lost now. *How easily we are broken*, Camila thought, by the mangle of life and the disregard of others? Then with that break, we fracture even further, at the flick of a wrist. It seemed to Camila she'd always been broken and there had to be something she could harvest from the break that would end the horror of her circumstance. If not for herself, then for Julia and Joe. It wasn't any longer just about herself. She couldn't throw her life away the way she had once longed to do, because others depended on her. Being depended upon felt better than knowing she had no one.

"I was abused by my two brothers for years" Julia eventually told Camila. *"They raped me and I couldn't do anything about it because I was too young. It fucked me up real bad, even with therapy I felt I was responsible for it." "Nobody can be responsible for something like that,"* Camila countered. *"No child asks to be molested or raped. No adult wants that either. It's not the same as sex games, it's not comparable. When someone rapes you, they make that decision and do it, regardless of what you want. That loss of choice is what makes it rape and it can happen whether you are a kid or adult, whether you are awake or asleep. It's easy to say don't blame yourself, but seriously, blaming yourself gives them the power over you, you don't want that do you?"* Camila looked at Julia. She held herself perfectly still, she never cried.

"Yeah. I've heard all of this before. It doesn't change that it happened, nothing will. It changed me and I've spent a lot of time trying to accept it's going to be a part of me and get on with my life irrespective. It's not easy though. I find myself here and it feels like I was heading to this place all of my life." Julia said. *"You haven't asked for this. Neither of us asked for this!"* Camila responded, *"You need to remember that bad things happen not because we want them or bid them, but because others want them. We're part of Rafael's sickness, we don't have it ourselves." "You sure about that Camila?"* Julia said. "*Sometimes I think the only thing I have belonged to is sickness."* She breathed in deeply and didn't say anything else. After a while Camila said *"Julia? Even if that's true. Wouldn't you give your life to get away from it? I know I would. That's what we have to do. At any cost."* Julia stared at her for a while. Then she reached across the distance and they touched fingertips. *"At any cost,"* Julia echoed.

The two of them gradually launched into unfolding their plan. Every day doing what they could to appear to be attracted to the other. It wasn't as hard as it seemed, they did care about each other. They were far less repulsive than he was, and the succor of one another's company had become all important in recent months. Camila couldn't say she didn't need Julia and she knew the younger woman needed her. The first time they kissed she was surprised that she liked it. Albeit she was nervous of feeling a slap across the face from him and she was still demented with the feel of his assaults on her person. But the kiss was innocent. She tried hard to make it seem passionate, that wasn't hard either. It was much easier than faking it with him like she had done years before. *I got away from you once.* Camila thought. *I will get free again.*

The maddening thing was, every time they did things to begin their plot, he didn't happen to catch them. They must have had to do it at least ten times before he caught them, but when he did all the fears they had about punishment, were nothing in comparison to his rage. *"What the fuck are you two doing?"* Rafael screamed, rushing over separating them, totally falling for it, maybe they really were convincing? Maybe he'd had a bad experience with another woman? *"You ingrate sluts! You whores! How dare you!"* He beat them both black and blue, beat them within an inch of consciousness, beat them for the sheer pleasure of beating and then some. Usually, he stopped — because he had some sense and knew he needed them up for working around the house, but this time nothing stopped him.

They lay in a ragged pile, bleeding from so many places, his wrath savage and relentless. He kicked them; Camila was sure she heard a rib bust. He broke Julia's nose, he split her lips, he blackened their eyes. They looked like they had survived a bomb. They had hardly survived; they were the living dead. *"Not such a good idea after all,"* she said, sounding funny even to herself, feeling her teeth wobbly in her mouth, knowing Julia had lost two. Hurting so bad she couldn't even cry because that made it hurt worse.

"You'll see," Julia said in an equally frail voice, *"I know men,"* and then she lost consciousness.

When Rafael hit her, Camila had learned to leave herself and go back into the past and retrieve a moment there that was not as intolerable. She would watch that moment as a film, instead of witnessing her own debasement, it would be the way she coped. She wondered if Julia did the same thing, or switched off her mind altogether. She knew that was how years later, people still carried trauma, by learning to switch it off, and still, it remained, slightly out of reach, a canker that wakes you in the night in a hot sweat. She didn't even have the luxury of being traumatized, she only had this moment, to ready herself for any way to engineer her freedom. Now it had become important that they both survive, not just herself, they were a team. They had grown attachments through the bitterness of their ordeal and she was not going to let him hurt Julia.

A few days later, painkiller free days – Rafael did that deliberately of course – they began to be able to think clearly again. Camila wondered how her poor head would endure with all the beatings, how much it had taken out of them both. They didn't try to touch again because she feared they would be put in separate rooms. Suddenly the plan didn't seem like a good one at all – and she cried silently – opening her wounds on her face with the force of her salty tears. She couldn't bear the idea of Julia being gone. That afternoon Rafael came into the room naked. He stood there reveling in himself. He thought he was irresistible and she didn't have the guts to tell him otherwise. Rafael grinned widely and said, *"okay whores you got me good with this one,"* he laughed and laughed before lifting their heads up so they would have to stare at him.

"You want each other? You sick bitches, I hate that and I fucking love that. I want to see it so bad. I tried not to want to see it but I can't stop thinking about it. Shame on me I'm such a predictable man." He laughed at that. *"I thought I was immune but lesbian sex turns me on, what can I say? I want to see what you got ladies; I'm determined to. I won't let you get away from me and do this behind my back."* He licked his large teeth. "*You're doing it all right but I'm going to be part of it and you want to hear the best bit? I'm going to fuck you both so hard you'll have the worst memories of your sordid little love fest that you can't even imagine. Get ready, goddamn you. I'll give you an hour to clean up your dirty little holes and then I want to see you put on the best goddamn show you got, before I piss all over it, literally and figuratively. Now get to it!*"

Horror films are based on reality, we forget that. We think

horror is an extension of imagination, but as time goes on, our horror worsens. As we learn what else we can do, how far we can go. Back in the sixties, Hitchcock's *Psycho* shocked audiences, the visceral sound of the knife piercing Janet Leigh's stomach. *It was the sound,* they said, *the sound you couldn't get out of your head.* Brian de Palma in the 1980s carried on the genre; tipping his hat to Hitchcock, he employed an electric chain saw. *It was the sound,* they said, *the sound you couldn't get out of your head.*

Come the 2000s, films like *Saw* and its sequels decided to up the ante and go for mock-snuff. *Why make it palatable when you can make it disgusting and repulsive?* Beyond gore, the greatest horror lies in torture. We've always known this, going back to the London Dungeons or the heads mounted on sticks as warning. We say we're not capable of it but within us all, there is a line that can be crossed, you just have to wait your turn, one day you'll know what it'll take to cross over. Become the doer instead of watcher. Surprise yourself at what you're capable of? Completely 'normal' people killed in WW1 and 2. Completely 'normal' people murdered in the name of their country, their race, their religion. It's not so unusual.

A cadre of the human population have always been interested in watching others being tied up and tortured, maybe subtly but enough that those kinds of films have always existed. Be they snuff films or films pretending to be horror rather than torture. Be they hard-core porn exchanged from hand to hand, the market exists and more than you'd think, flock to it. That irony wasn't lost on Camila as she thought of what they were going to do. The chains, the desperation, the man with the hard-on masturbating as they screamed. There has to be something that will work, Camila thought, there has to be a way to end it.

She didn't think she could do to others what they had done to her. Once upon a time she wasn't violent, once upon a time she wasn't vengeful. When ghosts refuse to stay dead, and pain does not release you into oblivion, you are the dog backed into a corner, bearing fangs. You are at your most dangerous then, though the predator does not know this, because the predator has brought you to this place and believes he's just finishing you off. He underestimates you even if he's learned before, not to do that. His ego, his sense of power, they blind him to the corner you find yourself in and he forgets what dogs do when they are backed into a corner. They become the wolf they always were.

Chapter 55

The two of them, like dancers who know the others' moves as well as their own, perhaps borrowed from the electricity of fear and survival impulse, acted as one. As if instead of two separate, virtual strangers, they had eight limbs like a spider. She'd watched the old film *Black Widow* and briefly it struck as humorous through the sick lens of irony (what we think about in the most inappropriate moments?). That they should seek to erase him joining together to blot him out once and for all, an infamous avenging spider, not permitting him to endure. When this is exactly what he did to them. *How things turn*, Camila thought, as Rafael came toward them with his large knife and they fondled each other, with one rolling eye like a skittish deer on the sheen of his blade.

Theory tends to play out smoother than reality, no exception when you haven't practiced your aim. But they both had the urgency of terror nipping at their heels, and maybe the agility of the broken-limbed females they were, disarticulated and savage in their last attempt. There is something about knowing there will be no other chances, that you only have this moment. On the one hand an incredible nervous energy, shaking because failure is signing a death warrant. On the other, the anticipation of fighting to the death. Rafael did not match their energy because he did not believe he was in a fight for his life. He believed he was the man with the large knife and they were the dumb lesbo bitches chained to the wall. I guess he hadn't ever seen that James Bond film after all …

Odd to touch the body of someone you like, for the wrong reasons. Like an actor practicing on someone he will later marry, she touched Julia's thin ribs, her sharp nipples. She knew she shouldn't hold back and be modest, that he would need to be drawn in, that he needed to see enough to entice him further. She began to imitate pleasure, subtly, remembering the last time she tricked him, ensuring she didn't overplay her hand. Julia, the more experienced, bent her neck and kissed Camila's thighs, she ran her tongue across her and Camila moaned. Not falsely but with a pleasure at feeling herself touched so gently. Julia took her in her mouth, she felt herself swell and build, forcing herself to stay sentient of their larger goal. An odd feeling of pleasure and terror, mixed with repulsion at Rafael's presence.

Rafael began to shift about uncomfortably, his breathing rapid. He watched Julia between Camila's legs, intently, touching himself. She moved his hand and replaced it with her own shackled hand, rubbing him hard the way he liked it, feigning her own rising pleasure. She knew she had to remove the feeling and prepare herself. Julia had said when she stopped going down on her and came up and kissed him with her wet mouth, that would be the signal. Julia's head rose from between her legs, she moved to his mouth and kissed him. Roughly, the way he liked being kissed; at first, he probably felt a twinge of suspicion, but his desire urged him on, the smell of Camila on Julia's lips intoxicating him. He kissed Julia back, biting her lips hard, penetrating her with his dirty fingers.

Now.

Julia. Younger and more agile, looped her thin legs around his neck as if urging him to eat her. Her thighs pressing into his cheeks — he seemed to like it, *"so you think you warrant pleasuring from a God, do you?"* Rafael said, and tried to lower his head to touch her with his tongue. Then Camila, lightning fast, a synchronized dancer, threw her legs over Rafael's head too. *"You both want to be pleasured by God?"* he said, laughing, momentarily distracted, until they pressed tighter. His face began to grow red, and first pleasure, then a question, was seen in his eyes, turning them darker than ever, he began to understand, he tried to move, held fast by their double grip, his anger rose, not yet fear though.

He began to protest, tried to bite their thighs, only able to make a muffled gurgle. Fear began to come into his eyes like smoke, Camila rarely saw it there. It was his job to entice and coax out fear in others, not experience it himself. He knew little fear, aside the destruction of himself, he sensed now something was tipping the scales, fear installed itself, he began to thrash wildly. His hands reaching back and seeking his knife that he had put by his side as they coyly asked him to join them in their play, that Julia's long leg had kicked free of reach when he was fully engaged watching them.

They pressed with every muscle they had, straining the fragile thin strength in their groins, a burning sensation, turning righteous. It gave them renewed strength, irrespective of their empty bellies and savaged faces, they worked together as one fist, pressing down on him. Camila was pressing the top of his neck with her legs, her useless arms bound behind her, she put all her energy into pressing as hard as possible. Julie twisted and pushed, flinching every time Rafael tried to bite her. Time slowed and every quartered second seemed an eternity, surely their strength would not last, surely, he would buck their combined weight and find purchase and revenge. But combined, they were heavier. Despite the pain it caused to arch unnaturally toward him, they didn't stop. They pushed with all the pain they had felt at Rafael's hands, all the anger of their humiliation and debasement, straining with quivering muscles, suffocating his muffled screams, turning him purple with rage and lack of oxygen.

Long after he ceased thrashing, they continued to bear down as if giving birth. He was after all, a Devil who had come back from the dead. Dead wasn't enough. Camila thought briefly of the day of her son's birth, of Rafael standing above her, delighting in her agony of the feeling of being ripped open without relief. She recalled the many violations since, and she pressed with every ounce of her resentment and ire. He had failed to die, failed to end, they had to be sure, they had to ensure there was no doubt. With the strength of their fear and nothing else, they squeezed, until something popped like the sound of a sore shoulder being rotated and his head went as limp as a rag doll, hanging at an unnatural angle. It was done, it was finally done, The Devil was undone. The Devil's neck was snapped, his pulse quiet, this final time, he was not coming back.

This did not resolve the issue of their capture, as they were both still bound to the walls by inviolate chains. They removed themselves from their idol embrace of Rafael's neck. They'd resembled an Indian God in their sprawling legs and appendages, but there was nothing Godlike about what they had done. Quenching a Demon was a gory, awful job. They'd had no choice, but killing wasn't a joy. The fact that they weren't relishing the kill separated them both from Rafael. He had lived to maim, torture, and kill. His brutality had not rubbed off on them, no matter how hard he tried to turn them.

They were still chained to their respective walls. Rafael had let the chains out some, but they were attached too heavily to ever pull the chains out of the wall. Camila produced from her mouth a thin piece of wire that she had picked up whilst cleaning the floor with her tongue. *It is amazing what you find on dirty surfaces* she said to herself, as she worked the wire in the locks until they stiffly eased apart. Julia was catching her breath; she had done most of the leg work. A joke they would never laugh over. *I never thought I had the strength*, she said, looking at Rafael's limp body. Both of them were thinking the same thing: Was he going to rise up and reanimate? This man who didn't die? Or would he stay dead?

What you cannot do, says more about your level of effort than it does the impossibility of the task, Camila's teacher had once told her. At the time she had not believed him because she was facing exams, she thought she could never pass — even if she studied for the rest of her life. But when it comes to survival, the saying fit well. They had both exceeded what they were capable of physically because the alternative was unacceptable. In a sense they had both died and been reborn as a warrior within, stepped out and proclaimed ownership.

When you stand on the side of a very bad thing, looking at the debris – when you have stood there before and trauma is repeating trauma on top of old trauma, like a stalagmite of scar tissue – you don't think very much. You certainly don't high-five each other and smile ecstatically and proclaim your freedom, because you have seen enough in the world to know, lying beneath trauma, nobody is free. Despite that, there was a feeling of release if nothing else. They were perfunctory in their endeavor to release themselves from their manacles and chains and set about getting the hell out of their prison. Out of Rafael's prison for them, forever.

This time, before leaving, Camila went back to Rafael's corpse. She knew logically he was dead. His head was at such an unnatural angle nobody, but nobody, could still be alive. *Rafael isn't like everyone else*; she said to Julia. *"He really is The Devil, if not in a Biblical sense, then in every other way. I can't leave him here again."* She sobbed without tears. *"I have to be sure. I need to know we're going to be safe." "Do what you need to do,"* Julia said, but she looked away. Neither of them relished violence. Camila took a deep breath, she stood over Rafael and with one sure movement, she drove the sharp kitchen knife she'd got from the kitchen drawer through his chest. It made a strange sucking sound and then nothing. Silence. Driven nearly to the hilt, to ensure, Rafael would never, never find his way back into their lives. If they could have crushed him to dust, they would have, to blot out any remaining stink of his existence.

There was no point in looking around, seeing if bodies were indeed buried in the garden. They would contact the authorities, they could do it, Camila and Julia's part was over. They needed to get as far away as they could, not stay a moment longer. Like those released from prison walk out, smelling the fresh air, their first dreams tainted by fears of waking up and it all being a bad dream. They needed to escape now, to ensure there was no way of returning. To leave behind the shadows of themselves, chained to the wall, bound to his evil. Bleach themselves clean of his reek and know they had survived him. For Camila, twice. She had been re-captured and finally finished the job.

They stole his car, that probably wasn't his anyway, and dust flew about as they pealed out in search of a long highway and kept on driving until they couldn't go any further. They holed up overnight in the car, sleeping like urchins on one another, with car lights lighting them as they went past the layover. As light came up over the mountains they continued to drive, deciding to return to New Mexico. Julia said she had been picked up in Vegas but had no desire to ever return there, so they were going to stick together. As they drove Julia told Camila that she had so many bad memories of Vegas, she had decided from this moment forth she was going to stop being the person she used to be. *"I'm not the same person any longer. I want to inherit a new future. One that didn't require I eradicate my memories, but choose to survive them." "We're both going to survive,"* Camila replied. This time underneath the trauma that kept shaking her shoulders as she drove, she really believed it.

They held hands as they took turns driving, breaking speed restrictions when the roads were empty, driving carefully when they were full. Their entire bodies were covered with scars, scabs, bruises, welts, they were alive in possession of broken pieces of themselves. It felt like being witness to their own near extinction, impossible to have survived it. When they pulled into Camila's own town to her old house, it seemed surreal. As if no time had passed since Camila had last been living a normal life here and the horrors of the last weeks had not occurred. But that was brief. Soon the terrible certainty that they had been taken up into horror, drove a knife through Camila's chest as she thought of where Joe would be, and all the days she'd spent thinking she and Julia would die.

As she came up to her house, she saw the 'for rental' sign out front and almost lost it. *"Calm down,"* Julia said. *"You've been gone ages, this was inevitable, but we can set things right. We're going to find Joe. We're going to get your life back Camila."* Julia put her hands on Camila's shoulders and forced her to face her. *"Let it out. And then start the car and let's go talk to the police."* Camila screamed. Then she went really quiet. Staring into the sun until she couldn't see anything but brightness. The hot air around her was suffocating but she welcomed it. She turned the key in the ignition, flipped the car around facing back into town, and drove to the police station; reporting everything that had happened to them.

Chapter 56

They stood, both filthy, unwashed, matted hair, blackened mouths, missing teeth, swollen eyed, and let it all come tumbling out, like venom onto the lino floor. Miranda, the bright and compassionate detective who had worked Camila's son's case drove down from Santa Fe that same day. Seeing Camila's and Julia's split lips and bust noses, Miranda bit her own lips in fury, only loosening slightly when they told her what they did to end him. *"Joe is safe Camila. Your son is safe."* Miranda told her. *"He's in foster care, but has only been with one family, he's been here in Albuquerque the entire time, I've called for him to be brought to the station."* Camila screamed. A guttural, primal sound that echoed through the police station. She screamed from the pit of her bruised, beaten stomach. Physical pain meant nothing to her any more. The fear of losing Joe, of never finding him again, of Rafael having lied and killed him, had been a madness awaiting a quiet release. Knowing he was safe, split her apart more than any horror could. It was the release of everything and a wide, inescapable joy. Something she hadn't felt in as long as she could recall. Joe was safe!

Why had Rafael not killed him? *It didn't matter, it didn't matter,* Camila thought. *He's alive and that's all that counts!* But Julia and Miranda wondered the same thing. Both knew Rafael the narcissist was exquisitely capable of killing his own but maybe being his blood stayed Rafael's hand. Put a pause on the inevitable. Maybe it was a trump card Rafael planned on pulling out in the future when he wanted to reintroduce pain. It certainly wasn't decency that made him keep his promise to Camila. Rafael didn't know how to keep a promise if it was the most sacred thing on earth, he relished breaking them. So why had he let Joe go? Nobody was sure. The miracle of his being alive seemed sufficient, although Julia knew, one day they would have to consider these things in light of understanding the psychopath who lurked behind the mask.

Miranda listened to their account of what happened: The women Julia said had come through the house, most likely trafficked as part of a larger conspiracy. Of the girl Julia felt had not made it alive out of the house. Of his connections that he had for drugs. When they got to the part where they suffocated and snapped Rafael's neck, Julia took over and she told the story with dispassion in her eyes. Miranda put her hands on top of both of theirs and saying nothing, spoke volumes in the wetness in her eyes and the shaking of her palm touching them. It was a turning point. There would be no come-back legally, they had survived. Whilst sometimes the law gets it wrong and seeks to blame the survivor for their choice of defense, this was not one of those times. Miranda would ensure they received no query for their actions and that the necessary follow-up concerning the snuff-films of old, the trafficking of women and possibly underage girls, was fully investigated in both Colorado and any other state they found involved.

Finishing the long tedious necessary legalities, Camila was reunited with Joe. He came running up to her as if no time had passed, his honey-colored hair longer and slightly dirty. He didn't cry, he just looked up at his mom, washed clean but by no means undamaged and said, *"Mama, don't leave me again."* Camila tensed and held him as hard as she possibly could, trying not to cry, there would be time for that, but not in front of him. She just wanted to feel his body in her arms, feel his beating heart against her own chest and know there was something Rafael hadn't taken from her. Julia watched them, tears in her own eyes. Miranda left the room, obviously feeling some of what they all felt, being together, surviving Rafael one last time.

Camila signed the papers that put Joe back into her custody, ensuring the state could not take him from her, and that everyone knew this was not a case of neglect or abandonment but an abduction at the hand of his hideous biological father. She had to tell Joe this, she could not keep it secret. That didn't seem right and maybe he had known all along but it didn't matter, he was not his father's child, he was all hers. In his eyes she did not see the terrible dark cloud of smoke rolling through, but the lightness of the sun catching and turning his irises a warm milk chocolate brown, the color of home.

They got Camila's stuff out of storage, went to their old landlord, who was told the story briefly by Miranda by phone and asked to ignore the missing rent. He didn't hesitate, giving them their old keys back. It wasn't like there was a thriving market for those kinds of small low-end houses at the best of time. They re-let their house, seeing no reason to leave a place that had held such joy before Rafael's return. It wasn't there the nightmares came from. It was in the dark heart of a man who lay lifeless somewhere on a mortician's slab, soon to be meal for worms. Going to the storage where the police had kept Camila's belongings, they brought them out in boxes and unpacked their life again, filling in the gaps, touching each other repeatedly as if to affirm their truth and existence once more. The three of them, bashed up, distraught, and damaged, moved back into their life and strung chili lights around the outside, and a very, very expensive alarm system. It felt like Julia had always been part of their life. The trauma hadn't erased the ability to care, it had made them turn toward each other, rather than away.

It turned out Julia had some money in a bank that she could access, and they lived on that until both of them got jobs. She had to go to the bank and prove she was who she said she was, which included getting new ID and everything else, since Rafael had taken everything. For a time, it was a series of proving she was alive, explaining why she didn't have ID. Camila had hers in storage. This wasn't a simple, seamless return to sanity. There were more nights spent shaking and crying than peaceful. They both tried to hide as much of the trauma from Joe as they could. He was still young enough and stable in himself from the years Camila had brought him up right, to feel safe and settled. Kids are resilient, especially if the majority of their memories are positive. Camila and Julia were carrying the weight of their combined trauma around every single day. Only the urgency to give Joe the rest of his childhood without blemish, urged them to keep it together. The longing not to let Rafael have the final word and for everything they'd fought for to fall apart, even with him dead. *"He's not going to get us from the grave."* Julia said. *"We have to thrive in order to keep him dead."* They both agreed, no matter the scars, they weren't going to let this ruin a chance for a future.

Miranda knew a woman who was an ex-cop who now worked with trafficked women. She became a friend and a therapist to them both. Miranda also. Eventually, they talked about what happened, exorcising the horror piece by piece, until the quilt of their experience wasn't as suffocating. Camila knew she'd never be able to regain everything. There were too many scars. Her ankle was bad, but Rafael hadn't cut it all the way through so it had healed and with a surgery she was able to walk with a limp. Julia healed well but both had scars on their skin and in their hearts that would never completely scab over. Some ghosts you live with, because you cannot send them away. It's not ideal, but nothing about surviving that degree of trauma is normal and life as they once knew it, was irrevocably changed. The only thing now was to make with what they had left, the best they knew how. To do that would be to vanquish the desire Rafael had to disfigure everything they knew. It wasn't enough to have survived. They had to try for more.

Camila went back to her quiet, steady, easy unquestioning bookkeeping. Julia began taking night classes to be an Licensed Vocational Nurse, volunteering at the local rape crisis center and getting paid work to answer the crisis hotline. It was a broken thing, repaired and disfigured by its damage, but like the Japanese art of putting broken pottery back together, the repair sustained them in their relief of surviving and destroying him. Rafael, the ghost of their continued nightmares, the Chupacabra on dark corners, the Sandman with malignant intention. He'd come out of nowhere, abducting them, destroying them, even killing them. Stronger in their resurrection they endured, proving that if once you felt like ending your life, if you survive that feeling, you can survive anything, even your own death. Such is the power of a mother; such is the strength of a woman.

Chapter 57

Ten Years Later

Julia was cooking huevos rancheros with borracha beans, her son was out collecting late-season avocados from the trees that they had planted not long after returning. It took five years for an avocado to give fruit and maybe that is how long it took Julia and Camila to realize that their bond went beyond that of survivor and friend and had a lasting edge to it that felt a lot like affection. When you've been brutalized, physically, mentally, it may seem natural to shun any emotion, least of all one where you are vulnerable. It may be impossible to imagine yourself able to be intimate, having survived rape. The brutality of Rafael had wrecked their bodies and the scars were an irrevocable reminder. But the endurance of human beings, despite atrocities, is a real thing. Our ability to exist beyond trauma. It's something you can't even describe; it may not make perfect sense. But the heart and soul wills itself to be heard, even when broken. It is the urge of life. To live!

It was five years to the day they had become more than friends. Ten years since Rafael. A strange anniversary of sorts. Five years since they'd escaped with their lives. On that day Julia told Camila that she was in love with her. Just like that, simple words, a hand on top of another hand. It was the comfort and the terror of opening a box labeled *'feel something despite everything'* and Camila surprised herself by lifting the lid of that box, and pulling out something dusty and forgotten. What she pulled out? That was her own heart, timorous and unused for so long, yet recognizing in echo, her own reciprocated feelings.

They privately wondered if the emotion was one of desperation. That no one except them would take them and that no one else could be trusted to understand. But the first night they spent in the same bed, it became clear that was in no way the case. Julia had been with women before, Camila had not. They both had legacies of rape and sexual abuse, both before Rafael and with Rafael. They had seen each other raped by Rafael. There were images that you might imagine were impossible to erase and replace with something undamaged. And whilst for many years the thought of being intimate with anyone was a repulsion, with time and affection grown in sunlight, and in each other's arms, they only found solace and gentleness. It wasn't desperation but a bond, deeper than underground water, reaching within, tindering feeling. Neither had experienced this in so long since Rafael's brutalization tore notions of gentleness into pieces. Yet there in the arms of each other, lay an impossible perfect feeling of unity.

That first night, Camila recalled the day they killed Rafael, how Julia had touched her between her legs, and she feared that this would trigger an awful repeated feeling if Julia did so again. But change is the one constant. It is thought without time, we could not reconcile many of the losses we endure in life. Time heals. It's imperfect but it has the ability to put distance between the intolerable and the future, if we let it. Maybe living was too great a desire to lose hope. Both of them had so much hope now. In Joe. In each other. And with some time behind them, and the familiarity and built trust of friendship, there grew a deep attachment. When Julia kissed her between her legs, Camila did not go back to that last night in captivity. It was such a sweet and unending pleasure, she surprised herself in how much she felt, how much she was willing to release.

Yes, as Julia's hand crossed the scars on Camila's skin, there was both the electricity of another's touch and a gentle reminder of how those scars were formed. Rafael no longer walked her dreams. She had tried with every month on earth, to erase his stranglehold of her. Since she had first met Rafael as a teen, he'd had that control. She'd left him and he'd manipulated her and found her again. All that she'd been through was worse than anything she could have imagined, and there were days she wanted to block it all out of her mind, forget it all. But Rafael had stolen her memories once, and Camila knew, part of being a mother, meant staying strong for Joe. Part of being a human was surviving and thriving. She wanted this. She wanted her life with Joe and she wanted her life with Julia. For all the triggers there were gradually, new pathways they created together.

They went slow. Nothing was rushed, nothing was assumed. You can make love fiercely and passionately or you can let yourself go in the arms of someone you love. They both sought the slow journey into each other's arms. Wild orgasms were less important than closeness. There was no longing for the kinds of explosive passion that could remind either of them of harm. Love didn't have to be loud to be legitimate. Love didn't need to break beds to be joyful. Their bodies were put back together but never quite whole. Being with each other lent a feeling of wholeness, that neither had experienced in such a long time. It was the resounding full completeness of being together.

When something is right you know it in a way that nothing can really explain fully. Camila didn't question that; life was far too short. Now she knew it could be snatched away overnight, she was going to live fully because she owed that to their son, for surely Julia was as much his mother now as she was by now. Julia was in so many ways the very epitome of her partner. They had endured and worked together to avenge themselves, they walked the same beat, they understood the same things, they finished each other's sentences and found humor in the inappropriate and the badly timed. Because sometimes all you had left – was laughter.

Her son had known before either of them admitted to themselves, there was a connection between them and Joe was relieved to see them no longer sleeping alone in their respective beds, backs to the wall, eyes wide and waiting for someone to switch the light on. He knew more than he let on, even as a child he knew his mom and her friend had survived Hell. All the time they spent together, only endeared Joe to Julia more. And he didn't want her to ever go away now that she was here. She was part of them both now. He had two moms and he liked it that way. He felt their family had finally begun to make sense, and things were shifting into the light now that they had found within the other the succor of damaged hearts, daring to grow again and flourish.

Joe had grown into a man and had his own lady whom he had been dating six months and had brought home to much approval and jaw nodding. He was on the cusp of becoming independent and he felt that when he did leave home, he could do so without a fearful heart that his mother or Julia would be alone, because they had each other. Joe knew nobody really needed to watch over either of them, *they were badass*, as his girlfriend liked to say. But he was their son, and he loved them and he knew, even the warrior has needs. Though they had not told him everything, he knew enough to know he would always watch over them both.

Everything was as unbroken as it was going to be. There were still bad days, days that just seemed to be forged wrongly and provoked the old fears as if no time had passed at all. But that was to be expected, and knowing this helped get through it, for all of them. Joe would sometimes get irrationally afraid of inheriting Rafael's madness, knowing of course who he was. Despite their wishes that he never find out, he had known early on. He remembered seeing his father, the way he'd been suckered into believing him to be a good person, which helped him understand the power he had over others, and also the choices people make. Joe knew he would never, never follow his father's example. In his mind, he didn't have a father, he was born of stars, he liked to say, and two women who watched him on the desert floor.

Julia and Camila. At times it seemed like something gorgeous had been born from Rafael's wrath. Set free long enough to cool on the road and taken off to join the stars. Camila would hold Julia close to her at night, listening to her heartbeat, touching her soft ebony hair, and stroking her sunburnt shoulders. She would think it incredible that miracles could come out of such repulsion. She felt despite all the bad, fortunate to have survived, to have ensured her son survived. In surviving she earned restitution for her suffering in Rafael's death and had done so with Julia, as a team. Julia meant more to her than a partner or a relative. She was the other part of her, the one who had outlived Rafael and gone on to feel joy in ways he would never have tolerated.

She saw herself in her lover, found a way to shave the years of horror away, letting herself enter a place of joy that she never thought in this lifetime she would experience. When she thought back to feeling suicidal, she understood it intellectually and how she had come to round that corner, but she knew she'd been given another chance. Perhaps in some ways she had made her own chance. This time with Julia, never taken for granted, always appreciated for the knowledge that so easily, we can lose it all. Julia was Camila's Isthmus, an island attached to the mainland by a thin stretch of land. Every time Camila felt she was losing touch with the world, she reached for Julia and the roundness of her arms holding her in her surround, brought her back.

Albuquerque has a long tradition of acceptance, and being same-sex did not present any difficulties for either of them. If anything, their world was less lonely than it had been when they walled themselves off from others. In trusting one another they began to let others into their life, and Joe would bring his friends over and they would have dinners and movie nights and watch the stars outside in deckchairs with root beer floats and occasional shots of tequila. Life would never be unblemished but the survivor who stares at the stars having run the gauntlet of hell and returned, will be like the pound dog, the mutt who thanks his new owner every day for his new lease on life.

Camila had never considered what a good relationship would feel like after being broken in her teens. Then during the drugged period with Rafael, she had only half been conscious of her part, before he revealed his demon. Julia was the first person she could trust, could let go with, and explore the inner working of a healthy relationship of two people who know they will not endanger the other. She had always been remote sexually — long before Rafael's abuse. Now she allowed Julia to share her secrecy and open her up to their attachment for one another. She loved Julia's strength and endurance, as much as her vulnerability and honesty. She had found a partner who both supported her and encouraged her to go beyond herself and not hold back waiting, for a do-over. They lived in the now, thinking less and less of the past and more of building a future both had been denied so long.

It may have seemed strange to anyone who knew their story, that two who were tortured together, would wish to stay so close, and become even closer. It might not make sense that they could with a lot of time, find a way back to responding and enjoying intimacy. We have expectations on victimhood and thriving isn't always one of them. But a human's capacity for survival is great, and in Julia and Camila there was a renewal of desire to survive, to do more than survive, to really feel and live. With Rafael dead, the terrible horror of their experience became gradually blunted with the years, and the choice to live without intimacy and love seemed to only give Rafael the final hurrah. Instead, they found with the other, a simpatico and genuine love that denied Rafael's horrific hold over them.

"It wasn't like Patty Hurst, was it?" Julia asked Camila one night after catching something about the cause-celeb on TV.

"The chick who was kidnapped by some radical group back in the day?" Camila responded, vaguely remembering the story.

"Yeah. She was the granddaughter of some famous guy in the media, lots of money. They kidnapped her and she ended up going on their side and agreeing with them."

"That's where Stockholm Syndrome comes from I think," Camila said.

"Wikipedia says that was another case, but it's the same concept and one of the more famous cases." Julia was reading from Wikipedia. *"When a kidnapped victim empathizes with their kidnapper and ends up siding with them, can you imagine? Nothing in this world would have persuaded me to believe in Rafael."* Julia looked like she'd sucked on a lemon.

"Yeah, I guess I can imagine" Camila held the spoon she was stirring pasta sauce with in the air, thinking of the time she rarely let herself think about. *"For a while I think I had that with him. With Rafael."*

"For real?" Julia spun to stare at her from the sofa.

"A bit I guess," she stirred the sauce without looking at it. *"I hated myself Jule. Rafael led me to believe so many things that weren't true. For a while I did see him as some kind of savior, I can't say I didn't."* The sauce began to bubble and she turned it down.

"Urgh and double urgh," Julia muted the TV and looked back at her. *"But that doesn't justify a damn thing he did. To either of us."* She bit her lip. *"Right? He made choices to deny ours. That puts the blame squarely on his shoulders not ours."* She sounded a bit like her therapist, but she wasn't wrong.

"I know." Camila walked over and kissed Julia's soft hair. *"It doesn't."* And she realized that she wasn't just saying it, she really felt it. She really felt she wasn't responsible for what Rafael did. Or what he did to Julia. Those were his decisions. His sickness. He'd played her from the start. Cleverly. And yeah, she'd fallen hook, line, and sinker initially. But anyone would. He was a versed psychopath. A narcissist with unlimited duplicity. The worst part was the guilt and if you let it, it would strangle you as surely as Rafael had. Camila had decided she wasn't going to let Rafael murder her from the grave. And she wasn't going to let him destroy what she and Julia had. *"I know."* She repeated to herself and she meant it. As surely as she meant anything.

Is it ever possible to emerge completely unscathed from torment? Unlikely. But the choices we make when we survive, are beacons in the darkness we carry with us. Choices to determine if we spend the rest of our lives watchful for The Devil lest he come to claim his survivors. Or able to move beyond horror and reclaim a world of balance and growth. Camila knew she'd spent years shutting down prematurely, her sadness too much for her to overcome. Now she had found a way to survive that sadness, not ignoring its existence but claiming life. There were still days she found it hard to get out of bed, but she had reasons that she had built with her own hands, her son, her partner, her life of many years ahead. Sometimes when you see your own ending, you appreciate the opportunity to once more stand and defy that preview, by thriving in spite of everything.

When they lay in bed together, folded in each other's arms, they did not always remember the past violations. Often, they saw only the future, and felt only the fingers of the other, kissing with gentle touching, the parts of them they thought would have died. If you do not die you grow stronger. You kick the beast that tried to consume you, until it is dead and you are the victor. In murdering the fear, it has no power over you anymore and even a brutalized body can recover and find redemption in the purity of truth and the solace of a real lover. Camila recalled the horror of pain and violation, thinking she could never crawl from under that shadow. Julia understood that better than anyone else, and when one of them would find themselves at its mercy, the other would hold on for dear life. Together, they said. They were whole.

Sometimes they would take in a movie, driving in their one vehicle, crowding in, and all grabbing for slices of cooling pizza as they watched the big screen set up in the desert. With the glow of night animals around them and the comfort of the car heater, rattling, it felt like the wide sky was a soft dream. They would cover themselves with the car blanket and let the story on the screen drift comfortably, a feeling of expanse and unbroken space all around them. Freedom from fear. The desert, a limitless land without edges, wild and untamed, bound by secret rules and miracles that urged life through dry dust. They felt as if they had become part of that desert, in the recess of their hearts, a desert rose, crawling from impossible places into the light and breaking open with such beauty and endurance. The desert was the right place to live, it held no dark corners, only a spread of watercolor, and warmth. Always rising and giving way to night chill and renewal. A place where confined souls could unfold their wings and feel the full moon on their skin, renewing and healing their silver scars and broken parts.

But those who say history has a tendency to repeat itself aren't wrong. Like a bad penny that keeps turning up when you thought you'd gotten rid of it; exchanged it, thrown it away. There it is again, in your pocket, soured reminder of doors that you can shut but still have the power to open even if you cannot see their design. One quiet evening the storm gathered her skirts and blew into town, scattering their peace every which way, like ruined pollen.

She came in the guise of The Devil's child. The one they had never known about. Sired before any of them had known of Rafael and his sick endeavors. Born in captivity, outside of time, inheriting Rafael's ire and his sickness, his child came for them on her twenty-first birthday like a dust Devil. She was bidden by ghosts, because her twenty-first birthday was when Rafael's letter to her was opened, along with the deeds to a house and a lot of money. That is where she read about two women *Whores*, who if she was reading this letter, had killed her father and stolen everything. He asked only one thing of his daughter. Hunt them, find them, make them pay.

Chapter 58

Mira, his daughter, had his darkness and none of her mother's light. Her mother had been alive without living, a doll inhabiting a human form, bruised of mind and deed. The young girl had turned to her father, Rafael, the one with the violence in his eyes. She had built him into a great God, a man whose very presence filled her with awe and expectation. She worshipped him as he urged her worship and though neither understood love, their bond was forged from the same desire, to be the greatest. To bend the necks of others, to their will.

Mira grew up talking to no one. At times she felt she could have severed her tongue and dried it in a tin on a shelf, for all the use it had. With her weak mother dead, her father left her with an acquaintance and she brought herself up. She saw her father when he visited, thinking about him when he didn't. During those visits he taught her things she needed to know and told her of the hate he held for them all. The girls who dared to mock him. He told her that she was better than a girl. She carried his blood; she was a God. She might have the misfortune of a vagina, but that was the only bad thing she had. Otherwise, she was all him, all of his strength, all of his ire.

She grew to hate her genitals, the weakness of her sex. She bound her chest so her small breasts were not visible. She wasn't Trans, this wasn't the same at all. Trans know they are meant to be another gender, it feels in their soul the right thing. Like being real with yourself, finally being who you were always meant to be. Mira hadn't wanted to be male because it felt like her real self. She wanted to be male because she wanted to be her father. Trans people wouldn't have related to Mira's reasons, they weren't the same at all, she was her own creature born of hate, not the light-footed helium rainbow children, seeking reconciliation with their anointed selves.

When she was old enough, Mira took a pill that made her menstruation cease, and she pissed standing up, learning to aim so nothing of her reminded her of those weak souls her father talked of. Pathetic weak women like her mother, a whore who betrayed him. Didn't they all? And Rafael's sister, another whore, whom he'd had to expunge, for fear her taint would spread. *"You see child, women are the inferior sex. They're weak. In mind and body"* he said, as they sat drinking beer when she was 13. *"You have to learn to be so hard that you don't need them and they still need you. You have to learn to hurt them and subdue them so they will bend to your will. You see this scar? This scar your aunt gave me when she was only 14. She gave it to me as she was protesting that I took what was mine to take. That is the way of women, they fight you, even when it is your right, they deny it. You must always be stronger, always carve out — from their weak flesh — your own destiny and have them fulfill your needs as if it were their own fate."*

After her womanhood was wrapped and hidden, Mira became Rafael's son. She didn't identify as Trans, in fact she was prejudiced against nearly everyone. She became his son as part of a campaign of hate, not transformation or growth. This was something different, not finding oneself, filled with light, but losing self, and plunging into the mind of a madman. He began referring to her as son, telling her that she had more courage than any of the shriveled specimens of manhood he'd sired in the past. *"I've had sons who were weaker than a woman. It's a horrible thing to find weakness in the bloodline but it's like a cat. There's always going to be a runt. You have to know when to drown them and when to let them live."* Her father said. *"It's who you choose to become. You have my blood; you can become anything. Choose wisely."* He endowed her with a confidence that she was more than those whores he taught to obey him. She had nothing in common with weakness, nothing of her mother, aside her beautiful eyes.

"Son, I will not break you the way I would another," he said. *"Because you are really of me. I can feel it. My DNA, my God's blood. I want you to carry on should I ever be unable to. You will represent me, you will continue the lineage, you hold our blood in your veins. I see myself in your face, in your hardness, more so than anyone else in this world and your obedience pleases me greatly. You will be my future. My true son. You will inherit me."* And after that he showed her how to pleasure him, with her mouth. He told her, this was not because she was a woman, or a girl, or his daughter, or his son, but because he was her God and she needed to worship him. And she did. She worshipped him completely.

It didn't perturb her to masturbate or fellate her father. She liked it. She didn't have the morals of the ordinary. She had the morals of her father's words and her own empty thoughts filling with images of violence and longing to be as powerful as he. She wasn't Trans, she didn't relate to that in any way, she related only to hate, she wanted to be a God. She knew acolytes must learn in their master's footsteps. It brought her enormous pleasure to know she could excite him with her mouth and hands that much. Sometimes Mira would ask why he did not break into her, tear the fragile hymen from her loathsome genitals and remake her in his image.

Rafael said that as her father he could not risk this. Their blood was so powerful should it mix and take life, it would burn them both to death. Mira didn't understand that, and some nights she touched herself wishing it was him touching her. The urges he gave her were never satiated, because he expected her to pleasure him without doing anything in return. Her selfish God lover, she would learn the art of holding back when someone stronger and more than yourself commands you. She worshipped his flesh so slavishly it felt like through her longing of him, she could keep him with her all the time. But he invariably left, for long periods of time, and the ache lay hungry.

When Rafael wasn't visiting, Mira would let local boys fuck her. At first it hurt and felt bad. She wanted their penetrating strength, not her own weak hole. They weren't her father; they didn't fill her mouth like he did. They just jumped inside her like scared frogs, and jumped back out. It was almost not worth it. But they would have to do. Something to sate her growing urges. Filling her up just enough to forgive them their inadequacy. After all they were just boys; stupid ungrown-things without sufficient resource to capture any interest beyond a five-minute tussle behind the playground.

For their part they saw her as an infinite source of pleasure, and practiced their rude unhinged art on her with great enthusiasm. It didn't occur to them that she was using them far more than they her, for they had been brought up to believe a girl was always the weaker sex. How mistaken they were. She hadn't been born in the wrong body, she'd been reborn as a God, she wasn't *just* a girl. Or a hole. When Mira learned how easy it was to end them, with one hard cut to the throat, she executed them. As they lay staring up at her with beseeching confused eyes, she watched their life dribble out from their pants in thin stream as if they were urinating on themselves rather than dying. *That was SO much fun*, she said, touching herself as they cooled.

Mira did not need to tell her father she had begun to practice. He read the newspapers, saw the infrequent deaths, usually ascribed to border violence or *homosexual* encounters gone wrong. She left no sign aside her juice, glistening on their withering parts. Even that, was untraceable as she was, walking away from them and not once looking back at their sad cold eyes. Rafael's pride in her awakening intensified. Sometimes he longed to pin her down and fuck out the violence in her, to harness her quiver for himself, but he stilled his urges and held back because she was a blossoming flower, readying herself to inherit him. He could no more destroy her than himself. *"I have created a mirror image, as if I were a lake birthing a miniature version of myself,"* he thought as he let her mouth roll over him and loosened his pride down her willing throat.

Sometimes people are so irretrievably messed up there is no going back. Social workers and psychiatrists never wish to believe this. They hold out hope, because the alternative would be what? Euthanasia? Permanent incarceration? They have to believe in order to do their jobs, that evil is not born. It is learned. And that once learned, like most things, it can be unlearned. But if you get them on a dark night when they are unable to sleep and they leave their bedrooms with a pain in their chest and drink a large glass of scotch when they really shouldn't. It is often because horrors they witness build up within them, threatening to strangle their preciously held hopes that everyone is redeemable.

In those dark nights, having drunk too much, then they might tell you. They might reveal the truth; that there are a small percentage of human beings, who look like us but are not of us. Something unfathomable that takes solace in darkness and the bringing of pain. They are Monsters and they do exist, even if we tell our kids they don't exist. Even as children, they are capable of killing. Or teens who laugh when someone is tortured, and join in. Adults who murder with a bored eye and a lusty soul. Those who haunt the recesses of therapist's minds. Those who are irredeemable. Nothing and no one, be it medication, therapy, or punishment, can reach their darkness and pluck it out of them. They are damned and it is of their own desire.

Therapists who have been in a room with such a creature, will remain calm but the creature will see the uptick in their beat at their throat and idly wish to tear it out and scatter it into a spray of life blood. The therapist will feel this urge, as keenly as a patient who desires them. They will wish to run screaming from the room, deadlocking the door, yelling at everyone to run. But we are pragmatists, and endlessly polite. We have ingrained social convention that absolves the natural urge to react. We work hard at underreacting, at smoothing over the bumpy lines of our nightmares and worst-case scenarios. Denying until we can no longer deny – that the monster sitting opposite us, is fantasizing about eating us.

Mira had attended a bad school where she didn't have to worry about close observation or kindly teachers worrying why she *wasn't right*. It is incredible how you can walk through life heavily damaged and just because you deny it, others, who are perhaps more willing for the lie than the truth, nod their heads in relief and pat you on the head. *There, there, good girl, go to class, do well.* She did do well *enough*. She was clever enough and *enough* is always sufficient to help the hider escape scrutiny. It is the one who cries out in the open, the one who beats to a pulp their tormentor, who is hauled away and paid attention to. The quiet ones who put their heads down and do what is asked of them? Even as they dream of turning the tables and making meal of you? Those are the ones harder to recall, most often ignored and let to roam in their extracurricular pleasures.

If you asked anyone what they remembered of her, they would say; *"Mira was a quiet girl."* Studious, well behaved, clean dressed, presentable. immemorable. They would have no cause for concern, no history of apparent neglect. She could be being banged by her father at home night and day and as long as she wore the proper smile she'd skate through. And so, she did. Sliding right through the requirements of her ages, until released and free from the tedium of learning what others already know, she left her books and pens in her locker and walked out, never looking back on the life she had only been passing through.

Now was the time. Nobody was going to come looking for a truant child because she had outgrown them and her destiny with her father could begin. They would hunt together, like the pack they were, the wolves who ran with other wolves, in a world of stupid sheep. She could hardly wait, and even if he would not grace her insides with his organ, she could work on that. Convince him that they were true partners. Nobody would make a better partner, it was her, her all along, the fruit of his loins, longing to return to them. A time where they could both kill without looking over their shoulder because they'd always be there for one another. Partners in destroying whatever they wanted to take. Devils.

But they never hunted together. It never happened because Mira's father was murdered. Rafael had talked once about how he nearly died when she was younger. Some bitch setting fire to his house, and escaping. He told her how he would track her down, but give her long enough to think herself free of him. He told his daughter that should anything like that ever happen again, she would know where to look and he left an envelope for her with the names and the details of those who had betrayed him. *"You must take over where I left off,"* he said, smiling into the sun because he felt then that he would never die. Never. This was idle talk and soon they would join together, and wreck together, the stillness of being. Mira promised him and he knew she meant it. Then he gave her what she had always asked for. A piece of him, growing in her womb. Perhaps deformed by the power of their entwined blood, but his gift to her. For her loyalty and her strength.

Mira did not know what love was, because as far as she knew, there were only two things in life worth noting: kill or be killed. Rafael had taught her that. He had shown her the fallacy of trust and gentleness, he had proved that honesty hurt and obedience trumped choice. She had a road, he said. A road to follow and anything else didn't matter. She was put here for a reason, she was his blood and his energy, and she inherited his rage with every molecule of her being. Truly, everyone else seemed weak and needy and she was without such qualms. When her father came to her and they saw each other face to face. He laid her down and opened her legs and eased himself inside her, she cried for the first time in her life since she was a little child. She cried from joy and pleasure, because the man who taught her not to love, was the only person in the world she did love. She knew that now, with every thrust he made, glad for his violence and violation like the Hindu bride of old, who climbs into her husband's fiery grave and burns with him.

That night Mira lay in his arms, feeling his energy coursing through her insides, knowing life was beginning to climb up within her. It was their destiny, they didn't have to say it, that's why they held off for so long. They knew it would only take one attempt — one union and she would carry his child. Her brother and her son. His son. From his daughter. *"The most natural thing in the world,"* he said. And because of that, it would not be deformed as she feared. Rafael had only held back to ensure she grew without needing him too much. Now that she had proven herself and come of age, she could be the place he laid himself, but she must never want that too much or he would need to extinguish that need and it would hurt. It would hurt a lot if he had to do that, so she must be mindful and obey him the way a good daughter would and she would become every part of him and gain his fire.

Mira's urges might even have surpassed her father's. Because of her youth she had the vigor and energy he once possessed and she lusted for him every morning, every night, and many times in between. Though she carried their child, she wanted him to break her apart. Being with her father, it felt more natural and right than anything she'd ever felt and she had to bite herself to keep from saying out loud how much she loved him and crying for him to say it back. He never did, because he was no more capable of love than a jackal spares the kin of another jackal, foolish enough to leave the den. Rafael would eat her whole if he let his true nature take over, he would fuck her until she died. He had to control those urges, if he didn't hold back and see a larger picture, forming through their union. At times his hate for all the world encompassed her, but she was part of his plan and as such, that hate was damped down by his self-control and his greater urge for spreading violence.

Though she tried to never fall into her idea of errors of womanhood and show weakness, vulnerability, fragility, emotion, Mira could not cover her gender when he lay her open and made her bleed with his sword. She was despite herself, still a woman. She knew he found her hole a disgusting place to lose himself, so she began to turn with every day, more and more like the man she longed to be. Not the way someone who is born Trans longs to become the person they always were, but through a series of twists and turns so sharp and brutal, she couldn't see herself, she only saw her father. Her body was slim, she always wore man's clothes. She kept her hair short; her breasts were hardly grown. She shaved her pubic hair and wore no makeup. She was very beautiful and she was without gender, except her betraying hole, getting wet every time her father got out of bed and walked to take a piss, mocking her.

Then she was just another Whore, like all the others. Wet and pathetic with her desire, she would spread her legs so wide that he had to look and he had to be lured. She knew it was a hateful thing and still she could not stop her lust, dripping from her onto the sheets and washing her with the obvious urges of his Whore. Weakening her, making her nothing more than the Whores he placed his hands around and squeezed until they turned mauve like the moon in Autumn. Oh God she wanted to be more than that, not to be trapped by her gender into weakness and Whoredom. It wasn't about transforming into the gender she felt right, it was about destroying the gender she was. She wanted to be his equal. She wanted to be his son.

One day, painfully aware she shared their loathed gender, Mira asked him what he would do to her if she were a boy. He stopped momentarily in his thrust and placing his hands on her hips looked at her with blackened eyes before turning her over onto her stomach and arching her toward him. He said, *"Once upon a time I was a boy who was fucked like a girl and I was the bitch to my possessor. The only way I gained my freedom was to learn from his strength. Do you want to learn from my strength? Do you want to change your gender as I did and stop being fucked like a little girl?"*

"Yes, I want to change my gender, show me how, show me." She

said. And Rafael reached within Mira, with his wet hands, and thrust his hardness between her buttocks until she screamed the high wail of a girl. Again and again, he thrust until she felt the hot blood of her insides land on her thighs and she heard herself screaming over and over and over, until she quieted and did not scream any more, learning through the intense pain to bite her lips and take each grind and thrust, leaning into the agony like childbirth. She gave him back what he broke into her, and they swung back and forth, like they were joined together, and he filled her sore insides with his rage and she took it in and it was good.

"Now you are my son in all ways," he said, twisting everything, deforming meaning. *"From here on out, I will never treat you like a bitch again. You have become a man, Mira and as a man, you will take your own bitches and we will ride them together, as stallions."* She didn't want him to stop doing her. She didn't want to have someone else, but she knew, that was his command, and she was his to command. Her worship of her father and his glistening phallus was the only prayer she made before going to sleep. She wanted to be more than his lover, she wanted to become her father, to inherit his violence and crush the world beneath her.

That night they found two drunk women in the local gay bars. Bi-curious and far too deep into their alcohol to care about much, they liked the idea of a dykey looking girl and her handsome older male friend. A four-some with cocaine and promises of ecstasy? Oh, sure they were well up for that. Coming back to a hotel, the out of the way last room next to a row of empties, sufficient to choke the screams out into the desert wind and away from living things, Rafael showed Mira how to destroy a woman and his obedient daughter followed him, step by step, peeling away their layers, their trust, their hope.

Mira found herself even more excited than her father's organ inside of her. The feeling of power, dominating the weak bitch beneath her. With her flaccid tits and her elongated hole, hurting her in ways she knew how bad it hurt. Then going beyond — to places where her eyes rolled up out of her head and her breathing got real shallow. Taking her to the edge of death and back again, waking her up and doing it all over. As she broke every bone with her lust, truly satiated, truly in control. She watched her father do the exact same thing in the bed next to her, closer to him now as a man, than ever she had been as a weak, stinking girl.

She wished only that she had the knife of a phallus. To spear the bitch beneath her, but even that, he showed her, can be accomplished. "*Nothing is forbidden to us Son,*" he said as he punched the girl beneath him. "*We are Gods. We are The Devil. We're fallen so far; we own the god-damn soul of the earth.*" She strapped on the dildo he handed her, feeling the leather bite her butt cheeks and she rode the dying girl. Feeling every bit of her penetrating and pain, until she climaxed in all ways, a true boy, her father's son, his pride and joy.

Chapter 59

After they killed together everything was set. He had to go back to deal with things, he said, but he would be back, and they would be together. Mira was to wait and earn money in his absence, learn and not draw attention to herself. Rafael had always been gone. He had a life somewhere else she knew, where he kept his collection of dolls, and he would show her one day but she had to earn it. Until then she was to wait and he was to return and touch his dolls and she was not to be envious because those were rights you earned, not rights you automatically inherit. She understood and she was good. As she waited, she thought of all the things they would do together and she touched herself pretending it was him, and thought of the moment the girl she took died, and how it felt to see her die and listen to her just as she crossed over, before her bowels gave out and the room rose in heady stink.

But her father never returned. That was when her father was destroyed. Rafael's plan, his ambitious plans, all gone, with his untimely shocking death. Mira had become Miro by then. She had become He. He never knew all the details but he filled in the blanks. Rafael had some whore at his house, she was there for his bidding, but then he'd found his old whore. The one who got away. Miro's father had kidnapped the Whore's son who was Rafael's son also and Miro's brother, ensuring the old Whore would come with him. "*You will meet them both,*" Rafael had said to Miro, "*because we will kill them together before leaving and going on with our voyage. But give me time to enjoy them first, I have history to wrap up first, grudges to settle. This must be in my time.*"

And Miro understood, but Rafael was wrong. Rafael had forgotten the first rule, never let your guard down and somehow, he had. Again, with that same Whore who had tricked him the time before. What was it about that woman? All the others so obvious, so weak, they had no chance against his father and his magnificent sadism, but she? The woman Camila. She was power, even though she was only a woman she had power over Rafael. He never explained it, didn't even realize it, but Miro could tell. The risks he took, the planning, as if obsessed by her. The echo of his sister whom he had been so besotted by.

Miro heard of his father's death. Strangled, stabbed. There had been two of them. Gone, no trail. And Miro opened the envelope and read what his father had written and then he packed his meager belongings and said goodbye to no one and left that same day. But all the addresses were outdated and all of the people had changed their names and Rafael hadn't taught him to know how to find people well enough, so he knew this was all wrong and premature and not how it was supposed to be. He lost his courage and his direction and began to spend his money on drink and sat at bars fantasizing about what he would do. Sitting there noticing how women weren't sure if he was one of them transitioning or a good-looking boy. Yet somehow, they would go with him, and somehow, they would end up lifeless and he was practicing on them, for the time he found those two who had taken his father from him.

If you really want to kill someone, it is said, it's not that hard. Perseverance is the only thing you really need. Nobody can hide forever. So it passed — that Miro found them, and he found the honey-haired boy Joe, who was his father's son and Miro's own brother. He saw as he watched, and was disgusted at his brother's light chocolate-colored feminine eyes and soft gait. He understood why his father hated his other son and why Joe too, would need to die. He waited as patiently as the fox that spies the rabbit, learns where the burrow lies and stays still for days on end waiting for the perfect time, the most unexpected moment. And he learned that the two women his father had captured before his death, were lovers and a plan hatched in his head, a plan that would hurt everyone all the more, which was most certainly the point.

Yes, this was good. This was not going to bring Miro's father back but it would be the first in a long line of homages he paid. Each homage, each murder, growing closer and closer to becoming his father entirely. He had a lot of money. He went to a surgeon that he had heard of that did things for money and didn't mind ethical issues. He told the doctor he wanted him to get rid of his stinking vagina, his loathed hole. He was a man. He didn't want to be a girl anyway. He was already transformed within himself now, he needed the last piece removed. Miro needed to be his father; he needed to have all of his power.

The surgeon who was a bad person who liked other bad people, took his money and built him a male organ. Not as long and wide as Miro's father's, not able to get quite as hard or as splendidly savage, but a functioning male organ. The doctor saved Miro's burgeoning womb that bore the growing seed of his father. The doctor replaced Miro's birth canal with a carefully carved phallus, glistening and violent. The surgery hurt as badly as when his father blessed him and called him his son for the first time. Miro was so happy he cried again, wiping away the tears with the back of his hand knowing that boys – boys and men, Miro, the daughter who became son – don't cry.

The bad doctor told Miro when the baby became full term he would be cut out of his abdomen. "You do realize it looks pretty weird to be a man carrying a child, right? You're going to stand out." The doctor warned. Miro had thought of that and had a long wig. Until the birth, Miro would be a pregnant woman with a phallus and a baby swelling in his thin, muscular stomach. An oddity that walked mostly at night, disguising his growing stomach with flannel shirts and layers, easy to do when thin and elastic. When people never suspect a man who is also a mother, of such strange nature.

Equipped with every asset of his father, Miro was tall and lean, muscular with perfect vision and strong forearms. He worked out every day in any gym he could find, be it hotel or climbing into apartment complexes and using their shared gyms. He was so strong of body and mind; he could hear his father's voice in his head and soon he understood. It was not just a memory of his father; it was his father. Talking to him through Miro's manhood, through the slow urge in his groins, growing stronger every day, gaining ground, learning how to be every bit his father's son.

At night lying alone in bed, Miro felt the hardness of his duality as man and woman. His child growing within him. The man and his male organ, on the outside, protecting and savage. She and he would bite one another's tails in a fluid snake claiming both genders. The child would turn in his belly, his new male organ would grow taut against his thigh and he would touch himself thinking of his father. Believing within him, his father lay, an acorn, bearing life, without and within, channeling himself through his power to defeat death, holding their child in a watery dream.

When the son Joe who had been his father's great mistake met Miro, he didn't know he was once a she. She had transformed so completely and Miro's child was layered beneath him in swaddle and secret. Miro was older than the failed honey-haired son Joe. His weak brother. The weak son of the murderess who had infected Rafael, taken out the quota that was Rafael and left a thin facsimile that Miro despised and ridiculed behind polite smile. Miro befriended him, becoming a familiar face at the local gym months before the abduction. Joe did not notice he always wore a baggy hoodie to hide his belly. Did not notice that when he changed, he did so without showering and showing his torso and chest.

They talked like guys do, in the bar afterward, and sometimes met on weekends to go skeet shooting. Joe, the weak son found something familiar and likeable about the young man he'd met. Liked how he was a little older, a little wiser, able to show him around notions of manhood in a way his two mothers were unable to. He didn't mention him to his parents, because there seemed no need. They met through the gym, they hung out sometimes, his girlfriend knew, everything was okay, everything was right. Until it wasn't.

Chapter 60

Miro had a beauty about him that reminded Joe of a girl, he seemed a little metrosexual and Joe guessed he might be gay, and felt nothing but protectiveness for the delicate boy with startling dark eyes and a mop of curly hair. Miro was a buddy, someone to hang with, but Joe could not open up and share what he and his family had gone through. That was a conversation he avoided altogether except with his girlfriend when they had first become intimate and she held him afterward as he cried and sobbed and revealed why he held back so many tears. He was guarded with others, enough to protect himself, but still he enjoyed the company of someone near his own age to have a drink with. It wasn't easy to find people who didn't ask lots of questions, Miro rarely did. He was careful what he said, and they talked easily like they'd known each other for some years.

The baby did not show enough to slow Miro down. He was agile as ever, strong and unrestrained. One day he went out for a coffee, meeting Joe and sharing the crossword of the day, over a latte, watching Joe drive off, light and easy, as if nothing in the world was bad. Then calm with an even pulse and soft walk, he went to the house where he knew Julia would be alone and knocked on the door. When Julia opened it, with a smile on her face, thinking Miro was a young effeminate boy, he punched her in the face with his fist. He hit her so hard she fell immediately, senseless, on the floor and he pulled her up by her long dark hair and stuffed her in the back of his waiting car, like she was a bag of dirt, and drove off. It took all of three minutes, in the middle of the day, with children playing in the street. Simply driving up to the side of the house and taking her, like one would a piece of chicken with fries and a coke. His father had taught him well.

His father Rafael The Devil said Miro's path would be natural though not easy. Taking the Whore Julia was a cakewalk. Carrying his father's seed, was an honor, having his father's gender attached to him in homage and re-birth, a pleasure he used nightly. As he drove away from their house, no sign of Julia having opened a door and been dragged out. The house exactly as it was, minus one person, he laughed and laughed and laughed. Seeing her flaccid unconscious arm, fallen out of the back blanket, he resisted an urge to pull over and bite her. Such was his mounting hunger to act, to carry on, to roll his terrible legacy down the mountain and crush the entire world with his violence.

When Julia was taken. When she was not home when Camila arrived. When the oven was on, and the food was burnt and the smell told her she was suddenly gone. Then she called Joe and he rushed over and they both felt the same as they had before. Reduced to ash like dinner, burnt in ways that calcified and burned beyond bone. *But it was impossible* Camila and Joe reasoned. Both women had stabbed him, they had killed him, *dead, dead, dead.* Could he have come back to life like he had survived before? Was that possible? Yet here the truth lay, like a gaping wound, or a maw of disfigured joy, Julia was gone.

Joe and Camila sat at the kitchen table with their palms

down on the wood, and didn't say a word. There was nothing to understand, everything was impossible. *Who? How? Why?* How could someone have done this? What malignancy still existed after him? Was it a curse that would never end, the flapping of butterfly wings, marking the ages, existing in chaos throughout time? Camila's son told her; the only rational explanation was that Rafael had had an accomplice. Camila thought back to what she knew of him, like delving into a box of tar, she felt dirty and her mouth filled with blackness at the thought of him. But she sat and thought, of everything he had ever said to her, everything she had ever known. It was like diving into a lake of insect parts, and swallowing them as you drowned to find a key at the bottom.

The office in the house by the lake, the one that had been locked and then opened to display without shame, his proclivity and his perversion. Sometimes he'd brought her in and forced her to watch disgusting pornographic exploitation films whilst he enacted upon her, his own response. Whilst he raped her, with unceasing enthusiasm, she tried not to cry out, and instead distracted herself by looking at the other things he had in the room. Taking herself out of the situation by focusing on things around her, was a coping method she'd used nearly every time and she still recalled what she'd seen.

Rows of books of pornography, and then photographs. So many photographs of women, some who looked dead, in leather bound journals with plastic inserts. Prior victims? Snuff pin-ups? She never asked him and then she thought she killed him and she couldn't bring them back, if she had indeed ever been in a position to help them. They predated her most likely — they were already in watery graves by the time Camila saw them. Yet she had taken the book when she burned the house down. It was the only thing of his she had taken. Not the videos but at least this, and she had put it in a lock box and put the lock box in a storage facility and she still had it.

They both raced to Camila's storage facility. The storage unit had survived her second abduction unscathed, as if denying that such a thing could have happened. It held things from her past, her recent past, and accumulated objects that she felt Joe might one day need. It was a very small unit, inexpensive and rent controlled, she paid up a year in advance, and had one set of keys that she kept and the number in her head. When she'd returned from killing Rafael, she'd briefly thought of getting rid of the book of snuffed pin-ups, but something made her stay her hand and keep it there, though she never went there and looked at it, in all the years since.

They opened the storage and there was the lock box, they drove home, not speaking and laid the albums out on the table. *"This is going to be very disturbing,"* she told her son, *"But it's the only clue I possess. I found this in the lake house. It was Rafael's album collection, I don't know who the women are, but maybe there is something in here. I haven't ever looked all the way through it. Back then I just took these, maybe as proof, the only proof, of what he did, thinking he was dead. Then when he wasn't dead and we killed him for real, I thought about throwing them away but something stopped me. I suppose it was this moment, this moment right now. Maybe I always thought it could happen, maybe I held on to these because I knew, we'd never be rid of him. If there is anything, anything at all connected to him, it will be here."*

"Didn't you show this to Miranda when you went to the police with Julia after you escaped?" Joe asked his mom. *"I didn't."* Camila replied. *"By then years had gone by. Remember, I took this book when Rafael first abducted me. When Julia and I escaped, I thought only of what we'd done then. I didn't think about this album." "But mom, it's so important"* Joe said. *"Miranda could have used this to track down the missing girls Rafael killed!" "I know that Joe,"*

Camila said wearily. *"Don't you think I know?"* She sighed deeply. *"Believe me. I know I fucked up. I do. I just didn't think about it. I had so much else to think about, it wasn't something that came into my thoughts. I realize I failed them. Now I've failed Julia too!"* Camila bent her head at the table and wept. Joe put his arms around his mom and comforted her. *"No mom. You didn't. You survived. I'm sorry. I'm sorry."*

After a while, they took an album each, and began. They were filled with the depraved repulsion of a man driven to extinguish women. Joe's biological father. The man who had abducted Camila twice. How had this level of violence and depravity begun? The first picture, in Rafael's album was of his sister. Camila only knew this by the striking resemblance to Rafael and to herself. It was awful to see someone who looked so alike, and yet, this was her, this was the beginning. This wasn't a pin-up book, this was a kill book. A list of everyone he'd ever erased. Next were Rafael's parents. The same picture of his mother and his sister together, a distant shot of his father with a label stating 'father' at the bottom. Then some people she didn't recognize, some of them children, some just flyers of missing pets.

As Rafael grew up, his murders grew up. Soon he was ending young women in their late teens and early twenties. So many faces. The whole book filled with faces, sharing a common look as if an entire swath of DNA were being extinguished. How did he get pictures? Some of them were dead, he took them himself afterward? Others were graduation pictures, happy smiling faces, he knew where they went to school? Ordered copies? Photos of missing women from newspapers. Pictures from missing posters. Anything to keep a record of his prideful history of slaughter.

Camila felt the guilt and relief of the survivor, a stupid, sick feeling in her stomach. The ability to have survived him twice, when so many of these women had never made it a quarter of the distance, through no fault of their own. What had stayed his hand with her? Kept her alive long enough to escape twice? How had she prevented her own death to become his concubine? What selected his mate? Wasn't it a disgusting thought to imagine there was something within her that drew him to her and made him want to live with her, have a child by her, rather than kill her? Something about that, made Camila feel complicit, somehow guilty of his crimes by having been selected for more than a quick death. No slice across the throat for her, or knife between the legs. She was groomed, kept in a box, she bore his child, she was his blood bride.

It made Camila wonder at her own existence. Was there something bad within her that he recognized? Would Joe eventually inherit it somehow after all? How could she ever remove the stink of him from her memories? Yet she would never do anything to touch her memories again. That is what Rafael had done, he had removed them and left her blank. Maybe that is why he allowed her to live, maybe her trying to kill herself was the key to unlocking why he chose her over all the other faces? The many, many women who were cut down by his urge to destroy. They could not speak; she was the only one who could avenge them. Maybe just because she looked like his sister, he had let her live and she had escaped.

"What's in your book?" She said to her son, who had maintained a total silence as he flicked through the pages. *"I shouldn't have let you see,"* she said, reaching for the book. *"Mom I've experienced worse, you know that. I know what you and mama Julie went through, I'm part of this. I'm invested in this whether you like this or not, we're doing this together, you're not doing this alone anymore."* Camila pushed her chair closer to him so they could read the book together. It began with a baby, a little, little baby who looked premature. A beautiful girl baby with a shock of black curls. The

next picture was of a woman. The baby's mother? Holding the baby, trying to smile for the camera. Holding two babies. The same age. Identical. She knew that smile, she knew that room, it was the room she gave birth to her son in. It was the same room and the same scenario.

"I know this woman." she said, *"that's his wife Carol, the woman before me, who Rafael killed."*

"Who are they?" Joe pointed to the infants. Camila was silent. *"Didn't he have a son with that woman, and didn't that son die?"*

"Yes." she said, and a cold streak ran down her back, *"I thought he did."* She swallowed. *"But it looks like he didn't just have Jacob. He had two babies."* She thought she was going to throw up.

Two babies. *Twins*. One kept home. One farmed out. Insurance.

The farmed-out girl, Mira become Miro. Spitting image of her father.

The other twin, Jacob. He was perceived as weak like the mother. Fodder for Rafael's murderous lusts, destined to be destroyed, no weakness permitted. Maybe Carol never knew they both survived. Maybe Rafael told her one of her twins had died. She'd given birth in the house. Camila knew how harrowing that was. Neither baby would have had any prenatal care. Carol was presumably heavily drugged. She may have thought one of the twins died. Rafael's classic manipulating hand. One he took, far away, to be raised by unknowns.

The next picture, the girl again, a little older, a savage smile on her face, she was holding a kitten but the kitten wasn't alive. She was laughing as if that gave her a lot of pleasure, as if she were the one who had … (*Daddy, I wrung its pretty little neck until it was dead*).

"Oh God, it's his daughter," Camila said.

"*No.*" Joe said, his face a sickly shade, whitening as he turned the page and looked at a picture of the same girl, grown up, 15 or so, *"No mom, it's not his daughter anymore. It's his son."*

Chapter 61

Joe explained that he'd met a boy called Miro a few years his senior, at the gym, and that they went out for beers sometimes, a few skeet shoots. *"It's her."* He said. *"They've either had gender-reassignment or they're pretending to be a man. But it's not about being Trans, I have a ton of Trans friends, I know this isn't what's going on here. I'm going to say they've had surgery because they've got muscles, they're not a girl anymore but it isn't because they were born in the wrong body, this is something else. I know them mom. Those photos are old, and they look a lot different now, but they're the same person. I know who has taken Julia! Miro got to know me, I wasn't suspicious, but I'm 100 percent certain that's the other twin. OMG how could I not have noticed the similarity between them and Rafael? But this isn't a Trans person mom, this is something bad."*

He stared at the photo of Rafael's daughter who was now son. Joe's face as pale as Camila had ever seen it. They sat there at the table, staring at the last photo in the book, a picture of Miro around 18. Tall and lean. Could easily be assumed to be a young male, with their strong chin and thick short hair. They were so like their father, and also not, because they'd done things to change themselves, things that made them look uncertain. Like shifting between two bodies and back again. His son who had been his daughter. "*They've come to avenge him,*" Joe said. "*Now they've got Julia.*"

Camila knew she should scream, but what was the good? How many unanswered screams went daily into the universe, imploring the silent Gods for mercy? Did anyone listen? Even if they did, was it within their power or pleasure to intervene? If one person prays and a person is saved, does that mean their prayer was granted, whilst millions more were not? Or is it simply a numbers game? One day your number is up, another day you might have got a pass. Do humans struggle with the notion of everything being random, without intelligent design? Or do they struggle against the idea of fate and the inexplicable choices fate has. Do we choose or is it random?

Neither outcome appears to satiate the screamer, who, into the void, asks the question we all ask at times. *Why? Why this person? Why now?* Maybe we should be asking *Why not?* Maybe we are asking questions into the void and nobody listens. Maybe we need to stand up and make change, if we want to see it. Praying for change is like steering a boat by hope alone, sometimes the storm needs a captain at the helm, to watch out into the roaring seas for the lighthouse.

It reminded Camila of a joke her grandmother used to tell. A man goes to Heaven. He says: *God I was sitting on top of my house, the flood was rising, I prayed to you and begged you to help me.* God said: *Did you see that boat that went past? I did*, said the man: *I told the people in the boat I didn't need help, I was praying to God, he would help me.* God said: *Did you see that helicopter that buzzed overhead?* The man said: *Yes, I did, I told the people in the helicopter I didn't need help, I was praying to God and he would help me. So why didn't you help me God?* Said the man, weeping at the doors of Heaven. God replied: *I sent a boat; I sent a helicopter* ....

She remembered laughing so much when she first heard that joke, finding the funny and getting none of the wisdom. Years later it hit her that during hard times, we often turn away from the hands that may be God given or otherwise, that seek to help us. Because we believe there is only one way we can help ourselves. But help comes in strange ways, we need to remain open to all messages, not just the ones that are palatable or fit our ethos. Even those that challenged it. When she told a priest once that she felt she lived the life Jesus would live, but found it hard to believe in God, he surprised her by saying, *Jesus would probably have agreed with you and felt much the same.* The empathy toward her struggle for faith drew her closer, rather than the judging, haughty answers many in the ministry had given her. She knew that if you ever wanted to overcome a prejudice you had to let go of your pride and be humble and open to all things. It wasn't easy when you were used to having control, nobody likes to be in unfamiliar terrain, but it taught her, often the most valuable lessons were found where you least expect them.

Camila thought of Julia, the idea of her being captive, again. An unbearable pain passed through her as if they were linked by their intimacy and experience. She felt she had let her down by not knowing the moment she had been held against her will and taken out of their home together. *"How can I be so blind as to have not seen this coming?"* She berated herself fruitlessly, knowing deep down there was absolutely no way she could have known Rafael had had twins. That one was living and grown and out to avenge him. Who would have ever considered such a thing? Or that his daughter would transform herself into a man? A carbon copy of Rafael, reenacting his atrocities on earth like an avenging angel? *What had he done to her?* What had he inculcated her with that she could have inherited his unending darkness and penchant for the purchase of pain and suffering? Was it truly possible to turn out an exact replica? In which case, was Joe going to reflect his father? Or would he remain in the light, as she had, despite every reason to be dragged ever more, into the world of shadow.

And Julia, gentle Julia who baked bread and touched her forehead with the lightest touch in the world. Julia whom Camila loved so deeply and unexpectedly, whom she held up as her salve from all pain. Julia whom she held protectively in her own once empty arms, her love, the girl who fought alongside her and conquered The Devil. *How could this be happening again?* What twist of life would fashion a child who took over where their father had left off? What would happen now? Was Julia even alive? There was nothing, it was as if she had been catapulted from existence, a figment of her imagination. Yet, here were her things, signs of her life, the dropped tea-towel, her shoes by the back door, waiting for her feet to slip into them and plod around the house, in her dressing gown with her long black hair, a silk waterfall behind her. Julia. Was Camila given her to love, only to see her destroyed by the DNA he sired, in his hate and his vendetta against her?

When you know your enemy, you can formulate plans. When you are shooting in the dark you can only wait and see what move they make and watch and observe with both eyes open. But waiting wasn't always an option for survivors. That meant being a victim again and that wasn't going to happen a third time.

"Mom," Joe said, *"Miro could go after my girlfriend. He knows her. I stupidly introduced them when we met at the gym one day and we went for drinks."*

"Does he know where you live?"

"No."

"Does he know where she lives?"

"No."

"Okay then. Call her now, tell her to go stay with her grandparents, tell her the truth. I know she knows our story; it won't be as hard as trying to think of something and make it up." Joe left the room and Camila heard his placating and urgent tones through the thin door.

Chapter 62

Was Julia conscious? Was she being hurt? Camila was surprised at the rage that coursed through her. Not the anger of a victim, but almost the fury of the aggressor. She wanted to strangle the person in the photo, scream at them, *how dare you take her? How dare you subject us to this again? If you are from him, if you are his monster, you need to go back to the hell you came from and stay there!* She imagined shooting Miro over and over and then she began to cry, because she knew, a daughter born of Rafael had no damn chance in this world, no chance at all. Was it any wonder that she had become a version of him? How far would we go to survive? Changing our gender? Could Camila really blame her or him when they had no chance? No chance at all. But this wasn't about pity, she may have felt an ache of regret for what this child of his had gone through, but Julia was missing, and he had returned from the grave to get his vengeance. The only way to meet that – was with equal fire.

At various times in our lives, we find ourselves at a crossroads. We may stand there a time wondering which road to take, weighing the pros and cons. We may spend time considering the bigger picture, second-guessing ourselves. Rarely are we so certain that we do not even stop to read the inscription of the road we choose not to take. Camila's focus was laser-sharp, everything else unimportant, irrelevant. She saw the crossroads, she recognized the sign that led to finding Julia, there was nothing more. Only this moment, her entire life reduced to this. Joe beside her, their minds working as one. They had changed color, their eyes were different, they were no longer living in the house, going through the motions. They were creatures of the flame, the ashes of the past keeping them aloft. They sought the tormentor with their every fiber, it was their only purpose, the return of Julia. That order be restored and those who sought to destroy be banished eternally from their destructive path.

They carried a gun each, everywhere. Camila didn't contact the police again, not even Miranda, what could they do? And by the time they had, it would be too late, or Miro would know and it would encourage him to act sooner. For the most part, the authorities had never helped before, they weren't going to now. This was their fight, hers and Joe's, the ancestors of Rafael's Devil. This had to be settled outside the lines. She might have to do things that weren't sanctioned, she didn't want anything to stop that from happening. She couldn't leave his child alive, in order to protect her own child, who was also from him but carried her heart not his. In order to find Julia, she might have to enter Rafael's world and become every bit as bad as he was. *"You've infected me, you bastard"* Camila whispered, *"you've finally done it and infected me. You tried so many times and I held back a part of myself, swearing I'd never resemble you, but you've succeeded. I give in to it, I'll let it happen. I will become you, if that is what it takes to right this wrong. I will fight it with your evil and not stop until I've obliterated it."* She gasped. *"Rafael? Do you hear me you bastard? You Devil? You might be dust by now but you're still here and whether you're Miro or Mira or the damn Devil himself, I'm coming for you."*

Time passed. Clearly their torturer was waiting it out, glad for the torment. They could not seek them out, they didn't know where they were, or where they had Julia. They only had to wait, until the tormenter grew tired of waiting and made their move. It was almost impossible to do nothing but there was no choice. Like a standoff they stood, longing to run out into the street and find them, but knowing the minute they did, they'd be picked off and lose. The greatest challenge was waiting it out. Waiting out the excited urges of the predator, drawing them into the light of the circle, ensuring they show themselves. You cannot fight shadows. You can only fight those who materialize and reveal their intention, then you fight, with everything you have, holding nothing back, with nothing to lose, because if you lose, you lose it all.

Miro, the daughter who became son, who became her father, waited as long as he could. He lasted a good long while, before the itch, a terrible, uncontrollable itch that ran through his senses like fire, began. He could not control the itch, it grew in intensity until it was outside of him, urging him to act. *DO SOMETHING.* It said, *I am impatient, I do not want to wait any longer for my fun!* But the daughter who became son replied; *no, we must wait them out, we must be patient like the wolf in the forest is quiet. We must let the prey think we are not there, watching them from the edges.* The itch satiated for a time but it began again, worse, and worse, urging him with every waking moment, a chant, a song, a command. *You must act, you must act, you must act. No. We must be sure*, he said. But his voice was not as certain as before, because like sexual desire, he could not control the itch. It ran from his sewn-on phallus to the tip of his itching fingers to the top of his frothing head and back down to his sewn-on phallus. *Itch, itch,*

itch. No scratch powerful enough to stay the urge.

Julia was in a small cupboard, bound and facing the wall. *Lead us not into temptation* he had said, as he closed the door, because he knew if he saw her, he would not be able to control the itch. He fed her by shoving food beneath the door. Hoping she could pick at it in her constrained position, knowing she must sleep in her filth brought him the same pleasure as it had his father. But the itch repeated and repeated*; oh please, open the door, just a peek, just a peek.* The itch was hungry, the itch demanded blood, it could smell Julia through the door, her weakness, her pathetic female genitals that he had rid himself of. Miro flexed his strong arms, he touched his sewn-on parts until they hardened satisfactorily and he thought, *maybe a little practice before the main course?*

After all it had been so long. But he couldn't eat his dessert before his *hors d'oeuvre*, so he went out and found himself a skinny, wan girl who reminded him of them all. His mother, his brother, Rafael's Whores with dark eyes and black hair and a damaged smile. And Miro paid the local Whore a lot of money to come back to where he hid with Julia. He knew when the paid-for Whore came in, she would not be leaving with breath in her chest. Because nobody could know he lived here, and nobody could know he existed and survive. After he doped the whore into compliance, he opened the cupboard enough that Julia, should she be facing the door, could see what he was going to do to the thin wan girl; *Yeah, an advance preview* he said. What Julia had to look forward to. Her and her beloved Camila. The murderers of Miro's father, the God. This would be their just end, as they had robbed Miro of her father, and that girl had become a man, who was his own father. *"My father Rafael. He is within me,"* Miro said loudly, *"he is right here, he did not die, you failed, I am he."*

Miro took out his sewn-on phallus and the drugged wan girl put it in her mouth obediently and sucked, thinking nothing much was wrong. She continued to suck even after he stuck the knife in, because she wasn't expecting that and it didn't hurt at first. As she bled out, he withdrew from her open mouth and she stayed with her lips, wet and open, in a silent scream. *Oh dear*, but she could not scream because he'd punctured her lung and all the air had gone and she could only hiccup a gasp for air. She began to fall, and lose consciousness, flopping down for him to open her legs and drive himself between them, abusing her in the exact same way his father had. Miro tried out his sewn-on phallus on the dying girl, showing his pregnant belly to her as he fucked out her last dying breath. *"See my belly Whore? You will NEVER have a child of your own, you will die, but I am both father and mother, alpha and omega! I will have a child in a few months' time and I will bring my son up to inherit the earth and he will plough the earth with your blood and burn your weak kind to their knees."*

Julia, in the cupboard, saw this. Saw the girl's eyes glaze over and die. She saw her pulse stop and the blood flow slow. She saw the daughter who became the son, so like her original tormenter, returned to life. She saw this version of Rafael, carrying his future. Pregnant and with a strange partial phallus, raping the dying girl before covering himself in her blood and wiping it on his growing stomach, and his tiny pointed breasts. *Oh my god* Julia said to herself, and she knew. She had not survived Rafael, none of them had. She had simply prolonged her own death before he destroyed her.

Could not The Devil himself bear a child, a demon? And this? This creature covered in blood before her, with his face, his wicked phallus that had hurt her and her beloved, and given seed to bear Joe. This tormentor, he was never going to be eradicated. He existed again. He had been reborn and he was stronger than ever, about to birth the greatest demon yet. It was a combination she guessed of his blood, twice mixed, twice stronger, **twice the**

evil of any of them.

The itch went away after Miro killed and satiated himself. The quiver of destruction a delicious high, sustaining his thirst for a time. He knew logically he had to bear his father's child before he made his final move, irrespective of impatience. He wasn't going to be strong enough whilst still pregnant and he couldn't afford any mistakes this time around. He couldn't jeopardize the life inside him either. Her son Joe and Camila, they were two against one. Whilst his might was more than both of them put together, he could not risk hurting his child, his and Rafael's ultimate legacy.

A few weeks passed. Julia slowly weakening back to her former self in her excrement and gruel, in the cupboard. The dead wan girl, removed and discarded, her blood staining the light wood of the floorboards. Miro felt the child kick, a hard kick, a kick of champions. It was too soon but this was not just an ordinary son. This was Rafael's son. He was a God. Anyway, Miro was growing tired of the weight around his stomach. He wanted to be strong again. He wanted to be the man he was meant to be. Pregnancy made him feel weak.

Miro went back to the bad doctor who had been expecting him and was both repulsed and fascinated by what he was about to do. He thought of Rafael's dead body, coming out of his sliced stomach and Miro longed for it to be so. Could he bring his father back into the world? To hold his father one more time, to infuse him with his power? Miro knew his father was already coursing through his veins, in every orifice. That he had *become* his father. This child, this would not be either of them. It would be more than them both, the product of their twinned purity of evil.

"You know we are going against everything here," the bad doctor

said, to himself, aware the child was purposed from a father and daughter, now a son. "*You are remaking yourself in the image of The Devil.*" He said this with a fear and an excitement, and the Daughter who was now Son, smiled a hideous, wide, loose-lipped smile and said, to the bad doctor; "*Shut up. I'm paying you what you want. Do it now, it is time, take this out of me, I need to be strong, sew me up tight, don't make a mess, I'm beautiful and I need to stay beautiful. Warriors can have scars, but they must be strong scars. Make mine a beautiful scar, and take the baby out of me so I can get myself ready for the engagement I have waiting.*"

The bad doctor did not know what the daughter who was now son, had in mind, nor the depths of his sickness. But he liked the excitement of doing elicit and well-paid surgeries, giving him a chance to tinker on the edge of what was ethical and moral. "*I could remove your breasts entirely*" he said, "*although they are already very small, mere protruding nipples really, they will reduce even that, when you wean the child.*" He whetted his lips at the idea of cutting into Miro's flesh. He loved the sound of the knife. He wasn't so far removed from those who do it for play.

"*No, I don't need that,*" Miro replied, "*I want to be able to feed my child, I want to be able to nourish my son to full maturation. He will come to rely upon me as both mother and father. He will be initiated as I was, and earn his manhood the way I did.*" The bad doctor did not understand what the strange daughter/son was talking about, but he bowed his sick and greedy head in acquiescence. The bad doctor injected Miro with painkillers and began to cut down into his tight pregnant belly and into the red meat. Miro's skin was taut from working out and his testosterone treatments, but his stomach opened like a pomegranate to the blade.

The baby was delivered easily, a large-headed thing despite being premature, crying without stopping like it knew its fate already. The bad doctor put it in an incubator whilst he sewed Miro up, making a double stitch to ensure the wound would not come apart. He applied every knowledge to sewing him up, knowing should he find a split in his side during his war, he would come back to the bad doctor demanding vengeance. He bound Miro the way people in Asia did after giving birth, flattening his bulging skin, and pulling everything tight like drawing in folds of skin as human fan, to press closely against the next, until all is well and ordered again.

"*You are all sewn up and ready to go,*" he pronounced, lifting the gas and air from Miro's face, *"I told you, didn't I? It didn't hurt a bit did it?"*

"Even if it had, that would be okay," Miro said humorlessly, his small breasts leaking milk, *"bring him to me now, give me my child."* He reached out his muscular arms and hands, grasping the baby to his chest. It disgusted the bad doctor, who wasn't easily disgusted by things, in that fascinating way the curious stare and stare, to see the man feeding his child with his tiny triangular breasts. The child suckled hungrily as if he had always known, he only had one source of comfort in this world. The blood in the milk was that of Rafael The Devil. The blood in the milk was that of Miro The Devil reborn. The blood in the milk was being drunk by the new Devil. The new Devil drank deeply.

The bad doctor left that day, thinking of Egyptian gods, with dog heads and shifting genders. Gods who didn't pay heed to rules, and slept with their parents, making their mother's their Queens. He'd done transgender surgeries in the past. He understood being born in the wrong body. He was sympathetic as much as someone of his guile could be. But this wasn't as simple or the same at all. What Miro had done was an abomination. He was evil, the bad doctor could tell even as his own heart was greedy and dark. There was much more at work here than gender reassignment surgery. Miro was mad. He was pestilence. He terrified him.

The bad doctor thought of how the ancient Egyptians resembled each other in artwork. With their eyes black, their hair black, their fingers long and covered with gold. He had done work for many bad people, that is how he earned his living since his license was taken, but he had yet to feel afraid of any of them. He always felt he was the real master of the scalpel, producing miracles. But this creature he made? He terrified him. His claw-like fingers, gently cradling his baby, suckling from his long nipples. A grotesque rebirth of a Devil, repeating throughout history. He knew, he was guilty of more than shifting boundaries, he was responsible for assisting the endurance of evil. That night when the bad doctor went to bed, he checked all his locks on his windows and doors. He slept uneasily and his dreams contained Egyptian deities, who ate him from his toes to his brain, slowly, and agonizingly.

Chapter 63

Days later, the wound healing fast, the new father Miro felt himself again. He put silver on his wounds. He kept them tightly bound. He used a UV light to speed up healing. He took steroids. Taking vitamins and doing all necessary to ensure his continued strength, he put the last act of womanhood behind him, the ugliness of birth. His child he farmed out for the duration of this war, to a woman who did his bidding or knew she'd live to regret it. A woman who had the hurt eyes of having known and survived his father. A woman whom his father had destroyed and reconstructed, so afraid, she would follow Rafael's every request, even from the grave.

Miro insisted on bringing his own milk to the baby's nurse, pumping it from his tiny titties, and giving her the small creamy bottles. She didn't know it was his milk but she fed it to his child unquestioningly. She was so weak it was hard not to want to kill her. But it was important she knew that this, Miro and Rafael's, child only drink from him. Nothing that was tainted, weak, or inferior. This child would grow universes in his stride. He needed the power of the blood. He knew this as he knew his father, lived through him and would again live through their child. He who is … never dies.

When Miro could again do sit-ups and squats, he knew he was back to fighting mode and he permitted the itch to return. The itch told him that if he didn't act soon, the itch would rush over to Julia and exsanguinate her as the itch raped her. That could only be avoided by action, said the itch, *"act now, I am impatient, I cannot wait."* Miro realized the itch was his father, telling him it was time. Time to erase the mistakes of his past, and put down those who ever dared rise up against him including his brother, a weak feeble boy who he would enjoy raping before he slit his throat and buried a knife through his chest. *"Ashes to ashes bitch,"* he spat on the floor and gathered his symbols of destruction.

At the tattooists Miro selected the words his father's letter decreed and the symbols. The pierced stoned artist faithfully replicated them onto Miro's small breasts and down his chest, looping through the freshly healed scar. "*We should wait until this is healed more, you might get infected, man,*" the tattooist said, but he shut up as soon as he saw the scorn in Miro's eyes. After all he had a fair share of hinky and kinky clientele; it wasn't the strangest thing he'd been asked to do, though what the man-woman had had cut out of themselves he didn't want to know. *"It's perfect,"* Miro said, looking at the fresh and sore tattoo on his chest and belly, and the tattooist once more wished that he had finished art school and become a graphic designer, because there were just too many freaks out there.

Julia saw the tattoo as Miro prepared himself. The faces of the dead screamed out, the words were a jumble of names and hate. The colors garish and bloody, like war paint, the sore skin puckering around the scars. It was a disgusting mess of rage and so like everything she knew of Rafael, now facsimiled and alive in the avenging form of Miro. Miro, the boy who had given birth and was sharpening his knives. Julia knew Miro was no progeny, he was the reincarnation of Rafael. Rafael again, readying himself to destroy as he had twice before, the life of Camila and Joe, with Julia as collateral damage. There was nothing she could do. She could not feel her limbs, they were tied so tightly they had turned a horrible blue and she was desperately weak with lack of water and food, lying there, impotent in her own filth.

"Don't," she managed to say through blistered lips, and Miro brought his face close to Julia's and she smelt the same smell as Rafael, as if he were inhabiting his daughter's body. She smelt the sickening smell of breast milk mixed with blood and she knew that nothing she said would do anything but excite the urge to hunt and destroy. "Don't hurt them," Julia said. *"I know you were hurt, you had to be, but this isn't the answer." "You don't know answers."* Miro said expressionlessly. *"You're just a woman." "You were a woman once, weren't you?"* Julia replied. "*I was never a woman. I'm not some sentimental Trans if that's what you're thinking. I was always my father. I hate Trans, I hate women. I've never been one of those sniveling lesbians or Trans who you revere so much, you stupid bitch. I'm a God."* Miro's eyes gleamed. *"It isn't wrong to be Trans or lesbian"* Julia said, but she already knew, he wasn't listening. *"I will be back for you darling"* Miro said, smiling, *"It wouldn't be right to hurt you now, not when you need to find out what happens. It would be like saving you before the kill, no that won't work at all. You need to all be together. I'll let you see it all, I'll bring you home their freakin heads!"* And Miro left, with Julia screaming behind the closed doors of the cupboard, to nobody, who could hear nothing.

That night Rafael was reborn. He walked the earth again. He wasn't a young girl become a man, this wasn't about that, this was about being reborn. He was Mira and Miro. He possessed a young body like a phantasma. He came to the house his family lived in, the house of his Whores and his mistakes. Where there had been love, but never love for him. Miro knew they would be waiting if they had put one-and-one together, but how could they have? Whether they waited or not, they would not expect him to be so emboldened. They would think him weak if they had found out about him. Maybe they would believe he was still a pathetic weak girl, maybe they would think he was a hapless, lost boy. Maybe they wouldn't know who he was. It didn't matter, they didn't realize who he truly had become.

His father, their father. Rafael the father of everything. Miro was stronger than they could ever be if there were ten of them in there, he could tear them apart. He had no fear only urgency and excitement. Sometimes directness paid off. He would break in as they slept. They couldn't stay awake every night waiting for news on Julia. He would break them and drag them back to the pit of their nightmares and he would take his time, slow, and easy, destroying every layer of them in homage to his nature. To his father. To The Devil.

It reminded Miro of when he was younger and his father would visit the people who took care of him. Back then when he wore skirts and dresses and didn't feel whole. His father, his great strong father who would lift him onto his shoulders and walk around the town like he owned it, with his easy swagger and his black eyes, telling him the names of everything they saw in the desert. Those moments, those brief moments they spent, before things changed, before he had to grow himself hard and take his father inside of him. Back then he could recall feeling a joy that he'd never known before or since. Now he felt the same joy, at the thought of cutting them open and offering them as sacrifice to the God of his father, watching within him, waiting for his courage.

Miro climbed like a cat with long dark legs, through the night. He drew himself as thin as a slice of moon, he placed the suction against the glass of the bathroom window. He cut with silent slice, the glass into the shape of an oval, he pulled it out, carefully like a warm fresh laid egg. He placed his hand and arm through the hole, as carefully as a virgin removing her shoes. He lifted the lock with whispering fingertips, and eased the window up, inch by inch, without a single squeak. Climbing in, stepping down, the light coming in from a chunk of moon, his feet sheathed in rubber, his clothes clinging to him like second skin. At no point did he waiver. He did not break a sweat, did not seem to breathe, such was his art. He moved toward the bathroom door, ajar. He stepped into the hallway, seeing both their bedrooms, his head turned toward the living room, checking to see if someone was up, hand on gun. Nothing. 3:00am, the quietest hour.

Camila, the Whore who was the very breakage in his father's strength. The link that undid him, was sleeping in her son's old bedroom. Joe slept with her. Sharing a bed together they looked like children again. She didn't look old enough to be Joe's mother, despite a few scars her lips still full. A beauty especially in the calm swell of sleep, her arm flung above her the way kids do when they are dreaming. Joe was turned toward the wall, slightly more protected, less carefree, or maybe, maybe a bad dream, a premonition. Miro smiled, only he was the purveyor of their bad dreams, and this would turn the page to the next chapter. He stood there a moment, seeing them both, tracing their lines. It was so easy, too easy, he turned to look behind him, nothing, nobody, and heard the slow rise of their breathing. Definitely asleep.

How to take them both? He withdrew from his pocket the stun gun. It was a smaller-than-usual version, shorter reach, same results. Compact. It whipped out like a lasso in the night, caught on fire, a lightning rush, hitting Joe in the middle of his chest, bursting the darkness, blinding everyone. Joe rose up in spastic jerk and seized, and then went slack and unconscious. Camila seemed to levitate from the bed, as if electrocuted at the same time, pouncing up like she'd been woken faster than a single thought can pull our strings. But Miro expected this and his knife met her jump, right in the sweet spot. If she moved any more, he'd slice her, fun or no fun, and she knew it and he knew it. The sickly familiar smell suffocated her as he sprayed ether into her face and she tried desperately not to breathe in the sickly smell, flailing uselessly in his muscular arms.

Chapter 64

Miranda, the detective.

Miranda hadn't been sleeping well. She would often dream of men in the night abducting her two children. She took them to the school gates every day before reporting to work in her Santa Fe office. She called once a month and checked in on Camila and Julia. She had to know they were okay; it was like the experience they all went through; they were part of her now. She'd even briefly thought of relocating to Albuquerque but she wasn't sure how they'd take that so she'd refrained. Maybe it wasn't healthy for her to care so much? After all, her kids were doing well here; was she going to relocate just because of two women she'd grown attached to? Isn't that just trauma attachment? Miranda didn't really care why, but she checked in, she always checked in. When she'd called the last time, she could hear a change in Camila's voice. *"What's happened?"* She'd said before anything was confirmed. "*Nothing's happened, we're fine, we're all fine,*" Camila unconvincingly reassured her. She was lying. Something was terribly wrong.

All day Miranda walked around feeling the same way, until her mind was made up. Her body knew it before her conscious mind did. She was packing an overnight bag for her kids; she was ensuring they had what they needed for the next day at school; she was calling her mom, and giving the key to her house to her neighbor. Her cat circled her boots, as she bent to take out the trash, she petted it absentmindedly. In her imagination she saw a darkness, it was slowly coming from the distance, it was filling their mouths. They were trying to ask for help, the darkness was absorbing the cries, drowning them with ash instead of water, they were choking, they were drowning on words that they could not spit out to be made heard.

Some years ago, Miranda had read about a Japanese serial killer, Futoshi Kobayashi. He had killed 9 women in 3 weeks, preying on suicidal women. Meeting them in chat rooms for those who were experiencing suicidal thoughts, Kobayashi has convinced them to come to his house for a suicide pact. Instead of dying with them, he had murdered them. It was the perfect prey, the article had said, people who were already thinking of dying. Miranda had thought of Camila and how she had been manipulated into attempting suicide. Until then Miranda hadn't understood how this was possible, but with everything she'd learned, she knew it was. Take the right person at the right time and you can manipulate the hell out of them. How else to explain extreme cults or mass child abuse? Fragile people weren't less than, they were often isolated, desperate, lonely. A friendly, understanding face could work magic. It was more an indictment of our society and our intolerance of suffering, than it was anything else. *Vulnerable people shouldn't be able to get to that point*, Miranda thought. It's our failing as a society that doesn't care that these murderers can gain traction.

That evening Miranda bundled her kids up and took them

over to her mothers. *"I'll be a few days at the most,"* she'd said at work and taken off. It's not like they didn't owe her. The drive wasn't long and it was beautiful, cutting through the deep red of the desert, how could anything ever be wrong with a landscape like this? She had frequently thought, listening to old songs on the radio and knowing how easy it would be to turn it to her favorite show on true crime and listen to the mountain of stories of bad people doing bad things. She knew bad things didn't mind if a place was peaceful and nice, they'd still act. They'd still steal the souls of their victims, never quite giving them back. She drove without stopping and her eyes stung from concern, and her hands stayed on the wheel not trusting herself and she kept her speed steady and five miles over the limit, because something was wrong, terribly wrong.

Driving at night you see things. You see shadows that don't make sense. You see lights that seem to come from nowhere and just as they appear, they disappear, leaving you wondering what it was you saw. She saw the red lines of the night sky plucking stings from the yellow of sun, over the mountain tops, she saw the caramel mix of snow and moon, she saw the shift of figures in the darkness, jack rabbits, coyote, lizard. She saw the tall spiny cacti growing high as a small tree silhouetted against her car lights like pleading people, thirsting near the road side. She heard the sound of prairie dogs howling, either at themselves or nothing, echoing once, twice, three times around the valley like a chorus.

As a child she used to ask her Tia, *"what does it mean when Papa says he sees the Chupacabra?"*

"Oh child, don't you worry about that," her Tia would say, bouncing her on her comfortable, cushiony knee.

"But Tia, Tia, he tells mama that he sees the Chupacabra coming to our house sometimes, he looks afraid when he says it Tia, who is

the Chupacabra?"

Her auntie looked her seriously in the eyes, all fun put aside; *"The Chupacabra child, is a monster within us all, a creature who is always hungry and when we open our mouths with our anger and our pain, the Chupacabra will be released and it will roam the desert in search of food. Finding no food, it will return to your city or your town and it will begin to eat away the edges of your city or your town until you can see the darkness of its big mouth."*

She crawled tighter against her Tia and listened; *"And that is why your papa is afraid of it child, because it is the monster on the edge of all of us, and we must keep our lights burning when times get bad, to keep away the Chupacabra who cannot be fed enough to stop. The only thing that will stop him is if we do not open our mouths with anger child, and we learn instead to help each other and not hate each other. Your papa may be afraid but he is not going to be consumed by the Chupacabra child, he is a calm and good man."*

Miranda was even more afraid then, thinking about a giant mouth eating the edge of the desert and every night she would look out of her little room and see the mouth of the night chomping at the sky line and she would cross her pudgy fingers and say quietly, *"I do not hate anything, so Chupacabra you cannot claim me,"* and she would go to bed hoping he heard her and passed by her house and leave her and her papa and mama and Tia alone.

Ever since then, as an adult, Miranda would scan the landscape every evening and see the slim river of light devoured by the dark and she would think of how all our stories, all our warnings are really metaphors for our emotional states. How some of the creatures of the earth, really are monsters, they are of us, and part of us. They seek for no good reason to destroy us, and we can never truly explain this, so we must make them larger, more monstrous to justify the evil they do. And Miranda drove, watching the entire world become absorbed into the mouth of night and roll back with a violet strain of cloud, brushing the darkness. Darkness like a residue bruise, aching to be touched and soothed, against the shimmering lick of night, thirsting for absolution. Her aching feet pressing the gas pedal faster, as she floored her car toward Albuquerque.

When she reached the familiar orange house, everything was still and undisturbed. 3:00 am. She'd wait in the car until 6:00 am and then go knock on the door. Julia was an early riser. But something moved, inside the house. A figure behind the curtain, lit by the moon coming in through an opposite window. A figure that was tall and certain, shifting like a question, not a person going to the bathroom at night, half asleep. Someone who was awake, their head, turning and turning again. Moving in Joe's old bedroom, closer toward where the bed would be, hidden by the wall. Miranda had her gun, ready to shoot, no safety, she held it with a hand that didn't shake and got out of the car as quietly as she knew how.

Going around the side of the house, she saw the open bathroom window, scaled it, gun first. Stepping into the small bathroom, following the feeling she had creeping down her neck. Suddenly light flashed everywhere, she couldn't shoot, she couldn't see who it was, it felt like it was as if someone had turned the light on and off, or maybe a flash of lightning but there was only a distant buzz, and then darkness. She knew that sound, *stun gun*. The word popped into her adrenalin-filled head like the flash it made. Miranda stepped around toward the bedroom she'd seen the figure in, there in the half-light she saw the shift of a blade against Camila's throat, saw Joe passed out, the prongs of a Taser, still attached high on his chest. Saw a man who was not a man, flickering between demon and window curtains, pressing the knife against Camila's throat, a strange smell of burning and chemicals in the room.

Against all protocol Miranda didn't announce herself. She didn't make careful calculation of distance between the flickering demon man with the knife at his victim's throat, and their own rising chests. She did nothing by the book. Instead, she aimed high and without stopping to query her action, she did not hesitate and pulled the trigger. The gun recoiled in her hand, sending her a step back, more out of shocking the silent scene than anything else. It was slow-motion after that. The demon with the knife, turning at the sound. At the same time, red spurting from his neck, like a pump, turning and falling sideways. The knife, pressed a little harder against Camila's neck then released and falling. The sound of a body hitting the floor hard, in the way unnatural falls sound, wrong and heavy. Miranda was turning on the light, blinding them all again, gun in hand, ready to shoot a second time. Knowing she'd broken every rule and not caring one wit. Just relieved, so damn relieved.

On his side Miro was turning the carpet crimson. Miranda went up and picked up the knife, put it on the bed, looked down at him, his eyes glazing over. The same eyes. How could he have the same eyes? He had the eyes her Tia told her about and the sharp teeth of the desert eater who stole the light. She checked over the two on the bed, Camila was unconscious but coming back, Joe already stirring close to coming awake, disorientated, but gaining awareness again. The blood on the floor darkening with every last dying pulse. Miro, grotesque in his death snarl. The stretch marks of his pregnancy a livid purple against his blanching skin.

Miranda sat on the edge of the bed and thought about how she could frame it in a way that wouldn't damn her and lose her the hard-won badge she was so proud of. She realized after all those years of service, after all the stories she'd heard, of people being cut up and left mutilated in the desert, she didn't care if one bad guy got his without due process. She almost felt righteous about it. She had saved them. She had saved herself. If he had come back to finish them off, she'd never have slept again. Her own and others children were safe, for now, another monster was down permanently. She saw her father's face and he said, *"Through time, good girl you have slayed the Chupacabra Miranda, I will go to bed tonight and I will not be afraid any longer."*

Miro did not feel the bullet pierce his neck. He felt instead a strange warm hand with incredible power, lift him from his intention and place him on the floor. It felt like the hand of God. He lay there, his black eyes clouding with a scarlet screen and heard murmurs all around. As he lay there, he felt a serenity he had never felt in all of his life, not even when his father held him down and drove into his soul. He felt the hand around his neck, a powerful heat like a metal, enveloping him and covering him in armor. He knew then that his father was an angel and he had come to bring him home. Miro smiled in his mind, though lying on the carpet bleeding out, his lips barely quivered. He felt the pressure of his father's hand around his neck cradling him, urging him to dissolve into the red womb and return.

He wanted to tell his father that he had waited all these years for that tenderness. That he hadn't really wanted to turn into a man, or a monster, but had wished his father would save himself and save them both. He thought he heard his father's voice, through the rush and whirl of blood in his head that seemed so very loud and so very close and his father's voice said, *"I am with you,"* and Miro, who wanted to cry but could not cry, closed his dark tired eyes on the world and followed his father into the night as a girl and as a boy. As a child who followed love with thirsty bewitchment.

Prologue

Afterward, they sat and talked, all four of them. Julia was found by Miranda's team and returned home. 15 pounds lighter, pale, shaky, traumatized by what she had witnessed. Ecstatic that her family had not been wiped out, with her unable to do anything, left bound and imagining the worst. After they were reunited and tears fell until everyone got dizzy headed and self-conscious and started to crack bad jokes and raid the fridge. Then they had come together to talk all through the horrors, around the kitchen table, Camila knew this was her family.

A strange family comprised of a murderer's son who was nothing like him (Joe), the two survivors of a murderer (herself and Julia) and even Miranda who knew when something was wrong and did what had to be done. In saving all of them from avenging the trauma of their experiences and having to kill again, Miranda maintained her law enforcement status and they, their roles as survivors and not double-murderers. It would not have sat right with them, much as in their hearts they burned to destroy. They would have come too close to being like the daughter who was now son, and their terrible legacy.

When Camila came to and found Joe stroking her face and Miranda speaking to other law enforcement personnel who swarmed the room, she also saw the death mask of Miro, lying on the floor, his brain bleeding into the carpet. She looked at the boy who was Rafael's daughter and she felt a deep sorrow, not hatred. "*Miro did not have a chance,*" she said, to her son, *"he only knew hate. Maybe genes weren't on his side, but it's what you do with those genes. He only knew he wanted to impress his father, imagine how he lived? What his influences were? He became what his father wanted, to earn his love, not realizing how he was capable of love after all and did not have to be like his father. I'm not even sure he wanted to change gender, he wasn't Trans, this didn't come from a place of self-insight and being born the wrong gender. This was something else. Miro was warped by his father into a parody of him. It's so different from Trans, who only seek to be their true selves. There was nothing true about Miro, he was lost because of what his father did to him, long before he changed gender."*

"*I wish that I had been able to reach him before it came to this, but I'm glad he's dead. If I had been able to help him."* Joe said, "*but he had the same dark heart as his father. A heart I always feared having myself. But I know I don't have that heart. I do not believe like you and Julia do, that everyone can be redeemed, I believe some people need to stop existing. It's the only way we will ever be free of them, I'm sorry mom but if he were alive, I would always wonder when he would come for us."*

She supposed Joe was right, and she understood. When a monster is unleashed, it is not sufficient to contain him, he will release spores and others will follow his call. Miro was a version of Rafael who carried in his heart, the same need to destroy. Following a life map, he was bound in his fate to continue his father's legacy, as ruinous as it was. How a child without any goodness within him, stands little chance at regaining goodness. But how she wished Rafael had not set into motion a train of destruction, killing nearly his entire lineage aside Joe, the one who got away, the one who would stand as her testimony, that not all who come from tainted blood retain the taint.

It made Camila sad to think Miro was Joe's rightful brother, and they would never have a chance to know one another, as they should have. All because Rafael sought to destroy everything that was good. *"You did not win Rafael,"* she whispered, *"you only erased yourself, the very thing you didn't want to do. You will not be remembered, you will be forgotten, you will not matter, you will cease."*

Bad acts are bad acts. If we commit one in self-defense, we are blameless, but it still leaves its stink. If ever you're in that situation, do your darndest but if someone who is trained to protect you can step in, all the better. Saving you having literal blood on your hands, or acting out in self-defense and vengeance and blurring the emotional ties that keep us from turning into the monsters who hunt us.

Julia came home. They changed the carpet in Joe's room and rinsed out the horror from their days and they held each other, for as long as they possibly could. Feeling their hearts beating in echo, wondering how they stood here, under their own roof, with The Devil cast out into diminishment.

Julia had dark circles under her eyes, but she curled into Camila's lap and they stayed there, as the light shifted across the room in layers. She knew it would take more time, more light, and Julia would regain her spirit and they would walk again through sun-setting rainbows and point out the desert birds cutting through low-lying clouds and the tops of thin silver trees, drawing water from the belly of the desert. Camila knew that like that, Julia would be sustained. They all would. They were children of the wind and they would grow with time, listening again to the hum of earth, the cry of wild things, and the song of them, enduring and powerful.

Miranda decided she would move from Santa Fe to Albuquerque and work at the local station there and she and her two kids bought a house in the neighborhood as their own. She began to work with local organizations who sought to track and find missing and exploited women. On the weekends they all volunteered, sifting through information on those of us who go missing and fade into obscurity. It became the outcome of their experience to find the light, the hope in their survival by bequeathing their time to looking for others.

They all knew, if someone had been watching closely, they may have seen the patterns earlier and saved lives. Because they had survived, they owed it to those who were still imprisoned to search for them when they were unable to free themselves. Even if they found one missing woman, one abducted child, it would right the order of the universe and define why they had survived Rafael. When things are so bad you cannot really give them description, you find in the light, places to put hope and you build those places, until the darkness is diminished into the very corners of your world.

So many people go missing every year, they are picked up like lost dogs on the sides of roads and by train stations and in shelters, where they trust someone when they offer them a meal. Instead, they find themselves trafficked across continents in the sex trade, chained, bruised, brutalized, they live short lives, often murdered or dying of disease. So many are never found, they simply wink out like stars in dark sky. Unmarked graves. If anything changes, it must be those who are willing to make change, and be that change, through advocacy and action. Miranda taught her children this. She helped them understand that living only for ourselves does not help heal the world. Giving back is the only way we all move forward together. Preventing cruelty and abuse, is how we find the light within us and without us.

When you pass someone in the street, find yourself taking note of their features closely. How often do you imagine they carry with them, a cage of horror, or incomplete soul, slices of them flayed by some assassin in their past? We assume completeness, we focus on positive, and have little time for those who are splintered. The ones who stay behind at the end of the day, lifting those who are still and unmoving – those are the heroes of the world, not the money-lenders, or the big spenders, but those who see in others a need and reach out and say, *I am here, let me carry your weight.* If we teach one thing to our children about goodness, it should be something of this; an urge to look beyond ourselves and whether we are okay. To think of others, and all the worlds outside our own where people suffer quietly without their tongues.

Camila was growing older, in the mirror she saw the residue of war, fracturing like feathers around her eyes, lending her a serious look that matured her face. It was not a bad thing, she decided, to bring life into this world and take life that had consumed and eaten goodness for far too long. An odd feeling perhaps, to be both giver and taker of life. But as she stood, a little stooped, sometimes tired for no reason, she felt a restfulness inside her. A restfulness she never experienced as a young woman, when jack-knifing through her was an urge to find meaning and a sense of futility. When she emerged from the river, she was reborn but still lost. Now she knew as part of her experience, she had found her way back, to herself and in time, to others.

If someone had told her Julia and she would stay together for all their days and retain a bond and lasting affection for one another, Camila would have marveled that she could be capable of such steadiness. Once the only steady thing she did was decide to end herself. Going through the gaslight of his rage and surviving Rafael, lent her an insight into what people face and the decisions they make. It helped her understand that nobody is all evil, but we can push ourselves so far down into darkness, that we are irretrievable and then comes the war. She knew she survived, just as the scars left from his abuse reminded her like crochet, of her existence. She no longer had an emptiness within her, because she had grown to accept the imperfection and wonder of herself.

When Camila looked at Julia, she saw herself before it had all happened. Only Julia was the way she should have been, learning to live with the pain and making something of it other than self-destruction. When the day turned blue, they would turn the TV on and switch off the world, watching *Lifetime Movie Network* shows until they rolled with laughter or tears. They would eat far too much sugar and raid the fridge for beer. Like best friends staying over together, the sadness would not completely go, but it would be valid and it would have its say. Then they would get up and clean off the bed and carry on, lifting the sheets high in the air and shaking them as we do ourselves in those lost times, we reach for another's hand. They reached for each other and they found, a tight grasp returned.

Joe did not inherit his father. The only legacy was his distant memory of what happened. He held a pride for the strength of those women in his life who taught him, *who you become is up to you*. His scars made it hard at times to trust, but he learned this was okay and taking life as a series of steps, was often the best way to soothe anxiety and make it through a rough patch. He grew into the kind of man anyone would be proud to call a son. He filled his life with the examples of his elders, and made a conscious choice to act as role-model for those other men he knew, who lacked the necessary lessons in life, helping us to respect each other.

As a group of survivors, all bonded by the same experience, they spent a lot of time together. The way people who have shared life and death often find themselves doing. None of them were without scars. None of them still didn't check the shower stall when taking a shower, or the window in the bathroom when they went to bed. But they were a cobbled-together family and they were alive, and this, this life, was good.

Postscript

The child who had lost its father, and its mother. The child who played by itself quietly for hours, seemingly lost in thought. That child grew swiftly and tall, with a mass of black hair and dark large eyes. Most of all, the child with dark eyes and no parents, liked to chase after little animals and see if one day it might catch one and see how it worked inside. And the frightened woman left in charge of this child, knew, when it became of appropriate age, or maybe just before, she would let it read the contents of the envelope left by the father. It was a large envelope, with a lot of writing in it. She kept it in her lingerie drawer next to her small can of mace. There was a name on the envelope. It read; *Rafael Jr.*

Acknowledgements

I've always worked more than one job at a time. Losing one afforded me the time to write this. Like many of my generation, we do multiple side-hustles, scratching a living from impermanent jobs with far too many hours, for far too little. I have taught critical thinking and international business, practiced psychotherapy in 4 countries and out of my garage, sold vintage toys on eBay and edited a wide variety of works from PhD manuscripts to economic forecasting papers by US Ambassadors, to eclectic poetry collections. When I look at earlier generations with their lifelong jobs, I can't imagine that kind of security. This novel is in many ways reflective of that lack of security. My time in immigration-limbo with the insecurity of no rights in a same-sex relationship, prior to legalization, taught me: We can never rest on our laurels. Rights are eroded the minute we turn our backs. When we support others, we raise us all. Those things that used to be forbidden to talk about, are the way out into the light. Codify Roe into law and stop dismantling women's rights and obviating the legacy of trauma. We are all equal.

I would like to specifically thank: Johann, Jia Li, Halle, Sun, Christine, Nitya, Eric, Tara, Susi, Belinda, Kalpna, Ruth and Shinny, Jo, Leah, Nic, Raili, Renee, Linda and Ashley, Tremaine, Dustin, Bob and Stephanie, Erik, Jane, Annette, Mark, Joaquin, Khusi, Susmita, Anthony, Kindra, Megha, Lakshmi, Laurie, Susie, Philip, Jodi, Allister, Robert, Susan, Derrick, Emily, Dom, Shayan, Rob V, MJ, Christopher, Lynny, and Lisa.

Thank you to Danny White and Rebecca Huston for reading

and giving invaluable feedback.

Thank you to all my colleagues at: Indie Blu(e) Publishing, Tint Journal, Raw Earth Ink, Queer Ink, Parcham Literary Journal, Lit Fox Books, The Pine Cone Review, Different Truths, Borderless Journal, Writers Resist, and all the wonderful people I have the honor to work alongside.

Deepest thanks to my eagle-eyed editor Nitya Swaruba. Thank you for catching so many things I did not.

My sincere appreciation to all at FlowerSong Press, I am truly blessed you believed in this book. Thank you for what you do to make the world a better place; especially Edward Vidaurre, Editor-in-Chief, Avery Castillo, and Priscilla Celina Suarez.

Author Biography

Candice Louisa Daquin is of Egyptian and French descent. Born in Europe, Daquin worked in publishing before immigrating to America to eventually become a Psychotherapist. Daquin is Managing Editor with *Lit Fox Books* (Austin, TX) and former Senior Editor of *Indie Blu(e) Publishing* for 8 years. She is also co-founder of Gay Questions, a site for LGBTQ+ youth. She holds advanced degrees in writing and psychotherapy.

Daquin is Editorial Partner with *Raw Earth Ink* (USA) and *Queer Ink* (India) and is Poetry Editor at *Tint Bilingual Journal, The Pine Cone Review, Writers Resist, Parcham Literary Magazine,* and *Life & Legends Magazine.* She also writes regularly for *Different Truths* and co-judges The Northwind Writing Award and the Silent River Poetry Prize. Daquin is former Writer-in-Residence for *Borderless Journal*; as well as former Consultant Editor with *Blackbird Press*. She's also guest-edited *SETU Bilingual Journal* and written for poetry periodicals *Rattle*, *SoFloPoJo*, *World Literature Today*, and *The Northern Poetry Review*.

Poetry Collections

A Jar for the Jarring (South Texas Press; republished by Palpitate Press), *The Bright Day Has Gone Child and You Are in for the Dark* (chapbook), *Pinch the Lock* (Finishing Line Press), *Tainted by the Same Counterfeit* (Finishing Line Press), *The Wound is Where Wholeness is Born*, Phylum Press (coming Winter, 2026).

Editor/Co-Editor Anthologies

Defy Definitions: Celebrating Extraordinary Journeys of Underrepresented Lives, with Dr. Khusi Pattanayak (Black Eagle Books), *Within Flesh: Poems in conversations with our selves and Emily Dickinson*, Al Salehi & Ivy Schweitzer, (Transcendent Zero Press), The 2023 and 2024 Northwind Treasury, Winners of the Northwind Writing Award, with Tara Caribou (Raw Earth Ink), *The New Condemned: Contemporary Albanian Poetry in English* (Ed. Dustin Pickering) (World Inkers Publishing), *Love Letters to Ukraine by Uyava*, Kalpna Singh Chitnis (River Paw Press), *But You Don't Look Sick: The Real Life Adventures of Fibro Bitches, Lupus Warriors, and Other Superheroes Battling Invisible Illness* (Indie Blu(e) Publishing), *The Kali Project: Invoking the Goddess Within* (Indie Blu(e) Publishing), *As the World Burns: Writers and Artists Reflect on a World Gone Mad* (Indie Blu(e) Publishing), *Through The Looking Glass: Reflecting on Madness and Chaos Within* (Indie Blu(e) Publishing), *SMITTEN: This is What Love Looks Like* (Indie Blu(e) Publishing), *We Will Not Be Silenced: The Lived Experience of Sexual Harassment and Sexual Assault Told Powerfully Through Poetry, Prose and Essay* (Indie Blu(e) Publishing), and *Unhoused: Yearning for home*, with Carrie Yang (Prolific Pulse Press).

Resources:

National Domestic Violence Hotline
https://www.thehotline.org/
(text START to 88788)

National Sexual Violence Resource Center
(nsvrc.org)

National Sexual Assault Hotline
1-800-656-4673

Anti-Sexual Violence Organization
www.rainn.com
800. 656.HOPE

Safe Horizon
https://www.safehorizon.org

Praise for *The Cruelty*

Daquin's debut novel *The Cruelty*, is outstanding in its perception of human-nature and the writers' innate awareness of the depravity of certain human behavior. This taut psychological thriller will keep you guessing and guessing, it's got the addictive quality of a best-seller, with the finesse of a writer who knows how to capture and keep her audience. This is a crucial book in our war against intimate violence and a brilliant read.

—**Megha Sood**, Poet & Literary Activist, Author of award-winning collection *My Body Lives Like a Threat*

Fans of psychological thrillers will relish this unpredictable, shocking and original novel *The Cruelty*. As a therapist I found it incredibly useful and insightful to shed light on the legacy of abuse. Daquin helps us understand and get to the core of abuse through generations. Her strong female protagonist is a sign broken people can recover and thrive. As a therapist to survivors, this book is one I would recommend to my clients and their families. It will trigger, it's not an easy read - but neither is what they've gone through. More of us should be aware of the extent of abuse and sexual violence; the toll it takes and the fight survivors go through. 1 in 3 women is the victim of some kind of violence in the homeplace. On a purely psychological thriller basis, this novel is exceptionally exciting but it's so much more than that, it's self-aware.

—**Jodi Roberts**, Licensed Professional Counselor

If you are disturbed by the things humans are capable of, *The Cruelty* doesn't pull any punches, but this isn't a horror novel, if you turn on the news you will see similar examples every day. Women are still the #1 victim of domestic and sexual abuse. Previous abuse, sets anyone up for future abuse. Until we understand this legacy, we cannot find ways to curb it. *The Cruelty* does a really thorough job of exploring this challenging subject with deep insights. As much as this is a work of fiction, there are many strands of lived truth, readers will be disquieted by. We need these kinds of books to cut a pathway through old tropes. *The Cruelty* is a fantastically exciting novel where you hold your breath hoping the protagonist will survive against literally all the odds. The unexpected twists and psychological depths are fascinating, terrifying and ultimately redemptive.

—**Dr. Belinda Román**, Professor, Committee Member with International Federation for Feminist Economics

Daquin's persona doesn't hold a high moral ground like a martyr; she also shares her vulnerability and imperfections; Resilience always comes to her with wounds. Her voice is well-formed, and her observation adds an overlooked fact or image that enhances the reader's understanding of the world. She brings her entire being into her writing.

—**Shweta Rao Garg**, Poet & Visual Artist, Author of *Goddesses and Women*, *Shakespeare Walis: Verses on the Bard,* & *The Tales from Campus: A Misguide to College*

The Cruelty is one of the most disturbing books I've ever read. I say this as a compliment. It's not a book you'd fondly recall, it's a book you need to read and recommend. Many people have experienced a bit of what Camila goes through or knows someone who has. The #metoo movement cannot be forgotten and our cancel culture often pushes sexual-assault-reform to the back burner. Novels like *The Cruelty* are social justice warriors speaking out. Truth can be in fiction as much as testimony and as I read Camila's story I read the story of many women. Cultural acceptance of violence has to end and awareness is one way it will. I couldn't put this book down; it literally gave me chills. I was so impressed with Daquin's handling of an extremely hot-topic and whilst she didn't hold back, neither did her protagonist. It's that courage that will eventually bring change. If you have a daughter, ensure she reads *The Cruelty* before she goes to college.

—**Susi Bocks**, Editor & Author of
Feeling Human & *Every Day I Pause*

As a big fan of psychological fiction written from the stance of a woman, I found *The Cruelty* an intelligent, feminist expose of modern culture. With a fascinating female lead, I was on the edge of my seat cheering her on, through the brutality of her experience, she grows in front of our eyes and fights back in ways unimaginable. I didn't see the ending coming, I don't think anyone can. Finally! A great book that has a finely crafted ending. Bravo! There is absolutely nothing disappointing about this riveting thriller.

—**Elizabeth Green**, Psychotherapist

The Cruelty kept me on tender-hooks. Its ability to pierce the inner-lives of survivors of domestic and sexual abuse, so viscerally, alongside an incredibly beautiful writing style, is riveting and wholly original. What Daquin's managed to do with her fiercely feminist debut novel is nothing short of outstanding. As a voice for her generation and for women, she's accurately nailed the reality behind sexual violence and given us an unforgettable story of survival, that's ultimately both redemptive and hopeful. Watch this author, she's the real deal.

—**Rebecca Huston**, Screenwriter & Author of
Prytain & *Legenderie*

Having worked with survivors I expected this to be a hard read, but what surprised me was how engrossing and compelling it was. Despite its challenging theme, this psychological thriller is a book you'll read in a few sittings and recommend to all your friends. Daquin's style of writing is lyrical, clever and provocative, in its examination of what humans are really capable of. I love psychological thrillers but it's hard to find one that accomplishes everything in a single book. This is exactly what *The Cruelty* has achieved. I can usually guess endings, but I challenge anyone to. Gripping, thrilling, informative. Everything you want. This is already my favorite book of 2025.

—**Didi Artier**, Author of
SMITTEN & *Defy Definitions*

As a man, I found *The Cruelty*, a sobering read; evidencing the hideous reality of male-on-female-violence. Whilst disturbing; the novel didn't seek to blame all men, but rather, a society that spawns monsters of any gender. This equality in handling such a tricky subject, is hard to successfully wrangle, but Daquin's writing is stunning, in its precision and comprehension of human nature. This isn't a book that blames men, it's a book about survival, for all survivors.

—**Eric Syrdal**, Author of *Pantheon*

This book is one I think all survivors of abuse would benefit from reading; because at its heart it is a story of overcoming impossible odds and finding yourself. The characters are really believable, their suffering compels you to root for them as they fight to turn the tide that's crashing down around them. I was swept away by her beautiful writing set against such a savage storyline; underscoring the importance of this subject for us all.

—**Chuck Smith**, Licensed Professional Counselor.

An incomparable writer, well before her time. Her writing is magnetic and pulled me in from start to finish. The words found in these pages will live on in one's mind for years to come; they have lasting power.

—**Tremaine L. Loadholt**, Author & Editor of
A New Kind of Down & Séduire

Candice Daquin's writing provides an exquisite blend of the delicate and powerful, of profound emotion established in simplicity, of eloquence and terror and wisdom born of experience and self-examination.

—**Robert Okaji**, Author of
Our Loveliest Bruises & *Scarecrow Sees*

The issues of identity and origins, the seeming reality of flesh and fabric… ultimately leaving nothing but subatomic particles neither from here nor from there, yet rooted, rooted deeply, in loss.

—**Donna Snyder**, Author & Director of the
Tumblewords Project, El Paso, TX

A suspenseful and fascinating exploration of character; this engrossing debut is packed with realistic psychological insights, tautly plotted and focusing on the central question; how far can cruelty go? Nothing about Daquin's debut novel feels done before, this is unpredictable, shocking and page-burningly addictive.

—**Dr. Joaquin Farrokhzad**, Editor

The enigma of how far Camile will go, keeps readers hooked until the very end. Daquin's pulse-quickening debut, is self-assured and preternaturally intelligent. It's a highly compelling read, brilliantly constructed and recommended to anyone who appreciates strong female leads.

—**Iris Bakalar**, Writer

At times, the author speaks to women, at times to men, sometimes to both. What conjures in our brain while we jostle between dream and reality is a tiny, sometimes unrealized space, wherein folks attempt an exploration of their assumptions and beliefs and draw conclusions on big and small existentialist issues. A master wordsmith, Daquin seems to be moving along with her words, creating a magic spell that is set in motion with the very first lines.

—**Anita Nahal**, Author of
What's wrong with us Kali women? & *Drenched Thoughts*

Daquin has elevated our expectations with her debut novel, expanding beyond entertainment to something breathing, meaningful and socially conscious. Her poignant clever writing is a like a painting that becomes more intriguing the longer you study it. This is an essential social statement with its gloves off.

—**Georgia Park**, Author of *Softly Glowing Exit Signs* &
Quit Your Job & Become A Poet (Out Of Spite!)

When you read Daquin, you will be swept along by the sheer power of her words, and you will return to reread for the connection you felt to those words whether you have similar experiences or not, for she reaches into our experiences, pulling them from us and holding them up for us to examine in the light. Thus, Daquin leads us to vicariously experience what she writes of here with her visceral use of language. Finally, one may return to her work here, reading again, for the simple appreciation of how masterful a writer Daquin is, to convey such powerful raw, honest emotion yet craft such unique figurative language.

—**Annette Kalandros**, Author of *The Gift of Mercy*

The first time I read Daquin, I thought of Lorca. Her writing possesses "duende" with a feminist edge. Brutal histories etched in cold acid glide alongside captures of love urgent and often fleeting, and social commentaries fast and tight as the flick of a switchblade.

—**Sun Hesper Jansen**, Author of
To Tune the Beast & *Fairy of Disenchantment*

I admit it, I'm a fan of Candice Louisa Daquin's writing, I've been following her work for several years. As different as our life experiences seem to be, I find that her writing goes deep to the places where the personal and universal meet, and I just "get" her.

—**Robert. G. Wertzler**, Retired Mental Health Worker,
Author of *The Comment Poems*

Daquin has a special understanding of and connection with the disenfranchised, the abused, the castaways of society. Quite possibly her extensive work in Psychotherapy honed her laser focus on what lies beneath the surface of things; the surface of people, the surface of behavior.

—**Linda Paul**, author of *My Life With an Enigma:
Unscrambling the paradoxes of an iron-willed romantic*

Daquin's writing is brave, honest, raw, intense, and at times even disquieting in her willingness to tell it like it is and discuss subjects some find might find distasteful. But that having been said, know that what she writes about, are often pieces of her personal reality, and to read Candice is to know Candice, not in part, but in all that she is and has been. Her writing is neither trite nor inconsequential. She is capable of telling stories that are charming as well as ones that are troubling but need to exist.

—**Clayton Terrell**, Actor

Daquin is that rare commodity, a person who writes what she wishes, how she wishes. Her work is all the more refreshing because of it. Her writing grips you by the throat and does not let go; delivered with brutal honesty and unerring quality.

—**Richard M. Ankers**, Author of
Britannia Unleashed & T*he Eternals series*

The Sylvia Plath of our times. Candice Daquin will be highly noted one day as one of our best contemporary writers.

—**Kimberly J. Steiner**, Trauma Therapist,
The Daniel Counseling Center, VA

Candice is a master of layered meaning, nuanced emotions and vivid imagery.

—**Stephan C. Anstey**, Author of *Learning To Do Without*

Incredible read, highly recommended. This book just pours with depth and talent.

—**Alysia Hutton, Writer**, Capital News Service,
Virginia Commonwealth University's
Robertson School of Media and Culture

The feminist, female, queer and BIPOC voice of Candice Daquin is breaking boundaries and insisting it be heard. Hers is the voice we need as women, as women of color, as queer angry females who demand unflinching, real role-models in modern literature.

—**Hera Hernandez**, Educator

Candice Daquin strings together lyrical, haunting, important prose following the life of an abused woman - Camila - told with care, exquisite detail, and the real weight of the cycles of abuse many women and girls have face throughout history to the present day. I found healing in the book from the experiences Camila goes through, as I'm sure many women will and can relate to. Social justice is so important, and the rights women are denied alongside sexual abuse and intimate partner violence is a tattered, torn threat *The Cruelty* seeks to explore. Candice handles the blade of the narrative and dark topics touched exquisitely, cutting into the deep fiber of Camila's soul. 10/10.

—**Allister Nelson**, Pushcart Prize-Nominated Poet,
Author of *Holy Diver*, Rebel Satori Press

FlowerSong Press nurtures essential verse from, about, and throughout the borderlands. Literary. Lyrical. Boundless.

Sign up for announcements about new and upcoming titles at:

www.flowersongpress.com

www.ingramcontent.com/pod-product-compliance
Lightning Source LLC
Chambersburg PA
CBHW030332040826
49266CB00030B/200

* 9 7 8 1 9 6 3 2 4 5 6 7 7 *